THE BATTLE OF THE SMOKEHOUSE

BOOK II OF THE KENTUCKY BLOOD SERIES

BY: ASHLEY THOMAS SHEIKH

The story, names, characters, and incidents portrayed in this production are fictitious.

1st Edition 2025

Dedicated to my Uncle Mark

(1962-2007)

He would have loved Charlie Young.

I am blessed by God to have such amazing Beta Readers. Thank you.

BETA READERS
Curtis Brown
Caitlin Marotte
Megan
C. Golo Naito
Shawn Miller
JBO
Trey W.
Jessica Brazell
Coralie Bengoechea
Aaron M. Carpenter

AUTHOR'S NOTE

This story was meant to close Book I, but proved too epic to confine to the finale. Though it largely follows the 70s timeline, rest assured that Book III, *It's Always Sunny in Kentucky*, will bring plenty more of the 90s.

For now, crack open an RC & tequila, toke up some Monkey, and prepare yourself—

—for The Battle of the Smokehouse.

- ATS

ORDER OF BATTLE

THE POSSE & Related Characters

Bill Cunningham *("Wild Bill")* — Leader of The Posse. Often wears a cowboy hat, boots, and aviator sunglasses, even at night. Convinced his dreams are prophetic, Bill believes cocaine theft and sales will fuel the rise of his Posse to dominate the Tri-County.

Charlie Young *("Young Charlie")* — Bill's right-hand man and best friend. OCD about cleanliness, loves dropping Spanish phrases, and hosts the Posse at his parent-free house, which he proudly rechristened *"La Hacienda."*

Graham Riley *("Graham Cracker")* — Famous across the Tri for his sheer size, Graham's presence alone inspires awe. Hated by underclassmen for extorting their lunch money as "tribute."

Kenny Moser *("Skinny Kenny")* — High-energy and eccentric, often bobs his head to a rhythm only he can hear. Favors RC and tequila—a combo that quickly became the Posse's drink of choice.

Wayne Cunningham — Bill's younger brother, who also claims to have prophetic dreams. Pesters Bill to play marathon sessions of Dungeons & Dragons.

Thomas Cunningham — Bill's father and Sheriff of Crow County. Known as a "hardass dude."

Bill's Mother — Like Bill, she claimed her dreams allowed her to see the future. Whereabouts and fate are unknown.

THE SMOKETOWN BOYS & Related Characters

Tommy Glick — Leader of the Smoketown Boys, haunted by visions of his dead brother Mikey whispering about a place called *"The Temple."* Runs his squad out of his late grandfather's house—now known as the Smokehouse—and dreams of leading them to dominance across the Tri-County.

Larry Knowles — Tommy's best friend and right-hand man. Towering and lanky, he's sometimes called "Larry Longface," a nickname he hates. Quiet but loyal, the kind of presence that fills a room without trying.

Jack Kindley — The freckle-faced, redheaded "brains" of the Smoketown Boys. Captain of both the debate and chess teams, Jack's obsessed with maximizing profits—and always ready to draw a line graph to prove his point.

Mitchell Mouse *("Mouse")* — The short but ultra-ripped "muscle man" of the Smoketown Boys. What he lacks in height, he makes up for in attitude. Prefers to be fighting or partying, and speaks loudest with his fists.

Leslie Henderson — One of the hottest girls at Crow County High. Known for her bombshell looks, carefree attitude, and frequent use of *"fuuuuck."*

Lacey Matthews — Leslie's best friend and fellow heart-stopper. Currently in a steady sexual relationship with Mouse; the two often eat together at Waffle House after hooking up.

Samantha Henson — Tommy's girlfriend. According to him, the most perfect girl in the Tri. A freshman cheerleader and straight-A student, she's currently working as a summer camp counselor at a distant Girl Scout camp without access to long-distance phone calls.

Michael Glick *("Mikey")* — Tommy's late older brother and founder of the original Smoketown Boys. Together, he and his squad grew powerful enough to nearly dominate the entire Tri-County—until Mikey ended his own life at the height of their reign.

THE POSSIBLES

David Brewster *("Asian David")* — The only non-white member of

Tommy's squad—and one of the few in the Tri-County. After Graham Riley smashed his glasses, his elderly foster mother sold her wedding ring to buy him a new pair.

Kevin Crowley *("Rich Boy Kevin")* — Born into money but drawn to danger, Kevin idolizes Tommy and the Smoketown Boys.

Wiley Simmons *("Wilin' Wiley")* — A top Monkey dealer with fists to match. Cool-headed and sharp, Wiley carries himself like someone who's already seen a lot.

Grant Mitchelson *("Good Guy Grant")* — Known as a goody-two-shoes. He's not so sure about snorting Miracle, swinging crowbars, or the war Tommy's starting.

NEUTRAL PARTIES

The Hazard Mafia — Top squad of Hazard County. The largest squad of the Tri in terms of numbers, but loosely organized.

The Zion Soccer Team — Top squad of Zion County. Deals high-quality weed, but has so far kept their business within Zion.

The Horse People — Sole marijuana suppliers of the Smoketown Boys, and once the trusted suppliers of Mikey's *original* Smoketown Boys. They haunt Bill's dreams in brief, terrifying flashes—visions that push him to recruit Graham, and possibly others, into their Posse.

Let's read Kentucky Blood!

* *indicates a flashback*

*** *indicates a scene change*

PART I

THE POSSIBLES

1970s

CHAPTER I

SAY IT

Crow County, Kentucky

"Parkin' lot. Six PM.

You fuck with my friends,

you fuck with me."

"FIGHT!"

"FIGHT!"

"FIGHT!"

Wiley Simmons wiped blood from his mouth.

Dude almost got the jump on me...

Almost.

"Get up!" said Wiley.

The crowd of students cheered louder.

"FIGHT!"

"FIGHT!"

"FIGHT!"

Crimson light bled into the horizon, casting everything in hues of red and orange. Wiley scanned the high school parking lot. No parents. No teachers. *Yet.* Didn't wanna get suspended for fightin' this jack-off.

"I said, get the fuck up, bitch!" said Wiley. "Ain't done with you yet!"

"FIGHT!"

"FIGHT!"

"FIGHT!"

The girls screamed over the guys. Fiercer. Like animals.

"Get the fuck up!"

"Don't let a freshman whoop you like that!"

"Show some fucking balls!"

Wiley spat blood on the pavement. Metallic tang coated his tongue—bitter, coppery. This guy just *had* to fuck with him, didn't he? Try to steal rep. Beat the ass of the freshman who stomped his buddy, prove he's loyal. Bullshit like that.

"He's gettin' up!"

"He's still gonna fight!"

"FIGHT!"

"FIGHT!"

"FIGHT!"

"I don't even know your name, man!" said Wiley. "I didn't do *shit* to you!" He had to say that—loud, in front of everyone. He wasn't the aggressor. This was self-defense. As a freshman, he already held the underdog status, but he had to protect it. *No one liked a shit-starter.*

"Come at me!" said Wiley. "Fuckin' come at me, you little bitch!"

Maybe that'd provoke the guy. Just needed him to make one clumsy swing, or a—

"UGGH!"

The dude tackled him like a freight train—shoulder down, football style. Air tore from Wiley's lungs as his back slammed against the pavement, hard enough to rattle his teeth.

Shit...

Didn't expect that...

Is this guy on the football team?

"My name is Josh, bitch!"

Josh pinned Wiley and cracked his cheek with a hard right.

"And you don't fuck with my friends!"

He drove another fist into Wiley's ear, leaving it crushed and humming.

The crowd shrieked.

"Fuck him up, Josh!"

"Teach him a lesson!"

"Freshmen need to know their fuckin' place!"

Blow after blow rained down. No pain. Only impact—numbing, dizzying. He'd been here before. It sucked. But there was one way out—

"AAAAGH!"

—fight dirty.

Josh screamed as Wiley's thumbs pressed into his eyeballs.

The crowd roared.

"Holy shit!"

"Fuckin' poked his eyes!"

"That's fightin' dirty!"

"Who cares!"

Josh staggered back, hands over eyes. Wiley bolted up, head spinning. *One chance. Only one.* He rushed forward and socked Josh straight in his gut—

"UUGH!"

—then drove an uppercut into his chin so hard it snapped his head back, sending him reeling to the pavement.

"WI-LIN' WI-LEY!"

"WI-LIN' WI-LEY!"

Sunlight glared off the blacktop.

Everything shimmered.

"Fuck!" Wiley flexed his fingers, wincing. Dude's chin was a fuckin' rock.

"Finish him, Wiley!"

"Beat his ass!"

"FIGHT!"

"FIGHT!"

"FIGHT!"

The crowd screamed. Girls jumped in place, faces flushed, fists pumping.

"Beat the shit outta him, Wiley!"

"Teach him a lesson!"

"Teach him a fuckin' lesssoooon!"

No. The lesson was taught. No more. He marched over and pressed his foot to Josh's throat.

"WI-LIN' WI-LEY!"

"WI-LIN' WI-LEY!"

"Say you're sorry!" said Wiley. "Say you give up!"

Josh's throat fluttered under his shoe—shallow, fast, like a cornered animal.

"Fuck you, motherf—*UAAGH!"*

Wiley pressed down harder.

"Say it!"

1970s

CHAPTER II

A DIFFERENT KIND OF FIGHT

The cowboy hat-shaped cloud passed before the sun, and for a moment, everything around the Smoketown Boys darkened.

WILEY BROUGHT HIS hand to his neck.

It'd been a while since he'd been in a fight. Josh was the last. Larry and Mouse had recruited him afterward, all hyped that he beat the shit out of two sophomores within a space of weeks. Mouse even re-enacted the throat stomp, which Larry applauded.

"*CROSS-ATTAAAACK!*"

DONG!

DONNG!

"We're up, Wiley," said Grant.

Wiley turned to the Smokehouse, sun bright in his eyes.

This time wouldn't be the same.

If Bill Cunningham made a move, it'd be a different kind of fight.

1970s

CHAPTER III

A NEW SCARECROW

"The Asian boy!" said Bill.

"Don't let him snort that shit!"

THE SCARECROW STOOD in the middle of the Smokehouse backyard—silent, still, and present. A battered cowboy hat slouched low over its head.

"CROSS-ATTAAACK!"

DONG!

DONNNG!

"Shit!"

A cool breeze rolled through. The scrap of paper pinned to its chest fluttered. *GRAHAM RILEY* had been scratched out, *BILL CUNNINGHAM* and *KENNY MOSER* scrawled beneath. The Possibles circled it, squinting against the summer sun, shirts drenched with sweat.

David Brewster twirled his crowbar.

He still imagined the scarecrow as Graham—

—Graham-fuckin'-Riley.

Didn't really know that Cunningham dude, and aside from his mad disrespect toward Tommy, couldn't muster much anger at him, either. But he *hated* Graham-f—

"My hand hurts," said Grant, bent over and panting.

"I'm tired," said Wiley, still catching his breath. A badass when it came to fightin', sure—but couldn't run for shit. Even the short sprints of the *cross-attack* wore him out.

"You know what'd be good right now?" asked Wiley. He spat, then leaned up. "That Miracle shit."

"I wanna try it, too," said Kevin. "Bet it'd give us a ton of energy."

"Me too," said David. Didn't know why, but he felt a *pull* toward it—as if the white powder itself was charged with energy.

They talked about Miracle some more, wondering what snorting it might feel like. *"Probably fuckin' good,"* said Wiley. Only Grant seemed hesitant. But Grant was hesitant about everything. David narrowed his eyes at Grant.

If shit did go down...

Could we really count on this dude?

"Alright, y'all," said Kevin. "Let's finish strong. Just a couple more reps."

David tugged at the front of his shirt, fanning air across his chest. Ever since the Dairy Queen incident, Kevin acted like the self-appointed "Leader of the Possibles." No one seemed to mind yet, though. Not even Wiley.

"And remember," said Kevin, "we have to run at him from *different angles.* That's key."

Wiley spat again. "This *cross-attack* stuff was for Graham, right? Why we practicin' for Cunningham and Moser?"

"Never underestimate your enemy," said Kevin. "Like Larry said, better to be *over*prepared, than under."

Wiley nodded—not in agreement, but to let it go.

"So is Jack still usin' his water gun?" asked Grant. "I mean, the whole Kentucky Blood in Graham's eyes thing, that's just for *Graham,* right? Jack squirts him, then we *cross-attack.* But if Bill's wearin' shades, is it even gonna work?"

David shoved his thick-rimmed glasses up his sweaty nose. Grant had a point—eyewear negated the whole strategy.

Kevin shrugged. "Maybe Bill won't be wearin' sunglasses. Not if he shows up at night."

A chorus of replies followed:

"He wore sunglasses at Dairy Queen that night!"

"Yeah, but why?"

"Who wears sunglasses at night?"

"Retards. And dumbasses. That's who."

"I thought it looked cool..."

"Can we chill for a bit?" asked Grant. "They got Kool-Aid inside. The purple kind. Why don't we take a break, and—"

"Nope," said Kevin. "They said no breaks until *after* we finished our reps." He picked up his crowbar and twirled it. "So let's finish."

"Well, I gotta pee first," said Grant.

"Me too," said Wiley. "And I'm gettin' water from the hose. Thirsty."

Mmm...

Hose water.

Sounded good right now. David didn't know why, but hose water always tasted better than tap. At least, it did when he was a kid.

"No breaks," said Kevin. "We gotta—"

"Kevin, *c'mon,* man," said David. "I'm sure they're okay with us drinkin' a lil' water from the hose. Just chill."

Kevin glanced around, like one of the Boys might be watching.

"Okay," he said.

"But let's make it quick, y'all."

***

One by one, the Possibles slurped from the hose like dogs. David hadn't drunk hose water in years, but it tasted like he remembered: cold and clear, with a metallic tang. Like an underground spring.

As the hose circled through the group, each Possible shared what they knew:

"Young Charlie wants to partner up on coke..."

"Cocaine? You serious?"

"Nah, Coca-Cola. Fuck you think?"

"I was just ask—"

"Wait. So he quit Bill's Posse, and *he wants us to sell his coke, too?"*

"I don't trust that guy..."

"Why not?"

"Somethin' about him..."

"I think he's funny."

"Funny?"

"Yeah. Always speakin' Spanish, makin' jokes to girls."

"Dude, he ain't funny. He's just full of himself."

"Think he might join up?"

"Young? You kiddin' me?"

"Him and Tommy used to be best bros. Back in the day."

"Nahhh, he ain't joinin' up. Not after Mouse took a giant shit on his living room carpet."

They all laughed. Mouse's poop had been *gigantic,* like elephant dung. David was surprised humans *could* poop that much. They talked about it more and decided that Young was likely desperate to sell his coke after his fallout with Bill, so tried to cut a deal with Tommy.

After one last session of slurping and complaining, they headed back. David's stomach swelled as the scarecrow came into view. *Too cold, too fast.* He lapsed into a daze, his thoughts drifting—

("adios, ese...")

—to the smell of cigarettes and the sound of lockers slamming shut.

1970s

CHAPTER IV

SOMETHING COLDER

"Is that David kid Chinese, or Japanese?"

"Fuck if I know.

Same shit, ain't it?"

"HEY, LITTLE ASIAN boy!"

"Little Asian Boy!"

David tensed. "Little Asian Boy" usually meant trouble. But the voice sounded warm. Friendly, almost. Not the tone of someone about to give him shit for being the only Asian kid at Crow County High *("you like fried rice, motherfucker?").*

"Hey, little man! *Hombrecito!"*

David adjusted his glasses, then turned. An older student—maybe a junior or senior—marched his way down the hall, cutting through the tide of backpacks and chatter. He'd seen this guy before. Mustache and goatee. Short, but still taller than him. Liked to speak Spanish, cracked jokes to girls. *"Mamacitaaa,"* stuff like that.

"Hold up for a second," said the dude. "*Un momento.*"

David shifted to his side, bumping into a locker.

This guy put him on edge.

Reeked of cigarettes, smiled too easily. His eyes twinkled, sure, but something *else* lurked behind them. Something colder. Smarter. And—

"Just wanted to say *hola* to ya, *ese,*" said the guy, dragging out *ese* so it sounded like *essaaay.* "Name's Charlie Young, but people call me Young Charlie."

He grinned bright enough to blind. Shark's teeth.

"Don't call me *Old* Charlie, 'cause I'm *Young.* Get it?"

He snickered, clearly amused with himself.

David stared, unsure of what to say.

"So," said Charlie. "Was wantin' to ask ya—hey, you can speak English, right? Fuckin', *hablas inglés?"*

David nodded. A group of girls walked past, whispering to each other and giggling.

"Bueno, fuckin' *bueno, ese,*" said Charlie. "I can speak *español,* actually. *Español,* and *inglés.* Ain't from Mexico or nothin', though. I just speak that shit. Anyway, where you from?"

David paused.

"Kentucky."

Charlie laughed. "That's funny, *ese! Qué* fuckin' *chistoso!"* He slapped his knee. The twinkle in his eyes grew brighter. "C'mon now, I mean where ya *really* from?"

David paused again.

"Kentucky."

Charlie's grin twitched, just for a second.

"Sí, but like, where you born and shit?"

David gripped his books tighter. He should be used to these kinds of questions, but no. Still annoyed the fuck out of him.

"Korea."

"Ah, *sí, sí,* that's cool, *ese. Annyoung*-fuckin'*-hasayo!"*

He held up his hand for a high-five.

"That's how you say that shit, right? *Buenos*-fuckin'*-días?* In Korean?"

David shook his head. *Didn't trust this dude.* There was a glint in those eyes—friendly, maybe, but cruel, too, and—

Charlie lowered his hand. "At least, I *thought* that was Korean. Maybe I got that shit mixed up."

"I guess." David adjusted his glasses, trying not to fidget. "Don't really know."

"You don't know?" asked Charlie. "You don't speak no Korean? Or shit like that?"

"Nope," said David. "Adopted when I was a baby."

"Oh," said Charlie. "By white people?"

David nodded.

Yes.

By white people.

Charlie's grin returned.

"Qué? You're fuckin' with me, right?" He laughed. "Fuckin', *estás jodiendo.* You're *Asian,* man. You gotta speak that shit! Like Chinese? Or Japanese? Shit like that?"

Lockers slammed nearby. The late bell rang. David just stood there.

Charlie narrowed his eyes. "You really don't speak *no* Asian shit? Not *nihow-ma?* Or *konnichi-wa*?" His tone sharpened. "Even though you're fuckin' Asian?"

David took a step back. He shook his head.

Nope.

Charlie's face darkened. He bumped past David, knocking his books to the floor.

"Adios, ese..."

*

1970s

CHAPTER V

HIT THAT SHIT

"You can't let shit slide," said Mouse. "If you let even one dude fuck with you, then everyone will, and you'll have zero-fuckin'-rep.

Get stuffed in lockers.

Maybe worse."

"DUDE," SAID THE tall, long-faced guy. "You kicked that sophomore's ass."

Crickets chirped as the sun's last glow faded through the trees. Wiley stared, dazed.

("FIGHT!")

("FIGHT!")

("FI—")

The short, stocky dude grinned. "And didn't even get no black eye. Those take *forever* to go away, man."

Wiley touched his swollen cheek and winced. He knew about black eyes—he'd had about twenty or so. But this time he lucked out: only a busted lip, a fat cheek, and a smashed ear, hot and throbbing. Both the fight and the aftermath felt like a blur. What were these dudes' names again?

The tall one—Larry.

The short one, Mouse.

Mitchell Mouse? Something like that.

Both upperclassmen. Not sure why they were talkin' to him. But also too tired to give a fuck.

"I've seen some fights in my day," said Mouse, "and I've beaten a *whole lotta* ass. But that was good."

"Fuckin' good." Larry pulled a blunt from a crumpled plastic baggie and lit it with a practiced flick. "Hit that shit."

Hit that shit. More like a command, not an offer, but Wiley would've hit it anyway. Risky, smokin' in broad daylight beside school property, but whatever. Still twitchy from adrenaline, needed to calm his nerves. The wooded enclave they'd led him to—a *"smokespot,"* they called it—should be secretive enough. He pressed the blunt to his lips and inhaled; smoke filled his chest like a warm, acrid fog.

"And you know what I really liked?" Larry's long face twisted into a grin. "When you stepped on his throat, man."

"Dude," said Mouse. "That was *awesome!"*

They went on for a while, hyped on how cool and brutal it'd been. Mouse even reenacted it *("fuck you, motherf—UAAAAAAAAGH!")* which Larry applauded.

Wiley stayed silent. He turned his gaze to the canopy, sunlight poking through leaves. Didn't need to tell'em he'd learned that trick the hard way, pinned down by his older brothers, throat crushed 'til he cried Uncle.

("learn your place, wiley!")

("stay the fuck d—")

He brought his hand to his neck.

"And that other sophomore," asked Larry, "Todd, or whatever? You stomped his ass last week, too?"

A squirrel scampered up a tree; Wiley watched it climb. Didn't know why, but fights always made him feel guilty. Especially the ones he won.

"That Todd guy," he said, "kept pushin' me in the halls. Talkin' shit when he walked by. So I beat his ass."

He paused. "*So we scrapped*" might've been better. Didn't wanna sound full of himself. These dudes acted friendly, but he sensed danger behind those smiles. Not the type you saw at church cookouts.

"Then his buddy Josh," he said, "fuckin' challenged me, so—"

("FIGHT!")

("FIGHT!")

("FI—")

The chanting.

Why did it both disturb, and excite him?

At the same time?

"So?" asked Mouse.

The squirrel halted on a branch above, staring at Wiley.

"So," said Wiley. "I did what I had to do."

"Nice," said Larry. "Takin' care of business."

The squirrel vanished into the canopy. Wiley hit the blunt again. Still didn't feel that high, just a weird tightness in his chest.

"You did fight dirty, though," said Mouse. "Pokin' his eyes like that."

A crow cawed, sharp and sudden.

Wiley tensed.

Mouse's tone had shifted—heavier now.

Accusatory.

Both he and Larry stared at Wiley, grins fading.

Wait a minute...

Were these dudes *friends* with Josh?

On the football team, too?

Actin' friendly-like?

Before they made a move?

The Larry guy stood tall as fuck and Mouse was short, but

super-ripped. Doubted he could take either one, much less both at the same time.

Wiley took a step back, blunt still in hand.

The blunt.

His only weapon.

If need be, he'd crush it into one of their eyeballs, then haul ass, try to lose'em in the woods. Or maybe—

"Buuut," said Mouse, "he did pin you to the ground, which is dirty, too. Kinda. So it's fine, I guess."

"Sometimes you gotta fight dirty, dude," said Larry.

("AAAAGH!")

Wiley grimaced.

Still felt the *squish* of those eyeballs under his thumbs.

("holy shit!")

("fuckin' poked his—")

But he *had* to.

No other choice.

Besides, he hadn't poked *that* hard.

Dude's eyes would be fine.

Probably.

"I don't start shit," he said. The blunt felt heavy between his fingers now. "I didn't start shit with *either* of'em. They started sh—"

"It's cool, man," said Larry. "Those dudes looked like little shits to me. Glad you beat their asses." He leaned on a tree, motioned for the blunt and took a hit. "And that Josh guy was just tryin' to steal rep. You know how it is, right?" He leveled his gaze at Wiley. "You ain't in middle school no more."

Wiley nodded. He knew. In high school, nothing mattered more than your rep. *Didn't need no fuckin' lecture.* He tasted copper, wiped his lip. Bleedin' again.

"You hear those girls cheerin' for ya?" asked Mouse. "Louder than the guys?"

Larry nodded. "Jumpin' up and down and shit."

"You *gotta* fuck those girls, dude," said Mouse. "You gotta." His face grew serious. "And get blowjobs, too. While your rep's still hot."

"Strike while the mouth is hot!" said Larry.

The two cackled and went on about blowjobs for a while.

"...and I ain't into that spittin' shit, they gotta swallow..."

"...dude, I think spittin' is hot...I like seein' my own..."

Wiley flexed his swollen fist, half-listening. The girls *had* cheered louder than the guys—but that didn't make him wanna mess with'em.

("WI-LIN' WI-LEY!")

("WI-LIN' WI-LEY!")

("fuck him up, wiley!")

("teach him a fuckin' less—")

Cold crept up his spine, slow and mean.

Bloodthirsty.

The girls had sounded *bloodthirsty.*

Didn't chicks used to be into Barbie dolls and shit?

What happened?

Mouse leaned against a tree. "Some of those freshmen were fuckin' hot, too. Girls weren't that hot when *I* was a freshman..." He sighed, blowing smoke out the side of his mouth. "Shit's changin'."

Mouse passed the blunt to Wiley. He took a hit, slow and silent. Personally, he found the junior and senior girls *way* hotter than the tiny, flat-chested freshmen. But hey, maybe the grass was greener.

"You know those chicks?" asked Mouse. "Think they like to smoke?"

Wiley nodded, passing the blunt to Larry. "I know'em. Dunno if they smoke. But I can ask."

"Let the Mouse know!" said Mouse. Then, for some reason, he grunted and pounded his chest.

Wiley stifled a laugh.

Who is this guy?

A gorilla?

Larry grinned. "We're always down to have more chicks at our place. Especially hot lil' freshmen that toke up."

"And hopefully suck dick, too," said Mouse.

They both cackled.

Wiley raised an eyebrow. "You got your own place? Like, to party at or somethin'?"

"Fuck yeah, we do," said Larry. "We throw badass parties, man. Shit gets *wild,* know what I mean?"

Larry handed Wiley the blunt. He took a deeper hit, letting the smoke burn his lungs. Finally started to buzz—like heat creeping into his skull, blurring his thoughts. These dudes seemed cool, but the vibe felt more like a friendly interview. Or an invitation? And they let him smoke shit for free...

"Hey..." said Wiley. "...are y'all the Smoketown Boys?"

Larry and Mouse cracked up.

"What gave it away?" asked Larry. "That we like to smoke?"

Mouse showed his teeth. "And gettin' you high as fuck?"

He slapped Wiley's back, nearly knocking the blunt from his hand. He'd heard of this squad before—caught glimpses in front of Walmart.

Smoked weed.

Played their music loud.

Threw *huge* parties with tons of hot chicks.

Pretty badass...

"You know what?" asked Larry. "You should come to our Smokehouse Party this weekend."

Wiley blinked. He'd never heard of freshmen that got invited to Smokehouse Parties. Not even the "cool kids" who played sports and shit.

"Join us, bro!" said Mouse. "The famous throat-stompin' *Wilin' Wiley!"*

Mouse stuck out his hand, grinning wide.

Wiley hesitated—then took it.

("WI-LIN' WI-LEY!")

("WI-LIN' WI-LEY!")

He touched his neck,

("fuck you, motherf—UAAAGH!")

("say it!")

and smiled.

1970s

CHAPTER VI

THE PATH TAKEN

"Hey slant eyes!

You use chopsticks, or fork and spoon?"

DAVID GAZED AT the scarecrow, belly full of hosewater.

What if he *had* spoken Korean that day?

Would he have made friends with Young Charlie?

Instead of Jack?

*

David waited for the red-haired, freckle-faced guy to fall for his trap. Joining the after-school chess club had never been a priority—few girls, none hot—but he did like chess. The pieces, how they moved, the need to deceive your opponent; every game a tiny battle of Napoleon-like complexity.

("you really don't speak no asian shit?")

("even though you're fuckin' asian?")

Heat prickled the back of his neck. Later, passing in the halls, that Young Charlie dude didn't even make eye contact. Which felt strangely disappointing. Sure, he didn't trust the guy—something about his eyes, that glint—

("adios, ese...")

—but having an upperclassman as a friend might've been useful. Especially when it came to girls, gettin' invited to parties. Shit like that. Maybe he should *study Korean a l—*

"Your move, dude," said the red-haired guy. An upperclassman he didn't know.

David pushed a pawn forward, then returned to his thoughts.

Might impress people, to speak a foreign language. Seemed to work for that Young Charlie guy. Sometimes girls (occasionally hot) asked David if he "knew Asian languages, too," *and not always in an obnoxious way, but with real curiosity, like they were about to unlock some rare exotic prize.*

But, no.

Try as he might, David really didn't give a shit about Korea.

Or Asia in general.

Getting asked "Which country you from?" *and then,* "Yeah, but where you *really* from?" *for the first thirteen fucking years of his life would do that to a guy.*

"Check," said the red-headed dude. "Not bad, man. Almost had m—"

"Checkmate," said David, moving his knight.

"What the..."

David stood. "Good game."

It really wasn't, though—and if that red-headed dude was any indication, the chess club had nothing to offer. Nerds with even less rep than him who didn't play that well. No thanks.

He strode past other players at their tables, wondering whether the school library had a Korean textbook. Probably not, probably only Sp—

"Hey, wait up!"

The red-headed guy caught up to him.

"*That was* smooth, *dude," he said.*

"*I'm Jack, captain of our team.*"

***

The evening sun hid behind a layer of clouds, casting the woods in a cold Kentucky gray. Jack passed the joint to David. He tried to bring it to his lips like he knew what he was doing and inhaled—

"KHACK-KHAACK!"

—then doubled over, hacking like his lungs were on fire. Hot smoke scorched his throat.

This shit is awful...

Why would anyone wanna—

"*You okay, little buddy?" asked Jack. "You smoked before, right?"*

"*Yeah..." David coughed again. "Just been a while..."*

A lie. But an important one.

Jack grinned. "Keep coughin', bro. Coughin' makes you more high."

David didn't understand the logic of that, but coughed some more, anyway. He glanced around at the "secret smokespot" *Jack had led him to, a wooded enclave past the parking lot. Decently concealed, but he already felt like a felon.*

"Dude, tell me," said Jack. "How'd you learn to play like that?"

A wave of dizziness hit David. Warmth crept up his legs and thighs.

"Just self-taught," he said, but it felt like someone else *spoke. His voice trailed behind like it didn't belong to him.*

Is this what it feels like...

To get high?

"*You heard of the Smoketown Boys?" asked Jack.*

David blinked slowly. The world felt a half-second behind. "...the squad that sells weed, right?"

"Monkey," *said Jack. "We sell Monkey. It's like weed, but better."*

David leaned against a tree, then stood straight. He felt like he floated now—a cloud.

*"You mean..." he said. "...*you're *one of the Smoketown Boys?"*

"Yeah," said Jack. "Why you look surprised?"

"Just, uhh...I thought..."

Jack's eyes flashed. "You didn't think the captain of the chess club would be squaddin' up, huh?"

David took another hit, coughed some more, then passed the joint back. Shit, maybe coughin' did *make you more high? Felt like he'd drifted to outer space now. Didn't know how to answer the question* (what did he ask again?), *so just nodded.*

"We're different from other squads," said Jack. "We run shit like a business."

He looked at David seriously, so David kept nodding. The "Monkey" or whatever was kicking in hard now. Getting him high. *All he wanted to do was nod.*

"And," said Jack, "we're lookin' to expand, *man. Get some younger guys in our ranks, help sell Monkey to the underclassmen, even get a foothold with the middleschoolers. Straight-up* diversify *our customer base." He emphasized* diversify *like it was some ten-dollar word. David nodded and mumbled something about the importance of diversification.*

"Diversification is *important, ain't it?" asked Jack. "See, you* get *that. I* knew *you would, man. The other guys—they don't..." He shook his head. "Hey, can I tell you somethin'?"*

"Sure," said David. But he didn't even know what they were talking about anymore. The air smelled of campfire, skunk, and something sweet he couldn't place. Damp bark? *Behind them a squirrel scurried through the brush, sounding both near and far at the same time. He felt hyperaware of everything—yet somehow detached from it all.* Like he was there, but not there.

"You gotta keep it secret, *though," said Jack. "Between you and me. You got that?"*

"Gotcha," said David. He wondered what Jack might tell him, but he

also wondered if he was really there, *standing in the woods. Or was this all a dream? Everything stood out, yet nothing felt real.*

"We don't grow our own weed, dude..." said Jack.

He lowered his voice, like someone might be listening.

"...we source it. From really fucked up *people."*

His eyes widened.

Cold fear fell upon his freckled-face.

"...I'm talkin' Texas Chainsaw Massacre *shit. But even* more *fucked up."*

David shifted, startled by the rough scrape of bark against his arm.

Where'd that tree come from?

He glanced at Jack, trying to read him.

Texas Chainsaw Massacre?

We talkin' about movies now?

Jack took a drag, eyes scanning the woods. "I been pushin' for us to find new suppliers, ya know? To straight-up diversify *our procurement. So we don't rely on them no more. The Horse People."*

"*...Horse...*People?" *asked David.*

The fuck?

He flicked his eyes to the trees again, imagining half-human, half-horse creatures. Centaurs.

Maybe this really was a dream.

"Horse People," *said Jack. He shook his head slow and strange, like he knew something terrible that shouldn't be spoken, then paused for what seemed like an eternity. David just stood there, unsure of the flow of time. Unsure of everything.*

Finally, Jack spoke again, looking like he'd returned from somewhere dark. "Anyway, you seem smart, dude. Like you get *shit. You're adopted, right?"*

Now David almost took a step back. Either he was really really *high, or Jack actually realized he hadn't immigrated from Asia yesterday. "Yeah...how'd you—"*

"Korea? Or Vietnam?"

"Korea."

"Cool," said Jack.

David blinked. Jack hadn't made a joke, hadn't asked "Which country you from, China or Japan?" *or if he* "used chopsticks, or fork and spoon?" *or spoke* "somethin' Asian."

This dude seemed cool.

Jack exhaled a plume of smoke, nodding like someone told him something.

"You like parties, David?"

"Hell yeah," said David. "I'm always down to party."

Had to say it like that. Cool and experienced. Pumped up. Bein' high helped his delivery. The truth was he'd never been to a party outside the occasional birthday, but he knew what Jack had meant:

Real parties.

Where wild shit happened.

With hot girls.

"You like makin' money?" asked Jack.

David nodded.

Fuck yeah.

*

David twirled his crowbar. Maybe, if he had spoken Korean, or at least *"some Asian shit"* as Young Charlie had expected him to, he would've joined Bill's Posse instead.

("adios, ese...")

No.

Something about that twinkle in Young's eyes—something *behind* that twinkle—put David on edge. Intelligence, sure, but a cruel kind, like the easy smiles and Spanish jokes were a mask for something darker.

Besides, Young ran with—or at least, used to run with, Graham Riley—

("huh huh huh...")

("smash your glasses?")

("or your face?")

("no, i—")

—and he fucking *hated* Graham-fucking-Riley.

"David, you're up!"

Cicadas whined from the trees. David shoved his glasses up his nose, gripped the smooth surface of the crowbar and entered the *cross-attack* stance. He locked eyes with Kevin across the lawn, then nodded.

Let's do this.

He tore across the yard, knees pumping, dirt kicking up behind him.

This time, he aimed for the scarecrow's head, imagining Graham's skull splitting open—

"CROSS-ATTAAAACK!"

—chunks of brain and blood flying through the air.

1970s

CHAPTER VII

TOKING SHIT UP

"Kevin!

Go for his fucking head this time!"

"DONG! DONG!"

The crowbar vibrated in Kevin Crowley's blistered hand. He slowed his run to a walk and glanced back.

Had David aimed for *the head* that time?

"D'you aim for his head just now?" he asked between breaths.

"Yeah," said David, still breathing hard.

"But we're supposed to go for the legs, right?"

David nodded. "If it's Bill or Kenny, I'll go for the legs."

Kevin thought about saying something, but didn't. At least David took shit seriously. Not like Wiley and Grant—always bitchin' about their hands or that they're tired or thirsty or whatever.

He was tired and thirsty.

And his hands hurt, too.

But he didn't bitch about it.

Things had changed now.

Ever since Tommy had praised him for charging Graham-fucking-Riley in front of everyone, things were *different*.

He was a *leader* now.

The leader of the Possibles.

Not just "Rich Boy Kevin."

*

"Don't look at'em, son..." said Kevin's mom. "Those types are dangerous..."

Stars twinkled overhead. From a nearby truck, The Beatles blasted as Kevin and his mom crossed the Walmart parking lot.

"Nothing but trouble..." said his mom. "...an embarrassment to the Tri... young people these days..."

She stole a glance behind her, then shook her head.

Kevin stared in awe:

The Smoketown Boys.

Smokin' weed in the Walmart parking lot.

Listenin' to music really loud and shit.

Awesome...

Two blondes in black tank tops laughed, smoke drifting from their mouths.

Hot girls with'em, too...

One bent over to pick something up, her breasts shifting with the motion. Kevin's jaw dropped.

...big boobs...

He squinted, trying to make out their faces in the dimly lit parking lot.

Leslie.

Leslie Henderson.

And Lacey Matthews.

Two of the hottest, sexiest chicks in the whole school.

And they had big boobs, too.

Kevin and his mom stepped through the glass doors into the harsh fluorescent light of Walmart. A wave of cold air hit his face, sharp with the scent of popcorn and cleaning supplies.

"*Mom, can I check out the books section while you buy stuff?*"

"*You sure? I was gonna buy you new underwear and—*"

"*I'm sure!*"

The last fucking thing he wanted was to be seen buying fucking underwear with his fucking mom.

What if Leslie and Lacey saw?

Or other hot chicks?

Or anybody?

"*Okay, son. I'll come find you when I'm finished.*"

But instead of checking out the books, Kevin lingered near the entrance, watching as his mom disappeared down an aisle.

He took a deep breath, then returned to the parking lot.

***

"*Hey, y'all...*" *said Kevin.* "*...can I...buy some weed?*"

His stomach twisted. He'd never actually spoken to them before—the Smoketown Boys—but he knew their names:

Tommy Glick. *Their leader. Usually wore a cap with a crow on it.*

Larry Knowles. *The long-faced, super tall and lanky dude.*

Mitchell Mouse. *The short, ultra-ripped guy. Had a mouth on him.*

Oh, and—

"*We ain't smokin' weed, little dude,*" *said Larry.* "*This is Monkey.*"

Kevin nodded. Mouse sauntered away from the group, Lacey's hand in his.

Must be his girlfriend...

Mouse pressed Lacey against the side of a car and ran his lips down her neck. She tilted her head back, locking eyes with Kevin before closing them again.

So...hot...

Wonder if she's gonna give him a—

"You tried it before?" asked Larry. "Monkey?"

"Uhh..." Kevin tore his gaze from the make-out session. "...what's 'Monkey'?"

"Weed mixed with tobacco." Larry leaned against his truck, blowing a perfect smoke ring. "Don't reek like straight-up MJ. Keeps the cops from sniffin' around."

"And," said a redheaded, freckle-faced guy, "the nicotine in the tobacco enhances *the THC of the weed. Keeps you sharp, while the weed mellows you out."*

Kevin nodded. The red-headed dude seemed smart. Knew shit about chemicals, stuff like that.

Jack.

That's his name—Jack Kindley.

Captain of the chess club.

He'd thought it strange the Boys had accepted someone so nerdy into their ranks, but that also appealed to him: the diversity *of their squad.*

Leslie stopped talking with Tommy and finally acknowledged his presence. "Did y'all pull in drivin' that BMW over there?"

"Yeah," said Kevin. "It's my dad's car."

He sensed the air shift. All eyes turned to him—even Tommy's.

Their leader...

He's noticing me now.

"Fuuuuck..." said Leslie. "Y'all must be rich to drive one of them..."

Kevin shrugged. "It's my dad's. Not mine."

He'd learned the hard way to act like that. Like wealth didn't matter. Came off better than flexin'.

Larry flicked ash onto the pavement. "So, Mr. BMW, you buyin' Monkey from us? Or not?"

Kevin tried to smile.

"S-sure..."

He'd never bought drugs before.

Nor smoked weed.

Felt dangerous.

And wrong.

But that made it even more *awesome.*

Jack glanced around, scanning the parking lot. "Your mom ain't comin' back, is she?"

"Nah..." said Kevin, praying to God that she didn't. "...should be cool..."

Larry pulled a backpack from his truckbed. "Don't fuckin' tell her about this..."

"I won't," said Kevin, reaching for his wallet. And then: "You have my word."

Felt important to say that.

Let'em know he took shit seriously.

"How much you buyin'?" asked Larry.

"Uhh...how much will..." He combed through the birthday cash in his wallet. "...thirty bucks get me?"

He felt the air shift again.

Jack whistled. "That's a lot, *dude. You gonna smoke all that by yourself?"*

"Um..." Kevin glanced at Mouse and Lacey in the distance. Mouse dry-humped her in plain view now, grunting while Lacey moaned.

Damn...

Like he's bangin' her with his clothes on...

Kevin gulped.

"...probably t-toke it up with my friends..."

Toke it up...

That's what the cool kids call it...

Tokin' shit up!

Jack and Larry both looked at Tommy, who seemed to appraise him now.

"You like smokin' with your friends, huh?" asked Tommy.

Kevin's eyes widened.

The leader...

The leader of the Smoketown Boys...

He's talking to me.

Tommy leaned off the truck and approached him. "What's your name, little dude?"

"K-Kevin."

Kevin's throat went dry.

Felt like he was talking to someone famous.

"Nice to meet you, Kevin," said Tommy. "You wanna roll with us sometime? Help us sell Monkey? To underclassmen and shit?"

Tommy extended his hand.

Kevin reached out and took it.

*

The midday sun blazed overhead. Kevin wiped sweat from his brow and squinted across the yard at the living room window, barely able to make out the Boys at their Table Meeting.

One day.

One day, he'd be a full-fledged Smoketown Boy.

Soon.

And then he'd join the Table Meetings, too.

He'd have a voice.

Everyone would respect him, and not because of his money, but bec—

"Y'all's turn," said Grant.

Kevin turned to face the scarecrow, feet digging into the grass, body coiled like a sprinter before the start whistle. He locked eyes with David across the yard.

Don't matter if it's Graham, Bill, or Skinny Kenny...

I'll destroy anybody *who fucks with the Smoketown Boys...*

Anybody!

"CROSS-ATTAAAAAAAACK!"

1970s

CHAPTER VIII

PLAYING WITH FIRE

"You think that Miracle stuff is crystal meth?"

"Nah. Larry said he got it for cheap. Crystal's more expensive than gold or diamonds, dude."

"Then what is it? If it ain't coke or crystal."

"He said it's like Heinz 57.

Got a lil' bit of everything."

GRANT MITCHELSON WANTED Kool-Aid.

The purple kind.

Cold and sweet on his tongue.

Grant tossed his crowbar aside and sank onto the Smokehouse lawn, his shirt clinging to his back, damp with sweat.

Hot.

Tired.

None of this made sense.

Not really.

No way Bill and Kenny would show up without Graham Riley, right?

He glanced at the jet-black crowbar beside him. Looked like a snake in the grass.

Are these really *necessary?*

Graham was a giant, so maybe it made sense for him, but for the rest—

"Man," said Wiley. "I'm tired of this shit."

Wiley plopped down beside him. Grant still didn't feel close to the guy, but there was a camaraderie now. And he trusted him. Dude could fight and sold his Monkey good, yet kept a quiet, humble vibe. Unlike Kevin, who'd turned into Mr. Badass ever since he charged Graham at Dairy Queen.

Why had Tommy praised him for that?

("aaagh!")

("aaaaagh!")

("huh huh huh...")

It was a stupid, crazy move and he got choked out in front of everybody.

("you're gonna kill him!")

("aaaaaaaaaaaaaaaaaaaaaagh!")

("huh huh huh...")

Something hard and tight coiled in Grant's chest.

By paying his lunch money to Graham every day, he'd avoided Graham's *wrath* the past school-year. They had an understanding. Was it fair? No. But he'd rather dip into his allowance to pay for lunches than risk a Graham-Riley head massage.

"CROSS-ATTAAAAAAACK!"

DONG-DONG!

He glanced up. Kevin and David had hit the scarecrow's legs at nearly the exact same time—the whole point of the *cross-attack.*

They were gettin' good.

Better than him and Wiley.

But whatever.

He was thirsty.

"I want some Kool-Aid," said Grant. "That purple flavor would taste so good right now..."

"I want that Miracle shit," said Wiley. "I wanna snort it *so fucking bad,* man."

Grant shot Wiley a sideways glance. He didn't see the appeal in snorting *anything,* much less a dangerous "mystery drug" the Boys got on sale from some weirdo in Alabama.

"I even like the name," said Wiley. *"Miracle..."*

Grant shuddered. Miracles were what Jesus performed. Drugs shouldn't be called that.

"How you know it's even a *drug?*" asked Grant. "Could be any white powder. Like laundry detergent."

"Nah," said Wiley. "Ain't no laundry detergent. Tommy's tried it, and it must be *really* fuckin' good if he don't wanna share it yet." His eyes flashed with hunger. "I'm talkin' *wild* shit."

Grant's stomach tightened. He didn't like the idea of ingesting *any* unknown substance, and he didn't like that Wiley seemed weirdly *hungry* for it, and he definitely didn't like the idea of—

"CROSS-ATTAAAAAAACK!"

DONG!-DONNNG!

—hitting people with *crowbars.*

He pulled his knees to his chest, digging his fingers into his sweaty shins.

This is insane...

What we're doing is insane...

Wiley went on again about how bad he wanted to snort Miracle and how "awesome" it probably was. Grant just stared at the scarecrow.

"...you okay, dude?" asked Wiley. "You been quiet lately."

"Yeah..." said Grant. "...just tired...that's all..."

But that wasn't all, was it?

Every day he hung with the Smoketown Boys was a day he faced *danger.* And the dangers kept piling up. He could get thrown in jail for drug possession, or die from that Miracle stuff, or get the shit beaten out of him by Bill and Kenny, or—

Wait a minute.

Bill and Kenny.

What if they *did* have some huge, epic attack plan for tonight?

Or what if Graham—

"We finished our set," said David, panting. "Y'all's turn."

Grant took in a long, slow breath. He flicked his eyes to the crowbar beside him.

Was this all really worth it?

"*Playin' with fire...*"

His mom's voice hissed through his head.

"You're playin' with fire, son..."

"...and you're gonna get burned."

1970s

CHAPTER IX

HOMEWORK PARTIES

"No..."

Jack's eyes darkened.

"...Smoketown Boys...never run..."

"A HOMEWORK PARTY?" asked Kevin.

Sunlight poured through the windows, hot on Grant's face. He leaned back on his bed and stared at the ceiling. Kevin sat in the chair across from him, eyes bright with disbelief.

"You *serious?"* asked Kevin.

"Yep..." said Grant. "...with party hats..."

"A homework party with party hats?" Kevin guffawed. "And your mom invited *girls* to it?"

Grant nodded slowly.

Yep.

Hot girls, too.

"She called other moms in the PTA," said Grant. "To invite their daughters over..."

He grimaced.

"...for a homework party."

"Damn..." said Kevin. "Did any show up?" He laughed and slapped his knee. "And did they wear the hats?"

"No," said Grant. "It was so lame, dude. Just me and my mom, wearin' party hats..."

He flicked his gaze around his bedroom.

Didn't even wanna say the next part.

"...some people drove by, though. Egged our house."

"Egged your house?"

"Yeah," said Grant. "Yelled *'Homework parties are gay!'* from their cars."

"Holy shit..." said Kevin. "That means other people heard about it, too. That can *kill* a guy's rep. You know that right?"

Grant sighed.

He knew.

Rep. Rep. Rep.

Why was everything in high school about *rep*?

Who you ran with. Who you fought. Who you fucked.

In middle school, things had been simple. Popular kids at the top, dorks, skanks and losers at the bottom, with a nice, sizeable gray area in the middle. *The middle.* He liked the middle. Felt comfortable. Safe. The top brought too much pressure, the bottom, too much shame. Less stress in the middle. But high school didn't work like that. You couldn't just stay in your lane, you had to keep your rep up and actively maintain it, or get eaten alive.

A guy with zero rep got bullied, picked on by everyone.

And never got any pussy.

Ever.

Kevin clasped his hands together. "You keep havin' these homework parties, you ain't gonna get no girlfriend, man. Probably not a date to prom, either."

Grant stared at the ceiling. He knew. He'd likely stay a virgin until college—lucky to even get a handjob. For the next four years he'd be reduced to asking others about their experiences and living through *them*. Like he did now.

"Oh, did I tell ya?" Kevin draped an arm over the side of the chair. "Goin' to a badass house party this weekend. You should join me."

Grant's eyes widened.

A house party?

Usually an upperclassmen thing—never heard of freshmen who got invited.

"Whose?"

"The Smoketown Boys."

"The Smoketown Boys?"

Kevin lifted his chin like he'd won something.

Grant frowned. The Smoketown Boys were *bad news*. Had seen'em at Walmart before. Blasted their music in the parking lot, acted like they owned the place. *Dangerous.*

He shook his head. "I heard those guys smoke drugs..."

"Monkey," said Kevin. "They smoke Monkey. It's like weed, but better."

"How?" asked Grant. "And why's it called Monkey?"

"I dunno," said Kevin, "somethin' about chemicals and shit. Anyway, they invited *me* to their Smokehouse Party this weekend, and it's gonna be *awesome.* There's gonna be so many hot girls, dude. Shit's gonna get wild."

He looked straight at Grant.

"The polar opposite of your mom's homework party."

Grant narrowed his eyes. Didn't need that "polar opposite" comment. But whatever.

"How'd *you* get invited?" he asked.

"'Cause I'm cool, man," said Kevin. "They see potential in me. *Possibilities.*"

"Possibilities? To do what?"

Kevin shrugged. "Help'em sell Monkey, earn money. Party with'em. Scrap if I need to. That kinda shit."

"Sell Monkey?" Grant's stomach tightened. "Sellin' drugs is illegal...you can go to jail for that."

"Whatever, dude," said Kevin. "It's not like we're sellin' on the street or somethin'. Just to people we know, who won't narc and shit."

Grant crossed his arms. "You shouldn't hang with those guys, Kevin. And I def—"

"See?" asked Kevin. "It ain't your mom. It's *you.*"

He leaned forward.

"You're the reason people call you *'Good Guy Grant.' You're* the reason why you got zero rep, and people laugh at you and egg your house while you have gay-ass homework parties with your fucking mom."

Grant's face turned hot. He looked out the window, away from Kevin. A line of red ants marched from a smear of yolk and broken eggshell on the driveway.

("homework parties are gay!")

He made a fist.

"...what time's the party?"

1970s

CHAPTER X

HE'S A GOOD GUY

"Snort it, Grant!

Snort that shit!

Fucking sn—"

GRANT STOOD IN the middle of the Smokehouse Party like an earlobe. Present. Wobbling. Unnoticed. Dread crept in as he scanned the chaos around him, every instinct screaming to get out before something *bad* happened. Pungent smoke clouded the air as older students danced to The Beatles, a band his mom said was anti-Christian. People in the backyard clustered in small groups, drinking, smoking, laughing too loud. One dude puked on the side of a tree.

"Let's get fucked up!" A short, stocky guy knocked back shots of a clear liquid with a hot blonde, then started making out with her in front of *everyone.*

Grant's stomach tightened.

Hedonism.

That's what his mom would call this.

Pure *hedonism.*

And yet...

("homework parties are gay!")

("homework parties are g—")

...this was *the scene* he had to join.

To be cool.

And gain rep.

He searched for familiar faces. *It's okay, Grant. You can do this.* Couldn't stand by himself like a loser. Had to talk to people. He knew that.

But to who?

About what?

It dawned on Grant that he didn't have anything interesting to say to anyone.

Slowly, he retreated to the safety of the wall behind him.

Gotta get outta here...

"This your buddy?"

One of the tallest, lankiest dudes in school peered over him. *Larry Longface.* And he *did* have a long face, like the rumors claimed.

After brief introductions, the questions began:

"Do you smoke?"

"How 'bout your friends?"

"Can you sell to'em?"

"How much?"

"Can you scrap?"

"How many fights you won?"

Grant lied through his teeth, answering in the way he thought Larry wanted to hear. He glanced at the Monkey joint in his left hand and the beer in his right.

Where'd these come from?

Didn't remember smokin'.

Or drinkin'.

And yet, *he did.*

He both remembered it, and *not* remembered it.

Larry asked another question, which Grant answered, but he didn't know what he said.

This...

This is what bein' 'fucked up' is.

He tried to focus.

Larry switched topics.

"How many hot freshmen you know?"

"Do they fuck?"

"Or suck dick?"

"What about anal?"

"Haha, I'm just kiddin, man."

"I know freshmen don't do anal."

"Or do they?"

Again, Grant's mouth spoke, but he didn't hear the words. *He didn't know what the fuck he was saying.*

Larry took a swig from an oversized red cup and offered some. Grant didn't want any *(gotta get outta here...)* but his mouth said *yes,* so he took a sip. Sweet. Tangy. But with a kick of gasoline. Different from beer. Where was his beer? He thought he had a beer. His joint, too, had vanished. *What the fuck's going on?*

Larry asked if he liked tequila and his mouth said *(no)* yes. *"How 'bout vodka?" Yes.* He said *yes* to a bunch more questions, maybe alcohol-related, maybe not. It wasn't him speaking anymore—it was his mouth. *His mouth had become a separate entity.*

At one point, Larry got pissed and said something dismissive. Grant wanted to run, but his feet stayed planted. Kevin tried to defend him.

"He'll help with sales!" said Kevin. *"He's a good guy!"*

A dude wearing a cap with a crow on the front walked up and shook his hand. "This is Tommy Glick," said Kevin. *"The leader..."*

Tommy asked him questions and his mouth answered. Tommy scowled *(uh-oh...)* and said something negative, to which Kevin said, *"He's a good guy! He'll help with sales!"*

Larry poked his chest and asked something in a sharp, accusatory tone. His mouth answered even as his mind screamed, *"What the hell is anyone talking about?"* Kevin handed him a cup of water. *"You look fucked up, dude..."* He chugged it. Felt nauseous. Queasy. Acid surged up. *Stomach so tight...* But words became clear again. He spoke—not his mouth this time, but *him.*

"Sorry, I'm too fucked up, y'all," he said. "But I want a chance. To help y'all sell shit. And *dominate.*"

Wasn't sure where that last part came from, but it seemed to have an effect. *Dominate.* Tommy and Larry nodded with approval, then asked him more questions—wasn't sure what, but he made sure to work in the word *dominate* every time he answered. Finally, Tommy shrugged and looked at Larry. *"Your call, Larry. You're the one who's been talkin' to him and shit."*

Larry took a gulp from his red cup, studying Grant.

"Alright, little dude," said Larry. "If you're a good guy, and wanna help us *dominate,* we'll give you a chance."

He extended his hand.

Grant reached to take it—

—but then scrambled outside, hot vomit spraying from his mouth like a fire hydrant.

"He's a good guy!" said Kevin.

"He'll help with sales!"

PART II

KENNY STUDIES GERMAN

1970s

CHAPTER I

EIN ZEICH, EIN LEISS

"If I can say somethin' cool," said Kenny, "somethin' real badass, in German, right before I knock a dude out, it'd be awesome.

Add some impact, ya know what I'm sayin'?"

"EIN ZEICH, EIN leiss..."

Kenny Moser bobbed his head to a special rhythm; a rhythm only he could hear.

"Ein schnell, ein krieg..."

This German shit sounded badass.

Heavy.

Powerful.

Evening light soaked the yard behind his family's trailer, fading gold over patchy grass, rusted junk, and weathered lawn furniture. He rocked in a sun-bleached plastic chair, grinning.

Felt good today.

Real fun learnin' new words, then makin' up new ones. Didn't matter if it was correct fuckin' German or not. Just as long as it *sounded* German.

Rule number ein *about foreign languages:* if shit sounded cool, and badass, that's all that mattered.

"Kenny!" His mom's voice rang out from the trailer. "Did you clean your room yet?"

Kenny clicked his tongue.

Fuckin' bitch...

He stood. "Mom, I—"

"You best clean your room! Or you can forget about dinner!"

With a scowl, he pushed his dark wavy hair aside.

Fuck.

He'd already cleaned his fuckin' room.

It was clean enough for him.

A fly buzzed near; he swatted it away. Probably more comin' soon. Drawn to the pile of rotten fruit in the corner of the yard, away from his mom's prying eyes. He sniffed. Didn't smell *too* bad; like sour wine, with only a hint of fresh puke.

He glanced down at his German book. The cover showed houses and apples and dumb-ass stick figures smiling. At the bottom, a cartoon owl wearing a graduation cap pointed at the word *Haus,* which, he assumed, meant the word "house." But he didn't care for German that sounded like English—no, no. *That was bullshit.* No reason to even study a foreign language if shit sounded the same. He didn't like *all* the German words, either. Only ones that sounded aggressive. Powerful.

Like *krankenwagen.*

Krankenhaus.

And *schmetterling.*

Badass shit.

Like weapons.

Addin' *ein* cranked the power up even further:

Ein krankenwagen!

Ein krankenhaus!

Ein schmetterling!

But he wanted more. Wanted to mash 'em together, make new ones, even more badass than before—

"Kenny!" said his mom.

"Gimme a minute!"

He tossed the book in his chair.

Just as I was learnin' more cool shit...

Still nodding to that rhythm only he could hear, he marched across the yard, picked up his baseball bat and took a swing. A whoosh split the air; sunlight glinted off the barrel in a cold metallic glimmer.

Nice.

Could beat some serious ass with this...

Glad they found the bats at the baseball field.

Saved money that way.

"Kenny!" said his mom. "Don't make me—"

"Just gimme five minutes, *ein mutter!* I'm studyin' German!"

"What?"

"German!"

Cussing in German under his breath *("fuckin' krankenwagen bitch...")*, he picked up a soft, caved-in apple off the lawn, its skin split and oozing. A worm wiggled out as he lobbed it in the air.

"EIN ZEICH!"

He swung—

"EIN LEIIIISS!"

—it exploded across the yard.

Fuck yeah...

German does *add impact...*

When I hit shit.

It played louder now—the rhythm only *he* could hear. He grinned. All outta apples. *Time for the big ones.* Nodding like he'd heard good news, he moseyed over to the pile of rotten watermelons, green shells sunken and cracked. Yellowjackets buzzed low over the pink mush weeping into the grass. The smell hit harder here: fermented, meaty. Alive.

Can't believe groceries give this shit away for free....

He raised the bat high, grinning wider, stretching his face.

"EIN ZEICH, EIN LEISS!"

"EIN SPRIGGEN, DIR SPRIGGEN!"

"EIN REISSVERSCHLUSS!"

"EIN KRANKENWAGEN!"

"EIN KRANKENHAUS!"

"EIIIIIIIN SCHMETTERLING!"

His chest heaved. Rotten watermelon lay strewn across the yard like chunks of brain and flesh. A yellowjacket landed on his cheek. He didn't flinch.

That last one—

—schmetterling.

That sounded truly badass.

Forgot what it meant (*butterfly? no, that'd be gay...*), but it hit hard. Would have to save that one for—

"Kenny!" said his mom. "What in blazes are you doin' out th—"

"EIN MUTTERRRR!"

He slammed the bat into the rotten watermelons with each word:

"I'M!"

"STUDYIN'!"

He froze, panting, skin sticky with juice and sweat.

Then, with full force—

"GERMAAAAAAAAAAAAN!"

PART III

PRELUDE TO CHAOS

1970s

CHAPTER I

PREPARATION

"Eeny, meeny, miny, moe.

Catch a weedboy by his toe."

TOMMY GLICK RAN his thumb across the lone crow etched into his cap.

("find it, tommy...")

("the temple...")

Still kept thinking about it—

("mikey...")

—that "temple" or whatever.

("why'd you do it?")

And Mikey,

("it was the pills, wasn't it?")

("the fucking pills made you t—")

trying to speak with him,

("FIND IT, TOMMY.")

to tell him—

("THE TEM—")

A cold shiver slid down his back. He turned to the Smokehouse meeting table. Jack Kindley and Mitchell Mouse bickered while Larry Knowles poked fun at both. Sunlight streamed through the windows, warm on the floorboards, while the Possibles outside hammered their crowbars against the iron limbs of the Bill-Scarecrow.

"CROSS-ATTAAAAAAACK!"

DONG!

DONNNG!

"Fuck!"

"My hand stings!"

A lava lamp sat bubbling on the windowsill, purple globs rising through red magma.

Mouse stared at Jack. "You keep callin' me 'Mitchey Mouse', thinkin' it's gonna rile me up. But it doesn't. You ever notice that?"

Jack reclined in his chair. "Mitchey Mouse, Mitchey Mouse, Mitchey Mouuuuuse..."

Larry chuckled, flicking his eyes between them.

Mouse continued. "Now, when other people call me that, it pisses me off. But not you, Jack. Because when you do it, it sounds like a pussy. Tryin' to speak. Flappin' its pussy-lips, ya know? Like—"

"Let's get back to business." Tommy put his cap back on. "What's next on the agenda?"

"Agenda?" asked Mouse. "So we got fuckin' *agendas* now? Like for classes, or bullshit like that?"

Jack slammed his fist on the table. *"Robert's Rules of Order!"*

"Yes," said Tommy. "We have agendas at fuckin' meetin's, Mouse. Get used to it."

"Agendas are good," said Larry. "Keeps shit organized."

Mouse returned to flexing his biceps. "Agendas are gay..."

Jack scrunched his freckled face as he flipped through his *SMOKETOWN BOYS — OFFICIAL MEETING MINUTES* notebook. "Looks like we gotta talk about...the ribbons. What color should they be?"

"Ribbons?" asked Tommy.

Larry stretched his long legs under the table. "The ribbons we're gonna tie around dudes' wrists. To show they paid the party entrance fee."

"Ribbons are gay," said Mouse. "Like agendas."

Tommy let out a slow breath. "That's why we changed it to paper bracelets, Mouse. Do y'all not remember that? Jack, you not writin' that shit down?"

Jack flipped through pages. "Whoops..."

"I remember now," said Mouse. "Yeah, I *guess* paper bracelets are less gay than ribbons. Probably why I voted for it."

"But what color should they be?" asked Larry.

"Fuck's it matter?" asked Mouse. "Just buy the cheapest sh—"

"Color's important, Mouse," said Jack. "It's the little things that can make, or break, a party. And in keepin' with our sales theme, I motion that we go with *purple.*"

Larry nodded. "Purple would be good. Purple Dream is gonna *sell*, y'all."

Tommy agreed. Purple Dream, the new weed strain they'd pick up from the Horse People, *should* sell—but he wasn't sure how much they'd supply.

"Fine," said Mouse. "Let's go with purple, then."

They all raised their hands and voted.

"Passed!" Tommy hit the table with his gavel. It was made of light, lacquered wood; low-quality, but fit his hand like it belonged there.

"Did you really have to buy a gavel?" asked Mouse.

Tommy shrugged. "It was cheap at Walmart."

Jack scribbled into his Meeting Minutes. "Alright, next on the agenda. Christmas lights. Should we buy'em for the Smokehouse, or not?"

"They did look cool at Young's place," said Larry.

"I dunno..." Jack tapped his pencil. "We already got a lava lamp. Why not buy a few more, make sure our style is synchronized?"

"Ambiance," said Mouse. "'Cause Christmas lights add *ambiance* to everything. Make people festive and shit."

They discussed it for a while. Larry said another lava lamp would be overkill, while Jack hammered the importance of *design synchronocity*. Mouse repeated *ambiance, ambiance* like it was a ten-dollar word, probably to show Jack he knew big words, too.

In the end, they voted to buy both: Christmas lights *and* another lava lamp. But not 'til the next party, once they knew how much budget was left.

"Passed!" Tommy smacked the table with the gavel.

The Possibles sauntered in through the side door, brandishing crowbars and looking exhausted.

Kevin wiped sweat from his brow. "We finished our fifty cross-attacks. Reportin' in."

"Fifty *each?"* asked Larry. "Or fifty *total?"*

Kevin scrunched his face. "...fifty total..."

The Boys erupted in commotion.

"We said fifty each!"

"Fuckin' pussies!"

"You best take this shit seriously!"

"Boy Scouts meet on Sundays!"

Tommy raised a hand, and the room quietened. "Y'all can take a break after this, there's snacks and Kool-Aid in the kitchen. But then do fifty *each*. Is that fuckin' clear?"

The Possibles nodded wearily.

"Sales reports this week," said Larry. *"Go!"*

Each Possible stepped forward, rattling off their numbers while Jack recorded them in his Meeting Minutes. Wiley had done the best, with David, Kevin and especially Grant well below target. Honestly, Tommy didn't expect *any* of the Possibles to hit their goals often, but it was important to set expectations high. Keep the pressure on, so they didn't slack off.

"Okay," said Tommy. "So everyone except Wiley sucked dick at sellin' Monkey this week."

"Y'all better step shit up!" said Mouse. "If y'all wanna be one of the Boys!"

Jack raised a finger. "We're a business. And if you don't perform, you get *fired.*"

The Possibles' eyes widened.

"How 'bout the new ratio?" asked Larry. "Any complaints? Or anyone noticed we're cuttin' the weed with more tobacco now?"

The Possibles mumbled no. Grant raised his hand.

"Grant," said Tommy.

"I mean," said Grant. "Not *yet*, but if they do...what do we say?"

Larry rolled his shoulders. "We're the only squad in Crow sellin' weed. They can bitch all they want, but they'll have to get used to it."

"A *monopoly,*" said Jack. "We got a *monopoly* on the market. Plain and simple."

"But what if..." said Grant. "...*another* squad starts sellin' weed? Without cuttin' it with tobacco? And claimin' it's more pure?"

Larry showed his teeth. "Then we ask'em to stop. Nicely."

The Boys chuckled. Grant looked confused, so Tommy spelled it out for him: "We teach'em a lesson," he said. "So they don't sell that shit no more."

"Problem solved," said Larry.

Mouse flexed, then patted his bicep. "We'll fuckin' *take care* of any squads that try that shit. Just tell us."

"Especially in Crow," said Tommy. "We already know about the Zion soccer team. They keep mostly to Zion, though."

"But y'all fuckin' tell us!" Mouse rose from his chair and pounded his chest. "If y'all hear about *any* of them Zion bitches sellin' in Crow! Y'all fuckin' got me?"

The Possibles nodded.

Mouse pounded his chest one last time, then sat back down—slowly.

Tommy drummed his fingers on the hard oak table. Like Jack said, they had a *monopoly.* They got away with cuttin' their weed with a shit-ton of tobacco because they were the only dealers at Crow County High.

People could buy from them, or fuck off.

***

Jack tapped his pencil against the chalkboard David held.

"So that's how sellin' Purple Dream," said Jack, "will straight-up *accelerate* our overall sales, over time, by addin' *diversity* to our product line. You can buy Monkey for normal price, *or* pay more for Purple Dream, *or* get the special combo with both. Ya know, to compare'em and shit."

Everyone applauded and praised Jack's line graph. Even Mouse. *"Makes shit easy to understand."*

"Any questions?" asked Larry. "Y'all best push that special combo, 'cause it's a good fuckin' deal."

Mouse glanced up from his biceps. "It's like the combos you get at Dairy Queen. Or Burger King."

Jack nodded. "Yep, and—"

"Or McDonald's," said Mouse. "Or Hardee's. Or Wendy's. Or—"

"They get it, Mouse!" said Jack.

"Pop quiz," said Larry to the Possibles. "When y'all sell Purple Dream to other underclassmen and middle schoolers and shit, how y'all gonna pitch it?"

"Differentiate," said Jack. "How y'all gonna *differentiate* our products?"

Tommy stroked his chin. He liked this pop-quiz thing Larry had started. Kept the Possibles sharp.

"Grant?" asked Larry.

"We, uhh..." said Grant. "...say that Monkey is good, ya know, to get you high and stuff, but Purple Dream, it, uhh...gets you *really* high."

"Uhh, uhh," mocked Mouse. "Gets you really, *really* high!"

The Boys snickered.

Larry's long face drooped in disapproval. "Grant, you couldn't sell water in the desert with that fuckin' pitch. No wonder you sold shitty last week."

Grant's face fell. He turned his gaze to the floor.

"Wilin' Wiley," said Tommy. "Your turn."

Let's see what you got, Wiley...

Hopefully better than Good Guy Grant.

Wiley stepped forward. "We tell'em that Purple Dream is a totally *different* high than Monkey. 'Cause it's purple, and dusted with shit, so it's more of a body high. Helps you feel relaxed and peaceful, like a dream." He paused. "And that's why it's called...*Purple Dream.*"

The room fell silent.

Slowly, the Boys began applauding.

"Not bad, Wiley," said Larry.

"See?" asked Mouse. "That's why Wiley sells his shit."

"Differentiate," said Jack. "That's how y'all *differentiate* that shit."

Wiley smiled, looking relieved.

As the applause faded, Grant raised his hand.

"Grant," said Tommy.

"What does 'dusted' mean?" asked Grant.

The Boys groaned.

"What?" asked Grant. "I...I dunno..."

"Asian David," said Tommy. "Tell him."

Alright, David...

You better remember what we taught you at Cracker Barrel...

David adjusted his thick-rimmed glasses. "'Dusted,'" he said, "means it's got stuff sprinkled on it. Usually pill powder."

"But, like..." said Grant. "...what kinda pills?"

The Boys erupted.

"Who the fuck cares?"

"Shit that'll fuck you up!"

"Or make you feel good!"

"Or both!"

Tommy leaned back in his chair. He'd forgotten that most of the Possibles still didn't know much about drugs. *Needed educated.*

"Usually pain killers," said Tommy. "Or muscle relaxants. Shit like that."

Jack held up a finger. "But don't *tell* people that. We gotta have a layer of mystery, of *intrigue* to our new product."

The Boys talked about it some more and agreed that the *mystery* and *intrigue* of Purple Dream was the icing on the cake.

"If kids ask what it's dusted with," said Jack, "you just laugh and say '*some good stuff, don't you worry.*' Y'all got that?"

The Possibles said they did.

As Jack continued lecturing the Possibles on the value of mystery and intrigue, Tommy turned his gaze out the window.

Feels like I'm missin' somethin'...

A pressure settled behind his ribs. He scanned the clear blue sky—no cowboy-hat-shaped clouds today, but he still felt Bill's presence. Like he was out there, watching. Waiting. For the right time to strike.

But without Graham?

And Young?

What could two guys do?

A cool breeze blew in from the window.

("desayunaste, glick?")

("YA DESA-FUCKIN'-YU—")

"...and it's *the way* you laugh," said Jack, "and say *'some good stuff, don't you worry'* that's really key. To spread the mystery. And intrigue. I want y'all to practice this, and—"

"Alright." Tommy waved the gavel, dismissing the Possibles. "Y'all get shit from the kitchen, take it out back and eat and whatever. Then do your fifty cross-attacks. *Each.* We got security issues to discuss."

He smacked the gavel against his palm.

Sure would feel good to pound Bill's face with it.

1970s

CHAPTER II

SECURITY ISSUES

"Besides, even if they do show up..."

Mouse flexed his bicep and kissed it.

"...I'll introduce'em to Muscle Man Mouse."

JACK LEANED FORWARD, his freckled face serious.

"Here's what *I'd* do, if *I* was Bill and Kenny..."

He paused and glanced around the room, like a spy might be near.

"...the night of the party, when everything's wild and shit, I'd hang back in the woods and snatch up the Possibles. One by one. Snatch'em up, tie'em to trees, shit like that. Then, after they're all strung up, go for us..."

He narrowed his eyes.

"...one by fuckin' one."

"Mmm-hmm," said Mouse. "And how would they 'snatch up' people, Jack? Without gettin' seen?"

Jack darted his eyes to the left and right, like the possibilities flashed before him.

"...a distraction."

He nodded like he agreed with himself.

"Start a fire," he said. "Out in the woods. So everyone says, *'Holy shit, it's a fire! We gotta put that shit out!'* And while everyone's focused on the fire, snatch up the Possibles, tie'em to trees. Maybe beat the shit out of'em. Then come for *us,* one by one."

He leaned back, clasping his hands.

"'Course, that's what *I* would do. Dunno if Bill and Kenny are that smart, though."

Mouse sighed and rubbed his temples. "Pretty sure people would notice Possibles gettin' 'snatched up,' Jack. Even with a fire. They'd probably scream and yell and—"

"Well, I'm just sayin'—"

"CROSS-ATTAAAAAACK!"

DONG!

DONG!

"Ahh! Fuck!"

"My hand!"

"Quit y'all's pussy-achin'!"

The Boys glanced out the window. The Possibles had slacked off after their break, so Larry went outside to whip'em into shape. Could still call him in for a vote, though.

Mouse clicked his tongue. "Do they *really* need to keep practicin' that shit? Shouldn't they be helpin' clean the house by now?"

DONG!

DONNNG!

"Aaah!"

"Let us wear gloves!"

"Fuck gloves! Y'all want tampons, too?"

"I mean," said Mouse, "now that Graham's not with the cowboy bitches anymore, no worries, right? And even Young's wantin' to partner up on coke, so who gives a fuck about Bill and Kenny? What can two guys do?"

"Guerilla warfare," said Jack. "Vietcong style. Even with only *two* guys, they could..."

While Jack and Mouse bickered, Tommy stared out the window at the treeline, the forest beyond shrouded in darkness.

("desayunaste, glick?")

("DESA-FUCKIN'-YUNAS—")

He took off his cap and ran his fingers through his hair.

Why do I keep hearin' that?

Over and over?

And the leaves, the leaves outside on the fucking trees, why did they swirl?

("i love you, tommy...")

("you're the only one I let do this...")

Samantha.

His Samantha.

("i love you, tomm—")

("you're the onl—")

She fucking said *he* was the only one who—

but her words?

Why did they swirl?

Like the leaves outside.

Just swirling, swirling, swirling sw—

("i fucked your girlfriend after prom...")

—did Bill really fuck her?

Did he really—

("she told me to bust on her face...")

("and in her mouth...")

—no.

("did you kiss her after that, tommy?")

("you didn't kiss *her after that, did ya?")*

No.

("i hope that bitch brushed her teeth!")

The leaves, why did they SWIRL into HER fucking face, her cum and blood-smeared face while Bill thrusted and thrusted and pounded her little body and she stared into her OWN FUCKING REFLECTION in his FUCKING SUNGLASSES and—

"Earth to Tommy!" said Mouse.

Slowly, Tommy's surroundings sharpened into focus. The leaves outside had fallen still, but his unease stuck with him, thick in his gut.

Gotta snap out of it...

"...Vietcong, right?" asked Tommy. "So we sh—"

"That was twenty minutes ago, Tommy," said Mouse. "Now we're talkin' about coke."

"Coke?" asked Tommy.

"Yes, Tommy," said Mouse. "And not Coca-Cola, either. You're smokin' too much."

Jack furrowed his brow. "You have been driftin' off a lot lately, T—"

"What *about* coke?" asked Tommy.

"How much we sellin' at the party?" asked Mouse. "We gotta train the Possibles to sell that shit, too, right?"

Ah, shit...

Tommy grimaced.

He'd hoped they wouldn't bring that up.

"Okay," said Tommy. "I know I said that Young wants to partner up on coke and shit. But..."

("no lo siento, cabrón...")

("por nada.")

"...somethin' don't feel right."

"Wait," said Mouse. "Now you think he was full of shit?"

Jack flinched, like the words stung. "Tommy, we already approved the coke deal via Table Vote. Now you're sayin' it was sketch?"

"Have you called him yet?" asked Mouse. "To talk about pricin'?"

"No," said Tommy. "I haven't called him yet. But—"

"You haven't called him yet?" asked Mouse. "But we were gonna sell *coke* at our party, too! Coke, Monkey, that new Purple Dream shit, everything! We voted on that shit, Tommy! We voted on it!"

"Technically..." Jack flipped through the Meeting Minutes. "We only voted to *discuss terms* with Young. Not on when we'd buy from him, or how much, or—"

"Technically," said Mouse, "that's some bullshit, 'cause Tommy *said* he'd call Young, and he fuckin' hasn't."

"We ain't sellin' coke yet," said Tommy. "First off, the whole focus of this party is supposed to be Purple Dream. We might get a shit-ton from the Horse People and we gotta focus on that before we fuck with coke. And second, coke don't go with weed, Mouse. They'd fuckin', counteract each other."

Jack nodded. "That is true. Cocaine is a stimulant, weed mellows you out. We should have a coke-themed party separate from a Purple Dream-themed party." His eyes lit up. "And have *white* bracelets, instead of purple ones. And have everyone wear white!"

"And," said Tommy, "this Purple shit *will* fucking sell, Mouse. Jack's already wrote up a long list of potential new customers."

"Okay," said Mouse, "but why don't we go ahead and buy at least *a little* from Young, to sample it, and—"

Tommy sharpened his tone. "How many fucking customers have *you* lined up for us? Huh, Mouse? To even sell fucking Purple Dream? Or, lemme guess, you're just invitin' girls to smoke our shit for free, like you always fuckin' do?"

Mouse's face turned red. A silence fell as Jack jotted notes in his Meeting Minutes, nodding approvingly.

"Alright, fine," said Mouse. "We don't gotta sell coke yet. Geez. But we *voted* on you callin' Young and settin' that shit—"

"I will," said Tommy. "But one new drug at a time."

He leaned back in his chair.

"Besides," he said, "if we make fuckin' bank from sellin' Purple, that'll give us more cash to buy from Young. Not like he's gonna front shit to us, given the recent history."

The others agreed that was a good point, and the discussion moved on.

"Next on the agenda," said Jack. "Trip to Nashville."

"Nashville-Cashville, baby!" said Mouse. "Fuck yeah!"

"Time to diversify our procurement," said Jack. "So we don't have to rely on the Horse People."

Tommy clenched his jaw.

Fuck.

Still didn't feel right about drivin' to places like Nashville to find new suppliers. Could get ripped off, or worse.

"Let's table that," said Tommy. "Until after the party. I wanna see how much Purple Dream we can sell and finalize shit with Young. Then we'll know how much cash we can take to Nashville."

Mouse and Jack bitched for a while, but finally relented.

"Back to security issues," said Tommy. "Jack's got a point. Bill and Kenny still pose a threat. And who knows? They might recruit guys from other squads, too. So we should do pre-party cleanup ourselves and keep the Possibles practicin'. Just in case."

"CROSS-ATTAAAAAACK!"

DONG!

DONNNNG!

"Fuck yeah!"

"Good job, David!"

"That's what I'm fuckin' talkin' about!"

Tommy spun the gavel in his hand. Sounded like Asian David had improved—maybe he had promise. Didn't seem to bitch and complain like the others. Quiet, but listened real good.

"Whatever," said Mouse. "But once the party starts, they gotta help with—"

"Nope," said Tommy. "Possibles are gettin' special security duties."

"*'Special security duties'?*" asked Mouse. "The fuck?"

Jack twirled his pencil. "This was my idea. We'll assign specific guard areas to the Possibles and have'em rotate every thirty minutes, so that way they're always checkin' in with each other. If somebody's not at their station, they'll know somethin's up and come get us."

"Mmm-hmm, mmm-hmm..." Mouse nodded like he'd heard some bullshit. "Sounds pointless and overly complicated. But sure, let's do that!"

Jack ignored him. "Now, Bill and Kenny *may* attempt an alternate strategy. So here's another thing I'd do if I was th—"

Mouse clasped his head. "Does this shit ever end? They're just *two* dudes now, they ain't doin' *shit* without Graham and Young, and even if they do—"

"Let him finish," said Tommy.

"Thank you, Tommy," said Jack. "Like I was sayin', an alternate strategy

I'd consider is recruitin' dudes to straight-up *infiltrate* the party. Pay'em in cocaine..." His freckled face turned cold. "...to help *sabotage* shit."

Tommy's eyes widened.

Sabotage.

From new *dudes in Bill's fucking Posse.*

With free coke as a recruitment driver...

This other theory of Jack's sounded way more likely than the earlier "Vietcong-like" strategy.

Tommy stroked his chin. "That *does* sound possible..."

But who would they recruit? Maybe the Bedford Twins, or maybe—

"CROSS-ATTAAAAAACK!"

DONG!

DONNNG!

"Good, Kevin!"

"That's what I'm fuckin' talkin' about!"

"So we make the party invite-only!" said Mouse. "Like, make it strict as fuck, so that *no one* shows up uninvited. Nobody—even chicks, even *hot ones*—gets in unless cleared by us, first. That way, we only have trusted people at the party, not random-asses who may or may not be new 'secret members' of Bill's Posse."

Tommy stroked his chin. "Not a bad idea. Makin' it invite-only might make it feel more exclusive, too. Jack, what you think of that?"

"You know," said Jack. "I'm actually okay with that. That's the first good idea I've heard from Mouse. Maybe he *does* have a br—"

"Your mother is a whore, Jack," said Mouse. "A red-headed whore who sucks dicks." He looked up from his biceps and glared. "And she swallows, too."

Jack's face darkened. "Listen, *Mitchey Mouse,* my mom's Catholic, so—"

"The fuck's her bein' Catholic gotta do with anything? Catholic bitches don't sw—"

Tommy hit the table with his gavel.

"Settle down, y'all! Settle down..."

He rapped the table a few times more.

Felt cool doin' that.

Like a judge.

"Alright." He rose from his chair. "Let's update the Possibles and Larry on the gameplan."

"Wait, wait," said Jack. "I just wanna say somethin'. For the record."

"For the recoooord..." mocked Mouse.

"I just got this feelin'," said Jack.

"I just got this feeeeelin'," mocked Mouse. *"In my pussssaayyy..."*

Jack grimaced. "Like, I'm a hundred-percent sure that Bill and Kenny are gonna *try* somethin'. Maybe snatch dudes up, tie'em to trees. Maybe recruit new Posse members. Or maybe..."

He leaned forward.

"...somethin' we ain't even thought of yet."

"My Catholic mom sucks diiiiiick," mocked Mouse. *"And swalloooows..."*

"This is *serious shit,* Mouse!" said Jack. "We gotta be *ready.* At all times. On our guard. Vigilant. And don't forget..."

Jack whipped out a green water gun from under the table. The Kentucky Blood sauce shifted inside, thick and heavy.

"...I'm packin' this baby, just in case."

1970s

CHAPTER III

CUATRO CUERVOS

"Somethin' bad's gonna happen.

I can feel it!"

TOMMY STOOD IN the backyard, twirling a vial of Miracle between his fingers. His Boys passed a Monkey blunt around while the sweat-drenched Possibles stood before him, all wielding crowbars. Behind them loomed the scarecrow, silent and still, its cowboy hat slouched low.

"Repeat after me," said Larry. "At the party, y'all are not to get fucked up on any drugs, alcohol, or shit like that..."

The Possibles raised their right hands and repeated in unison: *"At the party, we are not to get fucked up on any drugs, alcohol, or shit like that..."*

"And y'all will totally abstain from any of that bullshit, and focus solely on your party responsibilities..."

"And we will totally abstain from any of that bullshit, and focus solely on our party responsibilities..."

"...which are to keep an eye out for any drama, bullshit, people stealin' shit, and especially, above all—"

"Bill-fuckin'-Cunningham" said Tommy. "And Skinny-fuckin'-Kenny."

"...which are to keep an eye out for any drama, bullshit..."

While the Possibles repeated their oath, Tommy held the vial of Miracle to the sunlight. The white powder sparkled within, revealing hints of pale blue.

"Let'em split a vial?" asked Jack. "They don't need much. Just enough for a quick snort." His freckled face grew serious. "In case shit *goes down...*"

"I dunno..." said Tommy.

"Why not?" Mouse shrugged. "I mean, I don't think *anyone's* gonna fuck with us, especially not the cowboy bitches. But on the microscopic chance they do, they're gonna need that shit." He turned to the Possibles and pounded his chest. "Y'all still scrawny as fuck, don't got no *muscle*!"

"...and Skinny-fuckin'-Kenny."

The Possibles finished their oath.

The yard fell silent.

"You didn't snort this shit, Mouse," said Tommy. He glanced at the Possibles. Felt awkward now that they'd fallen silent. But whatever. "You don't know how it makes you feel, man."

He looked at his right hand and made a fist.

"My hands still fuckin' hurt from when I was punchin' trees and shit. And—"

Even now.

He wanted it.

Miracle had made him feel *alive.*

"No," said Tommy. He handed the vial to Jack. "Jack, you hold some on you. Or hide it somewhere safe. But they don't get *any* unless shit actually does go down."

"Is that Miracle?" asked Wiley. "Can we snort a little? To test it out?"

"No," said Tommy. "I—"

Young Charlie's voice, cold and clear, cut through his thoughts:

("no lo siento, cabrón...")

("desayunaste?")

("por nada...")

("YA DESA-FUCKIN'-YUNAS—")

Tommy took off his cap and ran his fingers through his hair.

The fuck was that?

His gaze drifted skyward.

God?

Mikey?

Are you tryin' to...warn me?

He turned toward the Possibles. "Do any of y'all got a Spanish dictionary or somethin'? At home?"

The Possibles looked confused and shook their heads no.

"A Spanish dictionary?" asked Mouse.

Larry's long face scrunched up. "You learnin' spic, Tommy?"

Tommy ignored them. "Or any of y'all take Spanish yet?"

Grant raised his hand.

"Grant," said Tommy. "Do you know what *'no lo siento'* means? Or *'por nada'*?"

Grant shot him a blank stare.

"Or," said Tommy, *"'desayunaste?'"*

Grant shook his head. "I barely passed that class."

"Guess that's a no, then," said Tommy. "Alright, whatever."

Mouse coughed from inhaling too much Monkey, then passed the blunt to Tommy. "The fuck we talkin' about? You got Spanish homework you need help with? Or you just want some tacos?"

Everyone laughed.

"El burritos, dos!"

"Los nachos, por favor!"

"Cinco de High-o, bitch!"

Tommy stifled a laugh, smoke slipping from the side of his mouth. That last one was good. Cinco de High-o.

Whatever...

Maybe I'm just overthinkin' shit...

Besides, *por nada* sounded like *de nada,* which he felt pretty sure meant "you're welcome."

Maybe something like that.

He turned to Larry. "So, who's the best? At cross-attackin' so far?"

"Asian David," said Larry. "And Kevin."

Both Possibles stood straighter, eyes wide.

"They bitch the least, too," said Larry.

Tommy nodded in approval. They should be praised. In front of everyone. As a leader, he had to make sure of that.

"David," he said, "that was good when you called that rally-up back at Walmart. When you saw Young. Showed initiative. And awareness. Keep that shit up."

David pushed up his thick glasses and squared his shoulders. He gave Tommy a firm nod.

"And Kevin," said Tommy. "Nobody forgets you chargin' Graham-fuckin'-Riley back at DQ. That took balls."

Kevin's eyes ignited with zeal.

Tommy turned to Wiley.

Might as well talk about'em all...

"Wiley," he said, "you're impressin' us with your sales. Help the other Possibles, too. Make it a team-effort."

Wiley nodded. "I will."

"And Grant..." said Tommy. "...you're a good guy, man." He tilted his head back, blew smoke upwards. "But you better step shit up."

The Boys jeered.

"You best step shit up, Grant!"

"Fuckin' Good Guy Grant!"

"Impress us, or get the fuck out!"

Grant cast his eyes to the ground. Tommy stared at him for a moment longer.

I ain't jokin', Grant...

You best step your shit up.

"We 'bout done yet?" asked Mouse, taking the blunt from Tommy. "I gotta pick up Lacey, we're gonna fuck and eat at Waffle House." He spat and looked at Jack. "We do that every day, now..."

Jack's freckled face turned red. He looked away from Mouse.

"Real quick," said Tommy. "I wanna assign officers for this party."

"Assign officers?" asked Mouse. "The f—"

"It's a good idea, Mouse." Larry stepped forward, his tall frame casting a long shadow across the lawn. "Just hear him out."

Tommy gave Larry a thankful nod. Felt good to have his support again. Lately, too many arguments split along the same lines: *Larry and Mouse vs Tommy and Jack.* That shit got old.

"For this party," said Tommy, "I wanna assign clear responsibilities. So we all stay sharp, organized. You can still party, but you got shit to stay on top of, too."

He looked at Larry.

"Larry, you're head of security. Keep the Possibles at their stations, rotatin' every thirty minutes. And keep any eye out for you-know-fuckin'-who."

Larry took the blunt from Mouse and hit it. "I'll keep shit under control."

"Jack," said Tommy. "You're head of sales and diplomacy. Try to get *new* customers. Best are people who throw their own house parties, so they'll buy in bigger quantities. And if you think you got a *big* sale—"

"I'll holler for you to finalize it," said Jack. "Might even get Hazard or Zion people to show up, sample the Purple. Straight-up *diversify* our customer base. Across the Tri."

Tommy raised an eyebrow. Hazard rednecks or Zion yuppies at the party posed a security risk. But, on the other hand...

"I'm cool with it," said Mouse. "As long as it's only a few of'em. And if they don't start shit. I mean, if we can sell to'em, why not?"

Huh. Didn't expect that from Mouse—especially not when it came to Zion bitches. Must be seein' dollar signs.

"Larry," said Tommy. "You cool with that?"

"Guess so," said Larry. "If it's only a few of'em. And if they show up respectful and shit."

CAW!

A crow landed on the Bill scarecrow, staring right at Tommy. Their eyes locked.

"Whaddya know," said Larry. "A crow in Crow County."

"A *raven,* actually," said Jack. "Seen'em around here before."

"Fuck's the difference?" asked Mouse. "Same shit, right?"

Jack went on a spiel about the differences between crows and ravens, then claimed Kentucky had a "Raven County," too, but no one believed him or gave a shit.

"Anyway, Professor Jack," said Tommy. "Try invitin' your Hazard and Zion connections, too. But just a *few.* Like, two, three from each, max. And let'em know we won't tolerate *any* bullshit. Not with us, and not with each other, either."

He felt a pang of worry. Hazard and Zion dudes had been goin' at it *a lot* this summer. A fight between'em could ruin the fuckin' party.

"Larry," said Tommy, "keep a close eye on'em. Don't let—"

"What about me?" asked Mouse. "Do I get an office, too?"

"So now you *want* an office?" asked Tommy.

"Well, yeah," said Mouse. "I like havin' power. And responsibility and shit."

"Okay," said Tommy. "Mouse, you're...uhh...head of—"

"Havin' a good fuckin' time!" Mouse did a little dance. "Mitchell Mouse is here, y'all! He keeps the party goin'!"

Everyone laughed while Tommy nodded.

He could work with that.

"Then you're head of social," he said. "Make sure that everybody's havin' a good time. And I mean *everybody.* If somebody's standin' by themselves, lookin' awkward or bored and shit, fuckin' talk to'em, introduce'em to people. Or get'em high as fuck, to help with sales."

"That," said Mouse, "I can do."

Larry exhaled a stream of smoke. "Anything else, Tommy?"

Tommy hesitated, all eyes on him.

"Boys," he said. "This might be the biggest party we've ever held. I dunno how much Purple Dream the Horse People'll give us, but if it's *a lot,* and that shit is *good...*"

CAW!

A second raven landed on the scarecrow.

"...this could take us to *the fuckin' top.*"

He paced before everyone, choosing his words.

"If we dominate Crow, that's great...but I want more for us."

Larry passed him the blunt without a word. He drew deep, the hot smoke filling his chest, locking eyes with his Boys, then switching his gaze to the scarecrow.

Mikey...

I want us to be more...

Even more than what you were, what you did, with your Boys...

He exhaled. Smoke drifted before his eyes, obscuring the scarecrow.

CAW!

A third raven fluttered down and perched on its head.

"...I want us to dominate *the whole fuckin' Tri,*" said Tommy. "I want us to be the *kings* of the fuckin' Tri."

He paused, letting his words sink in.

"...and the biggest risk to that now is Bill-fuckin'-Cunningham. And Kenny-fuckin'-Moser."

CAW-CAW!

A fourth raven flapped its wings from atop the scarecrow.

The fuck..?

Where these fuckers comin' from?

Tommy took a step back.

"Now," he said, "they don't got Graham, or even Young no more...and they might not even show up..." He took Kevin's crowbar from him. "But if they do...y'all got two choices."

Slowly, he approached the scarecrow.

"Call a rally-up..."

DONG!

He slammed the crowbar against the scarecrow's iron legs. All four ravens erupted skyward in a flurry of black feathers.

"...or *cross-attack* the fuck out of 'em."

"Or both," said Mouse.

Tommy shrugged. "Or both."

Grant raised his hand.

"Grant," said Tommy.

"What do they drive?" asked Grant. "We should keep an eye out for their cars, too."

Tommy nodded with approval.

Nice, Grant...

Finally usin' your head...

The ravens flew in a wide circle above, as if waiting for something.

"Good question," said Tommy, eyeing the ravens. "Don't think Kenny's got his license yet, but Bill drives a blue Ford Bronco." He turned toward the Possibles. "If you even *see* his fuckin' truck, you come get us. Y'all got me?"

The Possibles nodded.

CAW-CAW-CAW!

All four ravens returned in a rush of wings, feathers rustling as they descended onto the scarecrow. They fixed Tommy with a hard glare.

("desayunaste, glick?")

Tommy puckered his mouth. A bitter taste crept in, sharp and metallic.

"And..." said Tommy. "Just so y'all know..."

("DESA-FUCKIN'-YUNAS—")

"...Young Charlie drives a black Camaro."

PART IV

BILE

1990s

CHAPTER I

PUSH

Raven County, Kentucky

This one seemed different, though.

Hadn't cried yet.

Oh, he was scared shitless, alright. Beyond a doubt. So why no tears from him?

Rhonda shook her head.

Oh well.

We'll see if you end up cryin' or not, AB...

THE VOICE COMMANDED Bobby to push.

"Unnnffff..."

It urged him—push *harder.*

Said he had to get it out.

"...I...I d-don't wanna do this..."

The voice asked why not?

"...d-don't feel right...p-poopin' my dang ol' p-pants..."

Bobby winced. The dang ol' ropes bit into his arms every time he shifted. If only he had long-sleeves. If only the Kentucky Manson family would give him a jacket or somethin'. *Or a sweater.* A sweater'd be nice, now that it got cold at night. Could buy one real cheap at Walmart these d—

The voice insisted that it was life or death, part of the plan, and that they had to stick to the plan.

Bobby sighed, then listened for sounds outside. The hose they washed him with drip-dropped water in the corner of the garage while birds chirped outside. Always liked hearin'em. The birds. Bet they wouldn't have trouble poopin' on command. Birds pooped all the time.

Poopin' my dang ol' pants...

So much harder than I imagined...

For Bobby's entire life, he'd been conditioned to never poop his pants. Somehow, his butthole just knew: *don't poop the pants.* Like it had a mind of its own. He may have been a sweaty kid *("swea-ty bo-bby!")* and puked a lot *("barf-in' bo-bby!"),* but he *never* pooped his dang ol' pants.

Never peed in'em, either.

Not a single dang time.

Good thing, too. "Poopin' Bobby" sounded even worse than "Barfin' Bobby."

("barf-in' bo-bby!")

("barf-in' b—")

The voice urged him to try again—*to push.*

Bobby pushed.

"Ughhh..."

Dang it.

Sphincter wouldn't budge.

Who knew poopin' your britches would be so—

He sniffed.

What's that?

He sniffed again.

Smoke.

Cigarette smoke.

Marlboro Mediums—the red and white label kind.

The only kind the Kentucky Manson family smoked.

She's here...

He didn't hear her, but he knew.

The smell told him.

The tension in the air.

Her.

"H-How much t-time we got?" asked Bobby.

The voice wasn't sure. Could be hours, maybe minutes.

Bobby's heart raced.

Freedom.

Finally.

Dang ol' *freedom.*

No more SpaghettiOs!

No more garage!

No more *awful* things they did to him!

No more!

"Fuckin' thing won't light..."

Her voice!

The psycho-demon-woman's voice!

"Piece of shit cheapo lighter..."

Bobby's chest heaved.

Rhonda...

Didn't even like thinkin' the witch's name.

Creatures like her—*she-demons of pure evil*—didn't deserve no name.

The voice remained steady. It reminded Bobby that today was the day. That's why he had to stick to the plan, and poop in his drawers.

"Uggh!"

Bobby pushed again.

Dang.

Dang-dang-dang.

Not even a turtlehead.

"C'mon, motherf—"

Her voice!

"Shit..."

Something fell.

Landed on the gravel.

Her lighter?

Probably her right hand shakin' again. He knew about that. Likely Parkinson's, but he hoped it was rabies, so the witch would die a terrible, painful deat—

The voice whispered: she stared at the garage door now, tried to see him through it.

"...I know..." said Bobby. "...I know..."

He *felt it* when they did that—looked at the garage or tried to see him through the door. Like how blind people knew somebody nearby watched'em. One of the perks of being blindfolded and tied up so long: all his other senses had sharpened. Especially his hearing and sense of smell.

Even when they talked inside the house, or trained up on the hill, at their shooting range—he heard'em.

Heard every phone call, every channel they watched on TV.

Every looney-bin conversation about their dang ol' *"Quest"* for some dang ol' *"Temple."*

He heard all the weirdo culty-stuff they recited to their God during target practice. He heard every comparison between him and the past fellas they'd kidnapped, like FB (the weirdo), GB (the handsome one) and MB (the one who'd *escaped.*)

He heard'em.

And he *smelled*'em.

He smelled the sharp, tinny tang of the SpaghettiOs can the moment it opened. They fed him straight from the can, with the same plastic Dairy Queen spoon every time. *"So we don't gotta wash more dishes,"* they said.

He smelled their pizza, hot and greasy. Usually Domino's, occasionally Pizza Hut. And he smelled the toppings: sausage, green pepper and onion—usually supreme, but *without* the black olives. Oh, how he wished they'd share a slice with him. Never did though. Only SpaghettiO's for him.

Dang ol' SpaghettiO's...

He smelled every cigarette they smoked, and he even smelled Taleiah when she circled the garage, staring through the windows like he didn't notice, like he didn't *feel* her there. Her deodorant gave her away—*Secret,* a brand lots of girls used. Appropriate for a girl who hid so many *secrets,* even from her own family.

As he listened, and smelled, he came to understand.

He understood their smoking rituals better than they did, and learned to approximate their stress by how many they smoked and how fast they smoked'em.

He understood other things, too.

He understood that the most psycho demon-woman in the world had a name:

Rhonda.

He understood that even Rhonda's own Daddy didn't know what to do with her, and he understood why: some creatures couldn't be fixed. Only caged. Or killed at birth.

Bobby shook his head.

The Daddy—

—he understood him, too.

Bill.

Bill Cunningham.

He understood Bill the most, and he understood that Bill didn't *like* to hurt people, didn't get off on it like the psycho demon woman did. He understood that Bill wasn't crazy the same way she was; not the should've-been-killed-at-birth-type-crazy.

He understood that something in Bill's life had *made him* crazy.

And he understood that Bill suffered from an injury—some sort of trauma—both physical and emotional, and that it still caused him pain. Real bad on some days. Less on others.

He understood Bill's mind, and that it was damaged.

Especially his memory.

He understood that Bill seemed dang ol' *lost* in memory most of the time, wandering in a haze, trying to make sense of his past.

He understood that Bill buried himself in questions:

What happened to his ol' buddies?

Where were they now?

And was everything *his* fault?

He understood those buddies' names:

Young Charlie.

Skinny Kenny.

And Graham-cracker, among others.

He also understood those "ol' buddies" of Bill's might never have even existed.

He understood this from the way Bill's kids reacted when he said their names. He understood that meant those "ol' buddies" may only exist in Bill's imagination, the kind of buddies Bobby himself used to play with as a child.

(i don't do that no more, though...)

(everybody is real in my life...)

He understood that if Bill's ol' buddies *weren't* imaginary, then they'd likely died long ago.

He understood that perhaps Bill had killed them.

He understood that something might've triggered a *dang ol' psychotic break,* making Bill murder his friends and embark on his crazy "Quest" for an imaginary "Temple."

He understood that sometimes, Bill did remember things.

Usually bad things.

He understood how those bad things haunted Bill, because he himself was haunted by bad things, too.

("bar-fin' bo-bby!")

("swea-ty bo-bby!")

("i'm sorry, momma!")

("you've been a bad boy, bobby!")

("I'M GONNA MAKE YOU CLEAN")

He understood that haunting, and how it made Bill drink and chain-smoke and talk to himself. He understood how it worsened—evident from how he spoke when he *thought* no one listened, his voice thick with regret, frustration, and shame.

He understood that Bill must've led a wild life, filled with hard livin'.

Lots of drinkin'.

Lots of drugs.

Lord knows what else.

And he understood that—

DING!

"Oh, God!" said Bobby.

He jolted. The ropes creaked as they dug into raw grooves around his wrists, crusted with scabbed-over blood.

The voice told him it was alright, th—

"What w-was that?"

The voice guessed she'd kicked a rock at the door. Told him to relax.

"G-God..."

Now he knew how fish felt when you tapped the sides of their dang ol' tank. He'd never do that again. *Poor fish...*

The voice reminded him: if he wanted to keep his body parts intact, he had to fulfill *his part* of the bargain. Either poop his pants, or—

"I know, I-I know..." said Bobby. "Get c-chopped up and b-buried in t-that S-Strawberry Fields place..."

The very thought of the word "strawberry" made Bobby shudder, and with the shudder came an involuntary *push,* finally establishing a beachhead in his britches.

"I did it!" said Bobby. "I-I got a turtlehead p-pokin' out!"

The turtlehead emerged soft and without form, like it always had since his SpaghettiO's-only diet began, punctuated by the occasional Flintstones vitamin. *"For your immunity and shit..."* Bill had said.

The voice praised him, reminded him that he had endured so much, that he was stronger now. Smarter. Tougher. Not the same guy that masturbated on a Barbie d—

"I was feedin' Little Stacey!"

The voice fell silent.

"...but I-I done good, d-didn't I?" asked Bobby. "I d-did what ya a-asked of me..."

The voice reassured him.

He'd done good—*real* good.

But Bobby's britches felt warm, wet and wrong. In some ways, it felt worse than when he used to puke on himself, but in other ways, not as bad. Even a little comfy. Something about *the warmth.* Probably start itchin' soon, but for now—just warm.

Huh.

Maybe it *would've* been better if he'd been "Poopin' Bobby," instead. Unlike puke, this bodily eruption remained invisible to the—

"Yesss..."

Bobby jerked his head toward the garage door.

The psycho-demon-woman?

Did she...*whisper* somethin'?

The voice commanded him to keep pushing. Said it had to smell, so she'd notice.

"O-okay," said Bobby. "S-still got a little left, I th-thi—"

"I'm-usin'-Daddy's-long-diiis-tance..."

Oh God.

Bobby sucked in air and blinked. His eyelashes scraped the blindfold's fabric.

The psycho demon woman—

—she's *singin'.*

"I'm-usin'-Daddy's-long-diiis-tance..."

Singin' about callin' someb—

The voice commanded him to *push*, to poop more in his britches.

Bobby pushed.

"Unnnnnf!"

His poop came out easier this time, spreading a pancake-like layer of wet warmth, mushy and sticky, between his buttcheeks and tighty-whities. Like mashed potato under—

"Darla!"

Darla.

Must be the girl she's callin'.

Probably lived far away, in that "Tri-County" place they always talked about. Likely one of the worst places in the whole dang world. Couldn't imagine an area that produced people as crazy and nasty as them.

"Wait, how'd you know it was me?"

He'd look up that Tri-County place after he escaped.

He'd look *a lot* of things up, and figure *a lot* of things out.

"Yeah, right! How'd you know?"

That Darla girl knew it was *her* callin' because she probably had Caller ID.

"Oh, come on! Really?"

That meant that Darla, who lived in Tri-County, knew the phone number and therefore the address of the Kentucky Manson family that had kidnapped him—

"Darla, you ain't no psychic, I bet you got that, fuckin', Caller ID thing."

—the Cunninghams.

"Why'd you get that? Ain't it expensive?"

Heck yes it was. Either that Darla girl was rich, or she *really* wanted to know the names and numbers of whoever called. Or—

"Twenty dollars a month? That's a lot!"

—she wanted to know *when the psycho demon woman* called her.

"Girl, I am so happy I was able to reach you!"

The voice praised Bobby: he'd done good, *real* good.

Step One was complete.

"I can only talk real quick, I'm usin' Daddy's long-distance..."

"W-What about...Step Two?" asked Bobby.

"He don't know, though..."

A violin began playing.

Softly at first.

Then faster.

Sharper.

"I am, Darla. I really am..."

The voice promised that Step Two was the easy part.

"I c-can't cry!" said Bobby. "I done t-told ya! I can't cr—"

The violin screeched.

"I can't!" said Bobby.

The voice insisted he could, if he—

No!

No!

Fading!

Fading again!

"D-Don't leave me!" said Bobby.

The voice rose and fell, distorted and warped by the violin, but commanded Bobby to obey—

"I'm-just-a-little-ninjaaa, walkin'-through-these-wooooods..."

—to honor their deal.

"Hopin'-I-don't-get-cauuught..."

"I-I'll honor it!" said Bobby.

"...usin'-Daddy's-long-distaaance..."

"B-but d-don't leave me b-by myself!"

Now barely a whisper, the voice promised Bobby all would be well,

"Please!"

that he would witness The Void again,

"N-not with *her!*"

and that he
"Don't leave me!"
would be the one
"Don't go!"

to find

The Temple.

FIVE MONTHS EARLIER

1990s

CHAPTER II

DRANK

Mapleville, Alabama

"YOU DIRTY, DIRTY LITTLE BOY!"

BOBBY SAT AT the bar and tried to act normal.

Most nights he just watched TV. Well, more like pretended to watch.

Usually he just thought. And observed.

Tried to be invisible.

A man could observe a lot if he was quiet enough to turn invisible. Could *learn* a lot through such observation, too. Observation offered solace from the weight of words and people, gave him time and space to think about what he wanted—

—and what he wanted was Little Stacey.

(little stacey little stacey)

Tonight he tried to *see* her *(LITTLE STACEY)* in his mind's eye, to *witness* them together as he fed her breakfast, as she swallowed every last drop like a good girl, but every time he hit a wall:

Mr. Stannis.

Dang ol' Mr. Stannis.

Still wouldn't give him Wednesday mornin's off—

still wouldn't let him *feed* her.

(feed her...)

(i gotta feed her...)

(little stacey little stacey)

His breathing turned rapid.

Not a Barbie doll...

The real *Little Stacey!*

He squeezed his hand into a fist.

That dang ol Mr. Stannis!

He doesn't know nothin'!

Nothin' at all!

Didn't know the first thing about the complexities of the *creative accounting* his employees handled, the nuances of all the tiny loopholes and exceptions. Just used his Daddy's money to attend a fancy school and start his own firm where he could be the big, bad boss and tell people what to do.

Bobby had encountered his type before.

Many times.

But he *tolerated* that type, just like he *tolerated* a lot of things and people and crap he didn't like. As long as he acted how Mr. Stannis wanted and did his work good and fast, they could've kept their distance.

Until now.

Now, Mr. Stannis had forced his hand.

Little Stacey was *hungry.*

She needed feedin' and needed it *now.*

(little stacey little stacey)

He drained the double whiskey and slammed the glass on the bar counter. The way cool guys did.

"G-gimme another one, S-Sammy..."

Good ol' Sammy the bartender...

He'll fix me up good...

Sammy smiled. "You're knockin'em down tonight, ain't ya, Bobby?"

"S-sure am..."

Sammy made Bobby's drink fast and Bobby drank it fast. About half in one gulp. Whenever he drank, the world got dreamy. Things looked and sounded softer, and the alcohol imbued a sense of detachment, as if he hovered outside himself. Sometimes this was good. Sometimes bad.

Tonight?

Good.

Good and numb.

Couldn't feed Little Stacey, nor even use the dang ol' Barbie doll again, so might as well get *numb.*

He glanced at the guys near the pool table.

That's what us good ol' country boys do, right?

He nodded, took another sip.

Ain't that right, boys?

"Yep, that's right, Bobby..." he imagined they'd say. *"We're just gonna get good and numb tonight..."*

Those were some good guys.

Even if they weren't *really* talkin' to him, he felt their friendship.

Didn't need talkin', anyway.

Words were pointless.

Dang ol' useless most of the time.

Didn't even *feel* real.

Not like numbers, or the drink he held, or his thoughts, or *especially* Little Stacey.

Those felt real.

He scanned the bar. Words weren't his thing, but he'd mastered the art of silent observation.

Take the guys playin' pool. One girl had joined'em, not bad but no knockout, either. Ponytail. Decent boobies. Mildly slutty-lookin'. Could tell by her smile and the way her eyes flicked that she tried to work her charm and work it hard, but the guys seemed genuinely more interested in the game.

Two other dudes shot darts towards the back. They played Cricket—the only darts game worth playin'. People who excelled at Cricket not only had to be good at throwin' darts, but at numbers, too. He respected a game like that, one that required strategic use of numbers.

Numbers numbers numbers numbers.

Numbers felt concrete.

Felt real.

Like Little Stacey...

One guy was ahead big time; the other tried to act like he didn't care. He likely cared, though. *Cared deeply.* The more someone acted like they didn't care, the more they usually did.

Yep, yep.

Cool gals and tough dudes all across the bar. Eatin'. Drinkin'. Minglin'. He turned his glass towards'em, said *"Cheers, fellas,"* and took a sip. Enjoyed their company. Didn't have to talk with'em to enjoy their company. *No sir.*

Just enjoy.

Round and Round by Ratt played from the corner jukebox. One of his jams. He nodded to it. That jukebox was his friend, too. Played good tunes for everybody and didn't complain none. Played *real good* tunes. Mostly easy listenin'. Country. 80s jams. Although sometimes the younger crowd would play that *Nirvana* or *Alice in Chains* crap.

Didn't need none of *that* bullcrap.

Not tonight.

Not *ever.*

He shook his head and took another sip, savoring the harsh taste as it burned his throat.

Yep.

This bar was a good one.

Not too rough.

Not too fancy, neither.

People left him alone here, which was fine with him. *Just fine.* Watching everyone made him happy. *Pretending* like he talked with them felt fine with him, *just fine.* Better than tryin' to join'em. He'd tried that before. At this bar and others, at other places and times in life. Almost never worked. Even in the best of situations they'd merely *tolerate* him. Out of politeness. They could tell he wasn't good with words, and he didn't really like nor need their words, either. Just liked bein' with'em. Even the rare nice ones who tried to know him made him nervous with their words, *their words,* their DANG OL', DANG OL' WOR—

He shook his head.

Took another sip.

Nope.

Nope nope nope.

Didn't need to join'em.

Felt better this way.

To pretend.

Pretendin' *always* felt better. When he pretended, he exercised a degree of control over their words.

Control.

Control control control.

The whiskey flowed down his throat like a river, cold and sharp, burning a trail into his belly.

"G-Gimme another one, S-Sammy..."

Good ol' Sammy...

He'll fix me up real good...

The control his imagination provided eased things. *Always.* Didn't need real friends if he could imagine'em. Learned that as a child. He could *control* friends that he *imagined.*

Sammy the bartender smiled. "Knockin'em down tonight, ain't ya, Bobby?"

"Yes s-sir, I-I suuuure am..."

Oh, how nice it'd be if he could *control* people in real life. Especially their words. Then words wouldn't be bad. They'd be like numbers. *Numbers could be controlled.*

"Comin' to ya, Bobby!"

Sammy slid his glass across the bar; it coasted across the polished wood like a puck on a shuffleboard table. Bobby caught it and took a swig.

Nice and smooth.

Like one of them good ol' boys.

Always liked it when Sammy did that. Made him feel cool. Little Stacey would think it was cool, too.

Little Stacey...

Little Stacey wasn't good with words, either. They communicated through their eyes, their souls, through energies and emotions and even chemicals in the air he didn't understand but knew were there.

(little stacey little stacey)

They didn't need words.

They already knew each other.

Deeply.

(littlestaceylittlestaceylittlestacey)

Gosh-dang, I need you so bad...

He squeezed his whiskey glass.

Feedin' Little Stacey was the only thing that mattered.

Not Mr. Stannis.

Not his job.

And not his Ruining.

He *needed* Little Stacey.

And The Void.

(littlestaceylittlestaceylittlestacey)

He needed to *touch* The Void again...

(are you feedin' little stacey, bobby?)

(or the void?)

His hand felt wet.

(little stacey?)

(or the v—)

"Whoa! You okay there, buddy?"

The voice startled him.

"Hey man, you okay?" asked the voice.

Bobby glanced down to see the base of his whiskey glass encircled by jagged edges. Blood and whiskey ran down the counter, forming a puddle on the floor.

"Hey, bartender!"

Bobby stared into the bottom of the glass. The whiskey looked like a shallow lake; the jagged edges around it, mountains.

"Hey, bartender! Can you take care of this guy?"

Blood dripped from his hand into the whiskey-lake, forming tiny red clouds. He saw himself there, inside those clouds—together with Little Stacey.

Together...

The red clouds turned black.

Together...

In The Void...

In The V—

A hand shook his shoulder. Bobby tore his gaze from the blood-red clouds to see a stranger beside him.

"Hey, bartender!" said the stranger. "Can we get some napkins to clean this shit up?"

Sammy didn't reply.

Guess he couldn't hear over the music.

"Is the bartender deaf or somethin'?" asked the stranger. "Why can't he fuckin' hear me?"

"S-Sammy," said Bobby. "I d-done made a mess..."

Sammy walked over. "Damn, Bobby..." He began cleaning up the blood and the whiskey and the broken glass.

"G-guess I squeezed the g-glass too hard..." Bobby chuckled and tried to smile. Tried to *act cool* about it. "I-I'll be more careful n-next time..."

Sammy mumbled something under his breath.

"Your hand okay?" asked the stranger.

Bobby lifted the broken glass to his lips, slurping up the shallow lake of whiskey and its crimson clouds. A stray rivulet ran down his chin, staining his shirt.

"Don't drink from the broken glass, man!" said the guy.

"C-Can't waste it..." Bobby grinned. The jagged edge of the glass cut a small, near-painless tear in his upper lip. Blood tasted coppery. Metallic. He swallowed it down with the whiskey.

("can't waste it...")

He tried to smile and laugh.

Tried to *act tough* as he swallowed more of his own blood.

("can't waste it, bawww-by...")

Little Stacey had said that once, when she spilled her breakfast on the floor. She'd made sure to clean it *alllll up,* though. Like a good girl. Wipin' her lips and lookin' up at him with those purty and sweet and special eyes of hers.

("can't waste it...")

("can't waste it, b—")

"Bobby, you okay?" asked Sammy.

"I th-think so..." Bobby looked down at the bar, then jerked his head up. He forced a wide grin.

"A-ain't nothin' another d-drank can't fix..."

Finally.

Had been waitin' to use that one.

Sounded *cool.*

And tough.

He'd rehearsed it plenty—had to say *"drink"* like *"drank,"* with a stronger Southern twang than usual.

Both Sammy and the stranger beside him looked surprised, then laughed.

It worked.

It dang ol'worked!

A bucktoothed, big-boobed waitress sauntered over, smacking on pink bubble gum. Didn't know her name yet, still new and the turnover was high.

She flicked her eyes up to his. "Did you get a little *boo-boo?"*

Her breath smelled like sweet, sweet watermelon. Bobby chuckled and felt his face turn hot. "Yeah, I g-got a little *boo-boo...*"

"Aww..."

Upon hearing *"Aww..."* something *tingled* within Bobby. Her breasts jiggled while she wrapped gauze around his hand.

Big knockers...

And they jiggle...

She smiled like she knew what he looked at, and approved. "You want some hydrogen peroxide, honey?"

"Nah," said the stranger beside him. "I think the whiskey done disinfected it real fuckin' good!"

Bobby stared at her massive, beautiful knockers. "No, I'm-I'm good, ma'am...th-thank ya..."

Heat crept up Bobby's neck and tightened low in his gut. He liked that. Her takin' care of him. And her boobs were real big and nice and juicy and he wanted to squeeze'em and suck'em and touch'em and feel'em and—

No!

Can't think like that!

Gotta save myself for Little Stacey!

And only *Little Stacey!*

Always and forever...

He swallowed the blood from his lip.

No one could compare to Little Stacey.

No one.

He sighed and tore his gaze from her boobies to stare at the TV. The gauze's scratchy fibers rasped against his skin as she wound it tight, each turn squeezing until his heartbeat pressed back. When she finished, he mumbled, *"Th-thank you,"* then asked good ol' Sammy for another double whiskey.

"As long as you don't break it this time," said Sammy, laughing in a way that showed he was half-joking, but half-serious, too.

"You always breakin' your glasses like that?" asked the stranger.

Bobby thanked Sammy for his new whiskey, then tried to speak like other people did. Like normal people.

"J-Just been one of those d-daaays, I guess..."

"Amen to that, brother," said the stranger. "Cheers."

Bobby said *"Cheers"* as they clinked their glasses and turned'em back. Felt good now. Just one of the regular guys now, havin' a regular ol' drink at the regular ol' bar. One of the good ol' boys. Yes he was.

He took another swig of whiskey, swishing it in his mouth like mouthwash before swallowing it down with the blood from his lip. The more he drank, the less he tasted it.

Numb.

A guy and his gal came up and ordered two beers. They said hi to Bobby and he said, *"How y'all doin'?"* right back. Like one of the good ol' boys. Alcohol was one of the few things that helped him talk to people. Eased his stutter, and words in general slid out faster, greased, not seeming to matter as much either way. He wanted to drink all the dang time, but alcohol made almost everything else *other* than words worsen—his vision, hearing, ability to process numbers and financial statements—and, worst of all, he suffered terrible hangovers. Even from just two or three dang ol' drinks.

Or was it four?

Maybe five...

Anyway, tomorrow he'd feel like he got hit by a truck. But if it wasn't for the hangovers, he'd probably drink all day and turn into a dang ol' alcoholic. All for the best, m—

"You come here a lot?" asked the stranger.

"Yep," Bobby took a sip. "This here's my s-spot..."

The guy obviously wanted to talk to him. A rarity. Usually people left Bobby to himself. Maybe it was his aura, or maybe because he tried to be invisible, to observe. Didn't mind it, either way. Just enjoyed havin' a good ol' time with everyone. Enjoyed their company.

(you wish you were normal...)

(don't ya, bobby?)

I am normal.

I am.

Just a normal, good ol' boy hangin' out at the normal, dang ol' bar.

"You from around here?" asked the man.

"Yep," said Bobby. *"Born-and-r-raaaaised-here..."* He tried to draw out *"born-and-raaaaised"* the way cool guys and tough gals did—the ones that were good with words. And frequented bars.

The man sipped his drink.

Was he the one that ordered RC and tequila?

Weird combo.

Probably expected him to ask the *"You from around here, too?"*-type question, too, but Bobby didn't feel the need when he already knew the answer: people from around *here* never asked that question to begin with.

The man called over Ms. Bucktooth Bigboobs and chatted her up. Must've said somethin' funny 'cause she laughed and laughed and her boobies bounced and her cheeks turned red. Then the guy said somethin' in Spanish (likely somethin' *dirty...)* and when she asked what it meant he whispered in her ear and she laughed and laughed some more. Maybe charmed by him. Or maybe acted that way to everybody. Bobby had learned the hard way, too many times, that just because a waitress seems like she likes you doesn't mean she actually does.

He gulped his whiskey, pushing down the flood of awkward memories. The whiskey did its job. *Numb.* He returned his attention to the man.

Plaid shirt tucked into his jeans.

Sleeves rolled up.

Rough, blue-collar type.

But the tucked-in shirt—that said a lot.

The man wiped crumbs off the bar with a frown, mumbled dirty words under his breath.

Hmm.

Liked keepin' things clean, too.

Maybe one of them neat and tidy types, despite his rough around the edges vibe. A goatee connected with his mustache (a *"circle beard"* was the proper name for it, but even this guy probably didn't know that), and he kept it trimmed—not hippie-style or long and scraggly like them grunge boys. Thank God.

The jukebox played an Alice in Chains tune. Bobby knew this one—the most depressing dang song he'd ever heard—but at least it wasn't that headbangin' bullcrap. It was called *Down in a Hole* (or somethin' dark and "deep" like that), and was likely about drugs, suicide, depression, crap like that. All the rock songs popular with kids nowadays revolved around the same stuff: misery, angst, feelin' sorry for themselves 'cause their daddy didn't love'em enough when they were little.

Buncha bullcrap.

("are you gonna be a good boy, bobby?")

He didn't have the best childhood, either.

("yes momma, i am...")

Didn't even *have* no daddy growin' up.

("i promise, momma...")

But he didn't waste time feelin' sorry for himself.

("please don't hit me, momma...")

("momma, please!")

No sir.

("i said i'm sorry!")

("dirty boy!")

("dirty, dirty boy!")

("momma, no!")

("i'm gonna make you clean...")

And he definitely wouldn't write no song about it.

("i'm gonna make you clean!")

Bobby grit his teeth.

("I'M GONNA MAKE YOU CLEAN")

Didn't even need to *think about* that dang ol' st—

("I'M GONNA MAKE YOU CL—")

(push it down, bobby...)

(push it down...)

Bobby sipped his whiskey.

Pushed it down.

(good, bobby...)

(good...)

Numb.

The man beside him nodded to the song. Looked wistful, satisfied even. Probably the type that liked this feelin'-sorry-for-yourself-grunge-nonsense.

"Shit," said the man. "I'm 'bout ready for another fuckin' drink!"

As the man motioned for the bartender with his left hand, Bobby caught a detail that likely escaped everyone else: the absence of his pinky and ring finger on his right.

Dang ol' guy's only got eight fingers!

He imagined the rough, blunt ends brushing his palm if they shook hands. Would feel mighty weird...

The man kept his three-fingered hand at his side or in his lap, favoring his left. Since he sat at the bar's end with no chairs to his right, most people wouldn't notice.

But Bobby had noticed—

—and his mind raced.

Had never met a guy with *missin' fingers* before.

Now, how'd somethin' like that happen?

Maybe got cut off in an accident, or a dog bit'em off, or lost'em to Iraqi machine guns in Desert Storm, or maybe just born that w—

"Uno más, por favor!" said the man.

Sammy the bartender smiled. "You speak that Spanish stuff real good, *hombre!*"

Bobby raised an eyebrow.

Unusual.

Unusual that this rough lookin', eight-fingered man spoke a foreign language.

Maybe part-Mexican.

Or maybe...

...more clever than he looked.

***

Bobby found himself in front of the jukebox, putting a quarter in.

Don't remember walkin' here...

Oh well.

Didn't matter.

Had enough of that grunge bullcrap. No more *Down in a Hole.* People wanna be in a hole, they could go crawl in one for all he cared. He shuffled through the songs.

There it was.

There it was.

Just the song he wanted.

"What you playin', man?" asked a guy with a pool stick. Looked like one of them grunge dudes. *"Whatever I dang well please!"* is what Bobby wanted to say, but instead he mumbled *"S-some g-gooood stuuuuff..."* and scampered back to the bar.

The eight-fingered man had been flirtin' with Ms. Bucktooth Bigboobs again, callin' her a *"mamacita"* or whatnot, but now he sipped his drink alone, nodding to the music. For one surreal moment, Bobby wondered if the man had ever really talked to her—or if all the drinks were gettin' to him, and he'd just imagined it, wishin' he was him.

(is he even there, bobby?)

(or are you imagining him?)

(because you need the void?)

(the void, bobby, the vo—)

Bobby grimaced. Sipped his whiskey.

Numb.

The guy seemed real talkative, but it paid to be careful with folks at bars who came off too friendly. Folks who smiled too much.

Like this guy...

The man pulled a red-and-white cigarette pack from the front pocket of his flannel—*Marlboro Mediums.* Probably the started-smokin'-in-middle-school type. Maybe earlier. Goin' bald up top, like Bobby was, but thin, like Bobby wasn't. Thirties, maybe early forties, but his face, his aura told tales of *hard livin'* in his twenties.

Lots of drugs.

Lots of drinkin'.

Lord knows what else.

Still, the way he carried himself showed he'd moved past all that. Something about the twinkle in his eyes, something *behind* it.

A glint.

A glimmer.

Maybe he'd found God. Or Jesus. Or—

"Whatcha drinkin', *ese?*" asked the man.

Bobby fought the urge to stare at the guy's three-fingered hand.

Didn't wanna be rude.

"...w-whiskey..." he said.

"What kind?"

"...n-not sure..." Bobby tried to chuckle. "...w-whatever they d-dang ol' gave me..."

Wasn't used to guys tryin' so hard to converse with him. Must be *real* lonely. Maybe a truck driver. Or here for a construction project? A wedding band glinted on the man's left hand. Bobby had been so focused on the man's *missin'-finger-hand* that he'd almost missed that.

He relaxed a little.

Guess the guy wasn't no homo.

Thank God.

Had been runnin' into them homos more and more often now. So many times the dang ol' homos thought *he* was a dang ol' homo, too, and talked all friendly-like to him, puttin' their hands on his shoulders, leavin'em there *a bit longer* than necessary. They even rubbed their legs against his under the bar like it was an accident, testing the waters to see if he was okay with it.

He wasn't.

Sure as heck wasn't.

He wasn't no dang ol' homo, never would be, and feedin' Little Stacey was more than enough for him so he didn't need other girls, either.

Little Stacey...

(littlestaceylittlestacey)

He took another gulp.

The whiskey scorched his throat, settled in his belly like lava.

Numb.

Maybe he should open up to the guy. Just a little bit. Might learn somethin', a new method to use words in a cool and tough way he could copy later. Like the *"Ain't nothin' another drank can't fix"* line he'd finally used today.

That was good.

Real good.

Bobby grinned when his quarter more than earned its worth: the opening chorus of *We Built This City* by Starship blared across the bar.

Now this is a song!

A song from when music was dang ol' music!

Not that long-haired grunge crap!

Just good ol', dang ol' music!

A pump-you-up tune that makes ya feel *good!*

He raised his glass toward Sammy.

"Now this s-song *gets ya goin',*" said Bobby. "D-don't it, S-Sammy?"

Sammy pursed his lips and nodded, staring at the drink he poured. Someone yelled, *"Who the fuck played this shit?"*

"Te gusta esta canción, amigo?" asked the man.

Bobby chuckled.

Felt funny bein' spoke to in a foreign language.

"That means, *'do ya like this song?'*" said the man. He flashed a smile bright enough to blind. Maybe a little *too* bright.

Or maybe he liked *We Built This City,* too.

"Sí..." said Bobby. *"...m-muey* dang ol' *bueno..."*

That was about all the Spanish Bobby knew, so he switched back to *inglés.*

"Yep, yep..." said Bobby, "...I s-suuure do..."

***

As Bobby drank, fantasies of wreaking vengeance on Mr. Stannis played in the theater of his mind. He imagined storming into Mr. Stannis's office with *We Built This City* blaring in the background, like he starred in his own MTV music video.

I'd just storm in there!

Wouldn't even bother knockin'!

Maybe he'd wear sunglasses and a cap. Maybe even wear it *sideways,* show Mr. Stannis he meant business. Could even carry a boombox on his shoulder, blast *We Built this City* extra loud.

I'd just bust up in there!

And flip Mr. Stannis the dang ol' bird!

Bobby grinned.

Drool gathered in the corner of his mouth.

Felt good now.

Real good.

"Está bien tu mano, ese?" asked the man beside him. "Your hand alright, man?"

Gradually, Bobby's MTV fantasy faded and his bandaged hand came into focus. Blood had seeped through the gauze, the throbbing distant, softened now, like a dream.

He made a fist.

The bloodstain expanded.

Felt like a battle wound.

Made him seem *tough*.

Tough and strong.

Maybe *that's* why the guy wanted to talk to him.

"W-What ya d-drinkin', *brother?"* asked Bobby.

Brother.

He'd heard guys at the bar use that word sometimes. Usually with dudes they didn't know and wanted to seem amiable. Felt like a good word. Disarming. Peaceful. *Safe.* Still wasn't too sure about the man, or why he kept speakin' Spanish to everyone, or why he lacked *two dang ol' fingers,* but if he kept on stonewallin' him it might seem rude.

Rudeness led to trouble—

—and he definitely didn't want no *trouble* with this man, either.

Bobby didn't know why, but something told him that this wide-smiling, Spanish-speaking eight-fingered *amigo* could be the most lethal dang fella in the whole bar if you ticked him off.

Best not get on his bad side...

The man raised his glass. "*Salud!*"

Bobby guessed that meant *"cheers."* He muttered *"S-Salud!"* then nodded for a while, not to the music, but just nodded.

"You must've had a hell of a fuckin' day," said the man. "I ain't never seen no *ese* break a glass with their hands like that before."

Bobby didn't know what *"ese"* meant, but guessed it didn't matter. The guy probably just liked sayin' it.

"Sí," said Bobby. "M-more like a heck of a w-week..." Inspiration flashed and he swiveled to face the guy.

"Actually," he said, *"m-more like a heck of a m-month!"*

The man's eyes twinkled and he laughed.

Bobby tried to laugh with him.

That was a good one...

Not as good as the other one, but good...

The man nodded. "Heck of a life, *ese*..." He blew smoke out the side of his mouth. "We go through that bullshit every damn-fuckin'-day..."

He caught Bobby glancing at his missing-finger-hand and dropped it to his side.

"La vida es cabrona," he said. "But we all been there, brother."

There it was again—that word.

Brother.

Bobby liked that.

Brother brother brother brother brother brother.

Would use it more from now.

Sure would've been nice to have a brother growin' up. Maybe a brother's guidance could've helped him avoid his Ruining.

"Somethin' at work," the man asked, "or some fuckin' bullshit like that?"

"S-sí..." said Bobby, imagining Mr. Stannis's face and his shiny boots and that dang ol' Rubik's Cube.

"...m-my dang ol' boss..."

"Lemme guess, is he sick?"

"Sick?" asked Bobby.

"Sí."

"What do ya mean?"

"I mean," said the man, "*is he sick?*"

"N-no..." said Bobby. "...I d-don't think he's sick..."

"Oh, I bet he is..."

"W-What do ya m-mean?"

The whites of the man's eyes flashed; his teeth showed beneath his mustache. Something about that grin bothered Bobby, something behind it...

(be careful, bobby…)

"W-what do ya mean?" asked Bobby. "S-sick with what?"

The man's voice lowered.

"…well, I bet he's got *AD…*"

"AD?" asked Bobby.

The man nodded.

"You m-mean, *ADD?"* asked Bobby. "Dang ol', A-attention D-deficit Disorder?"

"Nope," said the man, "I mean fuckin' *AD…*"

"W-what's *AD?*"

"You don't know *AD, ese?* It's what he's sick with…"

"W-well…w-what is it?"

"You know…"

The man leaned in.

"The Asshole Disease."

The man smacked the bar and laughed.

Bobby laughed, too. A natural laugh, a *real* laugh. Not the clown-horn kind.

He sipped his whiskey.

Maybe this eight-fingered guy with his blinding grin was alright.

Maybe okay to open up to him.

A little…

"Y-You sure do know h-how to make a g-guy laugh…" said Bobby.

The man smiled and winked.

"I sure fuckin' do."

1990s

CHAPTER III

BILE

"I'M GONNA MAKE YOU CLEAN..."

BOBBY SIPPED HIS whiskey.

Burned good, *real good* as it went down.

Warmed his belly up, too.

He looked around, his vision blurry, yet sharper somehow.

The bar was gettin' *wild* now.

Like it always did.

The later it got, the more the wildness seemed to *awake* within people, even within the energy of the dang ol' bar itself.

Two guys had started shovin' each other and ol' Sammy the bartender broke it up. Somethin' to do with that slutty lookin' girl with the ponytail. Had seen that play out before. Paid to be careful with women at bars.

He smacked his lips and poured more whiskey down his throat. Tasteless now, but it imbued a dreaminess upon his perception.

The whiskey lacked flavor.

But the dreaminess endured.

"So this asshole *cabrón* boss of yours," said the smiling, eight-fingered man beside him, "with his, fuckin', Chinese Ivorywood desk, won't let you take Wednesday mornin's off no more?"

"S-Sí..." said Bobby.

African Blackwood, *not* Chinese Ivorywood, but that was okay. Best not to correct someone on a roll. Even Bobby knew that.

"Even though you got a good reason," said the man. "A *reeeeal* good fuckin' reason?"

"S-S-Sí..."

He hadn't told the man the *real* reason, not even the half-lie he'd told Mr. Stannis, but he'd hinted about its nature, and the man seemed to understand.

"And you're in charge of one of the most difficult clients," said the man, "of the whole motherfuckin' company?"

"S-Sí, sí..."

He'd made sure not to mention the client's name, though—wasn't that drunk, and probably never would be.

"Well," said the man, "I'll tell ya what ya need to motherfuckin' do..."

Bad words usually bothered Bobby, but he tried to tolerate it at bars. Just how the good ol' boys liked to talk. And tonight, he really was one of the good ol' boys. All thanks to this smiling, eight-fingered man.

"What's that, *b-brotherrr?"* asked Bobby.

The man blew smoke sideways. "You tell him, *'Now you listen* here, *motherfucker. I got two pieces of news for ya: one, you can suck my dick! And two, I fuckin' quit!'*"

Bobby chuckled. Sipped his whiskey.

"En serio, amigo!" said the guy. "You tell him to give ya your goddamn Wednesday mornin's off, or you'll fuckin' quit!"

Quit?

Bobby couldn't quit.

No other firms nearby, and movin' was out of the question.

Had to stay within the radius of Little Stacey.

Had to.

At all times.

Little Stacey...

"Can't quit, b-brother..." said Bobby. "N-no dang ol' *b-bueno...*"

He chuckled. Felt cool, speakin' Spanish. Like a super power.

"Por qué, amigo?" asked the man. "Fuckin' *por qué?* People quit their jobs all the time, go someplace better."

Bobby narrowed his eyes.

Hard to explain. Even this new *amigo* wouldn't get it, wouldn't understand how he had to *feed* Little St—

"Lemme ask ya somethin'," said the man. "Who was in charge of that real difficult account before you was?"

Tim Thanos.

"G-guy named Tim..."

"And where's he at?" asked the man. "What's that Tim-guy doin' now?"

"H-he went up to one of them b-big fancy firms...in N-New York..."

"Well, shit, *ese,*" said the man. "Why don't you do what he fuckin' did? Go up to one of them big fancy firms, make ya some *mucho dinero?"*

Bobby shook his head.

"*...n-no bueno, amigo...*g-gotta stay nearby..."

The man looked like he wanted to probe further, but didn't.

Good.

Dang ol' *bueno.*

Bobby appreciated that, someone who respected his privacy. So he'd do the same and avoid asking what happened to the man's hand. Lord knows he'd likely been asked a million times before.

The man lit a new cigarette.

"Sí, fuckin' *sí..."* he said. "So you really don't wanna move, huh?"

"C-can't move..." Bobby brought his glass to his lips.

Couldn't and *wouldn't* move away from Little Stacey.

Not for a million dollars.

Not for anything.

The man's eyes flashed. "But your asshole-*hombre* boss don't know that, does he?"

Bobby paused, holding his glass mid-air.

Good point.

This guy was smart—*street smart,* likely earned the hard way, in his hard livin' days.

"...but..." said Bobby. "W-what if he c-calls my...my dang ol' b-bluff, then?"

The man's eyes darted to the left and right, as if a multitude of scenarios played before him.

"Necesitas una palanca..." He held up a finger. "You gotta get *leverage* over him, *ese.* Fuckin', threaten his ass..."

Something cold and terrifying darkened the man's smile. Bobby once again got the feeling that there was something *beneath* that smile, something horrif—

The man leaned in and lowered his voice:

"...find somethin' he's *weak* against..."

Bobby brought the glass to his lips and held it there, letting the harsh smell of cheap whiskey waft up his nose.

What was Mr. Stannis weak against?

***

Bobby ended the night puking in the parking lot while the smiling man patted his back. Then he couldn't stop dry heaving.

("bar-fin' bo-bby!")

("bar-fin' bo-bby!")

On his fourth dry heave, bile crept onto the back of his tongue: bitter, hot, and sharp enough to make his eyes water. A barrage of images played before him:

The Rubik's Cube,
"...the office would devolve into chaos..."
Mr. Stannis's polished black shoes,
"Chaos!"
his desk,
"...vigilance at all costs..."
that immaculate African Blackwood desk,
"...vigilance is the only inoculation against chaos..."
his window with the view of sunshine, trees and grass,
"...ever-present and everlastin' vigilance..."
him lording over everyone,
"...you understand that, don't you, Bobby?"
and then, in the center of it all—

—the Rubik's Cube.

(chaos!)
"...we all have to do our part..."
That dang ol', dang ol' Rubik's Cube.
(chaos!)
"...even me, Bobby..."
(chaos!)
"...even me..."
(chaos!)
(chaos!)

Upon his last dry heave, when the bile tasted the most bitter,

(CHAOS!)

Bobby knew what he had to do.

PART V

SUNDAY MORNING

1970s

CHAPTER I

FIND IT

"Temple above all."

TOMMY WAS EIGHT when his older brother killed himself. He placed their dad's pistol in his mouth and pulled the trigger. There was no note.

"Mikey..."

It'd been a while since Tommy had thought of Mikey. Like, *really* thought of him. Sure, Mikey crossed his mind whenever he had a problem, like with leading the Boys or with Samantha or when some bullshit happened with his parents he'd think to himself, *"What would Mikey do?"* or *"How would Mikey solve this?"* It wasn't usually a conscious thought; more like Mikey had become a part of him that switched on when needed.

"Mikey..."

"Is that really you?"

Mikey's squad, "The Smoketown Boys," (the *original* Smoketown Boys) disbanded after his death. They claimed they didn't know why Mikey did it. The doctors said he didn't take his pills correctly, but with time, Tommy suspected it was *because* he took the fucking pills.

"It's been a while, Tommy..."

"I've missed you..."

Tommy's parents divorced afterwards. Maybe they blamed each other, or maybe themselves. Maybe both. His sister Suzie was only two when it happened, so neither the divorce nor Mikey's death impacted her like it had Tommy.

"I can't stay long..."

"But I need to tell you things."

After Grandpa died, Tommy spent a lot of time in the house he'd inherited.

Alone.

Grasping at fragments of memories of watching Mikey roll with his Smoketown Boys, wondering what it felt like to *be* him, to *be* Mikey.

"Important things, Tommy..."

Slowly, he started to act like Mikey, think like Mikey, and then, by degrees—

he *became* Mikey.

The leader of the new Smoketown Boys.

***

"Where are we?" asked Tommy.

Fog-shrouded mountains covered with lush green lay before him. A gray sky hung heavy above.

"Is that...really you, Mikey?" asked Tommy.

Before Tommy stood a figure wearing Mikey's cap, the same one Tommy now wore with the crow on the front. The figure's face melded into a blur, like he had no face.

But it was Mikey.

Something told him so.

"Do you see that, Tommy?" asked the faceless Mikey.

The voice resembled Mikey's, yet emanated from *inside* Tommy, resonating in an unsettling, otherworldly way, as if spoken through a distorted microphone.

But it sounded like Mikey alright.

You never forget the sound of your brother's voice.

"Do you see *it?"* asked Mikey.

Mikey pointed at a thin beam of light piercing the sky from a distant mountain crevice.

That light...

Tommy felt a yearning for it, like something unspeakably good waited there. Something that would make everything better.

"I see it, Mikey..."

"You have to find *it,"* said Mikey.

Tommy ripped his gaze from the beam of light to Mikey's face, a swirling blur of shifting skin and shadow.

"Mikey..."

He wanted to find it, but first he wanted to ask Mikey a million questions, and all of them were *"Why did you do it?"*

"I know you have lots of questions..." said Mikey. *"...but we don't have much time..."*

Why?

Why don't we have time?

Just let me fucking ask you!

It was the pills, wasn't it?

It was the pills, the pills the doctors fucking gave you and they fucked you up and made everything fuzzy and numb and when you stopped taking them the comedown fucked you up even more and then when you started again they didn't *feel* the same they didn't *work* the same, just tell me, Mikey, *just fucking tell me,* it was the fucking pills wasn't it—

"Something bad is gonna happen, Tommy..."

Thunder rumbled.

The gray sky darkened.

The mountains now seemed ominous.

Threatening.

"What do you mean?" asked Tommy.

The distant beam of light drifted away.

"Live through it, Tommy..." said Mikey. *"...live through it..."*

"Live through *what?"* asked Tommy.

"What are you talkin' about?"

"What's gonna happen, Mikey?"

"What *bad thing* is gonna happen?"

"And why did you fucking do i—"

"Find it, Tommy..."

"The Temple."

1970s

CHAPTER II

SOMEONE WHO MEANT HIM HARM

The Void was silent and still and perfect.

FOR A WHILE, there was only darkness.

Oblivion.

Silent and numb and perfect and still.

Perfect.

Oblivion.

("find it, tommy...")

("the temple...")

Tommy tried to scream and yell and speak and breathe but the surrounding darkness, *The Void,* kept him locked in a numb, strangely pleasant paralysis.

For the first time in his life, he felt nothing.

And feeling nothing felt good.

I could stay here forever...

In The Void...

Deep down, though, he knew that remaining in The Void served no purpose, acting merely as an *escape*—an escape from the terrors and stressors and colors and *risks* of the world—but it remained *only* an escape, not an answer, not a purpose. Tommy understood the difference. Just like he understood the difference between people who smoked weed and did drugs out of enjoyment, versus people who used them to *escape.*

He refused to run away from his life.

He refused to lose himself in the *escape*—

in The Void.

I'll find it, Mikey...

The Temple...

He reached inside himself and pulled at something.

Then we can talk again...

And you can tell me what really *happened...*

A speck appeared in the distance.

Light?

The Temple?

No—

something else.

He reached inside and pulled again.

The speck moved closer—a person.

Not a speck of light, *but a person.*

Who?

Mikey?

Tommy felt cold.

No—

not Mikey.

("something bad is gonna happen, tommy...")

Someone else.

Someone who meant him harm.

("live through this...")

Despite his fear, he reached inside himself and *pulled* again.

Pull.

Pull.

The person moved closer.

Pull.

Pull.

The face became clear.

Pull.

P—

Tommy left the safety of The Void.

1970s

CHAPTER III

LO SIENTO

"Buenos-fuckin'-días, Glick..."

"I'M SORRY ABOUT your brother, *amigo,*" said Young Charlie. "That's some fucked up shit."

Charlie and Tommy lounged on the back porch of Charlie's dad's place, joints in hand. The sun hung low through the trees, casting long shadows across patchy grass. School had let out an hour ago, and the air still held that dry, restless heat of late afternoon.

"Thanks, man..." Tommy blew smoke down. "...I don't tell many people about it..."

"I bet you're right," said Charlie. "Likely them psych drugs them fuckin' doctors put him on. Drugs like that'll fuck up your mind, *ese.* Probably made shit worse."

"Yeah..." said Tommy. "...or traded one mental problem for another..." He watched smoke curl from his joint. "I'll never know for sure, though..."

A silence passed. Young had turned his boombox down when they started talking about Mikey, and still hadn't turned it back up. *Thank God.* Hated that heavy metal screamin' shit. But whatever. Young was cool. Didn't wanna bitch about small things.

"Man, I'm about all-natural stuff," said Charlie. "Fuckin', *cosas naturales.* I take my Flintstone vitamin every day. Ya know, for my immunity and shit. And I read that fish oil pills and vitamin D helps ya mentally, so I take that shit, too."

"Think it actually works?" asked Tommy.

Charlie nodded. "Once I started takin' all that, I just wanted to learn more. About everything. And I started gettin' good at *español,* too. Like, shit that I studied actually stuck with me."

"Huh..." said Tommy.

Would Mikey have listened to that, though?

Mikey loved weed but wouldn't touch Tylenol—supposedly why he didn't take his psych pills like he was supposed to. Even fish oil and vitamin D might've been a bridge too far.

"You can pop them pills with me, *ese,*" said Charlie. "So how 'bout we cook up some fried chicken TV dinners, put Tabasco on'em to make'em *mucho delicioso,* and fuckin' munch on those while we pop them fuckin' pills?"

"Sounds good to me, *amigo.*" Tommy could already taste the Tabasco—tangy, sharp, the kind that stung the cracks in your lips.

Charlie then launched into a spiel about how they should also put extra virgin olive oil on their chicken dinners because it had something called "omega 3." Tommy just smiled and nodded. Sounded like New Age bullshit, but whatever. Only Young Charlie would wanna drizzle olive oil on a fucking *fried chicken TV dinner.*

"I'm always impressed with you, Young," said Tommy. "You know nutrition and speak that Spanish shit real good, too."

Charlie's eyes twinkled. *"Gracias. Muchas*-fuckin'-*gracias*. I do know a lot of shit. And I like sharin' what I learn, too."

They took deep drags of their joints, holding it in to increase their high. The smoke burned Tommy's lungs, hot and acrid, then dulled into a syrupy haze behind his eyes. Charlie coughed. Tommy didn't. Tommy never coughed when he smoked. Not even the first time.

"I appreciate you tellin' me all that, man," said Charlie. "About your brother. That's what real friends, *mejores amigos,* are fuckin' for."

He locked eyes with Tommy and nodded.

Tommy nodded back. He thought about revealing more—like how the cap he wore used to be Mikey's—but no. Wearing your dead brother's cap might seem weird. People didn't need to know that shit.

Charlie frowned. "*Ten cuidado.* Be careful, now."

Tommy glanced down. A pinchful of ashes from his joint had fallen on the table.

"Oh, my bad, dude..." He brushed them off.

Charlie stared at the spot where the ashes had fallen, still frowning. Tommy glanced down again.

A *tiny* bit of ash still lay on the table.

Damn...

How the fuck can he even see *that?*

Gotta be so careful even when I'm smokin' with him...

"My bad, dude..." Tommy wiped the table clean, not a speck left.

Gradually, Charlie's face relaxed. He leaned back in his chair and took another hit of his joint.

Tommy wondered, with a bit of dread, how pissed Charlie might get if he accidentally spilled something. Had to be extra-fuckin'-careful with those chicken dinners—a single drop of Tabasco on the carpet might make him go *blitzkrieg.*

Charlie squinted through the smoke. "Dude, were you fuckin' with me earlier? About your brother knowin' a dude with a pet monkey? Who taught him to cut weed with tobacco?"

Tommy shrugged. "That's what he said. And that's why he called it Monkey."

"Ya know," said Charlie, "my dad said he used to sell to a guy with a pet monkey. But I always thought he was jokin'. I mean, that shit's gotta be illegal, right?"

They talked it over for a while and figured it probably was illegal, at least in the state of Kentucky. Charlie thought owning one would be *"cool as fuck,"* but Tommy kept picturing a rabid monster—the kind that ate people's faces—and changed the subject.

"Hey, uhh, *amigo..."* Tommy shifted in his lawn chair. Mixing in Spanish always felt awkward and forced. *Amigo* was the only word that came semi-naturally. "I got somethin' I wanna roll past ya."

"Adelante," said Charlie.

Tommy hesitated.

He hadn't revealed this to anyone yet.

"So...I'm thinkin' of formin', like, a group of friends, ya know..."

Fuck...

A "group of friends" sounds so lame...

"...that, uhh, tear shit up..." said Tommy. "Ya know? And do cool shit all the time..."

Charlie raised his eyebrows. "Tear shit up? And do cool shit all the time? I'm all about that, *ese.* Sign me the fuck up."

"And we'll get high," said Tommy, "and work together on stuff..."

"Work together on stuff?" asked Charlie. "Like, homework and shit?"

"Nah..." said Tommy. "Well, okay, maybe..."

He wasn't against helping each other with homework, but that wasn't what he meant. He meant badass, *epic* shit. Not quite sure what—just knew that Mikey and his Smoketown Boys smoked, sold weed, fought other squads, and got into all kinds of secret adventures they only whispered about. Whatever it was, it had to be *awesome.*

Awesome and badass.

All the time.

He was sure of it.

"More like..." said Tommy. "Cookin' up schemes and shit...like, sell weed and use the money to, I dunno, buy more weed…and booze, shit like that…"

Charlie just looked at him and nodded.

Tommy's face grew hot.

I suck at explainin' this…

He had a vision, but it was hard to articulate without coming off as fake or corny. He wanted to say he dreamt of building a badass brotherhood—one that ruled Crow County and, eventually, all of Tri.

But to suddenly *say* shit like that…

Didn't feel right.

"I was thinkin'," said Tommy, "maybe we could throw parties at my grandpa's house. He left it to me and it's just sittin' there, empty."

"Bueno, fuckin' *bueno, ese…"* said Charlie. "We gonna chase some *mamacitas,* too?"

"Nope," said Tommy. "We make *them* chase *us."*

Charlie cackled and slapped his knee. *"Sí,* fuckin' *sí.* I like that, I do."

Charlie then told a story about some chick that used to live nearby, said he got her to give him head through *reverse psychology.* Kept teasing her that she wasn't good at sucking dick until she took it as a challenge. *"Best dick suckin' I ever got,"* said Charlie. *"And that bitch swallowed, too."* Tommy smiled and nodded. Might've been some truth to it, but Young's stories had to be taken with a grain of salt. Conveniently, the girl had moved to Hazard and no, he didn't know her new phone number.

"Anyway," said Charlie, *"De todos* fuckin' *modos,* what ya gonna call it?"

"Call what?" asked Tommy.

"Your group. Your squad you're thinkin' of."

"Oh," said Tommy. "I got some ideas…"

Still didn't wanna say it—not yet. Not until he felt certain he had a solid lineup to recruit from. That's how Mikey had done it.

Probably…

"Wanna recruit more guys," said Tommy, "before I come up with a name…"

Charlie swatted at a buzzing fly. "Who else you thinkin' of?"

"Not sure yet…" said Tommy. "Me and Larry Knowles been hangin' out, though."

"Longface, huh…" Charlie looked away, as if he'd lost interest in the conversation.

"His face ain't *that* long, man," said Tommy. "And definitely don't call him that when we hang, because—"

"How about Bill?" asked Charlie. "Bill Cunningham."

"Nahhh," said Tommy. "The Sheriff's son? Fuck that guy."

"He's cool, *ese.*"

"Don't matter," said Tommy. "He'll fuckin' narc on us the moment—"

"Nahhh," said Charlie. *"Estás equivocado* on that shit. Bill ain't like that. He don't even get along with his dad, man. They barely fuckin' speak."

Tommy shook his head. "I just don't like the dude..."

And he meant it. Bill Cunningham was one of those guys he didn't like from the moment he fuckin' saw him. Everything about the guy pissed him off. As if his very *existence* annoyed the shit out of him. Didn't know why, wasn't like they had any beef. But didn't matter.

Fuck Bill Cunningham.

"Hmm..." Charlie stroked his chin, then shrugged. "Well, maybe we can all hang out a couple times, see how we gel. *Hacerse amigos,* ya know what I'm sayin'? Maybe holler at them sweet *mamacitas* a few streets down, see if they wanna smoke with us."

Tommy stared off as the joint smoldered between his fingers, heat nibbling the skin. He had no fucking intention of hanging with Bill Cunningham *what-so-fucking-ever,* but didn't wanna hammer the point, either. No need to ruin the good vibes today.

"Sounds good, *amigo...*" said Tommy. "Maybe get them *mamacitas* to play spin the bottle with us or somethin'..."

"Oh, hell yes," said Charlie. "First we spin for kissin', then we spin for fuckin'!"

Charlie slapped the table and cackled. Tommy couldn't help but crack up, too. They made a few more explicit jokes involving spin the bottle *("Don't forget that dick suckin',"* said Charlie, *"gotta make'em spin for that shit, too!")* and laughed and laughed and smoked some more.

"I like your way of thinkin', Young," said Tommy. "And we might be able to pull that off, man. Just gotta slowly escalate things every time we spin, ya know what I'm sayin'?"

"I sure fuckin' do," said Charlie. "And hey, speakin' of escalatin' things, *lo siento, amigo."*

"'Lo siento?' What's that mean?"

Charlie didn't answer.

Just stared.

"You teach me that yet?" asked Tommy. "I forgot that one."

Charlie sat perfectly still.

Not blinking.

Not breathing.

"Young," said Tommy. "You okay, dude?"

("i'll teach you some easy español, *man...")*

("'gracias' *means thank you")*

("and 'lo siento' *means i'm sorry")*

"What's wrong?" asked Tommy.

("lo siento")

("lo siento")

("no lo siento")

"Why you starin' like that?"

Tommy tried to rise.

Nothing moved.

Huh?

A cold pressure spread across his chest, like someone lay a slab of stone on him. Everything stood still, as if time had stopped.

Why can't I move?

From somewhere down the street, a shriek, like a monkey. Or maybe a laugh. Charlie didn't react.

"Young, wha—"

The table, porch, trees, grass and sky—*even the sunshine*—melted into darkness.

The Void surrounded Tommy.

Young Charlie stood before him.

("desayunaste, glick?")

("desa-fuckin'-*yunaste!")*

"Lo siento, Tommy..."

"...for what I'm about to do."

1970s

CHAPTER IV

SUNDAY MORNING

"I like the way your sister cries, Glick..."

("FIND IT, TOMMY...")

"Bubba?"

("the temple...")

"Bubba, wake up!"

("the temple")

("the temple")

("all for the temple")

"Bubba!"

Tommy tried to open his eyes, but couldn't.

"Ho...ry...fuuuurrrck..."

His tongue didn't work right.

"Bubba, are you okay?"

"Ahm...*try'intosplaghmfaghm...*"

"What? What're you sayin', Bubba?"

Fuck...

Can't even talk...

Am I still there?

...in The Void?

With great effort, he forced his eyelids open.

Suzie...

His little sister Suzie leaned over him, bathed in pale morning light. He tried to speak again.

"Whart...tarhm...irs-it?"

Holy fuck.

Could barely move his tongue.

"It's moh-ning time..." said Suzie.

No shit, Suzie...

But why are you *here?*

He felt both warm and immobile, like a stone heated to a gentle glow.

"I'm hahn-gwy..." said Suzie. "...and I wanna pway in the pooool..."

Fuck...

Bitch stepmom wasn't supposed to drop her off 'til Monday...

Tommy moved his head first, slow and careful, rolling it clockwise, then back the other way. The house smelled like weed, stale beer, and something sweet he couldn't place, like perfume, but earthier. Dudes and chicks lay crashed out all over: on the floor, across couches, chairs, and beanbags. Some half-dressed, most familiar. For some reason, everyone wore purple bracelets…

Then the memories hit.

They'd thrown a party last night—

—a badass Smokehouse Party.

*

"Let's smoke that Purple uuuuuuup!" said Lacey.

"All Day and All of the Night" *by The Kinks jammed from Mouse's jumbo-sized boombox. Tommy strained to hear Lacey over the music and chatter. They'd never had this many people at a Smokehouse Party before.*

"Purple-purple-purple fuuuuuuuck!" said Leslie. "Give it to me!"

"Give it up, Tommy!" said Mouse. "We gotta smoke that shit!"

"No!" Tommy shouted over the noise. "We gotta wait until later! That shit'll fuck us up!"

"Whoa, whoa, whoa!" Mouse shoved Lacey and Leslie aside. "What'd you just say?"

"I said we gotta wait until later!" said Tommy.

"And why'd you say that?"

"'Cause it'll fuck us up!" said Tommy.

Mouse placed both hands on Tommy's shoulders.

"That's why we fuckin' smoke it, man!"

*

"Mau…se…" said Tommy.

Mouse lay on the floor, eyes closed, mouth open, drooling.

He looked dead.

Lacey lay beside him.

Also drooling.

Also looked dead.

Am I droolin', too?

"Ahmmm…" He tried to tell if slobber clung to his chin.

"I'm hahn-gwyyyy…" said Suzie.

Fuck.

Gotta feed Suzie or she'll start cryin'...

Feeling.

Feeling returned to his hands and feet.

He wiggled his fingers and toes.

Man, I only took one hit of that shit...

That purple stuff—*Purple Dream,* yeah, that's what it was called—must've been dusted with strong shit. Muscle relaxants, pain killers, and maybe—

Horse tranq.

That's what they dusted it with.

The Horse People.

*

Tommy pressed on the gas. The engine surged, its low, visceral hum vibrating through the floorboard. Sunlight poured through the windshield, too bright and hot on his arms. Didn't wanna break the speed limit, but he did wanna get the fuck home.

Larry rolled a Bic lighter between his fingers. "I think Jack was right."

He fidgeted in his seat.

"About the diversification shit," said Larry. "Ya know what I'm sayin'?"

Tommy shook his head.

The steering wheel felt slick under his sweaty palms.

Just gotta focus on the road...

"Did you hear me, dude?" asked Larry. "Jack was right. We should find a new supplier. Fuckin', diversify and shit."

Tommy bit his lip.

Didn't wanna talk about the Horse People. Or what they saw out there.

Just wanted to get home.

Focus on the party.

They had a shit-ton *of that purple stuff—needed to figure out who to sell it to, how much to charge.*

That's all that mattered.

("you boys like horses?")

("pretty, pretty little horses...")

"Tommy," said Larry. "You listenin' man?"

("all little boys like pretty horses...")

"Who gives a fuck, dude?" asked Tommy. "They fronted *us this shit. Can you believe that? Trunk's packed, and we didn't have to pay a dime up front."*

He rapped his knuckles on the steering wheel.

They trust us...

They trust us to deliver...

He cranked the music up. Bass thudded against his ribs like a warning.

Larry kept yappin'.

"Tommy—"

"Don't wanna talk about it."

"Let's just sell this shit."

*

"Bu-bba!" said Suzie. "Hahn-gwy!"

"I can...feed you..." said Tommy. "...gimme...time..."

Good.

Improvement.

At least he wasn't slurring his words anymore.

"What's *wahng* wid you?" asked Suzie. "What's *wahng* wid *ehbery-wahn?* Why they sweepin'?"

"Par...ty..." said Tommy.

"Pahty? Like a birf-day pahty? Whose birf-day? Mine?"

No, not yours, Suzie...

Catch a clue.

"What we gonna eat, Bubba?"

Tommy raised his forearms. Up, then down.

Could move'em okay, but didn't *feel* anything.

"What we gonna eeeeeeaaaaat?" asked Suzie.

"Pizza..." said Tommy.

"You can't eat pizza for bwek-faaast!"

"Yes, you can..." said Tommy.

"Lots of...pizza..."

*

"Hey Tommy!" said Jack. "The Zion dudes are here! The ones I told ya about!"

Jack yanked Tommy away from the girls he chatted with and dragged him toward the front yard, the summer night air thick with sweat and smoke. Mouse's boombox rattled the porch boards beneath their feet.

"You sure these guys are cool?" asked Tommy.

"I'm sure, dude," said Jack. "I was right about the Hazard Maf guys, wasn't I?"

Jack had *been right about the Hazard dudes. More or less. Not "cool" exactly, but they weren't startin' shit. Minded their manners.*

*They did seem like...*Hazard *dudes, though.*

Fit the stereotype perfectly. Confederate flag bandanas, Marlboro and Budweiser t-shirts. And that super-strong Hazard drawl of theirs...kept yappin' about "ridin' their backs in the mountains," *took nearly five minutes to realize they were sayin'* "bikes." *Even their names sounded redneck as fuck: Zane and Zeke.*

Who named their kids that these days?

Fuckin' booney shit.

They'd brought hot girls to the party, though; public property chicks, not their girlfriends and shit. Nice of 'em.

"The Hazard Maf dudes seem alright," said Tommy. "But I ain't sure about Zion bitches..."

"Dude," said Jack. "Even Mouse *is okay with 'em. He fuckin' met 'em and you know how Mouse is..."*

Tommy clenched his jaw. He'd avoided Mouse since their argument about the Purple—still didn't want any of his Boys smokin' that shit 'til later in the party, when it started to die down.

Just in case.

Jack clenched his freckled face, jaw twitching. He was amped tonight. "This is the biggest PR and sales event we could ever imagine! This Purple shit is gonna take us to a whole new level, man!"

Once Jack had seen the trunk crammed with huge bags of Purple, he spent days campaigning on the phone, promising cheap samples to both current and potential customers. "It's called Purple Dream, man," *he'd said.* "And I'm not fuckin' kiddin' you, it's really *purple,* dude. Purple as fuck. And dusted with shit, too." *When asked what it was dusted with, he assured everyone that it was* "just some good stuff," *and with a hearty laugh, added,* "It'll fuck you up, that's for sure..."

Per the Table Vote, Jack had insisted the party remain "exclusive" and "invite only," and that anyone wanting to bring a friend needed to clear it with him at least one hour before the party. Unapproved guests would be asked to leave—although the Boys later decided they'd enforce that rule selectively, and it didn't apply to hot girls, or pretty much any girl in general.

"They called us beforehand," said Jack. "Just like the Hazard guys did. That's a sign of respect, *my man. That's how* big *we're gettin'..."*

Tommy looked around, taking it all in. The Smokehouse pulsed with energy. People drank and smoked and danced and laughed not only inside, but across the front and backyards, too. Sales surged harder tonight than ever before, mostly off the combo pitch. They'd hyped it up heavy: smoke Monkey first, get grounded, then hit Purple Dream when it dropped, see how far it takes you.

"Ride the Purple Wave!" *Mouse had said.*

As they headed toward the driveway, Jack whispered in his ear. "Dude, you know those girls the Hazard Maf guys brought?"

"Yeah," said Tommy. "They're fuckin' hot..."

Leslie and Lacey had bitched about the Hazard chicks ("They'll give ya somethin' Ajax can't scrub off!"), *likely jealous and shit. That's girls for ya.*

"Especially that Gina girl..." said Tommy.

As if on cue, Gina strode across the lawn, wiping her mouth with the back of her hand, eyes glassy and lipstick smeared, bare legs streaked with dew from the grass. For a moment, they met each other's gaze. Tommy nearly looked away.

"...she's got nice tits..."

"Yeah, her tits ain't that big," said Jack, "but they're real nice, ain't they? Like, shaped real nice."

"And she knows how to show'em off, too," said Tommy.

"Well, guess what?" said Jack. "They were givin' blowjobs to guys on the side of the house."

Tommy eyes widened. "You serious?"

Jack nodded. "Them Gina and Sarah girls were. I don't think that Tracey girl was, though. She was on her knees in front of a dude, just jackin' him real slow-like, lookin' bored as fuck while she was doin'—"

"To who?" asked Tommy. "The Hazard Maf guys?"

"Nope," said Jack. "Underclassmen. But honestly, the handjob was pretty hot, too. Her lookin' bored actually made it hotter, like— "

"To underclassmen?"

"Yep," said Jack. "Dunno their names. Friends with Kevin and Wiley."

"Holy shit..." said Tommy. Girls givin' straight up blowjobs on the side of the Smokehouse, and to underclassmen, at that?

Next-level shit.

Kissin', makin' out real intensely, and yeah, maybe fuckin' and shit behind closed doors, that happened. But girls suckin' dick on the motherfuckin' side of the house?

Set a whole new precedent for a Smokehouse Party.

"It's so awesome," said Jack. "This whole party—is just awesome. *Even just* watchin' *those girls suck dick was hot..."*

Tommy agreed.

Even just watchin' that shit would *be hot.*

"You gonna try to get some of that?" asked Tommy. He made a mental note to hit up those Hazard girls for their numbers—just in case things went south when he confronted Samantha about that bullshit with Bill.

"Hell yeah I will," said Jack. "But tonight I'm prioritizin' business, ya know what I'm sayin'?"

Tommy shot him a thumbs-up. He loved that about about Jack. Business first. Always.

"These Zion dudes," said Jack, "said if the purple stuff was good, they'd be interested in buyin' two *fuckin' bags to sell to kids up in Zion."*

"Excellent," said Tommy. "That's what we need." He patted Jack's shoulder.

Good, Jack...

Good...

Sellin' two fuckin' bags out the gate would be real *fuckin' good. They'd cut it with tobacco, too, to sell twice as much. First, let'em sample the pure shit, then sell'em bags cut with tobacco. But he didn't need to tell Jack that. Jack stayed two steps ahead when it came to that shit.*

"Hey Tommy, nice to meet you, dude," said one of the Zion soccer team guys. They shook hands and the Zion dude told him his name, but Tommy forgot it instantly ("Bryce," or some bullshit like that). While Jack did his sales pitch, Tommy studied the Zion bitches, searching for anything that might trigger an alarm. Predictably, they'd over-dressed for a house party—Ralph Lauren bullshit, with khaki pants to boot—and reeked of expensive-smelling

cologne. Typical Zion yuppies livin' off their daddies' money. Even spoke with a diluted, almost Midwestern accent, as if half-tryin' to pretend they weren't from Kentucky.

Other than that, they seemed alright, though.

For Zion bitches.

"Hey," said a Zion bitch, "my uncle manages the North Crow Domino's, he can give us discounts and shit. If it's cool with you, I can order a bunch of pizzas, on us. If you could throw us a few samples of the purple stuff for free."

Tommy gave him a slow nod, imagining the greasy cardboard scent already.

A peace offering.

He could accept that.

No.

Even better:

Tribute.

He'd accept tribute *from the Zion bitches.*

*

Tribute.

Pizza from Zion.

Hot-ass, slutty girls from Hazard.

Both offered as tribute.

A show of *respect.*

Likely how Genghis Khan felt when he received the emissaries of other nations; when he received their *respect* and *tribute.* Those Hazard and Zion dudes understood now—fucking *understood* that the Smokehouse Boys represented power, *a force not to be fucked with.*

He squeezed his hand into a fist.

This is how it feels...

To be on the path...

The path to becoming the Kings of the Tri-County.

"What kinda pizza is it?" asked Suzie. "I waike peppa-woni..."

"We got all kinds..." Tommy patted his head to make sure his cap was on straight *(Mikey...),* then slowly brought his knees up.

Good.

Could move his legs again.

And he wanted pizza, too.

"Where's Samantha?" asked Suzie.

Samantha.

("i love you, tomm—")

("you're the on—")

Even high on purple weed dusted with horse tranq, he still saw *her* fucking face—that bloody, cum-smeared face of hers.

"I waike Samantha..." said Suzie.

("after prom...")

("i took her fuckin' cherry...")

A hot spike of anger surged through him, and he used that anger to push himself upright, shifting into a sitting position. Sweat slicked his back. Muscles twitched like they were barely connected.

God...

So hard to even sit up...

"Samantha ain't here..." His vision pulsed at the edges, breath thick in his throat.

But when she comes back...

I got some fuckin' questions for her.

He grimaced and attempted to rise—

"Bubba!"

—then fell flat on his face.

*

"Hey, come here..."

Deanna took his hand.

"...I wanna show you somethin'..."

Tommy's cock grew hard at Deanna's touch.

Something had sparked *between their hands—sharp and electric.*

She rubbed her finger slow across his wrist.

Damn...

Deanna led him through the crowd toward a back bedroom. Good Guy Grant stood blocking the door.

"Grant, the fuck you doin' man?" asked Tommy. "You're supposed to be outside, keepin' an eye out."

Tommy wasn't that pissed, though. Pretty obvious that Bill and Kenny wouldn't do shit tonight, so keeping the Possibles on guard around the perimeter didn't seem necessary anymore.

Still...

"I was just—" said Grant.

"My baaad," said Deanna. "I asked him to guard the bedroom for us. Michelle's changin' in there and didn't want no one walkin' in..."

"Gotcha," said Tommy. "It's cool, then. You can go back outside, Grant."

"I'm sorry, Tommy, I—"

"It's alright," said Tommy. "Just keep an eye out, man."

Grant nodded and headed out, crowbar jutting from the back of his jeans.

Deanna ran her fingertips across Tommy's chest, then guided him inside and shut the door behind them.

Holy fuck.

Tommy's jaw dropped.

Michelle knelt on the floor mattress, her bare ass facing him, pale in the dim light.

Holy fuck.

Is this real?

She moaned.

Deanna yanked her skirt up and dropped beside her, ass out, mirroring Michelle.

"You can fuck us both, Tommy..." Michelle swayed from side-to-side.

"...we'll keep it secret..." said Deanna. "...we promise..."

Fuck.

God, how those asses swayed.

He wanted *that.*

For the first time since him and Samantha started going steady, he actually wanted *to cheat on her.*

("i love you, tomm—")

("you're the on—")

After all, that's what she fuckin' deserved, *wasn't it?*

("I took her cherry...")

("and done loosened it up for ya...")

The fucking cunt.

Slut.

*Piece-of-ass-*whore *who gave her virginity to Bill-fuckin'-Cunningham when they went to Prom* "just as friends."

"...fuck us both, Tommy..." said Deanna.

"...give it to us both..." said Michelle.

Hell yes.

He'd fuck'em both tonight.

Like he'd never fucked before.

He dropped his hand to the cold brass button on his jeans.

(no)

A force *took hold, maybe God, maybe something else, and dropped him to his knees.*

"We'll suck your dick, Tommy," said Deanna. "We'll both suck your dick and you can c—"

"You're both beautiful..." he said, feeling as if something else *spoke through him.*

Without thinking, he kissed both their ass cheeks the way one kisses a baby's forehead.

Michelle moaned again.

Tommy gazed at the spectacle before him a bit longer, then rose.

"But I ain't gonna cheat on my girl."

He turned to leave the room.

Not until he knew whether she really *fucked Bill Cunningham or not.*

*

Tommy's face lay on the cold hardwood floor.

Holy shit...

Why didn't I hit that?

Not many guys would pass that up.

Most never even got the chance.

Ever.

Maybe he'd never get that chance again—not for the rest of his fucking l—

"Do you need a baaaand-aid?" asked Suzie.

"No..." Tommy struggled to push himself up. "...I'm fine..."

The room spun like the floor tilted beneath him—heavy, slow, unreal. He felt sleepy, *blurry* again.

God...

Feels like I slept for a hundred years...

And I could sleep for a hundred more, easy....

"Wait," he said. "What's today?"

"What do ya mean?" asked Suzie.

"What day is it today?"

"Sunday..."

He breathed a sigh of relief.

Good.

It'd be *insane* if they'd all been out for like, thirty-six hours or some shit.

"Aghm..."

A mumble escaped Mouse as a strand of drool dangled from his lips to the floor.

Tommy chuckled.

How long would it take Mouse to wake up?

***

"Mmm..." said Tommy, mouth full of pizza.

Thankfully, someone had the sense to toss the leftover Domino's in the fridge. Probably Larry. Thank God for bros like Larry.

"This pizza's *sooo* gooood..." said Tommy.

The pizza was cold. Tasteless. Rubbery.

And yet, somehow—

—the best fucking pizza he'd ever eaten.

Maybe the Purple both dulled *and* enhanced his tastebuds?

He inhaled slice after slice, cramming them into his mouth, nearly crying tears of joy.

"Fuuuuuck..." He bit into another slice.

Now he was talkin' like Leslie.

This must be how she felt, all the time.

Just like, *"Fuuuuuuck..."*

Now he knew.

Now he understood.

"You sure it's okay?" asked Suzie.

Tommy snatched another slice of pepperoni. "What is?"

"Pizza..." said Suzie. "...for bwek-fast..."

"Why wouldn't it be?"

"My stepmom says—"

"Well, she ain't here, is she?"

The fuckin' bitch.

"So eat up," said Tommy.

Suzie poked at the pizza, nudging it across her plate.

"I never ate *cohde* pizza before..." said Suzie.

"Well, now you will," said Tommy. "So eat and be happy."

He crammed another slice in, unsure if he even chewed—just felt it slide down, heavy and perfect.

***

"That's your eighth slice..." said Suzie.

What?

Had he really eaten *eight* slices?

A *whole* fucking pizza?

"You sure?"

"Yep!" said Suzie. "You eat like a gahhh-bage truck!"

"Whoaaaaaa..." said Tommy. The world shifted—blurry again. His body felt like it drifted toward the sky.

Am I...

...floating?

Like, spiritually-fuckin'-floating?

He glanced down at his half-eaten slice of mushroom pizza.

Maybe the mushrooms?

Increased my high?

He took another bite.

And then another.

And another.

"Whoaaaaaa..."

Every bite of mushroom goodness seemed to multiply and intensify his high, like someone cranked the volume up in his brain.

Maybe some kinda...chemical reaction?

Between the Purple Dream and the mushrooms...

He had to share this.

With his Boys.

***

Tommy shuffled through the house, stepping over passed-out partygoers while laying mushroom pizza slices on each sleeping Smoketown Boy. Felt like an Italian Santa Claus.

Larry...

Mouse...

Jack...

Pizza presents...

For all of y'all...

The Possibles hadn't been allowed to smoke the Purple—needed 'em alert, in case Bill and Kenny showed up.

He shook his head, pizza box under one arm.

Never showed, though...

Of course they didn't. Not without their walkin'-fuckin'-tank, Graham-fuckin-'Riley. Didn't even have Young on their side anymore. In the end, all of Jack's big-brain theories had blown away like bullshit in the wind.

No Vietcong-style guerilla warfare.

No fire-in-the-woods distraction.

No Possibles tied to trees.

And no—

A cold flicker ran through Tommy, like ice water down his spine.

Recruitment.

Jack's other theory: Bill was out recruiting new guys, using free coke to pull'em in.

And what if he *did* have an epic plan?

To use those new guys?

To do somethin' big...

Or—

—maybe Mouse was right.

Just him and Jack overthinkin' shit.

He shook his head.

Could worry about that later.

Kevin's eyes cracked open as Tommy laid a pizza slice on his chest.

"What's this...?" asked Kevin.

"Your breakfast..." said Tommy. "But it's still early, dude...go back to sleep..."

"Cool...thanks, Tommy..."

Kevin moved the pizza slice to a nearby pillow and rolled to his side, the crowbar jutting from the back of his jeans.

Didn't need those crowbars, after all...

And when they wake up...

They'll have a nice slice of pizza, good and ready for'em...

Larry snored from a hammock in the corner, his favorite spot. He'd shifted in his sleep and knocked his pizza slice to the floor, but whatever. It was still good. *You could still eat that shit.*

Next—get'em all glasses of water?

Might have cottonmouth.

Nah...

Seven glasses of water was a lot of work. Besides, *he* didn't have cottonmouth, so they probably didn't, either. Maybe another sweet, sweet salespoint of the Purple Dr—

"Aah!"

Tommy bent over and clutched his head.

("the temple")

("find the temple...")

*("*lo siento, *tommy")*

("temple above all")

("live through it, tommy")

("live through it...")

("for what I'm about to do...")

Slowly, he straightened up.

God...

What the fuck *was that dream about?*

Mikey?

That Temple place?

And then it all went black, like a *Void*...

And Young Charlie sayin' *lo sien*—

"...fuuuuuuck..." whispered Leslie, asleep on a beanbag.

Wait.

Was it *lo siento?*

Or *no lo siento?*

Tommy scratched his head, trying to recall the *español* Young had taught him back in the day. *Lo siento* meant "excuse me," right? So maybe *no lo siento* meant "no excuses," or "I got no excuses."

Made sense.

"Bubba!" Suzie burst from the bathroom in a pink Barbie bathing suit. "I put on my bay-ving suit!"

"Cool, Suzie..." said Tommy.

Anyway. Didn't matter.

Just a fucked-up weed-dream.

Probably why they call it Purple Dream...

Gives you fucked-up, crazy-ass dreams...

"Lemme make some Kool-Aid before we go out..." said Tommy.

Still felt high as fuck—hard to even walk straight. But he could chill this morning. Let Suzie play in her kiddie pool while he took a nap, maybe catch another crazy-ass Temple dream. Morning had barely begun, and he couldn't imagine the state of guys who'd took *multiple* hits of Purple.

Probably wouldn't budge all day.

***

"Fuuuuck..."

Tommy stared at the empty pizza boxes, gut heavy and fingers greasy while stirring Kool-Aid powder and sugar into a cloudy pitcher of tap water. Purple felt like the right flavor today.

"Can't believe I ate all that pizza..." he said.

"You keep sayin' dat!" said Suzie.

"'Cause it's true..."

Shocked that much pizza even *fit* inside his stomach.

Gonna take the mother of all dumps today...

"I want Kool-Aid. And wanna swim in the pooool..."

"Sounds good..." Tommy took a sip of purple Kool-Aid—*damn.* The flavor exploded in his mouth. Electric-sweet, sharp with citric acid. It didn't just taste purple, it *felt* purple.

Even the Kool-Aid tastes better than normal...

Purple Dream makes everything *taste better...*

Wasn't sure what to do with Suzie after the pool, though. She could watch cartoons and shit, but that'd only last so long. Maybe take her to the skating rink? Could invite chicks along, like those Hazard girls who'd sucked dick on the side of the house.

"Whoaaaaa..."

The kitchen swayed.

Walls breathing.

Light melting.

Fuck...

Still so high...

Could he even fucking *skate* tonight?

"Blu-aagh!"

Tommy half-burped, half threw-up in his mouth—immediately tasting pizza crust, stomach acid, and purple.

"Eugh..." He grimaced. "I gotta brush my teeth."

He handed Suzie a glass of purple Kool-Aid.

"Drink your Kool-Aid, chill for a bit."

Tommy ambled across the house, passing Jack sound asleep with a slice of mushroom pizza on his chest.

"Whabbafuckadudga..." Jack grasped at something in his pocket, something—

The water gun.

The Kentucky Blood-filled water gun.

Jack still had that.

A look of satisfaction crept across Jack's peaceful, freckled face as he cradled the water gun to his chest.

Tommy smiled.

You can squirt that on your pizza, Jack...

Won't be needin' it for anything else now.

***

"Arhmmm..." said Tommy as he brushed his teeth. Even that simple motion demanded strength and focus. But the toothpaste—

Goddamn.

Tasted incredible.

Cool and sharp, clean and minty, like normal toothpaste dialed up to the millionth degree. He felt each individual bristle, each stroke like a tiny miracle.

"Fuuuuck..."

He brushed deeper, slower.

Euphoric.

Feels so good to brush my fuckin' tongue...

Later on, it'd be fun to compare the effects of the Purple with everyone else.

That Purple Dream shit was somethin' else.

*

"Dude, it's one a.m.," said Mouse. "Can we fuckin' smoke it now?"

Tommy surveyed the scene. The party was finally winding down—most people had moved inside, with a few scattered groups still in the front and back yards.

The Zion and Hazard guys had behaved...until they ran into each other. Then came the shit-talking. The drama. The false bravado.

Luckily, Jack and Larry stepped in fast, telling both sides they "didn't want no bullshit tonight" *and threatening to withhold the Purple if they started some.*

"Larry," said Tommy. "What you think? Time for the Purple?"

"Time for the Purple," said Larry. "Maybe just enough so everybody gets one hit. Don't know how powerful that shit is yet."

Tommy narrowed his eyes. As their leader, he had to consider the worst-case scenario. The threat of Bill and Kenny had all but vanished, but he didn't want his Boys blasted outta their minds and then other shit go down, like getting robbed by Hazard or Zion guys.

"Okay," said Tommy. "Bring the Possibles back inside, they'll stay sober while we toke up. Just in case, ya know—"

"The Hazard or Zion bitches start shit," said Larry. "I'll round'em up."

Good ol' Larry.

Read his fuckin' mind.

"Jack," said Tommy.

Jack leaned an arm against the wall, chattin' up that Gina chick in the corner. She arched her back and pushed her chest out, tilting her head like she already knew what he wanted—and just might give it to him.

"Hey, what's up, Gina?" said Tommy. "Sorry to interrupt y'all, but—"

"Great party, Tommy!" Gina hugged him tighter than necessary. Her breath smelled like beer, weed and cum.

"Thanks, thanks..." Tommy patted her back. "I just gotta holler at my boy Jack real quick."

Gina stepped back, looking tipsy. "Hey, lemme introduce my friend, Tracey..."

"The one with tattoos?" asked Tommy.

"No, that's Sarah," said Gina. "I meant my other friend..."

Damn. He liked that Sarah chick—she had tattoos, and style. *Like a badass girlfriend of a Hell's Angel. Exactly the kinda girl that should roll with the Boys. That other chick, Tracey or whatever, was hot, but acted like she had better places to be.*

Didn't have time for bitches like that.

Especially if she gave boring-ass HJ's on the side of the house while her friends actually sucked dick.

"Uhh, yeah, cool," said Tommy. "Lemme holler at her later, then..."

He pulled Jack over to Mouse and they huddled up.

"Okay," said Tommy. "We're gonna smoke the Purple shit."

"Yes!" *Mouse's eyes shone like stars.* "Fucking. Finally!"

"You sure?" asked Jack. "Maybe we should—"

"I'm sure," said Tommy. "Larry's roundin' up the Possibles. They'll keep watch while we toke."

"Gotcha," said Jack. "Just in case."

Tommy nodded.

Jack fucking got it.

Leslie crashed into their huddle, wild-eyed and swaying. "Purple-purple-purple! Fuuuuuuuck..."

"Let's smoke that purple shiiiiiit." Lacey floated in behind her.

Mouse looked deadly serious. "Dude, we barely smoked shit tonight. We just wanna experience the Purple."

"Like, pure," said Lacey.

"Only the purple," said Leslie. "Nothin' else mixed in,"

"We want the purity," said Mouse,

"of the Purple."

*

"Ohhhgfm..."

Tommy knelt on the cold garage floor, the concrete chilling his kneecaps. Drool dangled from his mouth, thick and warm.

"What's *wahng* with you?" asked Suzie.

A secondary high.

That's what's wrong with me...

I hit a second wave.

Something about food in his belly, or maybe the mushrooms on the pizza, must've pushed him into it.

But I only took one hit of that shit...

Didn't I?

He raised his gaze to the pink plastic kiddie pool, its sides decorated with faded decals of Barbie riding a dolphin. Most of their smiles had half-peeled from wear.

("tommy, that was a pussy hit!")

("hit that shit again!")

("fuuuuuck, you gotta inhale *that shit, tommy....")*

Wait a minute...

Maybe he'd taken *two* hits.

Or three?

Strong, solid, *deep* hits of that shit.

He wiped his mouth with the back of his hand, then smeared it on his jeans.

Just gotta make it to the front yard...

Then I can fuckin' chill.

***

"Put the watah in! Put the watah in!"

Suzie bounced barefoot in the damp grass like she was at Disneyland.

Tommy stood over the kiddie pool at the crest of the sloped front yard. The sun felt good on his face.

But God, he was *tired.*

Shuffling around the house all morning made him feel like he'd run a marathon.

"Alright," said Tommy. "I'm gonna need your help, Suzie. Bring me the hose, then turn it on. Can you do that?"

"Okay!" Suzie marched over to the hose.

Beer cans, cigarette butts, Ziploc bags, and Dairy Queen cups littered the front yard. Still, not *too* bad, all things considered. Easy cleaning for the Possibles later.

"Here's the hoooose," said Suzie.

"Alright," said Tommy. "Now go turn it on."

After a few moments, water spurted from the hose, sparkling in the sunlight.

Damn...

That water looks so good...

"Aaaahhhh..." Tommy opened his mouth.

Couldn't help but drink from the hose.

"Mmm..."

The water hit his tongue cold and sharp, carrying that hose-smell; rubber, rust, and summer.

Holy fuck...

This is the best water ever...

Crisp, clear, with a hint of iron—like water *should* taste, or how it used to taste, back in the day, when people drank from waterfalls.

"Put the watah in the pool!" said Suzie. "I wanna swim!"

She climbed inside as Tommy filled it up.

"Aaah!" said Suzie. *"It's cohde! It's coooohde!"*

Tommy grinned. "You'll get used to it..." He returned his mouth to the hose, gulping down its pure, delicious goodness.

Gonna drink from the hose every day now...

Tastes so fuckin' good...

"A buhdie!" said Suzie. "A wed buhdie!"

"Wha?" asked Tommy.

A cardinal—the biggest he'd ever seen—perched on the rim of the kiddie pool. It tilted its head at Suzie, then him, then back again. Watching.

"A budhie! A wed buhdie!"

"It's a cardinal..." said Tommy. "...Kentucky's state bird..."

Suzie clapped her hands. "So pwetty! Pwetty wed bird!"

The cardinal hopped across the edge of the pool toward Tommy.

Maybe thirsty or somethin'...

"I saw it in my dweam!" said Suzie. "Mikey told me!"

Mikey?

Tommy blinked. "You dream about *Mikey?*"

"Sometimes!" said Suzie. "And about The Temple!"

His grip on the hose slackened.

The Temple?

("find it, tommy...")

("find it...")

"Suzie," he said. "What did Mikey tell you about a Tem—"

With a beat of its wings, the cardinal vanished into the treeline.

A low thunder rumbled in the distance.

What the...?

Rain?

Not a cloud in the sky.

The thunder drew closer.

What is *that?*

The thunder advanced, following the road beyond the treeline.

No...

The sound of metal—

Oh, no...

—*heavy* fuckin' metal.

Oh God, no.

A black Camaro screamed onto the driveway like a bad dream.

PART VI

THE BATTLE OF THE SMOKEHOUSE

"Bill, I'm tellin' ya, we've gotta exercise straight-up fuckin' brutality *on Glick and his weedboys...*

If we don't, this shit'll never end."

Blackbeard: The Man Who Scourged the Seas
By: Roberta Stevenson
CHAPTER 13
Why Was Blackbeard So Brutal?

(pg.120) "Okay, I understand why Blackbeard had to kill people," you might be thinking, *"but why did he do such brutal things? Like make people eat their own hearts while they were still alive?"*

That's a great question!

Why *did* Blackbeard go the extra mile and commit such terrible acts of brutality?

Why didn't he *just* kill them?

Blackbeard's actions might sound brutal, but they were key to his success—and the reason you're reading about him today. Believe it or not, there was method to the madness.

→ ***Did You Know?*** *Sometimes people do bad things, but for good reasons. That's why you should never judge someone for their actions until you know why they did it.*

Blackbeard: He Didn't Play Around

In the last chapter, we discussed Blackbeard's tendency to *flay* people—to peel off their skin, *slowly and carefully,* the way one might peel a carrot.

Sounds terrible, right?

But he didn't stop there.

Blackbeard didn't play around!

After flaying his victims, he'd hang their skinless bodies across the sides of his ship—*while they were still alive!* It's no wonder that after the first few times he did this, most ships surrendered to him without a fight. Blackbeard was more than a pirate—he was an *international terrorist.*

→ ***Vocabulary Question:*** *Do you know what a "terrorist" is? A terrorist is someone who uses fear to accomplish goals. For terrorists, the* threat *of horrific violence is more important than the act itself—it compels compliance with their demands. This is why terrorists aren't as bad as serial killers, since terrorists kill people for specific causes or reasons, and not just for fun.*

Remember Captain Stannis, the British Captain mentioned at the beginning of this book? He wore an overly large wig and commanded the *HMS Zion.*

Using the power of your imagination, pretend that you're Captain Stannis!

Imagine: You Are Captain Stannis

Your name is Captain Joseph Peter Stannis, and you're not only a proud officer of the Royal Navy, but also the commander of Her Majesty's largest and most well-armed treasure ship, the *HMS Zion.* You and your crew have pledged to safeguard the Queen's treasure with your lives, and you aren't afraid of anything—even pirates! The *HMS Zion* and her cargo are to be defended at all costs.

But as a pirate ship approaches, you can't help but stare in horror at the skinless bodies hanging across its sides. You can't stop hearing their moans, their cries for the release of death. And then Blackbeard himself emerges on deck, smoke rising from his menacing beard.

A chill runs down your spine.

He appears *otherworldly,* like a wraith of the sea—just as fearsome as the tales portray him.

And, although you try not to, you *remember...*

You *remember* the stories, the legends of Blackbeard's brutality.

And you wonder...

...what would he do to *you?*

You aren't afraid of death, but you *are* afraid of being skinned alive. Or being force-fed your own beating heart!

It's no surprise that the real Captain Stannis, upon identifying Blackbeard as his adversary, surrendered his ship's treasure without a fight. Since Blackbeard attacked during a storm, he didn't even have his cannons ready!

→ ***Did You Know?*** *Whenever you attack someone, try to make it a surprise. History is filled with instances of smaller forces triumphing over larger ones just by catching them off guard!*

In return for Stannis's surrender, Blackbeard showed mercy, allowing him and his men to keep their lives. He even gave them a free ride to a nearby colony!

→ ***Did You Know?*** *Upon returning to Britain, Captain Stannis underwent a court-martial for surrendering his treasure ship without a fight.*

Following a lengthy trial, he received a six-month prison sentence, but later returned to the Royal Navy as a First Mate, where he died off the west coast of Africa in 1722.

His cause of death?

Severe diarrhea!

Now that you've used the *power of your imagination* to experience what Captain Stannis must have felt, you can understand why Blackbeard cultivated such a fearsome reputation. If enough people knew the horrible things he'd done, they wouldn't dare give him any trouble, and nobody would get hurt.

Blackbeard: Forced by Destiny

Although considered cruel at the time, scholars now believe that *destiny* forced Blackbeard's hand, compelling him to commit acts of legendary brutality.

→ ***Vocabulary Question:*** *Do you know what "destiny" means? Destiny is something that's meant to happen in your life—usually something big, important, or even epic. It's what you're meant to do or become. Many people who became famous or powerful did so because they followed their destiny—they didn't run from it or hide. They faced it head-on.*

Blackbeard didn't *enjoy* flaying people, or forcing them to eat their own hearts, or even cutting off their heads and placing them on the bow of his ship. In fact, maybe he hated those things (we'll never know), but *destiny called upon him* to commit those atrocities in order to achieve his status as the most legendary pirate of all time.

When destiny calls, you better answer!

Brutality: It Saves Lives

Looking at the big picture, we can now see that Blackbeard's brutal tactics actually *saved lives.* If he had merely killed the people who defied him, it wouldn't have been enough, and more ships would have fought back—ultimately resulting in more deaths on *both* sides.

→ ***Did You Know?*** *Back in the 1700s, killing people was more popular than saving lives. In fact, people killed each other all the time! Men even challenged each other to duels to the death over liking the same girl.*

Blackbeard wasn't the only one who understood that brutality saved lives. Throughout history, other nations and leaders have understood this, too.

Turn the page to learn more!

Discussion Exercises—Talk With Your Friends!

1. Blackbeard exercised brutality to achieve his *destiny* as the most legendary pirate in the history of the world. Do you believe in destiny? Why or why not?

2. Have you ever felt that you, or someone else, were *destined* to do something?

3. If you felt destiny beckoned you to do something *legendary*, would you do it?

4. People who follow their destiny usually achieve great success, fame or fortune—or sometimes something simpler, such as peace and happiness. Why do you think that is?

5. If destiny called upon you to exercise brutality, would you heed her call?

1970s

CHAPTER I

PLAY WITH THE COWBOYS

"No lo siento, cabrón.

Para nada."

LA HACIENDA

"You wanna do *what?"*

Bill stared at Charlie, mouth agape.

"You heard me," said Charlie. "Don't think it needs repeatin'."

Bill's gut twisted.

"Charlie, that's—"

"Oh, *what now,* Bill?" Charlie kicked broken glass across the porch. "Is Wild Bill goin' pussy on me? Huh? *'Oh, that's too much, man,' 'Oh, that's too ruthless, Charlie,' 'Oh, that's too fucked up, dude.'* Is that what you're thinkin'?"

Bill stared at him.

Yes.

That is what I'm thinkin'.

"Well, guess what, *motherfucker,"* said Charlie. "That's exactly what Blackbeard would fuckin' do if he were fuckin' here right now. If we can't *kill* them motherfuckers, then we gotta do the next best thing."

Bill took a step back.

"Charlie..." he said. "...that's...that's..."

Charlie laid a hand on Bill's shoulder. His face appeared calm now, serene like the surface of a lake.

"Epic," said Charlie.

"And *justificado."*

"And it's what Blackbeard would do."

TOMMY

"Cowboys!" said Suzie. "I wanna pway with the cowboys!"

Tommy couldn't make out the faces of the people in the car, not at first, but he saw their cowboy hats, and that was fucking enough.

Four.

Four fuckin' cowboys.

Not one, not two.

Four.

"Suzie," he said. "Get inside the house."

"No!" Suzie splashed her hands in the water. "I wanna pway in the pool!"

"Suzie! I said get in the—"

"I wanna pway with the cowboys!"

BILL

Heavy metal blasted from the car speakers—so loud it rattled the windshield, shook the fucking air. Basslines thrummed in Bill's chest.

"*SNRRKT!*"

Charlie and Graham snorted coke off a cassette case and threw their heads back, eyes wide and electric. Kenny grinned and bobbed his head to a rhythm separate from the metal, a rhythm only he could hear.

"Just like you told us, Bill!" Kenny shouted over the music. "That little kiddie pool and everything!"

"*SNRRKT!*"

Charlie wiped coke off his mustache.

"Just like you prophesized, Bill!" said Charlie. "Prophet Posse! We're the fuckin' Prophet Posse!"

Him, Kenny, and Graham started chanting.

"Prophet Posse!"

"Prophet Posse!"

The chant fused with the roar of the heavy metal.

"Prophet Posse!"

"Prophet Posse!"

Bill shut his eyes.

Clasped his hands tight.

Please God...

Grant us victory...

And the strength we need to obtain that victory...

Cocaine burned in his sinuses.

The chant grew frenzied.

"Prophet-fuckin'-Posse!"

"Prophet-fuckin'-Posse!"

Charlie screamed like a preacher on fire.

"Prophet-fuckin'-Posse!"

Graham hooted like a drunken gorilla.

"Prophet-fuckin'-Posse!"

Kenny howled like a rabid hyena.

"Prophet-fuckin'-Posse!"

Their voices crashed together—raw, ecstatic, a wall of noise that buzzed in Bill's teeth.

"Prophet-fuckin'-Posse!"
He reached deep inside himself,
"Prophet-fuckin'-Posse!"
to find that speck,
"Prophet-fuckin'-Posse!"
that speck of darkness needed,
"Prophet-fuckin'-Posse!"
"Prophet-fuckin'-Posse!"
to do what destiny required of them today.

("we follow your dreams, Bill...")
("just tell us what to do...")

He opened his eyes.

Time to go Blackbeard.

TOMMY

"Suzie," said Tommy. "Get in the fucking house!"

"No!" said Suzie. "Don't yell! And don't say bad words!"

The heavy metal ceased.

A deadly silence filled the air.

Like a bad dream playing in slow-motion, Bill Cunningham, Young Charlie, a shirtless Kenny Moser, and Graham-fuckin'-Riley stepped out of the car, all donning backpacks, cowboy hats, and aviator sunglasses.

No.

No.

No.

Graham heaved the boombox onto his shoulder. He hit play.

Heavy metal blasted from the speakers.

"Suzie!" said Tommy. *"Get in the fucking house!"*

"Don't say bad words, Bubba!"

Bill and his Posse ascended the hill toward Tommy, aviator sunglasses glinting in the sunlight.

Fuck no.

God no.

No.

They all wielded baseball bats.

LA HACIENDA

Bill gazed into Charlie's bathroom mirror, unable to see himself. He sighed, closed his eyes and dragged a hand down his face.

Charlie had demanded the most insane, fucked up, brutal, and yes, *legendary* thing he could imagine.

If he did that, *if he helped Charlie do that,* there'd be no turnin' back.

"We go there tonight," said Charlie. "We ride to their Smokehouse and *go Blackbeard* on them motherfuckers."

Bill shook his head. "We already dropped Graham and Kenny off."

"So?" asked Charlie. "We pick'em up again."

"They both gotta work in the mornin'," said Bill.

"So the fuck what, *ese?"* asked Charlie. "They can go to work fuckin' sleepy. Or they call in sick. Who the fuck cares?"

"They're probably already sleepin'," said Bill.

"Well, *I'm so goddamn sorry* to interrupt'em past their fuckin' bedtime," said Charlie, "but this is *serious shit,* man. This is the kinda stuff that *defines* us."

"Charlie, this don't *define* us, it's just—"

"It *does,* Bill." Charlie spoke in a voice Bill didn't recognize now. "It *does* fuckin' define us."

Bill looked away. For the first time in their friendship, he felt intimidated—almost afraid.

"This is what makes us a *real Posse,"* said Charlie, "or just some bullshit group that fuckin' *acts* like we're real when we're fake as fuck."

Charlie glanced again at the brown stain on the carpet. He'd been glancing at it every five seconds or so. The stain seemed to fuel him.

"Somebody steps on our fuckin' toes," said Charlie, "we cut off their fuckin' legs! That's how it's gotta be! If we wanna be a *real* fuckin' Posse, we have to go over there with *over-whelmin'-fuckin'-force,* man! Overwhelm the shit out of'em! Then do somethin' fuckin' *legendary!"*

Bill grit his teeth.

There's legendary, Charlie...

Then there's cruel and extreme...

And you can't seem to tell the difference.

"No," said Bill. "That's too much, man. You're lettin' your anger get the best of ya."

"Qué es esto, ese?" Charlie pointed at the brown stain on the carpet. "What's that, huh?"

The stain seemed darker than before.

"What the fuck is that, Bill?"

"It's a fuckin'—"

"Falta de respeto," said Charlie. "It's *disrespect,* is what it fuckin' is. Disrespect to the Posse. We can't tolerate that shit. Disrespect, when you tolerate it, only invites *more* disrespect. If all the other squads across the Tri hear about this, that the fuckin' weedboys fucked up our *La Hacienda* and got away with a mild ass-beatin' and eggs thrown at their Smokehouse, then *everybody's* gonna try fuckin' with us, man! Gonna wanna step up to us, and fuckin' challenge us!"

"Now, that's an exaggeration, Charlie, and—"

"Everybody in the *whole damn Tri-County's* gonna wanna fuck with us, Bill! And throw eggs at my house and brick my fuckin' windows! And poop on my goddamn carpet!"

"That won't happen," said Bill. "And I'll tell ya wh—"

"And then they'll fuckin' challenge us," said Charlie, "and try to gain rep from beatin' our asses!"

"Now Charlie," said Bill. "You're makin' a bigger deal about this than ya sh—"

"No, I fuckin' ain't, Bill," said Charlie. "And you know damn well I'm not. People are gonna be like, '*Hey man, what's goin' on tonight?' 'Oh, not shit man, what you doin?' 'Oh, nothin' much, hey, why don't we go egg Young Charlie's house? And poop all over his place? Let's fuck with him and his weakass Posse!' 'Well yeah, we ain't got nothin else goin' on tonight, so why the fuck not? Sounds like a plan!"*

"Charlie, people ain't gonna talk like that, you're over—"

"They fuckin' will," said Charlie. "You *know* they will, *ese.* And then it just won't stop. It won't stop and our fuckin' senior year is gonna be fuckin' *ruined.* We're gonna be known as the cowboy bitches, man. *The Bitch Posse!"*

Bill sighed, burying his face in his hands.

Charlie...

He felt almost certain that none of those scenarios would come to pass, that Charlie was makin' a *way* bigger deal of it than he should. But the predictions carried an uncomfortable ring of truth; an undeniable possibility, however remote, that Glick and his weedboys braggin' about what they did might invite more trouble. More disrespect. More challenges from other squads.

Squads lookin' to gain rep, and dominate the Tri.

Lowering his hands from his face, he looked into Charlie's eyes.

Murder.

Fuckin' *murder* in them eyes.

Bill took off his cowboy hat and ran his fingers through his long hair.

One last try.

"Charlie," said Bill. "Under normal fuckin' circumstances, okay, you might be right. *But my dreams, Charlie.* My dreams ain't shown me shit about this. It's all just a distraction, a fuckin' sideshow, distractin' us from our mission to rob Stevie Baker and other guys down the road, so we can—"

"Our mission?" asked Charlie. *"Our mission?"*

He stared at Bill in disbelief.

"Our mission," said Charlie. "Is to kick ass and take names, brother. To be the most *badass Posse* in the whole fuckin' Tri. You fuckin' *told me* that when you told me about your dreams, *ese.* You *told me* that God's got a long-term plan for us, and th—"

"He does," said Bill. "God, the Ethereal, whatever it is, *somethin'* is communicatin' with me, Charlie. Has been for a long time now, ever since I can remember. And it ain't said *shit* about this."

"So, what if somethin' happens to me?" asked Charlie. "Or if one of our Posse gets real fucked up? If your dreams didn't say shit about it, guess we shouldn't give a fuck, right?"

Bill started to speak, then paused.

What if one of us did *get killed?*

Or truly fucked up?

And my dreams didn't tell me shit about it?

What would that mean?

"Bill," said Charlie. "I'm gonna tell ya right the fuck now, there's only three ways shit's goin' down tonight:

"First way, fuckin' *la primera manera:* I call up Kenny and Graham, tell'em what happened, and get'em to roll with us. Tonight. If they do, *vamos.* Let's fuck shit up.

"Second way, fuckin' *la segunda manera:* If they say they can't roll out 'cause of their parents or they got work in the mornin' or some other *bullshit* like that, then me and you go. Alone. And we'll *still* fuck shit up.

"Third way, fuckin' *la tercera manera:* If you don't wanna roll with me..."

Charlie stared at the spot on the carpet, a look of pity falling upon his face.

"If my best friend," said Charlie, "my *mejor amigo,* won't roll with me... then I'll go there by myself. Tonight. Fuckin' *yo solo,* man."

He closed his eyes and shook his head.

"Just gonna *yo solo* that shit..."

"Charlie, you can't go over there alone, they *will* fuck you up, and—"

"I don't give a *fuck, ese,"* said Charlie. "I'm gonna do, what I'm gonna do. And if you're with me, then you're fuckin' *with* me. But if ya ain't, then ya fuckin' ain't."

"Charlie, I'm with you man..."

(are you?)

(are you really gonna do that to someone?)

"...but if we go there tonight," said Bill, "just like them weedboys want us to, on *their* fuckin' territory, then *they* got the advantage. That's exactly what they want us to do. We'd probably get our asses kicked, even with Graham and Kenny, 'cause we'd be fallin' into some fuckin' trap, or some bullshit they got planned."

"Don't give a fuck." Charlie yanked his keys from his pocket, strode to the phone, and started dialing.

"Charlie—"

"I'm just gonna call Kenny and Graham one time each," said Charlie, "and I ain't gonna argue with'em, neither. Not like I am with you, *ese.* Ain't got time for no bull—"

Bill pressed the receiver down.

"Charlie," he said. "Lemme try to talk with it."

"Talk with *what?"* asked Charlie. "The fuck you tal—"

"The Ethereal."

TOMMY

Tommy's stomach churned.

This can't be real...

Wearing smiles of murder, Bill and his Posse ascended the hill toward him and Suzie, their cowboy boots thudding heavy with each step.

No.

No.

I'm not gonna let this happen.

His Boys.

Some had probably woken by now.

The Possibles hadn't smoked that shit.

They were *ready.*

Ready with their crowbars.

They'd *trained* for this.

He dropped the hose and balled his hand into a fist, raising it high.

"SMOKE-TOWN-BOYS, RALLY—"

Kenny bolted forward, bat swinging in a shining arc.

"EIN LEICH, EIN ZEIIIIIIIIIISS!"

SUZIE

"EIN LEICH, EIN ZEIIIIIIIIIISS!"

Suzie watched in horror as the shirtless cowboy swung a shiny bat upward, cracking Bubba across the face.

"URRMFFFF!"

His cap flew off and landed in the pool. Blood arced through the air and spattered her Barbie bathing suit.

"BUBBAAAAA!"

The cowboy grinned at her—a crazy, terrifying grin that made her stomach turn.

Then he raised the bat and brought it down on Bubba's chest.

Over

and over

and over

again.

"EIN ZEICH, EIN LEIIIIISS!"

"EIN SCHNELL, EIN KRIIIIEG!"

"EIN ZIECHEN, EIN LIIIIIIIIEGEN!"

"STAHHHHHP!" she cried.

Tears streamed down her cheeks, mixing with Bubba's blood. They trickled into her mouth, salt and copper, thick on her tongue.

LA HACIENDA

"The fuck's *that* gonna do?"

Charlie paced in circles across the living room, his shoes crunching over broken glass. "Talkin' to the damn fuckin' etherment, or—"

"The Ethereal," said Bill. "And, technically, I don't really talk to it—*it* talks to *me."*

"What's *that* fuckin' mean?" asked Charlie.

"It tells me what it wants to," said Bill. "Like watchin' TV or listenin' to the radio. You can turn it on, and you can try to tune it and change the channel and shit, but you can't really *talk* to it. It just talks to you."

"Well, what-the-fuck-ever, *ese,"* said Charlie. "The fuckin' etherment or God or whatever the fuck it is, this is some serious shit, and if your dreams ain't sayin' shit about it, I'm gonna tell ya right now, I'm startin' to fuckin' doubt your whole fuckin' 'dreamin' thing. I'm talkin' *tengo dudas, ese. Tengo-*fuckin'-*dudas..."*

Bill's face darkened. Didn't know what *tengo dudas* meant, but didn't like the sound of it.

"I don't see *everything,* dude," said Bill. "I'm not a fortune teller. I can't see the Lotto numbers or who's gonna win elections or shit like that. I just see what it *wants* me to see, or—"

"Or?"

"—or sometimes, it's just stuff that's spillin' out. Like it doesn't want me or *not* want me to see. It just spills outta somewhere, and I just happen to see it."

"Sí, fuckin' *sí."* Charlie nodded. "Sounds like bullshit to me."

"Charlie," said Bill. "Gimme thirty minutes to—"

"Thirty minutes?"

"To try and reach out to it," said Bill. "See if it can tell me somethin'."

Charlie flicked his eyes to the spot on the carpet.

"I'll give ya twenty."

***

Engulfed by the dark woods near the *Hacienda,* Bill fell to his knees and clasped his hands.

Wasn't sure who—or *what*—he should pray to.
But God seemed like a safe bet.
So he closed his eyes and prayed.
Please God...
Show me what I can do...
What we *can do...*
To pay those weedboys back...
He waited.
And waited.
Nothing.
Just crickets chirpin'.
He opened his eyes, took a deep breath, then closed them again.
God...
I need your power...
I need your wisdom, and your glory...
Show me the right path...
The path to victory...
The right time, and the right way, to strike'em...
Nothing.
"Goddamnit!"
He pounded his fist into the soft earth.
Felt like a damn fool.
He looked around as his frustration flared, then cooled.
One more time.
He closed his eyes and focused his thoughts.
God, please, please show m—
A rush of images flooded his mind:
Blood.
Water.
Sunlight.
More...
Show me more...
Blood clouding water.
That's it...
Clouds of blood,
strings of vomit,
floating in water.

More....
Bags of weed.
Purple weed.
Sprinkled with white powder.
Shit that would fuck you up.
That's—
Crowbars.
Jet black ones.
Cryin'.
Someone cryin'.
A little girl?

"Bubba..."

BILL

"EIN ZEICH, EIN LEIIIIIIIIISS!"

"BUBBAAAAA!"

Glick curled into the fetal position, arms over his head, trying to block Kenny's blows.

"EIN SCHNELL, EIN KRIIIIEG!"

"STAHHHHHP!" cried Suzie.

Charlie smiled and nodded.

"EIN ZIECHEN, EIN LIIIIIIIIEGEN!"

"Huh huh huh…" chuckled Graham.

"That's enough, Kenny," said Bill.

"EIN ZEITGEN, EIN SM—"

Bill caught his arm mid-swing.

"Stop."

Kenny's arms trembled. Something wild flickered in his eyes—a kind of unhinged joy.

"*Remember the plan, Kenny,*" said Bill. "Me and Charlie'll talk to Glick. You and Graham go inside."

Slowly, Kenny relaxed.

He lowered his bat and nodded.

"And remember," said Bill. "If any of 'em are awake, don't let'em call that *rally-up* bullshit, either."

He spat and glared at Glick.

"It's like their goddamn superpower or somethin'…"

Kenny grinned. "Let's go inside, Graham. Time to fuck shit up."

He twirled his bat, heading for the stairs. Graham stomped behind him.

"Huh huh huh…" Graham popped his knuckles. "…this is gonna be fun…"

Glick moaned.

Blood burst from his mouth.

Suzie screamed.

"MY BUBBAAAAAAAAAAAAAAAAAA!"

Kenny lifted his shades, flashing her a smile and a wink.

GRAHAM

Graham stomped into the Smokehouse living room. The stench of weed hit him hard—pungent and earthy, tinged with somethin' else. *Somethin' purple-smellin'.* Weedboys must've burned through pounds of the stuff last night.

He scanned the room. Everyone was out cold, slumped across couches, chairs, beanbags, and the floor. They all had cheap strips of purple paper wrapped around their wrists, like they'd checked into some birthday party for losers.

A lava lamp bubbled red on a windowsill. Graham stared, slack-jawed. He liked how the blobs moved. *Nice and slow...*

Kenny strutted ahead, nodding and twirling his bat. "Just like Bill's dreams told us..." He grinned, his smile twitchy and off. "All dead asleep... even the music don't wake'em up..."

"Huh huh huh..." chuckled Graham. "Smoked too much stupid shit." He set the heavy metal-blasting boombox by the door. Each bassline rattled empty beer cans.

"Look," said Kenny. "It's Mickey Mouse!"

Mouse sprawled beside that weedchick Lacey, both droolin', mouths wide open.

"Mouuuse..." Kenny dragged his bat across Mouse's cheek. "...oh, Mickey Mouuuse..."

"Huh huh huh..." chuckled Graham. "He can't even feel yo—"

"EIN ZEITGEIST!"

Kenny slammed his bat onto Mouse's nose. Blood spattered Lacey's cheek and forehead.

Mouse groaned.

But didn't move.

Kenny twisted the bat into Mouse's face, smearing blood.

"I could kill you, Mouse..." said Kenny.

He pushed the blood-slick bat into Mouse's open mouth, twisting it.

"...I could fuckin' kill you right now..."

A wild glint flashed in his eyes.

"I'll find the rest!"

TOMMY

Tommy lay in a broken heap on the ground. Metallic warmth spilled down his chin.

"Bubbaaaaaaa..."

"...it's alright, Suzie..." His words came out wet and slurred. "...just stay in the pool..."

Pain—sharp, dull, and everything in between—radiated through his ribs. But without the Purple Dream, he'd be screaming. Something in the horse tranq, or maybe the purple weed itself, seemed to dull the pain.

"EIN SCHMETTERLING!"

Glass exploded inside the house, shattering the air.

Tommy crawled toward the kiddie pool.

His cap.

Mikey...

"Bubbaaaaa...."

"...Suzie..." He pulled himself over the side and reached for his cap, but it floated away.

Suzie smacked her hands into the water.

"I don't wiiiike dis!"

"...just stay in the pool..." said Tommy. "...it's gonna...be alright..."

He coughed, spraying blood onto the pool's surface. Droplets floated for a second, then sank, forming clouds of red that rose to the top again.

"Gimme your arms..." Bill twisted Tommy's hands behind his back. His shoulders screamed.

"Fuck you!" Tommy thrashed, trying to break free, but Kenny's blows—and the numbing pull of the Purple—had made it hard to fight back.

"You do what we say, Glick," said Bill, "and this won't be as bad as it could be..."

Coarse rope bit into Tommy's wrists, grinding his skin raw. Suzie screamed *"Bubbaaaaaa!"* and splashed her hands in the blood-strewn water.

"Buenos fuckin' *días,* Glick..."

Charlie towered over him, framed by the rising sun.

"Tiempo de pagar, hombre..." said Charlie. *"Tiempo. De.* Fuckin'. *Pagar."*

Tommy coughed, spraying the grass with blood.

Young...

All that shit we talked about at Walmart...

"Young, you lyin' piece of sh—*aahhhh!"*

Bill yanked the ropes tighter. A warning jolted in Tommy's ribs, but the Purple softened the edges.

"Shh..." Charlie raised a finger across his mouth. *"Cállate...silencio..."*

Tommy grit his teeth and glared.

I'll kill you for this, Young...

I'll fucking kill you and burn your goddamn house down...

Suzie shrieked, slapping at the blood-slick water.

"I don't wike dissssss!"

"Staaaahhhhp!"

"I don't wike dis game!"

Charlie grinned.

"Don't hurt my Bubbaaaaaa!"

GRAHAM

Graham swept his gaze across the numerous sleeping bodies, most of them familiar. He stomped his cowboy boot.

CLOMP!

A tremor ran through the house.

No one budged.

Just like Bill's dreams said.

CLOMP!

And the boots—Bill was right about those, too.

They felt good.

Powerful...

CLOMP!

Time to wake the weedboys.

"*Buenos días,* y'all," said Graham. "Huh huh huh..."

Felt funny speakin' one of them foreign languages.

CLOMP!

"Ti...tiem-po..."

Fuck.

What was it?

Tiem-po or *tiem-pe?*

"Tiem-po...tiem-pe...de..."

He scratched his head.

"...tiempe de—"

"EIN SCHMETTERLING!"

Glass shattered in the distance.

Fuck it.

Focus on beatin' weedboys.

Kenny's racket clanged on the far side of the house as Graham stomped over to Longface, snoring in his hammock.

"*Rise and shine,* weedboy..." he said. "...huh-huh-huh..."

That was good.

"Rise and shine."

Didn't need no Spanish.

He raised his bat high.

Hit the weedboy.

Good and hard.
Then tie him up.
But first—hit him.

"Wha?"

From the corner of his eye—

—a black blur.

TOMMY

"Tommy," said Bill.

A strange undercurrent of sympathy ran under Bill's voice when he said that:

"Tommy."

Not "Glick," but *"Tommy."*

Something about that note of sympathy unsettled Tommy. Like the way people used to say *"Tommy"* when they talked about Mikey's death.

("tommy, sometimes these things happen...")

"In case you ain't noticed," said Bill, "you ain't got much of a choice here. Either agree to swear to everything I just told ya, in front of everybody, or shit's gonna get *real* bad, *real* fuckin' fast for y—"

"Go fuck yourself, cowboy," said Tommy.

He coughed and spat blood on the grass.

Just gotta give the Possibles more time...

They trained *for this...*

"Kill me," said Tommy. "Beat the shit out of me. Send me to the hospital. Do whatever the fuck you want, man. I ain't swearin' shit."

A look of sadness darkened Bill's face.

Not fake, either—genuine sorrow.

Something's not right about that look...

"Alright..." said Bill. "...I tried..."

He nodded at Charlie, and they both took a step back.

Charlie smiled.

Bill didn't.

"Beat the fuck out of me," said Tommy, "I don't give a fuck, you fuckin' gay-ass, limp-dicked wannabe cowboy fagg—"

THWACK!

The bats cracked across his back, driving him to the ground.

"BUBBAAAAAAAAAAA!"

("something bad is gonna happen, tommy...")
("something really bad...")

Bill and Charlie raised their bats again,

morning sun glinting off the metal.

KEVIN

Kevin lay on the couch, pretending to sleep.

He'd woken the moment Bill and his Posse rolled up—cowboy hats, aviator sunglasses, the whole damn look—but something told him to stay down. No point takin'em all head-on, not when they carried fucking *baseball bats.*

Clomp.

Clomp.

As Graham's boots pounded the floor, Kevin's heart kicked up.

("aaaagh! aaaaaaagh!")

("huh huh huh...")

For some bizarre fucking reason, Graham had tried to speak Spanish while that Kenny guy yelled shit in...*German?*

What the hell?

What kind of drugs is that Kenny guy on?

"EIN SCHMETTERLING!"

Glass shattered across the living room.

Drugs.

The Miracle.

They didn't have their vials, but the Miracle was here, somewhere in the house, and—

"EIN KRIEGS, EIN SVEEEEDERLAAAAAND!"

Another window burst. Kenny's yells grew distant—likely at the back of the house now, while Graham—

Clomp.

Clomp.

—still stomped nearby. Slowly, Kevin twisted on the couch, eyes slitting just enough to glimpse Graham drop the metal-blasting boombox by the door, then lumber toward Larry's hammock.

("huh huh huh...")

("aaaagh! aaaaaaaaaagh!")

Cold fear gripped Kevin's chest.

("let him the fuck go!")

("you're gonna fuckin' kill him!")

His breath turned shallow.

Panicked.
("huh huh huh...")
("aaaagh!")
His heart hammered in his throat.
("aaaaaaaaaaaaaaagh!")
("aaaaaaaaaaaaaaaaaaaaaaaaaaaagh!")
("aaaaaaaaaaaa—")

No.

Graham had his back turned this time.

This time would be different.

Didn't even need that Miracle stuff.

He reached behind him, grasping for the reassuring chill of the crowbar tucked in his jeans.

Just gotta be quiet about it...

Slowly and carefully, he slid off the couch. A slice of mushroom pizza hit the floor with a soft, greasy *flop.*

Fuck!

He froze.

Graham didn't move.

Still watched Larry in his hammock.

Thank God...

Heart hammering in his ribs, he approached Graham from behind, hands slick with sweat, clutching the crowbar in a death grip.

"Rise and shine, weedboy..." Graham raised his bat high above Larry. *"...huh huh huh..."*

Kevin rushed forward, pulling the crowbar back,

"Wha?"

aiming not for Graham's knees,

but his fucking head.

TOMMY

"...I'll never swear to that..." said Tommy. "...you're wastin' your time..."

He coughed and spat blood on the freshly cut lawn. Thanks to the Purple, Bill and Young's fucking baseball bat party hurt less than it should.

Still hurt, though.

Hurt like hell.

And that Skinny Kenny guy had knocked the fuck out of his mouth. Probably fucked up on some mean coke they snorted.

Or meth.

Maybe they did crystal meth.

Why else would the dude be screamin' in *German* and shit?

"EIN KRIEGS, EIN SVEEEEDERLAAAAAND!"

Another window shattered inside the house.

Tommy coughed again, spat more blood. Might've lost a tooth—wasn't sure. Too much blood and couldn't feel his tongue.

I can take this, though...

I can take whatever they wanna dish out...

He glanced at his cap still floating on the pool's surface.

Mikey...

Mikey wouldn't bitch out in a situation like this.

Neither would he.

"...it's gonna be okay, Suzie..." Blood spilled down his chin. "...just stay in the pool..."

The Purple dulls the pain...

They don't know that...

Tommy glanced behind Bill and Young to catch sight of someone slinking across the living room toward Graham.

Was that—?

Kevin.

With his crowbar.

Yes.

God, yes.

He glanced back down.

Didn't wanna make Bill and Charlie notice.

Knock his fucking brains out, Kevin...

Go for his fucking head.

1970S

CHAPTER II

JOIN THE FUN

"Every single window, Kenny...

Every single goddamn window."

LA HACIENDA

A guitar solo whined from Charlie's boombox. Bill, Graham, and Kenny lounged on the couch, listening to Charlie recount his run-in with Glick in the Walmart parking lot.

Bill asked, "Did Glick *really* say all that to ya?"

"He sure fuckin' did," said Charlie. "So I said, *'Oh, you for real, man? You wanted* me *to be one of the Originals? One of the Original Smoketown Boys? Well holy-fuckin'-shit, everything's* real *cool now, motherfucker!*"

Bill and his Posse cackled.

"And then he turned around," said Charlie, "and he looked at me *reaaal fuckin' dramatically,* I swear to God, like a fuckin' movie, with the sun settin' behind him and shit, and he turned back to me and said, *'You still could, Charlie. You still could be...one of us.'*"

Everyone slapped their knees and stomped their feet.

Kenny nearly fell over.

"'You still could be...a Smoketown Boy.'"

Their laughter roared.

"That's funny, Charlie-boy!" said Graham.

Bill couldn't stop laughing. "I wish I could've seen that!"

They laughed till they cried, wiping tears, then went back to snorting coke—except Kenny, who sipped his RC and tequila, nodding to a rhythm only he could hear.

"Man," said Kenny. "If this fuckin' works, Glick is gonna shit his fuckin' pants today!"

"They're *all* gonna shit their pants, *ese...*" Charlie poured a line of coke across a chipped plate. "...especially once we get to the *good* fuckin' part..."

Bill's laughter faded.

His face darkened.

Kenny asked, "When you gotta tell us what that *is,* Charlie?"

"Yeah, Charlie-boy," said Graham. "What's this big *thing* you got planned?"

"I'll tell ya soon enough..." Charlie bent over the plate, crisp dollar bill in hand, folded once, clean and sharp.

"SNRRK!"

A line gone.

"Man, that's good shit..." He wiped his mustache and flipped another page in the Blackbeard book.

Graham followed with his own snort—*"SNRRK!"*—using a wadded-up, sweat-softened bill that barely held shape.

"K-Boy," said Graham. "You sure you don't wanna coke up with us?"

Kenny twirled his baseball bat. "Nah, I'm good..."

Graham watched the bat spin, hypnotized by the shimmer and whirl of aluminum.

"Hey," said Graham. "How come you don't do drugs?"

Slowly, a bizarre grin spread across Kenny's face. Like the smile of a demented clown.

"Don't need'em," said Kenny.

His grin widened.

KENNY

(COME ALONG)

"EIN ZEICH, EIN LEIIIIIIIIIISS!"

(JOIN THE FUN)

"EIN SCHNELL, EIN KREIIIIIIIIIIIIIG!"

(FUCK SHIT UP)

"EIN STURGEN, EIN STRAAAAAAAGEN!"

(ALL DAY LONG!)

Kenny pranced around the back bedrooms, his bat feeling light as a feather. A sick, fucking awesome *rhythm* tore through his mind, *through his very being*—a rhythm forged by heavy metal and violins and cellos and *(THE STARS, THE STARS)* a choir of angels, *beautiful fucking angels,* singing along *(SING ALONG WITH THE STARS)* with *something else,* something both electronic and ethereal *(THE STARS)*, pulsing deep out of deep space *(THE STARS THE FUCKING STARS),* rocketing from another galaxy—

"EIN VOLKSTAMMMMMMMMMER!"

—and above it all, a rhythm, a *sick fucking awesome rhythm, (A RHYTHM ABOVE THE STARS)* pounding louder than the orchestra and driven by those angels, those *sick fucking angels* screaming and screaming beneath otherworldly beats *(THE BEATS ABOVE THE STARS),* all of it feeding *the rhythm, the rhythm (THE RHYTHM OF THE STARS, GIVE IT TO ME)* the fucking rhythm that only existed in his skull, that no one on Earth would ever replicate,

until,

perhaps—

"EIN ZEITGEIIIIIIST!"

—the far future.

DAVID

"EIN ZEICH, EIN LEIIIIIIIIISS!"

David woke to the sound of glass shattering and heavy metal pounding from a boombox.

"EIN SCHNELL, EIN KREIIIIIIIIIIIIIG!"

And some guy yellin' shit...

"EIN STURGEN, EIN STRAAAAAAAGEN!"

...in German?

The fuck?

"EIN ZIECHEN, EIN LIEEEEEEEEGEN!"

He slipped his hand to the crowbar behind his back.

Cold. Solid.

Ready.

Someone do some bad drugs?

That Purple Dream?

Maybe made—

"Huh huh huh..."

Oh no.

Oh God, no.

He took a deep breath, put his glasses on, and rose from his mini-couch.

("aaaaaaaaaaaaagh!")

("huh huh huh...")

("aaaaaagh!")

("aaaaaaaaaaaaaaagh!")

Heart pounding, he crept through the house—just in time to see Kevin draw back his crowbar, aiming for the back of Graham's head.

Yes.

Oh God, yes.

Bust it like a fucking watermelon.

GRAHAM

The crowbar stopped an inch from Graham's face—caught in his fist.

Kevin stared up in disbelief.

"Huh huh huh..." chuckled Graham. "...that could've hurt..."

A metallic clang echoed through the house as Graham dropped his bat to the floor. He yanked the crowbar from Kevin's grip with his left hand and flung it aside. With his right, he grabbed Kevin's throat, lifting him into the air.

"Aaaaaaaaaagh!"

"Huh huh huh..."

You are like an ant to me...

An ant that I will squash.

Kevin squirmed and kicked his legs out as his face turned pink, then deep red.

"Aaaaaaaaaaaaaaaagh!"

"Aaaaaaaaaaaaaaaaaaaaaagh!"

"Huh huh huh..."

Movement.

Behind him.

"Wha?"

Longface!

In the hammock!

He tossed Kevin into the wall and attempted to spin around—

—too late.

Longface coiled his right arm around Graham's neck, flinging Graham's sunglasses off with his left.

"Jack!"

"I got his sunglasses off!"

"Use the water gun!"

Graham reached back toward Larry's long face.

Did he say—

"water gun?"

TOMMY

Tommy lay curled in the front yard.

More baseball bat strikes.

More pain.

More demands that he swear to that *bullshit.*

His face rested in a slimy pool of spit and blood. Grass poked through, blades tickling his cheeks. The sweet, earthy scent of the summer lawn filled his nostrils.

("something bad is gonna happen, tommy...")

("something really bad...")

"Ugmmf..."

The Purple's numbing effect was fading. Sharp aches now outnumbered the dull; his whole torso lit up with pain.

"Damnit, Glick!" Bill's voice cracked. "We will *pound* you into the fuckin' ground, boy! Just swear to it!"

("live through it, tommy...")

("live through it...")

Suzie screamed and cried and for one terrible, weak moment Tommy thought, *"Fuck it. I'll just swear to it."*

But then Larry's voice rang out:

"Jack!"

"I got his sunglasses off!"

"Use the water gun!"

A smile curved across Tommy's face, pressing his lips into the blood and saliva-soaked grass.

Yes.

God yes.

Jack still had the water gun, and knowin' Jack, he'd probably only taken one hit of the Purple, if that. Likely ready to throw down by now. Larry must've not smoked much, either—or maybe his freakish height dulled the Purple's effect.

"Ughhh..." Tommy forced his head up. Bill and Charlie stood staring at the house, faces turned just enough to catch their expressions.

Bill looked worried.

Charlie, less so.

Tommy smiled again, blood sticky on his teeth.

Y'all got surprises comin' for ya...

BILL

A water gun?

The fuck?

Dread gnawed at Bill as he lifted his gaze to the Smokehouse. It loomed larger now, casting a cold shadow.

His dreams, The Ethereal—none of it had shown him anything about a *water gun.*

He glanced at Charlie, who didn't seem concerned.

Maybe it's nothin'...

Besides—

the fuck could they do with *a water gun?*

LARRY

"Jack!"

"I got his sunglasses off!"

"Use the water gun!"

Larry maneuvered his face left, then right, evading Graham's hands.

"Jack!"

"Use the fuckin' water gun!"

Jack had only hit the Purple *once*—right?

He had to wake up.

He *had* to.

"Jack!"

"Wake the fuck up!"

Graham staggered backward, slamming Larry into a wall.

"Fuck!"

The impact loosened Larry's headlock, and Graham nearly broke free, but Larry tightened his arm.

"No-you-don't, motherfucker!"

Graham grasped for his face, but Larry had one option left. With his long legs locked around Graham's waist and his right arm tight around Graham's neck, he raised his left fist high:

"SMOKE-TOWN-BOYS, RALLY-UU-AAAAAAAAAAAAAGH!"

Graham's heavy hands found his throat and *squeezed.*

JACK

"That sounds great, Tanaka-san." Jack put his feet up on his desk. *"Ii desu ne.* And as soon as you convince them Tokyo politicians to *get down* with your plan to legalize weed, I'm sure we'll be able to find an exclusive agreement that benefits both our companies..."

A red light flashed on his phone, indicating he had another call.

"I'm so sorry, Tanaka-san. *Sumimasen,"* said Jack, "Got another *real* important call, this time with the Prime Minister of Korea, Kim Whats-his-face. You know how *he* is! Yep, yep...uh-huh...but gotta let ya go. You tell Honda-san I said hi—I mean, '*konnichiwa.*' You tell him I said *konnichiwa.* Uh-huh. *Sayonara!"*

He hit the line switch.

"Mr. Kindley?" asked a sultry female voice.

"Yes, Gina?"

Mmm.

Gina.

Even *her voice* made his dick hard. He could almost smell her perfume through the phone—sweet, thick, like overripe peaches and sweat. Ever since he saw her sucking dick on the side of the Smokehouse, way back in high school, he *knew* he had to have that. Hiring her had been one of his best moves yet, as she served not only as his secretary but also his personal di—

"It's your wife, sir."

Jack's eyes widened.

"Ohhh..."

Shit.

He swung his feet from his desk and stood.

"Wait a few minutes, then send her in. Tell her I'm on a—"

"Will do, sir."

Click.

That a girl, Gina.

She knew how to play it.

Probably got a little nervous whenever the old wifey-wife showed up. But nothin' to worry about. In fact, it usually made it *hotter* when they fucked right after his wife visited. Increased the intensity somehow.

He grabbed the *TIME* magazine from his massive African blackwood desk and strode to the window where the New York City skyline stretched before him. Skimming the article while glancing at the view made him *feel* something—powerful, grand, epic. For the hundredth time, he reread the title: *"From High School Line Graph Prodigy to Global CEO Phenomenon: The Story of Jack Kindley."*

Line graphs.

That's how it all started, wasn't it?

He'd made that clear in the interview—it all began with him presenting line graphs to his marijuana selling "gang" (he hated that term, preferring "squad," but they used it, anyway) and then grew into a region-wide *enterprise.*

An illegitimate enterprise, perhaps, but still an *enterprise.*

During the interview, he'd also made it clear that the path to becoming the President & CEO of the *first and most successful marijuana company in the entire world* was never an easy one. So many obstacles thrown his way—battles with other "gangs," bailin' his Boys out of jail, and of course, the stubborn Kentucky state politicians, who refused his bribes to legalize marijuana but responded quite positively to violence and blackmail.

Left *that* part out of the interview, though.

They didn't need to know every little detail.

Knock-knock!

"Come in," said Jack, not bothering to turn around.

The door swung open, heels *click-clacking* across the room. A sharp whiff of her perfume followed her in, so different from Gina's: flowery, expensive, suffocating.

"Jack..."

Jack counted silently to three, then spun around.

"Samantha! What are you doin' here, baby? What's goin'—"

"Don't give me that crap, Jack!" Samantha folded her arms. "I barely see you anymore! You're never home! You're never with the family!"

Jack sighed, holding the magazine so the cover faced outward.

"I am *so* sorry, baby..."

He paused, still holding the magazine face-out, giving her a chance to notice.

"It's just been *so* crazy since the interview with *TIME...*" said Jack. "...

all the phone calls, people wantin' to meet me, presidents of other countries and shit wantin' to do business with me..."

He stretched his arms out for a hug, but she slapped them away, her palm stinging against his skin.

"I am your wife, Jack. Don't you understand that? You should put *me* above your work. Above everything else."

"Of course I understand that, baby..." said Jack. "I put you *way above* all them famous people and world leaders tryin' to *bother me* about shit. But it's just that—"

"No 'buts,' Jack. I'm tired of it. It's been this way for too long now, and—"

"Let's go to dinner tonight, baby. I'm gonna take you to a nice place, we're gonna get Italian, and—"

"Dinner? And then what? You fuck me? And make me do all those *nasty* things for you?"

"Well, I—"

"And then you disappear again? For weeks? Months?"

"Baby, I—"

"Sometimes I wish I'd stayed with Tommy!"

Jack's face dropped.

Uh-oh.

The T-bomb.

Now was *his turn* to get pissed.

"I'll be damned." He tossed the *TIME* magazine to the floor. "That's a hell of a thing to say."

He returned to the window and stared out at the skyline, shaking his head.

"If you'd like to divorce me," said Jack, "and date one of my *subordinates,* go right ahead. Tommy's a good guy. A *decent* sales manager. I'm sure he'll take *decent* care of you."

"Jack, I—" Her breath caught. She sniffled.

Jack counted before he spoke again—

one.

two.

three.

four.

five.

"My secretary will contact you with the divorce papers," he said. "And if you'd like to—"

"Jack!" said Samantha. "I don't want a divorce! I just want you! *You!* I need *you,* Jack! *More of you!"*

Jack shook his head. "Samantha, I don't think tha—"

"Shut up," said Samantha. "And fuck me."

Oh shit.

Jack's breathing grew rapid.

He turned to face her.

"I need you *inside* me, Jack." Samantha slipped off her heels and gave a teasing shake of her hips—just enough to send her panties down her legs.

"I need you to *fuck me."*

Biting her lower lip, she sauntered over.

"Fuck me. Right here, right now. In your office."

("jack!")

She glided past him and pressed her face to the window, then hiked her skirt up.

("jack!)

"Fuck me hard. Doggystyle."

("i got his sunglasses off!")

"So we can look out at the skyline together."

("use the water gun!")

"While you fuck me."

("jack!")
("jack!")
("jack!")

"And cum inside m—"

("wake the fuck up!")

TOMMY

From the yard, Tommy spotted Larry's lanky frame wrapped around Graham, clinging to his back like a cape.

Yes.

Larry.

Thank God for Larry.

Kill him.

Kill the fucker.

"Might wanna help your cowboys..." said Tommy.

With great effort, he leaned up. Something sharp pressed inside his left ribcage. Felt like a fishhook in there, or a jagged chunk of glass. Probably fractured somethin', but didn't give a fuck. Could smoke Purple later, kill the pain. Smoke Purple for days and weeks, see if it healed on its ow—

"Shit!" Bill turned to Charlie. "I'll go inside, you stay here."

"Relájate, amigo..." said Charlie. "I'm sure Graham-cracker's *está bien*. And I definitely wouldn't worry about no water g—"

"You don't know that, Charlie." Bill's face tightened. "We might have a fuckin' problem."

Tommy smiled.

Yes.

Yes, you do *have a fuckin' problem, Bill.*

Your problem is that we've prepared for Graham-cracker for a while now.

We're ready.

"Listen up, gay cowboys," said Tommy. "I'll give y'all one last chance before shit gets outta hand. If y'all leave now, and I mean *right the fuck now,* we can call it square and—"

"UUUUUUUUUAAAAAAAAAAAAAAAAAAAAAAAHHHH!"

Larry crashed through the window in a shower of broken glass, landing in the yard with a sickening *thud.*

"Larry!" Tommy's mouth fell open.

Charlie grinned.

"No gracias to your offer, Glick..."

"...*no* fuckin' *gracias."*

BILL

Longface lay on the ground, limbs twisted like a rag doll.

"Graham?" he called out. "You okay in there?"

Graham's deep voice bellowed from inside the house.

"Yeah!" he said. *"Think I'm good!"*

"You need some help?"

"Nah!"

Bill narrowed his eyes and headed toward the stairs.

Best check and see what this water gun business is all about...

Just in case.

GRAHAM

Graham took deep breaths as he recovered his cowboy hat, sunglasses, and baseball bat.

So some weedboys are just pretendin' *to sleep...*

Best be careful, then.

He leaned back against the wall, resting for a moment. Tossin' a guy as tall as Longface was hard. Took a lot out of him.

"EIN STURMEN, EIN STRAAAAAAANGEN!"

Glass shattered on the other end of the house.

"...fuuuuuuck..." said a female voice.

A hot chick—that weedchick from Cracker Barrel, Leslie—shifted on her beanbag, still sleeping peacefully, mouth agape and drooling. A string of saliva dangled from her chin to the top of her left breast, then slid down her cleavage.

So...hot...

"EIN SCHMETTERLIIIIIIIIIIIIING!"

Glass shattered again.

Graham shook his head like a dog shaking off water.

Gotta remember the plan...

Gotta find weedboys.

He took a few steps forward, broken glass crunching under his feet.

So many sleepin' people...

Could pop up and surprise me...

He gripped his baseball bat.

I don't like surprises...

*

Graham squeezed *the soft monkey doll's neck with both hands.*

"I am more powerful than you..." said Graham. "...bigger and stronger and more powerful..."

"Now Graham-cracker..." His mother flipped through a magazine. "Remember what we talked about. You need to be more kind to your stuffed animals and playthings..."

Graham narrowed his eyes.

Kindness?

He didn't need to show kindness *to those less strong than him.*

Those less powerful...

"...and to your classmates in kindergarten, too..."

No.

Even they must fear him.

They especially, must fear him.

"BRAAAAP!"

He belched.

"I'm hungry, Momma..."

His mother clicked her tongue.

"Now Graham-cracker, I just fed you breakfast an hour ago. You're not gettin' any more food until lunch."

"ARAAAAAAAAAAAH!"

With a mighty yell, Graham body-slammed the stuffed monkey onto the floor.

"I'm hungry, Momma! I need food! Now!"

His mother looked up from her magazine, face as cold as a refrigerator.

"Now Graham." Her tone sharpened. "Do you want me to tell your father what a bad boy *you've been today?"*

Graham's eyes widened.

His palms started sweating.

No.

Not Daddy.

Daddy would hurt *him again...*

Because Daddy was stronger *than him...*

"...no..."

"Goooooood..." His mother returned to her magazine, lips pursed in a tight smile.

Graham plopped back down to the floor, unsure of what to do next.

No food.

Nothin' good on TV.

Had to be nice to his toys.

Nothin' to do...

"Why don't you play with that new toy your grandma bought you?" asked his mother.

A strange box-like contraption sat on the shelf with a handle jutting from its side.

"What's it...do?" asked Graham.

"Turn the handle," said his mother. "And you'll see..."

Graham placed the box-like contraption on the floor and slowly turned the handle. A light, cheerful melody began playing.

"Makes...music?" asked Graham.

His mother flipped a page of her magazine.

"...keep on turning..."

Graham turned the handle again.

More lighthearted, cheerful music.

"A music box..." said Graham. "Can it play other son— "

A terrifying clown-like figure burst from the box.

"AAAAAAAAAAAAAAAAH!"

He slammed the box down and stomped on it.

"AAAAAAAAAAAAAAAAAAAAAAAAAAAAAH!"

His mother tilted her head back and cackled.

*

Graham shuddered.

Who thought a toy like that would be fun?

Bein' surprised is the *opposite* of fun.

"Graham?" asked Bill from outside. *"You okay in there?"*

"Yeah!" said Graham. "Think I'm good!"

"You need some help?"

"Nah!" said Graham.

He looked around.

Where's that Jack guy?

The one that's supposed to have a water gun?

He turned his gaze to the beanbag in the corner of the living room, near a hallway.

Could've sworn he was sleepin' over there...

A delicious-looking pizza slice lay on the beanbag—but no Jack.

"Graham," called Kenny from the other side of the house. *"You okay, man?"*

"I'm good!" said Graham.

"Okay!"

Graham stomped over to the pizza slice. It had mushrooms on it—lots of 'em.

"EIN HAUSCHLUSS!"

Kenny kept on smashin' stuff and yellin' in German, but it all faded in the background now.

Graham liked mushrooms.

And he *loved* pizza.

He crammed the entire slice into his mouth.

"Mmm..."

So good...

Domino's—not that Pizza Hut stuff. The cheese, tomato sauce, buttery crust and mushroom toppings all melded into a savory union inside his mouth.

"Mmm..."

Hadn't eaten cold pizza in a while.

Pizza tasted good cold, too.

Almost forgot that.

"BRAAAAAP!"

He belched and patted his belly.

Maybe more?

In the kitchen?

A sudden gust of wind—*movement?*—behind him.

"Wha?"

He whirled around, inspecting his environment—

—nothin'.

Just people sleepin' their stupid drug-sleep.

He chewed the rest of his pizza and swallowed.

(jack)

(jack in the box)

The hairs on the back of his neck stood.

What if that Jack guy planned on *surprisin'* him?

Like that awful toy did...

He didn't like surprises.

("aaaaaaaaaaaaaaaaaaaaah!")

("ahahahahahahahahahaha!")

("you don't like your new present, *son?")*
("ahahahahahahahahahahahahahahahahahahahaha!")
No, he didn't like that stupid present and he *hated* surprises.
Something wasn't ri—
Wait.
Where was that one kid?
The weedboy he threw against the wall?

Kevin.

WILEY

Wiley slept beside the window on the mattress usually used for fuckin'—thin, squeaky and vaguely sweat-smelling. He opened his eyes to see Suzie in a kiddie pool out on the front lawn, screaming and crying as Bill and Charlie, dressed like cowboys and wielding baseball bats, stood over a kneeling Tommy.

"EIN STURMEN, EIN STRAAAAAANGEN!"

A raw jumble of noise battered him: heavy metal, Graham's slow, dumb chuckle, Kenny screamin' shit in German (what the fuck was *that* guy on?), Larry yellin' for Jack to use the water gun—then glass shattering, sharp as gunfire, then Larry *flying* into the front yard.

"EIN SCHMETTERLIIIIIIIIIIIIIING!"

More glass shattered. The sound of heavy cowboy boots *clomp-clomping* on the floor drew near.

Fuck.

That crazy Kenny guy—closer now.

Probably to smash the window near him, then smash *him.*

Clomp.

Clomp.

Kenny's footsteps drew nearer. Slow, heavy, each one vibrating through the floor.

Fuck.

If only I had that vial of Miracle...

He *really* wanted to snort that shit. Even just holding the vial had seemed to energize him, as if it pulled back the curtain on a hidden reservoir of power, pure pow—

Clomp.

Clomp.

Shit.

Real close, now.

Can't just lay here, though...

Miracle or no Miracle...gotta fight back.

He could fight. One of the reasons the Boys recruited him. Wasn't much he was good at, but he could fucking fight. And he could *hurt* that Skinny Kenny dude.

Then hide from Graham.

Hide from Graham as quickly as fuckin' possible.

Or maybe call a rally u—

Clomp.

Clomp.

Heavy cowboy boots halted beside him, creaking on the floorboards.

Fuck.

Adrenaline hit. His senses sharpened. The sharp stink of sweat and spilled beer clawed at his nose.

Had to think like a fighter.

Like last time.

Had to remember *hurting* someone.

("say you're sorry!")

("say you give up!")

("fuck you, motherf—UAAGH!")

("say it!")

He gripped his crowbar, cold metal biting into his palms.

Time to throat-stomp a cowboy.

TOMMY

"I like the way your sister cries, Glick..." said Charlie.

He ran his fingers through Tommy's hair.

"Laaaa, laaaa bamba..."

Tommy knelt before the pool. Suzie screamed and cried. His mind raced.

The water gun.

Larry was out, but Jack was still inside.

With the water gun.

And the Possibles were still inside, too.

With their crowbars.

They could still *win* this.

"Laaa, laaaa, bamba..." sang Charlie. "Do you know that song, little girl?"

Suzie screamed.

"Shh..." said Charlie. *"...cállate...silencio..."*

While Young resumed humming *La Bamba,* Tommy worked through his options.

Bill had gone inside—which meant he only had Young to deal with. But what could he do fucking *tied up* like this? He needed *both* of'em to go inside before he made a move. He needed—

"Little girrrrrl..." said Charlie. "What's your name?"

Suzie shook her head, staring at Charlie like he was the boogeyman.

"*Niñitaaa...*" said Charlie. *"Es tu nombre...?"*

Bill's voice echoed from inside the house, screamin' somethin', but couldn't make out what.

Fuck.

Best to draw Bill back outside, give his Boys a better chance against Graham and Kenny.

Charlie stopped humming and clasped his hand around Tommy's throat.

"What's the bitch's name?"

Tommy strained against the ropes.

You know her name, Young...

You fucking know it.

"Suzie," said Tommy.

"Oh, that's right..." said Charlie. "Lil' Suzie...thought it was Suzie or Stacey...somethin' like that..."

He resumed humming *La Bamba* while dragging his hand across Tommy's face and head.

"It's been a busy mornin', Glick..." said Charlie, "...so busy I'd forgotten Lil' Suzie's *nombre...*"

Suzie clasped the pool's edge.

"Lil' Suzie," said Charlie, "can you speak *español?*"

Suzie stared at him, sniffling.

"Lil' Suzieee..." said Charlie. *"Hablo españoool..."*

"She don't speak Spanish, you kn—"

"I was askin' fuckin' Suzie!"

Charlie *squeezed* Tommy's face.

Suzie squirmed in the pool, eyes filled with fear.

"Está bien, Lil' Suzie..." said Charlie. *"Está bien*, now..."

He returned to caressing Tommy's head. Every slow stroke burned like ice.

"When I was your age," said Charlie, "I didn't know no *español,* either..."

"...laaaa, laaaa, bambaaa..."

BILL

Bill stepped into the living room, nodding to the heavy metal just as Graham stomped toward the other end of the house. Place stank like that "Monkey" bullshit the weedboys smoked—pungent and sour, laced with somethin' sweet. *Somethin' purple.*

Everybody was knocked the fuck out, like his dreams had shown him, but the purple bracelets? Like some dumbass toddler's birthday party? That shit was new.

Whatever.

Not important.

Also—kinda gay.

He strode across the living room to follow Graham. A lava lamp glowed red on a windowsill. Looked cool, he had to admit. Might get one for the *Hacienda,* maybe mention it to Ch—

He halted.

A red-headed, freckle-faced guy crawled out of the hallway, droolin' and draggin' himself like his legs didn't work.

A weedboy.

Jack.

"Oh no ya don't!"

Bill dashed forward and slammed his bat across Jack's spine—a sharp crack, loud even over the heavy metal.

"UAAAGH!"

Jack collapsed to the floor.

Bill kicked him over and raised the bat again.

"Don't you fuckin' move!"

"Ummff..." Drool hung from Jack's lips.

Water gun.

Why had Longface been yellin' for Jack to use a *water gun?*

What *the fuck* was that about?

Somethin' ain't right...

Somethin' I didn't see...

"Where's the fuckin' water gun? Huh?"

"...what...water gun..."

Bill slammed his bat onto Jack's ribs.

"OOOMF!"

"Goddamnit, boy! Don't fuck with me!" said Bill. "Where's the fuckin' water gun? Why was Longface askin' for it?"

Jack clutched his side, tears streaking his face.

Bill winced.

Didn't mean to hit him *that* hard—way harder than he'd hit Glick.

Might've busted somethin'.

(it feels good to hurt people, doesn't it?)

(to show'em who's boss...)

(to show'em y—)

No.

He didn't like doin' this.

Didn't like hurtin' people.

Glick was an asshole, sure. Needed a lesson. But this Jack guy hadn't done shit—not directly, at least.

Didn't matter, though.

Had to be *Wild Bill* today.

Just like Blackbeard had to be fuckin' *Blackbeard.*

"You best tell me, weedboy!" Bill raised the bat again. "Or, *I swear to God,* I'll beat the fuck outta you!"

"...don't...know..."

"Yes, you fuckin' do! Now fuckin' tell me!"

Jack coughed, wheezed. Raised a trembling hand to block the next blow.

"...don't got it...no more..."

(LIES)

Bill squeezed the bat handle.

Something cruel and ugly bubbled up inside, something that—

No.

No time for this shit.

Best bring him outside for now.

He dropped the bat, pulled rope from his backpack, and bound Jack's wrists and ankles. The knots came easy, like tying his shoes. Like he'd tied people up before. *Lots of people.*

Maybe in a past life,

("we got a big one this time, didn't we?")

or maybe,

("i got the hammer and strawberries ready!")

in his future.

("time for his family welcome...")

He froze.

Whose *voice* was that?

A girl's.

Familiar.

Strong.

Like one of those chicks you didn't fuck with.

But wh—

Movement flickered outside—just past the window.

He turned.

A scarecrow stood in the backyard, half-sunk in dirt, shoulders slumped, straw pokin' from the sleeves. One arm pointed straight at the house. And on its head: a cowboy hat. *A fucking cowboy hat.*

The hell...?

A piece of paper flapped on its chest with words scrawled in black marker.

He squinted.

The fuck's that s—

A cold pulse shot through his arms. He snatched his bat off the floor and wheeled around.

"Motherf—"

Nothin'.

Just stoners, sleepin' their stupid weed-sleep.

Even with all this racket.

Feels like somebody's hidin' from me, though...

"Come on out, now..." Bill swept the room with his eyes. "...if you come out, I'll just tie ya up...won't hit ya none..."

The heavy metal pounded behind him. He nodded along—felt it in his chest.

"I promise..." said Bill. "...ain't gonna hurt ya if ya come on out, now..."

He scanned the bodies. Most of 'em he recognized. A few lay face-down. That Michael Mouse guy had blood on his face, looked comatose. The Lacey chick lay beside him. Blood on her face, too. Probably Mouse's. Hard to say, but—

Wait.

Did one of 'em move just now?

He peered through the tint of his sunglasses.

Maybe just *pretendin'* to be asl—

"Bill!"

Charlie's voice rang from outside.

"Hey, Bill!"

Fuck.

He headed back outside.

Behind him—

he could've sworn he heard movement.

DAVID

David lifted his head from the floor and watched Bill step outside.

"Okay!" he said. *"It's okay!"*

Kevin lifted his head, too. Together they scrambled to Jack, clawing at his ropes, but Bill had tied'em damn near perfect. Tight. Cruel. Practiced. Every knot locked like a trap.

Was he in the Boy Scouts or somethin'...?

"...hurry..." said Jack, coughing. "...drag me...through the hallway...back bedroom..."

Seconds ticked by like hours. They finally got the knots loose and dragged Jack across the floor, crunching over broken glass, eyes peeled for any bat-swinging maniac cowboys. Muffled voices and movement echoed from the far end of the house, but the heavy metal blaring near the entrance drowned most of it.

"Grant!" said David.

He flung the bedroom door open. Grant sat on the floor, back against the rear window, eyes wide with fear.

"Shut the door!" said Grant.

David and Kevin hauled Jack inside and leaned him against the bed. They slammed the door and pressed their backs to it.

"...that Purple...Dream..." said Jack. "...really...fucked me u—"

"Shh!" Sweat dripped down Grant's face. He lowered his voice to a whisper. "...we gotta *run.* I tried openin' this window but it's stuck, and breakin' it might get us caught. We gotta run out a *different window* into the woods and—"

Jack spat. The glob smacked Grant right on the forehead.

"No..." His eyes darkened. "...Smoketown Boys...never run..."

Grant wiped his forehead. "I don't got my crowbar, Jack! I lost it!"

"You *lost* your crowbar?" asked Kevin.

"I don't know where it went!" said Grant. "It don't matter, we can't beat'em, they got *Graham!* We gotta—"

"Shh..." said Jack. "Quit whinin'...just gotta use...*this*..."

He reached into his pocket and brandished the water gun. After a short coughing fit, he handed it to David.

"...full of Kentucky Blood..." said Jack. "Extra-hot kind..."

David rotated the water gun in his hand, examining it like an alien artifact. Thick red liquid sloshed inside like blood.

Would it even work?

Was it even worth try—

BOOM!

The house rattled.

Something big. Fast.

Far end of the house.

"*Cross attack* him..." said Jack. "...like y'all trained for..."

Pain twisted Jack's face as he shifted. Tears streaked down his cheeks. David hadn't seen Bill hit him—but he'd heard it, and the sound still echoed in his skull. A sharp, wet crack, like wood snapping.

"Go for his knees..." said Jack.

"He's got sunglasses on," said David. "The water gun won't w—"

"Then knock'em off..." said Jack.

"We can't," said Kevin. "Anytime we get close, he just choke-grabs us."

Jack coughed and wheezed. "...you can...just need...a little help..."

"There ain't no help, Jack!" said Grant. "Everybody's sleepin' and Tommy's tied up out front and Larry got thrown out a window and—"

"Shut the fuck up, Grant!" Jack's freckled face flushed crimson, then twisted as another cough ripped through him. With a trembling hand, he reached into his pocket and pulled out a vial.

White powder shimmered inside.

Miracle.

"Here..." Jack handed it to David. "...here's your help..."

David held the vial to the sunlight from the window. The white powder sparkled within, revealing hints of pale blue.

Miracle...

Jack winced as he pulled another vial from his pocket, then shook his head and stuffed it back.

"I can't snort it..." he said. "'Cause of my heart..."

"But y'all can..."

KENNY

Kenny nodded to *the rhythm* as he stood over a guy lying on a stained mattress. Looked like a weedboy. One of their "Possibles," or whatever the fuck they called'em.

Wiley.

That's this kid's name.

"Wilin' Wiley" or some shit like that. Heard about him after he'd won some fights against dudes older than him. Apparently throat-stomped a guy until he cried Uncle.

"Wilin' Wiley..."

Kenny dragged his bat across Wiley's back, starting from his tailbone and tracing up his spine, all the way to his head.

One good hit.

One good hit to watch him *squirm,* maybe cry, then tie him up.

No, *two* good hits.

Hit his arm real good, *then* his chest.

Yep, that sounded right.

Time to fuck shit up.

Kenny drew his bat back.

Wakey-wakey...
Eggs and bakey...

"EIN FLAMMEN—"

WILEY

"EIN FLAMMEN—AAAAAAAAH!"

Wiley swung the crowbar back as Kenny's bat descended, smashing into Kenny's right hand.

"Ahhh! Motherfuck!"

Kenny dropped his bat with a metal clang, bending over and clutching his hand.

"Fuuuuuck!"

Wiley didn't hesitate. He hopped up, drew back the crowbar and swung forward, hitting Kenny square in his stomach.

"BLUAAAAGH!"

Kenny collapsed to the floor, clutching his stomach. Tears streamed beneath his sunglasses.

"Uuuuugh...."

Wiley felt a rush of triumph.

Your balls hurt, don't they?

When you get hit in the stomach, your balls hurt!

He slammed his crowbar into Kenny's right arm, metal crunching bone.

Don't they?

Kenny screamed and collapsed into a ball of pain.

Wiley squeezed his left hand into a fist.

Now's my chance...

Before Graham comes back.

He raised his fist high.

"SMOKE-TOWN-BOYS-RALLY-UAAAAAAAAAAAGH!"

Kenny's cowboy boot struck him square in the throat.

"Ein...flammenwaffen..."

BILL

"Think he's fakin' it," said Charlie.

Tommy convulsed on the ground, eyes rolled back. A weird, guttural moan escaped his spittle-covered lips.

"If he ain't," said Bill, "we're in trouble."

Suzie had curled into a ball in the kiddie pool, burying her face in her arms.

"Suzie," said Bill, "does your brother got seizures? Or shit like that?"

Silence.

Didn't even budge.

"Lil' Suzie," said Bill, "if your brother's got like, a fuckin', medical condition or someth—"

"Might be that Purple shit they smoked," said Charlie. "Or whatever it was fuckin' dusted with."

Bill gripped his baseball bat and shifted his gaze from Tommy convulsing on the ground to the Smokehouse looming over them.

Something wasn't right.

Shit wasn't goin' accordin' to plan.

He didn't *see* everything.

WILEY

Wiley fell back, reeling from the cowboy boot-kick to his throat. He dropped his crowbar and brought both hands to his neck.

Can't...breathe...

My...my tr—

Trachea. That's what it was called. Maybe. Whatever it was, felt like it'd fucking *collapsed* on itself, like an anvil on his windpipe. He massaged his throat—didn't seem to help, but what the fuck else could he do?

This is how that dude must've felt...

When I throat-stomped him...

Kenny, still clutching his stomach, grabbed his bat and tried to prop himself up. He coughed and spat towards Wiley.

Still gasping for air, Wiley grabbed his crowbar and rose.

Gonna have to hit his head this time...

Knock his ass out.

"C'mon, motherfucker..." said Kenny, stooped over. "Let's get wild..." He twirled the bat with his left hand, nodding as a crooked smile spread across his face.

Wiley's eyes widened.

Is he...

Is he fuckin' enjoyin' *this?*

Kenny's eyes shone like a maniac's. "Let's dance, weedboy..."

Wiley gripped his crowbar and charged forward.

("fuck you, motherf—UAAGH!")

("say it!")

He knew how to dance.

DAVID

"You...you guys snort it first..." said Grant.

Jack shot Grant a look of disgust. "Grant," he said, wincing. "You're *really* disappointin' me, man..."

David stared at the thin line of white powder on the back of his hand. Hints of pale blue seemed to appear, then vanish.

"...y'all know how to *snort* shit, right?" asked Jack. "...close one nostril, and then—"

"Yeah..." David pushed his thick-rimmed glasses up. "We got it..." He looked at Kevin and nodded, then closed his right nostril and lowered his left to the back of his hand.

"*SNRRK!*"

("ga-ya dwae-yo!")

("ji-geum!")

He glanced back up at Kevin, now sporting white powder on his nose. "Are we supposed to feel someth—"

("GA-YA DWAE-YO!")

("JI-GEUM!")

David felt his pupils dilate.

KENNY

"Fuck..."

Kenny leaned against the wall of the kitchen, then slowly slid down to the floor.

His balls hurt.

When you got hit in the stomach, your *balls* hurt.

Almost forgot about that.

"You put up a good fight..." said Kenny. "...Wilin' Wiley..."

He clutched his right hand. The throbbing grew worse by the second.

"...think you might've broke my hand..."

Wiley lay facedown on the floor before him.

A pool of blood crawled across the floor.

GRANT

"Fuckin' snort it, Grant!"

"Snort that shit!"

"You guys are scarin' me!"

"I don't wanna snort it!"

"FUCKING SNORT IT!"

GRAHAM

Graham stomped into the kitchen, breathing hard, cowboy boots *clomp-clomping* across the floor. Kenny lay slumped against the kitchen wall, chest rising and falling fast, clutching his right hand, hunched like his stomach hurt. Before him lay a weedboy, one of their "Possibles" or whatever. A pool of blood spread beneath the Possible's face.

"You okay, K-boy?" asked Graham.

"Not really..." Kenny coughed, his words catching between gulps of air. "...think some of these Possible kids didn't smoke that Purple stuff...this Wiley dude about kicked my ass..."

Graham wiped sweat from his brow, still trying to catch his breath. He picked up a glass of a purple liquid, sniffed it, then brought it to his lips.

Mmm...

Purple.

Sweet.

Tangy.

Tasted like...not grapes, but...

Purple.

Tasted like purple.

"Can I have some?" asked Kenny.

"BRAAAAAP!"

Graham belched.

"Sure."

Graham handed him the glass. Kenny drank deeply.

Kenny gulped air between swigs, then wiped his mouth with his sleeve. "We gotta finish this up...I'll smash the rest of the windows...how many weedboys we got yet?"

Graham scratched his head. "Uhh...only one, I think."

"Only one?"

"No, two. I threw Longface out the window. So Longface and him." He gestured at the weedboy on the floor.

"No, we got Glick, too," said Kenny. "So we got three."

"How many did Bill say we gotta get?" asked Graham.

"Eight," said Kenny. "Eight total. Five more to go..."

Kenny grabbed his right hand and winced.

"Fuck..." he said. "Can you tie him up for me, man? I don't think I can tie a fuckin' knot with my hand like this."

"Huh huh huh..." chuckled Graham. "Sounds like you got *pussitis* in your hand."

He reached down to help Kenny up.

"Pussitis..." said Kenny. "The fuck is that..."

"Huh huh huh..."

"Oh, I get it now..." said Kenny, using the bat as a crutch. *"Pussitis.* As in, my hand hurts 'cause I'm a *pussy."*

"Huh huh huh..."

"Good one, Graham..."

Kenny hobbled over to the weedboy and poked him with his bat.

"Hey, dude? You awake?"

He poked him again. Graham unslung his backpack and took out some rope.

"Hey, dude?" asked Kenny. "Uhh, Wiley? Don't start no more shit. We won this. Graham's here."

Wiley lay perfectly still; his right hand folded under his stomach.

"Fuck," said Kenny. "I don't think I hit him *that* fuckin' ha—"

In one fluid motion, Wiley spun around and yanked the bat from Kenny, then hopped up, reared back—

"FURRRF!"

—and swung it across Kenny's face.

Kenny reeled. His sunglasses fell to the floor as blood flew from his mouth, splattering the wall.

WILEY

Wiley watched Kenny reel back.

Yes.

I showed you, motherfucker.

Now I'm gonna—

A heavy, calloused hand closed around his throat.

"Should've stayed down, weedboy..."

Graham choke-lifted him high in the air.

"Huh huh huh..."

Wiley squirmed in Graham's grip, suspended *("aaaagh!")*, then felt himself fly across the kitchen.

BOOM!

WILEY

Sprawled on the cold floor, wracked with pain, Wiley clung to one hope:

Miracle.

GRAHAM

"Fuck!" said Kenny from the floor. "I knew he was fakin' it!"

Graham dragged in a slow, heavy breath.

Throwin' guys was hard.

His back hurt.

"Fucker hit my nose!" Kenny rose just enough to lean against the door. He wiped blood from his face. "And my mouth!"

Graham glanced at the empty pizza boxes on the kitchen table, then the fridge.

Gotta find more weedboys...

But also want pizza...

And more purple drink...

A soft, fluffy thing hit his face.

What the...?

A pillow.

A pillow had hit his face.

A glasses-wearin' Asian boy stood panting in the doorway, lips twitchin' all weird. White powder covered his nose.

David.

Asian David. Or somethin'.

"Hey, four-eyes," said Graham. "Ya better—*umph!*"

Another pillow. Smacked him from the side.

Kevin.

In the other doorway.

"Huh huh huh..." chuckled Graham. "Pillow fi—*uumph!*"

Another one. From David.

Why they throwin' pillows?

He stomped toward David.

"Come here, four-eyes!" said Graham. "Lemme see those glasses!"

David turned and ran. A black crowbar jutted from the back of his jeans. Graham chased him into the living room, the floor quaking with each step.

"Huh huh huh..." chuckled Graham. "...I'm gonna catch ya..."

David whirled around, eyes wide and bloodshot, lips and mouth still twitchin'.

Graham halted, surrounded by sleeping bodies.
Wait a minute...
Somethin' don't feel right...
The music.
The heavy metal from the boombox, it wasn't playin' no mo—
Movement.
Behind him.
He spun around.
Another pillow in his face.
Kevin.
That Kevin boy.
Bloodshot eyes.
Twitchin' mouth.
What the...
Slowly, Kevin and David drew crowbars from the backs of their jeans.

A metallic resonance filled the air.

GRAHAM

"Hey, Graham-cracker!" said David. A weird, manic energy pulsed behind his voice. *"Take your fucking sunglasses off!"*

"Why would I do that, four-eyes?" asked Graham.

He stomped across the living room, stepping over people sleeping on the floor.

"Huh huh huh..." he chuckled. "Didn't I break your glasses one ti—"

"GRRRAGH!"

A roar tore through the room as someone launched up from the floor, mounted his back, and ripped away his sunglasses.

Not this shit again!

"Get offa me!" said Graham.

Fingers clawed at his face and pressed into his eyeballs.

"URRRAAGH! MY EYES!"

Grabbing his assailant by the neck, Graham slammed him onto the living room floor.

BOOM!

"Fuck!" Graham squeezed his eyes open and shut, blinking away radiant spots of yellow and red.

That's cheatin'!

Now these kids gotta pay!

The weedboy on the floor gasped for air.

I slammed you good, weedboy...

Now you—

"Now, Grant!" said David.

"Fucking now!"

GRANT

(kill kill kill)

(murder murder murder)

Grant lay on the floor, unable to breathe.

"Fuck!" Graham squeezed his eyes open and shut. His cowboy hat and sunglasses had fallen to the floor.

"Now, Grant!" said David. *"Fucking now!"*

Still gasping for air, Grant fumbled into his pocket, yanked out the water gun, and fired straight at Graham's eyes.

Gotcha, motherfucker.

DAVID

(kill kill kill)

(murder murder murder)

"Now, Grant!" said David. *"Fucking now!"*

As Grant brandished his water gun, David raised his crowbar, locking eyes with Kevin across the room.

"CROSS-ATTAAAAAAAAAAAACK!"

David bolted forward, propelled by rage, hatred and something else—something he'd never felt before, something the Miracle had blessed him with.

("GA-YA DWAE-YO!")

("JI-GEUM!")

The need to fucking *hurt* someone.

TOMMY

"Still think he's fakin' it," said Charlie.

"Why you think that?" asked Bill.

"It's what I would do," said Charlie. "He ain't got many options."

"Well," said Bill, "how can we know?"

"I say we hit him some more," said Charlie. "Or burn cigarettes into his arms and shit. See how he reacts."

"Okay," said Bill. "But what if he—"

"CROSS-ATTAAAAAAAAAAAACK!"

Voices charged with a frenetic energy rang out from the depths of the Smokehouse.

"Fuck!"

Bill and Charlie bolted toward the porch stairs.

Tommy stopped convulsing and opened his eyes.

"Suzie!"

"You gotta untie me!"

SUZIE

"Suzie!"

(don't think about the bad things)

"Please please please untie my ropes!"

(just think about the temple)

"Please!"

(the temple that mikey showed me)

"*Help* me, Suzie!"

"Please!"

(whenever bad things happen think of mikey and the temple and everything will be alright because one day we're gonna find the temple and mommy and daddy will marry again and mikey will come back and all the bad things will stop stop stop stop stop stop stop i just want it all to st—)

GRAHAM

"CROSS-ATTAAAAAAAAAAAACK!"

A blast of bold, tangy heat lit up Graham's mouth the instant the sauce hit his tongue.

Kentucky Blood—

the Extra Hot kind.

It came in fast: vinegar bite, pepper sting, and a creeping burn that danced across his gums.

"Mmm..."

Sauce oozed down his chin, warm and oily, just as David charged toward him with murder in his eyes.

Wha...?

Behind him, that Kevin boy charged forward, too.

Uh-oh...

KEVIN

"CROSS-ATTAAAAAAAAAAAACK!"

(kill kill kill)

(murder murder murder)

Kevin rushed forward, aiming for the side of Graham's left kneecap. He felt vaguely aware of his lips and mouth twitching and how fast his heart beat and how he couldn't stop *panting* but none of that mattered, *none of that fucking mattered now* because snorting the Miracle had *changed him,* it had changed him today and *today* they'd make Graham a fucking cripple, put him in a fucking wheelchair for the rest of his life and then torment him *every fucking day* for the rest of his fucking life.

(kill kill kill)

(blood blood blood)

Everything would be made perfect; everything *fixed* from today.

(kill kill kill)

(murder murder murder)

He brought his crowbar back for a mighty swing.

Time to fucking pay, Graham-cracker.

KENNY

"EIN WANZERFAUUUUUUUUUUUUUST!"

DAVID

"EIN WANZERFAUUUUUUUUUUUUUST!"

(kill kill kill)

(murder murder murder)

As David rushed forward, he glimpsed a metal baseball bat slam into Kevin's legs, sending him flying.

(doesn't fucking matter)

Graham looked at David in surprise, wide-eyed and stupid, crimson sauce oozing from his mouth—not his eyes, *but his mouth.*

(doesn't fucking matter)

As he swung the crowbar downward in a perfect arc toward Graham's right kneecap, he realized that none of those failures in their plan mattered, because today, fucking *today* he'd shatter Graham-fuckin'-Riley's right-fucking-kneecap into a thousand fucking pieces and make him *fucking pay.*

(JUG-EUL SIGANIYA!)

(JUG-EUL SIG—)

GRAHAM

"Ow!"

"That hurt!"

DAVID

Graham bent over, clutching his knee.

David stared in disbelief.

No.

That didn't—

—that didn't make sense.

A crowbar going that fast, that hard, should *obliterate* anyone's kneecap.

The sound it made—that wasn't *right,* either, not the sound of bone breaking, but more like—

"That hurt, four-eyes!"

Graham's fist collided into his face, shattering his glasses.

DAVID

David screamed.

"My eyes!"

"The glass is in my eyes!"

GRANT

Grant struggled to stand, barely able to breathe.

(kill kill kill)

(murder murder murder)

He missed.

He fucking *missed* Graham's eyes and got him in the mouth.

"My eyes!"

"The glass is in my eyes!"

Before him, Graham rubbed his kneecap while David writhed on the floor and Kevin assaulted Kenny with his crowbar in the neighboring room.

Crowbar.

He needed a weapon.

(kill kill kill)

(murder murder murder)

Something *better* than a crowbar or a fucking water gun.

Something to kill and murder and hurt people with.

A cold, dangerous thought entered Grant's mind.

BILL

As Bill and Charlie climbed the stairs, unease prickled through Bill—no heavy metal blastin' from Charlie's boombox.

Gotta have my heavy metal...

Can't beat no ass without it.

A stench crept down the stairwell: weed, sweat, stale beer, and the coppery scent of blood. He stepped into the living room and forgot about the music—

—too much goddamn chaos, all around him.

"What the..."

That Asian kid writhed on the floor, screamin' about his eyes, while Graham rubbed his knee and hopped on one leg, each hop shakin' the whole damn house, rattlin' the floor under Bill's boots. In the other room, that Kevin kid pinned Kenny to the floor, assaultin' him with his crowbar, which Kenny barely blocked with his bat. One weedboy crawled under the kitchen table while another rose up in front of Graham, clutchin' his chest like he couldn't breathe, then staggered toward the hallway. Bill nearly chased after him, but the *clang-clangin'* of Kevin's fuckin' assault on Kenny seemed a higher priority.

"I'll kill you!" said Kevin, slamming his crowbar against Kenny's bat.

CLANG!

"I'll fucking kill you!"

CLANG!

"I'll kill you!"

CLANG!

"I'll fucking kill y—"

Kevin raised his crowbar again, but Bill ran up from behind and struck the weedboy's grip with his bat. The crowbar went flying.

"Aaah!"

Kevin whirled around, clutching his hand.

"You ain't killin' shit, weedboy!" said Bill.

He kicked Kevin's legs out from under him, dropping him to the floor. Kevin pushed up quick, but Bill planted his heavy cowboy boot between the kid's shoulders and shoved him flat. Sweat drenched the kid's shirt, slick under Bill's sole.

"Arraaaah!"

Kevin thrashed and howled, spit flyin' from his mouth. Bill kept his boot planted, but it wasn't easy. Like tryin' to stomp down a rabid dog, all bone and rage.

"*I'll kill you! I'll kill you! I'll kill you!*"

"Charlie!" said Bill. "Tie this motherfucker up! Fast!"

"I'll fucking kill you! I'll fucking kill you!"

"And turn the heavy metal back on!" said Bill. "I can't beat no ass without it!"

He turned to see Charlie dash towards the kitchen.

"Charlie!"

WILEY

Wiley crawled across the kitchen floor.

His face *hurt.*

His head *hurt.*

His whole body *hurt.*

But he'd glimpsed David roll something toward him after throwing a pillow at Graham.

"My eyes!"

"The glass is in my eyes!"

Fuck.

David.

Where could it be where could it be where could it—

There.

There it is.

A vial—behind a table leg.

Miracle.

Yes.

Oh God, yes.

Finally.

Finally, he could snort that shit.

He crawled faster.

GRAHAM

Graham hopped around on one leg, struggling to maintain balance as his knee throbbed. The Asian David kid writhed over in the corner like an electrocuted worm, screamin' and cryin' while carryin' on about glass in his eyes or shit like that.

That's what you get, four-eyes!

Shouldn't have tried to smash my knee!

Bill ran off to help Kenny with that Kevin dude while Charlie stared at something behind Graham, toward the kitchen.

Huh?

What's behind me?

Just as he turned, Charlie rushed past him, a flicker of alarm on his face.

WILEY

(kill kill kill)

(murder murder murder)

Wiley's lips and mouth twitched. His veins felt like rivers of gasoline.

God!

It's even better than I thought it'd be!

Nothing hurts anymore!

Nothing!

I'M FUCKING INVINCIBLE!

Amidst his sense of *fucking invulnerability* arose a hunger—a *hunger* to hurt someone and injure them and maim them and kill them.

(kill kill kill)

(murder murder murder)

Fuck weed!

Fuck that Monkey bullshit!

I ONLY NEED MIRACLE!

ONLY MIRACLE FROM NOW ON!

A scream of agony drew his attention. David leaned against the living room wall, pulling a shard of glass from his eye.

It's gonna be alright, David!

We'll make these cowboys suffer!

WE ALL WILL!

Wiley tightened his hand into a fist, raising it high.

"SMOKE-TOWN-BOYS, RALLY-UUUUUUUUUUUUUUP!"

1970s

CHAPTER III

RALLY UP

"Kill'em, David!

Fucking kill'em all!"

DAVID

David's hand trembled as he attempted to remove the shard of glass from his right eyeball. He screamed.

"ARAAAAH GOD!"

Slowly, he withdrew the shard, leaving behind a thin trail of mucus and blood before tossing it to the floor.

Fuck!

"ARAAAAH!"

He tried to stop screaming.

Fuck!

"AAAAHHH!"

He couldn't.

Fuck fuck fuck!

"AAAAAAHHHH!"

That was the biggest piece, though.

That was the biggest piece and he'd gotten it out.

And he could still *see.*

Blood clouded his vision, *but he could still see.*

He picked at the smaller fragments in his left eye, still screaming. Blood wept from both eyes, tickling his cheeks, but he could still *see—*

(kill kill kill)

(murder murder murder)

—and the Miracle still *fueled him*, still helped kill the pain. He could still—

"SMOKE-TOWN-BOYS, RALLY-UUUUUUUUUUUUUUP!"

KEVIN

"Charlie!" said Bill. "Tie this motherfucker up! Fast!"

(kill kill kill)

(murder murder murder)

"And turn the heavy metal back on!" said Bill. "I can't beat no ass without it!"

I'll kill you!

I'll kill you!

I'LL KILL YOU!

"ARAAAAAAAAH!"

Bill pressed the heel of his cowboy boot into Kevin's spine.

"Best stop squirmin' now," said Bill, "and calm the fuck down, or else I'll—"

"SMOKE-TOWN-BOYS, RALLY-UUUUUUUUUUUUUUP!"

TOMMY

"Suzie," said Tommy. "Please, please, please untie my fucking ropes. Please. Please help your brother. *Please.* I'm gonna make everything better. I promise."

Suzie sat in the kiddie pool, motionless, face planted on her knees. Withdrawn from reality.

"Fuck!" said Tommy. "Suzie, you've gotta—"

"SMOKE-TOWN-BOYS, RALLY-UUUUUUUUUUUUUUP!"

Tommy's back straightened and his head jerked up.

Wiley!

Wilin' Wiley!

Yes!

Thank God!

I knew I was right in recruitin' that kid!

"Suzie," said Tommy. "If you untie my ropes, I'll buy you whatever you want, I'll take you to the skatin' rink *every day,* I'll take you wherever you want, *I will take you to Disney Land, Suzie!* Disney World *and* Disney Land! In Florida!"

Suzie didn't budge.

Fuck!

He turned to Larry, still face-planted on the lawn amidst a sea of broken glass.

"Larry!"

"Larry, they called a *rally-up!"*

"We can *win* this!"

"Wake the fuck up!"

LARRY

"I never fucked a Cracker Barrel girl before..."

The cool night air caressed Larry's long face as he sat on the parking lot pavement, leaning back against his truck with the Cracker Barrel girl in his arms. The full moon shone high above the dumpster before them. Some people might think it's weird that they fucked in front of a dumpster, that they *dumpster-fucked.* Some might even call it tacky.

But it was *appropriate.*

Poetic, even.

And *hot.*

Hot as fuck.

The Cracker Barrel girl traced her finger down his cheek. "I never fucked a boy with a face as handsome as yours, Larry..."

"You...you really mean that?" Larry reminded himself that her name was *Whitney,* not *"the Cracker Barrel girl,"* but deep down inside he preferred the latter.

"Sure do, honey..." said Whitney. "...you have got the most beautiful face of any man I ever seen..."

She kissed his cheek.

Larry felt himself blush. "You don't think it's...*too long?"*

"Noooo, honey, it's not too long..." said Whitney. "It's just long enough. That's why I fucked you, Larry. That's why I wanna *keep on* fuckin' you, and—"

"You *really* think that?" asked Larry. "Or you just sayin' it?"

"Of course I really think that, sugar..." said Whitney.

Larry returned his gaze to the moon. A single tear rolled down his cheek. No one had ever told him he was handsome *because* of his long face, the nuance of any compliment usually bending towards *despite it.*

"Some people at school..." Larry wiped his eyes. "...they...they call me Longface..."

"Larry," said Whitney. "Listen to me."

She turned his long face toward her.

"All those other people," she said. "They're just insecure. Because their faces are too short. They're *shortfaces.* Think about that."

"Wha—"

Larry paused.

He'd never thought about it that way.

His face was *normal,* and their faces were *fuckin' short.*

Shortfaces...

They're all shortfaces.

"Larry," said Whitney. "I can't ever accept the dick of no shortfaced boy again. Not inside me."

Gently, she kissed his forehead and gazed into his eyes with a dreamy, drugged-out look.

"Not after I had *you* inside me..." she said. "...and looked at your *long,* beautiful face while you fucked me with that *long,* beautiful dick of yours..."

Larry's cock grew hard. He wanted to fuck her again—to *dumpster-fuck* her.

"Me neither, Larry..." said a voice beside him. A younger, skinny girl leaned naked against his truck.

Samantha Henson!

I dumpster-fucked her, too!

I double-*dumpster-fucked'em both in the Cracker Barrel parkin' lot!*

A wave of guilt washed over Larry.

No...

Tommy...

He's my best bro.

What have I done?

"It's okay..." Samantha caressed his long face. "...I like it when you're inside me, Larry...*it feels good...*"

Samantha...

Had never heard her talk like *that* before. Didn't even know a girl like her *could* talk like that. Wanted to dumpster-fuck her again, too. Dumpster-fuck her *hard* and then—

No!

Best bro's don't do that!

He pushed Samantha's hand away.

"This ain't right, y'all..." said Larry. "...we shouldn't have done this..."

Whitney guided his face back toward hers. "Larry, when you get older, you'll realize you should've done *more* shit in high school, like more *feelin' good shit.* Just gotta focus on feelin' good, that's all. That's the secret to life."

"But Tommy's my best friend, and I—"

"Shh..." Samantha gently guided his face toward hers. "We'll keep it secret..."

She placed his hand on her A-cup sized breast.

"...we'll keep it secret from *everybody,* Larry..."

The heat from her breast traveled up his arm, stopping just short of his heart.

Fuck...

The overwhelming desire to *dumpster-fuck* swelled again.

But with Tommy's girl?

What am I thinkin'?

He pulled his hand away.

"Still don't feel right about this..." said Larry.

"Larry," said Whitney. "On a scale of one to ten, how was it dumpster-fuckin' us both just now? In front of that dumpster over there?"

"And havin' us both suck your dick?" asked Samantha. "We straight up *dumpster-sucked* it, Larry..."

Larry thought it over. Dumpster-fuckin' both an older chick and a younger one at the same time had been *epic.* They both *felt* so different, they both *fucked* so different. They both dumpster-fucked and dumpster-sucked *so* damn good, but in their own, totally different ways.

Whitney,

("you like this, larry?")

with her experience,

("you ever had this before?")

and Samantha,

("...am i...am i doin' it right?")

with her innocence.

("...i think...i think it feels good now, larry...")

Experience, *and* innocence.

Every guy craves both.

And the dumpster made it hotter.

So.

Much.

Hotter.

Larry gulped. "On a scale of one to ten, eleven or twelve, I guess, but—"

"No buts, mister!" Samantha clasped her hand over his, pressing her breast into his palm.

Oh damn...

Samantha was so fuckin' cute when she talked like that, callin' him "*mister.*" He'd always wanted her to call *him* that, ever since he'd heard her say it to Tommy.

"We love you, *mister...*" said Samantha. "And wanna make you feel good..." She lifted his hand to her lips. "...and for you to make *us* feel good, too..."

"...by dumpster-fuckin' us..." said Whitney, licking his face. "...on a regular basis..."

"...and we'll keep it secret..." Samantha guided his hand back to her breast.

"...our secret..." whispered Whitney, her mouth right beside his ear. She caressed his right inner thigh—his *"secret spot"* that when touched just right, got him rock-hard, *always,* though he didn't know why.

"We can do this forever, *mister!*" Samantha pushed her chest tighter against his palm.

"...and we can..."

Head tilted back, she grinded against the pavement.

"...keep it...se-cret..."

Fuck.

It was *time.*

Time to fuck both in front of the dumpster; to *dumpster-fuck* them, good and har—

"—ALLY-UUUUUUUUUUUUUUP!"

The sky flashed white, as if lightning struck.

Larry bolted up.

"What the..."

Was that a rally-up?

Samantha tugged at his thigh. "Sit back down, *mister!"*

Larry scanned the empty parking lots.

Where'd that come from?

"Larry," said Whitney. "Sit back down, sugar, we need your dumpster-fuckin'..."

"Shh!" said Larry. "Y'all be quiet, now. Thought I heard somethin'..."

If one of the Boys had called a *rally-up,* that meant they were in trouble.

("huh huh huh...")

Where was he before this?

("rise and shine, weedboy...")

Wasn't there some kind of...

("i got his sunglasses off!")

trouble...

("use the water gun!")

at the Smokehouse?

("use the fuckin' water gun!")

"You didn't hear nothin', *mister...*" Samantha rose and pressed her warm, naked body against Larry, guiding him back down.

Maybe...

Maybe it's just my imagination...

Whitney caressed his long face. "...just give us a good dumpster-fuckin', good and hard, on a regular basis..."

"At least once a week!" Samantha nuzzled his ear. "Hard and deep! We need it, *mister...*"

"Dumpster-fuck us," they said in unison, *"in front of the Cracker Barrel dumpster..."*

Everything felt blurry.

"...and let us touch your face..."

("larry!")

"...your long..."

("they called a rally-up!")

"...beautiful..."

("we can *win* this!")

"...handsome..."

("larry!")

"...face."

(wake the fuck up!)

LARRY

"Larry!"

"Wake up!"

Larry awoke to pain.

Agonizing pain.

"Larry!"

"Untie me!"

"We can win this!"

"We can fucking win this!"

With great effort, Larry struggled to push his face off the summer lawn, shards of broken glass sparkling before him.

...fuck...

...can barely move...

"Larry!"

...gotta go to the hospital...

"Come here and untie me!"

Larry rose, then fell back down again, then rose. Felt like he'd been hit by a truck. *A huge fucking truck.* The world was a blur. He felt nauseous. Weak.

Do I got a concussion?

"Larry!"

So dizzy he could barely walk, Larry stumbled over to Tommy—kneeling, bound, and positioned in front of Suzie, who sat curled in a kiddie pool like the whole world was a threat.

"Untie my hands first!" said Tommy. "Then we can both untie my feet!"

"Wha...?"

Everything spun around Larry; everything felt *blurry.* Tiny shards of glass jutted from his arms and face—but the worst of his pain radiated from his bones.

Every bone in his body *ached.*

So this is how it feels...

To be thrown out a fuckin' window...

He groaned while pulling at the knots binding Tommy's hands. The more he tugged at the knots, the deeper the shards embedded themselves into his hands.

"They called a *rally-up,* Larry!" said Tommy. "We can win this! *We can fucking win this!"*

Larry stopped untying the knots to remove a sizeable shard from his palm. Blood dripped onto the grass.

"We still got the Miracle!" said Tommy. "Inside the house! We can snort that and fuck'em up *bad*, Larry! We won't even feel any pain!"

Larry returned to the knots. Whoever had tied'em knew how to tie fuckin' rope. A goddamn expert.

"...these knots are fuckin' tight, dude..." said Larry.

Words.

It took so much energy, so much effort to even form them—*words.*

"They pulled it off, Larry!" said Tommy. *"The cross-attack!"*

Larry's heart quickened.

"They...they pulled it off?"

"They pulled it off!" said Tommy. "Just like we trained'em to! I heard it!"

Larry turned his gaze to the Smokehouse, everything still spinning. A cacophony of *clang-clanging* and yelling and screaming echoed from within.

Like a fuckin' warzone...

"Larry," said Tommy. "All ya gotta do is untie me, then we snort Miracle, then we kick their asses. *We can win this, Larry! We can still win this!"*

A wave of dizziness engulfed Larry, and he nearly blacked out, but then something *clicked* and he attacked the knot with renewed determination.

Untie Tommy...
Snort Miracle...
Beat the fuck outta cowboys.

That's all they had to do.

JACK

"My eyes!"

"The glass is in my eyes!"

David's screams pierced the air as the entire house quaked from Graham hopping on one leg, clutching his knee.

Jack crawled toward Mouse.

Why?

Why had their plan failed?

Grant had fuckin' missed with the water gun. That much was clear. Probably hadn't accounted for the stream *dropping* as it shot upward—straight into Graham's mouth.

But the cross-attack...

The cross-attack had fucking worked.

David had nailed Graham in the knee, *nailed him hard,* yet it seemed to inflict only mild-to-moderate pain.

Didn't make sense.

"...Mouse..."

Didn't even sound like *bone* breaking when David hit him.

Sounded like somethin' else.

"...ya gotta wake up, muscle man..."

Mouse's face lay in a shallow pool of spit, drool still leaking from his open mouth. His nose barely looked human—crushed cartilage, flared wide, one nostril clogged with dried blood. Jack's hands trembled as he opened a vial of Miracle and held it beneath the only nostril left open.

"...snort it...c'mon, muscle man...snort it..."

Jack caught a whiff from the open vial and nearly gagged. Sharp and chemical, like sugar set on fire.

"...I know you can hear me...snort it..."

Nothing.

If he can't snort it...

Maybe I should?

Just a little...

Even with my heart condition, just a little *might be al—*

"Mrrghhff..."

A low, wet moan bubbled from Mouse's throat.

"Mouse!" said Jack.

"...mmmrrghhff..." moaned Mouse.

"Mouse, wake up!" said Jack. "They called a *rally-up*! They fuckin' called it!"

"I know you heard it, Mouse!

"I know you fuckin' heard it!"

WILEY

"SMOKE-TOWN-BOYS, RALLY-UUUUUUUUUUUUUUUP!"

(kill kill kill)

(murder murder murder)

The air felt charged the moment the *call to rally* left Wiley's lips. Like electricity surging from him to all the other Boys within a half-mile radius.

Yes.

Now it's our *turn to fuck shit up.*

God, yes...

Crowbar.

He needed his crowbar.

Where was it—

"Rally this, motherfucker!"

BILL

"Best stop squirmin' now," said Bill, "and calm the fuck down, or else I'll—"

"SMOKE-TOWN-BOYS, RALLY-UUUUUUUUUUUUUUP!"

"Shit!" said Bill. "Not *that* bullshit!"

For just a second, *only a second,* Bill released a tiny bit of pressure from Kevin's back—

"RAAAAAH!"

—but that was all Kevin needed.

"Fuck!" said Bill.

Kevin rolled out from under his feet, hopped up and yanked away Bill's baseball bat.

"I'll kill you!" Kevin charged forward.

"Back the fuck up, weedboy!" Bill cowboy-boot-kicked Kevin in the chest, sending him flying back.

Fuck...

What're these kids on?

That crystal meth shit or somethin'?

"Kenny!" said Bill. "Need your help, man!"

Kenny rolled on the ground, moaning.

Shit...

No help from Kenny, then...

Bill snatched Kevin's crowbar, twirling it as Kevin circled him, mouth and lips twitchin' all crazy-like. Didn't like usin' a crowbar against his own fuckin' baseball bat—but didn't have no choice, either.

I didn't see this...

My dreams didn't show me this.

WILEY

"Rally this, motherfucker!"

Charlie's baseball bat careened toward Wiley's head, but he caught it in his bare hand.

Charlie looked shocked. "The fuck..."

(kill kill kill)

(murder murder murder)

Young Charlie.

Bill's right hand man.

I'm gonna beat the fuck out of you, Young Charlie.

He kicked Charlie in the stomach and yanked the bat from his grip.

First you...

Charlie bent over, clutching his abdomen.

Then that crazy Kenny fucker...

He slammed the bat downward, straight onto Charlie's back.

But first, you...

Charlie yelped like a fucking dog, collapsing to the floor.

First, you're gonna suffer...

With rabid, animal-like strength, he slammed the bat onto Charlie's back once more.

Suffer...

Charlie screamed.

Tears ran down his face.

I'm gonna break your fuckin' back, Young...

With a manic grin, he swung the bat downward with all his might, but Charlie blocked the blow with a kitchen chair. Wiley reared back for another swing, but Charlie bolted up and shoved the chair in his face.

"Aléjate! Aléjate, motherfucker!"

Wiley fell back, almost losing balance, but then ripped the chair from Charlie's grip and hurled it against the wall, smashing it into pieces.

Gasoline...

It's like goddamn gasoline in my veins!

Charlie seized the crowbar on the floor and took a swing, which Wiley easily deflected with the bat.

Gonna beat your brains out, Young!

With your own fuckin' baseball bat!

Hunched over and clutching his stomach, Charlie turned the kitchen table over between them, then dashed through the door into the garage.

(kill kill kill)

(murder murder murder)

"Run, Young Charlie!" said Wiley. "Run!"

His lips quivered and twitched, then parted to emit a wild cackle.

GRAPE-GRAPE-JELLY!
GRAPE-GRAPE-JELLY!

GONNA SMASH YOUR BRAINS INTO GRAPE-GRAPE-JELLY!

GRAHAM

"SMOKE-TOWN-BOYS, RALLY-UUUUUUUUUUUUUUP!"

Fuck.

Not *that* bullshit.

(*"and remember, don't let'em call that 'rally up' bullshit, either..."*)

(*"it's like their goddamn superpower or somethin'..."*)

Graham retrieved his cowboy hat and sunglasses from the floor. Amidst the chaos around him, signs of bullshit reared their heads in all directions.

So

much

bullshit.

Over in the kitchen, that Wiley weedboy chased Charlie into the garage.

Nearby, that Kevin kid looked like he'd turned the tables on Bill.

On the other side of the living room, that Asian David boy had started to stand. Blood oozed from both eyes.

"Mrrghhff..."

That Mouse guy on the floor stirred in his sleep.

"Mouse...snort this..." said Jack. "...you can do it..."

And that Jack dude kept tryin' to get him to snort crystal meth or somethin'.

Fuck.

Bullshit everywhere.

Knee still throbbing with pain, Graham hobble-stomped to Charlie's boombox by the front door. Out in the yard, Longface fumbled with Glick's ropes.

Double-fuck.

Double-bullshit.

"You best stop that, Longface!" he said. "Or I'll *hurt* you again!"

Longface and Glick glanced up, then yelled, *"Fuck!"*

Graham narrowed his eyes.

Should I go out there and stop them?

Or take care of things in here f—

Movement.

Behind him.

Probably that Asian David boy, all mad ‘cause he broke his glasses again.

Alright.

No more playin' around.

He cracked his knuckles.

("we gotta have the heavy metal playin…'")

("can't beat no ass without it…")

Graham bent over to press play on the boombox—

—and sensed someone *rush* toward him.

TOMMY

"You best stop that, Longface!" said Graham from the front door. *"Or I'll* hurt *you again!"*

Tommy and Larry looked up.

"Fuck!"

"I thought you said they pulled off the cross-attack!" said Larry, still struggling to untie even one fucking knot. "Why's Graham still walkin' around?"

A cold bead of sweat ran down Tommy's forehead. "...I dunno... maybe...maybe it didn't work..."

But why?

Why would the cross-attack not work?

Did they miss or somethin'?

Graham's voice echoed from the house. *"Damnit, Asian kid! Just give up!"*

"But they're *still* fightin', Larry!" said Tommy. "You just gotta untie me so we can join 'em!"

Tommy shifted his gaze to a near-catatonic Suzie—she hadn't budged from the kiddie pool—then to the Smokehouse, looming above.

"We'll snort goddamn vials of that Miracle shit!"

"Whole fucking vials!"

"And fuck their shit up!"

JACK

Jack shoved the vial of Miracle at Mouse's nose.

"Snort it, Mouse...just sn—"

"Damnit, Asian kid!" Graham's voice boomed near the front door. "Just give up!"

David flailed, limbs kicking as Graham hoisted him by the throat.

"Aaaagh! Aaaaaaaaagh!"

Jack's chest swelled with pride. Even with blood oozin' from both eyes, David still wouldn't quit. A true Smoketown Boy.

Keep fightin', David...

I knew I was right in recruitin' you.

In the next room, Kevin swung the baseball bat like a maniac at Bill, forcing the wannabe cowboy to dodge and stumble back into the kitchen.

Get him, Kevin...

Beat him to death with his own baseball bat.

Over in the kitchen, Wiley chased Charlie into the garage.

Good, Wiley...

Make Young Charlie run before you crack his skull open.

Near the front door, Graham yelled something at Larry in the front yard.

Hell yes...

Larry's probably untyin' Tommy...

And then we're really *gonna show these guys...*

Show'em whose fuckin' house this is!

Wasn't sure where Grant ran off to, not that it mattered. The kid was a disappointment. Had to practically force him to snort Miracle, and he *still* missed with the water gun. Probably off cryin' in the woods.

Didn't matter now.

They were turnin' the tables on these cowboy bitches.

We can win *this...*

Just need Muscle Man Mouse to wake up...

A pumped-up-on-Miracle-Mouse—*just* what the doctor ordered.

BOOM!

David flew across the living room and slammed into the wall. The house shook. He fell into a broken heap on the floor.

It's alright, David...
You did your best...
Now the Muscle Man's gonna wake the fuck up and take care of business...
"Mouse!" said Jack. "I know you heard the *rally-up!* Wake up, man!"
He jammed the vial into Mouse's only open nostril.
"Just snort!"
C'mon, Mouse!
"Snort this shit!"
"And wake up!"
We are so close to winnin' thi—
"AAAAAAAAAAAAGH!"
A heavy cowboy boot came down hard on his hand.
Bone crunched.
The vial exploded under his palm.

He screamed.

1970s

CHAPTER IV

THE PURPLE ROAD TO FUCKTOWN

Upon reaching orgasm, Rhonda often soared on a brilliant wave of light. Sometimes red, sometimes yellow, one time orange. This time, purple—a purple wave of light, freeing her from this realm and allowing travel elsewhere.

Elsewhere...

MOUSE

Mouse and Lacey rode a purple ray of light soaring through a sky of pink.

"It's beautiful, ain't it?" asked Mouse.

"What is it...?" asked Lacey.

The sky transitioned to soft shades of red, orange, and green, but its prevailing color lingered, a soothing pink.

"It's the Purple Road, Lacey..."

As the sky shifted among a spectrum of hues, the road below remained *purple*—a deep, dark purple, just barely translucent, as if made of grape Kool-Aid.

"The Purple Road..." said Lacey.

They scooted forward to the front of The Purple Road as it pushed through the air, its edges sparkling like fireworks, somehow gliding under its own propulsion—as if it self-created with each inch of sky.

"Where's it takin' us?" asked Lacey.

Mouse squeezed her hand.

"...to Fucktown..." he said. "...it's takin' us to Fucktown, Lacey..."

Stars appeared across the canvas of pink clouds, twinkling in response to Mouse's revelation.

"...Fucktown..." said Lacey. "...what're we gonna do there?"

Mouse grinned. "What do you think, baby?"

They laughed and tickled each other and laughed some more, then enjoyed holding each other for a while, marveling at the surrounding beauty.

"Things are gonna change, Lacey..." said Mouse. "...when we get to Fucktown..."

He kissed her forehead.

"Everything's gonna change."

"How so?" asked Lacey.

"Everything's gonna be *better,*" said Mouse. "But especially, in terms of fuckin'. Fuckin' in Fucktown is different, Lacey. *Everything goes.*"

"Everything?"

"Everything and anything," said Mouse, "that involves fuckin'. And of course, suckin' too. But mainly fuckin'."

"...I don't understand..." said Lacey. "...everything's so beautiful, but—"

"Lacey," said Mouse. "When we get to Fucktown, I'm gonna *fuck* you.

I'm gonna fuck you *so* hard, and it's gonna be *so* amazing, that you won't even know what to do with yourself."

"Okay, but—"

"And then, I'm gonna fuck Leslie, too."

Lacey's face dropped.

"But Mouse," said Lacey, "We already talked about this. We're only gonna fuck ea—"

"Lacey," said Mouse. "*Everything goes* in Fucktown. In terms of fuckin'. And suckin' and shit. So I'm gonna fuck Leslie, and a lotta other girls, too. And you're actually gonna be okay with it. And you're not gonna bitch about it like you used to. You'll see."

The sky shifted from pink to orange, then green, as if approving of Mouse's declaration.

"It's so beautiful..." said Lacey.

"Ain't it?" asked Mouse. "And that's why you're startin' to understand now, ain't ya?"

Understandin' how things'll really *go from now...*

In Fucktown.

"...I'm okay with Leslie, I guess..." said Lacey. "...but what *other* girls you wanna fuck?"

"Deanna and Michelle, for starters," said Mouse. "And those Gina, Sarah and Tracey girls that sucked dick on the side of the Smokehouse. And a few other girls I can't remember the names of."

Leslie's voice rang out from behind them.

"Fuuuuuck...where are we?"

"We're takin' the Purple Road to Fucktown, Leslie," said Mouse. "It means I'm gonna fuck you good and hard."

"Fuuuuuuuck," said Leslie. "Okay."

***

Mouse sat between Lacey and Leslie near the front, wrapped in their arms on the Purple Road to Fucktown. It felt damn good to watch the Road self-create before them, knowing they were headed to Fucktown.

"Feels good just ridin' the Road, don't it?" asked Mouse.

"Fuuuuuck..." said Leslie.

"I could ride it forever..." said Lacey.

Thunder rumbled in the distance. The sky darkened into a bluish-grey.

"EIN ZEITGEIST!"

The Purple Road quaked.

"Huh huh huh..."

"Mouse!" said Lacey. "What's goin' on?"

"Fuuuuuuck!" said Leslie. "This place is scary when it's dark!"

"It's alright, y'all..." said Mouse. "It's alright..." For a moment he tasted something metallic, coppery—*blood?*—but it faded as he pulled both girls in close, making sure to cup their breasts.

"The Road won't let us fall," he said. "The Road will *protect* us. Just trust in the Purple Road, and trust in me..."

He closed his eyes, trying to push the dark skies away. Truth be told, he wasn't sure of even half the shit he'd said—it seemed to come from somewhere else and speak *through* him, but, whatever.

"Trust in me..." he said. "...and trust in the Purple Road...to Fucktown..."

Slowly, the sky reverted to a comforting pink. The Purple Road's quaking dwindled, then ceased.

"See?" asked Mouse. "Y'all just gotta *chill,* and be okay with the Road, and be happy to go to Fucktown."

And that means bein' okay with me fuckin' other girls...

He kissed Leslie on her forehead and Lacey on her mouth.

"So are you *cool* yet, Lacey?" asked Mouse. "With me bangin' other chicks and shit? Because maybe The Road can *sense* that you're not, and that's why—"

"Okay, I'm cool..." said Lacey. "*Once* we get to Fucktown. *If* it's actually as awesome as you say it is..."

"It is," said Mouse. "I haven't been there yet, but in my fuckin' heart, I *know* it is. I just know it. And I know you can feel it, too. In your heart. And in your pussy."

"What?" asked Lacey. "Like, in my p—"

"You heard me," said Mouse. "And I ain't gotta repeat it. Do you *feel* it down there? Or not?"

Lacey turned her gaze downward.

"I think...I think I can, Mouse..." she said. "...I think I can feel it...*in my pussy...*"

"Fuuuuuck, y'all," said Leslie. "I can feel it, too! All up in my pussy and shit! Let's fuck in Fucktown, y'all!"

Mouse laughed and nodded. The Purple Road to Fucktown represented the greatest things in life. The greatest things in the world! Lacey and Leslie knew that now; they *accepted* it. And that brought them happiness. The Road would bring the whole world happiness!

"Oh," said Mouse. "And I'm gonna need to fuck Samantha, too."

"Samantha?" asked Lacey and Leslie.

"She needs it," said Mouse.

"Is she even your type?" asked Lacey. "I mean—"

"Honestly," said Mouse. "Nah, not really my type. Skinny, no boobs, and she's a, ya know—"

"A goody two shoes kinda bitch," said Leslie.

Mouse smiled.

"Y'all know what I'm tryin' to say," he said. "I like *badass bitches.* Girls who ain't afraid to get *fucked up.* But Samantha, she needs it. She needs my fuckin', too."

"Fuuuuuck," said Leslie. "Is she gonna be okay to fuck *you,* though? You know, with Tommy and everything."

"In Fucktown," said Mouse, "everything goes, Leslie..."

He turned his gaze to the pink sky, the clouds a canvas for his thoughts.

That's the beauty of fuckin'...

...in Fucktown.

***

Onward they rode; the Purple Road to Fucktown.

Gauging time proved difficult. Perhaps hours passed, perhaps days, perhaps minutes. All thoughts, feelings, and sensations melded together, making every passing moment seem both long and short, drawn out, yet fleeting. Only when someone spoke did time seem real again.

"Oh," said Mouse. "And I'm gonna cum inside y'all, too."

He narrowed his eyes.

"Deep!"

"Fuuuuuuuck!" said Leslie.

"You for real?" asked Lacey. "But what if I get preg—"

"Then we'll just *let-it-happen,"* said Mouse. "The same with you, Leslie. We're just gonna *let-it-happen..."*

The Mitchell Mouse DNA has to spread...

Gotta populate the world with kids as strong and cool as me...

And then, when they're in middle school and shit...

They can be Smoketown: The New Generation.

Lacey asked, "You're not gonna nut inside Samantha, though, are you?"

Thunder rumbled as the sky darkened. The Purple Road quaked again. A familiar voice charged with a manic, frenetic energy, echoed across the sky:

"CROSS-ATTAAAAAAAAAAAAAAACK!"

"What's goin' on?" asked Lacey.

"Dunno..." said Mouse.

He pulled Lacey and Leslie in close.

"Cross-attack?"

The fuck is that?

It sounds familiar, though...almost as if—

"Fuuuuuck," said Leslie. "I'm scaaaaared, y'all!"

"I think it's the Road..." said Mouse. "...it's *angry,* Lacey...because you're questionin' it."

"I ain't questionin' it," said Lacey, "I just can't believe you wanna bust a nut inside Sama—"

"I *will,* Lacey," said Mouse. "I *will* bust a nut *deep* inside of Samantha Henson. And you can't stop me! You can't *control* me anymore!"

Thunder rumbled louder.

Closer.

"But *why?"* asked Lacey.

"Because the Purple Road to Fucktown *demands it,* Lacey!" said Mouse. "And that's why it's gettin' angry!"

"But what about Tommy? Won't he—"

"He'll understand!" said Mouse.

Mouse closed his eyes and tried to *will* the darkness away.

"...once Tommy rides the Purple Road to Fucktown..." said Mouse. "... he'll understand, too..."

Slowly, the sky reverted to pink.

The thunder faded, then ceased.

"Goooood..." said Mouse. "...goooood girls..."

He caressed their heads, petting them like cats.

***

"My eyes!"

"The glass is in my eyes!"

Screams of agony rang through the heavens. The sky had darkened again—this time into the ebony of night.

"Fuuuuuuck," said Leslie. "Who's screamin' and shit?"

"It's alright!" said Mouse. "Just ignore it!"

Sounded familiar, though...

A younger guy's voice...

Maybe some Asian dude I know, but—

"Tommy, I'm scared!" said Lacey.

Cold raindrops fell upon their faces, tasting like metal. The Purple Road tilted and turned, weaving through a darkened sky illuminated by lightning strikes.

"Fuuuuuck!" said Leslie. "I don't like this Road anymore!" Wind blew her hair back.

"It's alright!" said Mouse. "The Purple Road's just mad! Because Lacey's still not cool with me nuttin' *deep* inside Samantha!"

"How could I be okay with that?" asked Lacey. "I don't even like that bitch!"

The Purple Road swerved harder, almost sideways. Mouse and the girls clung to it, as if gravity held them in place—but that didn't stop the screaming.

"Fuuuuuck!" said Leslie. *"I don't like that bitch, eitheeeeer!"*

Mouse pulled Lacey and Leslie in tight, making sure to cup their breasts.

"It don't matter if y'all like her or not!" said Mouse. "I don't like her, either! Not really! But she *needs* it! She *needs* my fuckin'! In Fucktown!"

The Purple Road began twirling like a ribbon.

"BLUUAGH!"

Lacey made an almost-barfing sound.

"Fuuuuuuuck!" said Leslie.

The wind and rain intensified, making it difficult to see or talk.

"You've gotta accept it!" said Mouse, yelling over the wind and rain. "Accept that I will fuck Samantha and all those other girls! And nut deeply inside them all!"

"I don't want to!" said Lacey. "I don't wanna accept that!"

"You have to!" said Mouse. "You can't bitch like you used to! That shit's gotta stop!"

The Purple Road zig-zagged like a roller coaster gone mad.

"Fuuuuuuuck!" said Leslie.

Mouse's heart raced.

Oh, fuck...

Are we gonna die?

Are we gonna die before we even get there?

Before we even get to Fuckt—

"Okay!" said Lacey. "I accept it!"

"You sure?" asked Mouse.

"Yes!"

"You're not gonna get mad?"

"No!"

"You promise?"

"I promise!"

"You swear?"

"I swear!"

"You swear to God?"

"I swear *to God,* Mouse!"

***

"Whoa..." said Mouse. "...that was intense..."

A serene pink hue had reclaimed the sky, occasionally shifting to warm shades of orange, red and green. The Purple Road ran straight ahead now; no more rollercoaster bullshit.

"Listen, y'all," said Mouse. "I know that was scary...."

He nodded and stroked both girls' heads.

"…but Lacey," he said, "you did a good job of accepting me, and accepting the rules of Fucktown. That's all I've wanted from you, from the very beginning, when we started fuckin' on a regular basis. To accept my needs, and accept *me.*"

"Okay…" said Lacey. "…I accept it…and I accept you…whatever you want…"

Mouse stroked her head harder. *"Goooood…"*

"Fuuuuuck…" said Leslie. "…that was scary, y'all…"

"It was," said Mouse. "But I've got good news. I *was* gonna keep it a surprise, but guess I'll go ahead and let y'all know…"

"Let us know what?" asked Lacey.

"That Fucktown…" said Mouse. "…has a Waffle House, too."

"You for real?" asked Lacey.

"I'm for real," said Mouse. "They have a Waffle House *and* a Dairy Queen and *everything* that you could ever wanna eat, ya know. After fuckin'."

"Fuuuuuuck," said Leslie. "Will they have a Cracker Barrel, too?"

"They sure will, Leslie," said Mouse. "I know you love them grilled Colby cheeses on real sourdough bread."

"Fuuuuck yeah, I do!"

"I'll feed one to ya," said Mouse, "real slow-like, after we fuck. How would you like that?"

Leslie nuzzled his arm. "Fuuuuck…"

"Wha—?"

They gasped.

A streak of light blazed across the pink sky, fading as quickly as it appeared.

"Did y'all see that?" asked Mouse. *"Tell me y'all fuckin' saw that!"*

"I saw it!" said Lacey.

"Fuuuuuck…." said Leslie. That probably meant she saw it, too.

"We *all* saw it, then!" said Mouse. "So we know it's real! We all saw a shootin' star while ridin' the Purple Road to Fu—"

The entire sky flashed white.

"*—ALLY-UUUUUUUUUUUUUUP!*"

Mouse bolted up.

"Did y'all hear that?" he asked. "Did someone just call a *rally-up*? One of the Boys?"

Lacey pulled him back down. "Mouse, you've gotta chill…"

"But did y'all *hear* that?" asked Mouse.

"Fuuuuuck..." said Leslie. "...I didn't hear shit..."

(*"they called a rally-up, mouse!"*)

"Well, I fuckin' did!" said Mouse.

("they called it!")

("i know you heard it, mouse!")

("i know you fuckin' heard it!")

Mouse balled his hands into fists. "And if the Boys are in trouble, I gotta—"

"Mouse!" said Lacey. "We're almost there!"

"We're almost to Fucktown..." they said in unison.

"...stay with us..."

"...stay on The Purple Road..."

The sky turned black.

"...to Fucktown."

Jack's screams filled the air.

1970S

CHAPTER V

CRUSH

"Huh huh huh..."

MOUSE

Mouse pushed his eyelids open.

Before him, a heavy cowboy boot crushed Jack's hand, grinding it into broken glass with a sickening crunch.

"ARAAAAAAAAAAAAAAGH!"

Jack screamed.

"AAAAAAAAAAAAAAAAAAAAAAAAGH!"

And screamed

and

screamed

and screamed.

"AAAAAAAAAAAAAAAAAAAAAGH!"

Graham's face clenched with effort.

"Huh huh huh..." he chuckled. "...no drugs for you..."

Sweat beaded beneath his eyes. He pressed his tongue between his teeth.

"Mmmraaf!"

Mouse tried to speak.

"Mmmraaaaaf!"

He tried to say *"motherfucker."*

But his mouth didn't move right.

He couldn't fucking *move.*

No...

Jack...

This isn't real.

This can't be real.

Jack's screams climbed higher—a sawblade shriek, ripping through the room.

This is a fucking nightmare.

DAVID

David lay on the floor. He wiped blood from his eyes.

He hadn't even *touched* Graham, not even when charging from behind. Like the oaf had a sixth sense or something.

(kill kill kill)

(murder murder murder)

It had to be a *cross-attack.*

They had to try it *again.*

One last time.

One last chance.

("juk-il geo-e-yo!")

("chi-reul geo-e-yo!")

But why hadn't it smashed Graham's kneecap?

Maybe...metal plates in his knees?

Or maybe his legs had *that* much fucking strength?

But it did hurt him—not severely, but it *hurt* him—and if they hit him in a different spot, it might—

"ARAAAAAAAAAAAAAGH!"

Jack screamed as Graham crushed his hand beneath his cowboy boot.

"Huh huh huh..." chuckled Graham. "...no drugs for you..."

Now.

It has to be now.

He struggled to push himself up. The stinging in his eyes—especially in his right—had worsened. Blood clouded his vision, and the room hadn't stopped spinning since Graham's fist collided with his face. Embers of pain smoldered in his joints.

The Miracle—its effects had started to wane.

He had to act *now,* while it still *fueled* him.

("JUK-IL GEOEYO!")

"Kevin!"

From behind an upturned table, Kevin halted his assault and spun around.

David's chest heaved.

He felt the weight of the world on his shoulders, the weight of his ancestors. They all watched him now; everything depended on this.

Everything.

He raised his crowbar high.

"Kevin!"

His voice—even his fucking voice—surged with power.

"Aim for his fucking head this time!"

Kevin nodded and turned toward Graham, entering the stance they'd practiced—this time with a baseball bat.

Graham's eyes widened.

"Huh huh *wha?"*

GRAHAM

"ARAAAAAAAAAAAAAAGH!"

Graham ground Jack's hand beneath his cowboy boot.

"Huh huh huh...no drugs for you..."

Hand parts crunched under his heel.

He counted the weedboys he had left to squash.

Jack—screamin' and cryin'. *Squashed.*

Asian David—bleedin' from his eyes. *Squashed.*

Kevin—fightin' Bill in the other room. *Needs squashin'.*

Longface and Glick—in the front yard. *Needs squashin'.*

Wiley—chasin' Charlie-boy outside. *Needs squashin'. But later.*

Was that all?

Felt like one more...

Oh well.

Best help Bill first.

Then Bill could help squash more weedboys.

"ARRAAAAAAAAAAAAAAAAAUUUUGH!"

Jack's screams spiked.

"MY HAAAAAAAAND!"

"Huh huh huh..."

Graham stuck his tongue between his teeth and pressed harder, twisting his heel.

The tendons gave.

Hand parts *snapped.*

I like squashin' your hand...

Because I'm bigger.

Stronger.

More powerful.

And ain't nothin' you can—

"Kevin!"

"Aim for his fucking head this time!"

"Huh-huh-*wha?*"

BILL

Bill nodded to the heavy metal, barely dodging Kevin's swings.

Fightin' with a crowbar against a weedboy cranked up on meth was *not* how the fuckin' mornin' was supposed to go.

"ARAAH!"

Kevin screamed like a wild animal and swung again, knocking Bill's cowboy hat off, barely missing his skull.

Thank God the heavy metal's back on, though...

Can't beat no ass without it.

"Come on, weedboy!" he said, backing up into the kitchen. Chairs and shit in there. Could use that.

"Fuckin' come at me!" Bill dodged another swing. "Pussy-ass weedboy!"

He grabbed a chair and hurled it at Kevin, hitting him in the face. He'd intended to follow up with a *surge-and-attack* kinda move, but Kevin barely reacted.

"Shit!" Bill narrowly avoided another swing. He maneuvered behind the overturned kitchen table, kicking it forward to close the space between him and the weedboy.

Once he tries to hop the table...

That'll be my chance...

Over in the livin' room, that Jack guy screamed and screamed like a dyin' cat. Graham must be hurtin' him bad—*real* bad. He'd have to hurt this weedboy the same way, *Wild Bill-style,* to settle him down.

It wasn't supposed to go like this...

Shit's fallin' apart...

Kevin tried to climb the table, but Bill cowboy-boot-kicked him in his chest, pushing him back. Would've preferred to whack him with the crowbar instead, but Kevin's reflexes were too fast—he deflected every one of Bill's swings.

Charlie's gettin' chased outside...

Kenny's still on the floor...

"C'mon, weedboy!" said Bill. "Come at me!"

All these Possibles hopped up on crystal meth bullshit...

And Longface is tryin' to untie Glick in the front yard...

Kevin kicked the table forward, swinging the bat wildly.

"MY HAAAAAAAAND!"

Jack's screams grew louder.

Thank God for Graham, though...

"Huh huh huh..."

Thank God thank God thank God for Graham-fuckin'-Riley...

He *knew* he'd been right to recruit him.

And as long as they had ol' Graham-cracker up and about, they still had a damn good chance of win—

"Kevin!"

"Aim for his fucking head this time!"

"Huh-huh-*wha?*"

KEVIN

"CROSS-ATTAAAAAAAAAAACK!"

Kevin surged forward.

(kill kill kill)
(murder murder murder)

Pulling the bat back with both hands,

(KILL KILL KILL)

aiming not for Graham's legs—

(MURDER MURDER MURDER)

—but his fucking skull.

DAVID

"CROSS-ATTAAAAAAAAAAACK!"

With his last reserve of strength, David dashed forward and *soared* through the air, jumping higher and faster than he ever dreamed possible.

("GA-YA DWAE-YO!")
("JI-GEUM!")

He pulled the crowbar back—

("JI-GEUM!")
("JI-GEUM!")
("JI-GEUM!")

GRAHAM

"CROSS-ATTAAAAAAAAAAAACK!"

Graham tore his gaze from a screaming Jack. The Asian David kid with bloody eyeballs ran and then *leapt* towards him.

Not this bullshit again…

He extended his right arm to try and catch David by the throat, or at least partially block his blow. With his left arm he reached to blunt Kevin's attack from behind—maybe even catch him by his throat, too.

They won't stay down…

Have to hurt'em more!

But as David soared through the air, for one split second Graham knew, he understood that something would crash into his skull.

No stoppin' it this time.

BILL

"Oh, no you don't, weedboy!"

KENNY

"EIN SCHMETTERLIIIIIIIIIIIIINNNNNNG!"

WILEY

GRAPE-GRAPE-JELLY!

GRAPE-GRAPE-JELLY!

Gonna smash Young's head!

Like GRAPE-GRAPE-GRAPE-JELLY!

(kill kill kill)

(murder murder murder)

Wiley emerged from the garage into the radiant sunlight of the driveway, searching for Charlie the way a predator stalks its prey. In the front yard, Larry appeared to be untying Tommy.

Good!

I'll bring Young's fuckin' brains *to'em!*

And then we can all eat GRAPE-GRAPE-JELLY!

He squeezed the bat's grip, his mouth and lips twitching.

GRAPE-GRAPE-JE—

Rustling.

Nearby.

In the woods.

Young Charlie.

Must've ran in there. Wouldn't go far, not with the wind knocked out of him like that.

"CROSS-ATTAAAAAAAAAAACK!"

David and Kevin.

Yes!

God, yes!

Kill Graham, too!

Turn'em all into GRAPE-GRAPE-JELLY!

He rushed into the forest, the trees melting into a blur of green and brown.

SMASH-SMASH-SMASH their heads into GRAPE-GRAPE-JELLY!

Brains-brains-brains like GRAPE-GRAPE-JEL—

"Sorpresa, motherfucker!"

JACK

Jack crawled past David lying on the floor.
His hand hurt beyond crying.
Beyond thought.
Miracle.
Fuck his heart condition.

Miracle.

GRAHAM

"Fuck!" said Bill. "Graham, we gotta tie these fuckers up! Help me with Kevin!"

Graham stood frozen, staring in disbelief.

The weedboys.

They almost smashed his brains in.

I almost died.

I almost died just now.

"Graham!" said Bill. "Hold Kevin down! And then we'll tie up the Asian boy!"

Behind Graham, Bill stood on the back of a squirming Kevin, pinning him down with his cowboy boot while the weedboy screamed, *"I'll kill you! I'll kill you!"*

"Graham!" said Bill. "Snap out of it, man!"

Before Graham, David lay motionless on the floor while that Jack guy crawled toward the hallway and the Mouse dude kept on sayin' *"Mraaf! Mraaf!"*

He swallowed hard, feeling his throat constrict.

I almost died.

He turned to Kenny sitting on the floor, his face a bloody mess, exhausted and bruised, but still nodding to some unknown rhythm.

Thank you, Kenny.

"Graham!" said Bill.

He turned to Bill.

Thank you, Bill.

"I'm comin'!"

BILL

"Alright..."

Bill finally finished tying Kevin up. It had taken the combined effort of him, Kenny and Graham holdin' the weedboy down just to tie the fuckin' knots.

"Y'all want some purple Kool-Aid?" asked Graham. He sighed, then poured himself a glass near the sink. Kenny and him said they did.

"Let's tie up the Asian boy next," said Bill, "then Mouse, and where's that Jack g—"

Kevin started writhin' on the floor.

"I'll kill you! I'll kill you! I'll kil—"

"Shut the fuck up!" said Kenny. He kicked Kevin across the face, sending blood flying through the air.

"...ughh..."

The kid finally stopped squirmin'.

Kenny coughed and spat blood onto the weedboy's face. "What *the fuck* are these kids on?"

"Some crystal meth bullshit or somethin'..." said Bill.

"Well, the Asian kid ain't a problem no more," Kenny coughed and clutched his hand as he wiped his bloody boot off on Kevin's shirt. "Neither is that Jack guy. And Mouse hasn't even fuckin' *moved* since we got here. We just need to find Wiley and that other dude."

Around them, several of the sleeping partygoers began to stir. Bill clicked his tongue.

Shit.

Not good if people start wakin' before we got all the weedboys tied down...

Have to make it like my dreams showed me...

"Alright, y'all," said Bill. "We need *all* the weedboys tied up real good before everyone comes to. And—"

His eyes widened.

"Graham, what were you yellin' about Longface out in the front ya—"

Glick!

Bill bolted toward the door, imagining Glick in the front yard, fist raised, about to call that *rally-up* bullshit again.

No!

We've almost fuckin' won this!

No!

TOMMY

A *second* cross-attack.

Why had it gone silent after the *second* cross-attack?

Either they'd finally taken Graham down, or—

"Got it!" said Larry.

"Yes!" said Tommy, pulling his hands free. He kicked his bound legs out in front of him, attacking the rope knots.

"Help me untie my legs," said Tommy. "Once we untie'em, we'll—"

Cold metal invaded Tommy's mouth.

"A dónde ibas, motherfucker!"

BILL

From the front door, Bill, Kenny and Graham watched Charlie beat the fuck out of Glick and Longface with his baseball bat.

"*A dónde ibas,* motherfuckers!" said Charlie. "Huh! *A dónde*-fuckin'-*ibas*!"

Bill nodded, relief washing over him.

Atta boy, Charlie...

Teach'em a fuckin' lesson...

Both in Spanish, and in that ass-whoopin'...

Off in the driveway, a tied-up Wiley writhed around, screamin', *"Grape-grape-jelly"* or bullshit like that.

"Kenny," said Bill, "go help Charlie tie those fuckers up. Line'em up with Wiley in front of the kiddie pool, just like we talked about..."

Like my dreams showed me...

"...me and Graham-cracker'll tie the rest up and find that other weedboy."

Just one *more weedboy still runnin' around...*

Hope he's not on that crystal meth bullshit.

GRANT

Can't stand still...

Can't stand fucking *still...*

(kill kill kill)

(MURDER MURDER MURDER)

Grant couldn't fucking stand still but he *had* to, *he had to for his plan to work,* because he'd missed with the water gun but he wouldn't miss again—

(kill kill kill)

—not with this fucking thing.

(MURDER MURDER MURDER)

He couldn't miss *(stand still)* he could never miss *(stand fucking still)* he wouldn't miss *(STAND STILL)* he would never miss again.

(STAND)
(FUCKING)

(STILL)

BILL

Bill peered under a bed. Lots of people sleepin' on this side of the house, but no weedboy yet.

"What's this last weedboy's name?"

"Dunno..." Graham sipped a glass of purple Kool-Aid while he helped search. "...maybe ran off in the woods or somethin'..."

"Well, if he pussied-off somewhere, that's fine," said Bill. "But let's make damn sure he ain't hidin' in the house before we do what we gotta do."

The last thing Bill wanted was *another* surprise. Too many surprises already this morning.

Too many.

"He might've went down that hallway," said Bill, "the one that Jack guy crawled off into..." He navigated around two sleeping girls to fling another closet door open.

"...let's just make sure he ain't on *this* side of the house first..."

He paused, glancing down at a dude wearing a Polo shirt and khaki pants collapsed on a beanbag. Now, who the fuck wears *Ralph-fuckin'-Lauren* to a goddamn house pa—

Zion boys.

That's who.

Probably one of their soccer team dudes—supposedly sold weed and shit. The so-called *"badboy squad"* of Zion County.

"What y'all doin'...?"

The voice came from the corner of the room—a dude on a beanbag wearin' a Confederate flag bandana.

Hazard Mafia.

Now, why were both them *and* the Zion soccer team dudes here at a Smokehouse Party?

Didn't matter.

Havin' other squads witness what came next would be even *better* than what his dreams had showed him.

"Hey dude," said Bill. "We're just lookin' for a weedboy. You can go back to sleep, man."

"Cool..." said the Hazard dude, closing his eyes again.

Everybody's startin' to wake up...

Gotta find that last weedboy...

Fast.

"Weedboy!" said Bill. "Come on out, now! Y'all' done lost this one! We got everybody tied up or knocked out! Except you!"

Bill flung a bathroom door open, ready to smack the shit out of anything that popped out. Instead, he discovered a girl with her head draped over the side of a toilet and a dude passed out beside her, naked from the waist down, still grasping his flaccid dick.

Damn...

Must've been a hell of a party.

"And we ain't gonna hurt ya," said Bill, "if ya come on out!" He pushed back the shower curtain with his baseball bat. "Just gonna tie ya up and talk to ya! I give ya my word!"

"Huh huh huh..." chuckled Graham from the other room. "We ain't gonna *hurt* ya, weedboy..."

Bill sighed and returned to the bedroom.

"Now Graham," said Bill. "If *you* say it, he definitely ain't gonna believe it."

Graham flung another closet door open. "Why not?"

"Because you're *Graham-fuckin'-Riley,* that's why!" said Bill. "If I was one of them weedboys and I heard you stompin' around claimin' you weren't gonna hurt me, you can be for damn sure that I'd—"

Bill froze.

Someone sleepin' on a couch—covered by a blanket from head to toe.

That's him.

The weedboy.

Bill looked at Graham, pointed at the couch, then placed his index finger over his mouth.

Silently, Graham set his purple Kool-Aid down. They both crept towards the couch, readying their baseball bats to *thwack* a fuckin' weedboy.

"Hey Graham..." said Bill. "He must not be in here...let's go check the *other* side of the house..."

"Huh huh huh..." chuckled Graham. "...the *other* side of the house... *sounds good...*"

Bill poked the blanket-covered figure with his bat.

No reaction.

He poked again—harder this time.

Nothin'.
Alright, weedboy…
If that's you under there, you better not fuckin' sur—

"ARRRRRAAAAAAAAAAAAAAAAAAAAAH!"

The war cry came from behind.

GRANT

(kill kill kill)
(MURDER MURDER MURDER)

Gonna SLICE-SLICE-SLICE his belly!

EATIN' BACON TONIGHT!

BILL

"Graham!"

Bill whirled around and charged forward as Graham uttered *"wha?"*—his massive frame pivoting just in time for the weedboy's kitchen knife to slice across his belly.

Fuck!

Graham!

Bill slammed his baseball bat against the weedboy's hand, knocking the kitchen knife to the floor, then swung upward across the weedboy's face, sending him reeling.

"Goddamnit!" Bill rushed forward and unleashed a torrent of strikes upon the weedboy.

"I'm!"

"so!"

"fuckin'!"

"tired!"

"of y'all's!"

"bullshit!"

GRAHAM

Graham gazed at the crimson river flowing from his mid-section.

"Graham, you alright?"

"Graham, how deep did he cut ya?"

"He didn't hit none of your insides, did he?"

The weedboy thrashed and screamed on the floor, pinned beneath Bill's cowboy boot.

"Can you help me tie this fucker up?"

"He won't stay the fuck down!"

Graham pressed his hand against the blood running down his belly, registering the pain.

That's the second time...

The second time I almost d—

He glanced up at the weedboy, thrashing and screaming, eyes burning with hate.

These weedboys keep on hurtin' me!

By cheatin'!

He stomped over to the weedboy and placed his boot on his skull.

Usin' knives!

Pokin' my eyes!

Cross-attackin' me!

That's cheatin'!

"Stop—"

He pressed his heel downward, shifting his weight to the weedboy's skull.

"—movin'!"

The weedboy screamed.

TOMMY

Pain wracked Tommy's body as he knelt on the lawn before Suzie in the kiddie pool. She hugged her knees and stared straight ahead, like the whole world had already ended. The Smokehouse cast a shadow over them both.

Four...

Four of my Boy's left...

We can still win *this.*

Larry, Kevin and Wiley knelt beside him. Wiley still squirmed, twisting against the ropes, mouth moving, lips twitching—mumbling something about *"grape-grape-jelly."* Kevin had started nodding off like he was about to pass out.

You fought hard, Kevin...

But when the Miracle fades...

You're gonna crash like a freight train...

When Tommy had tried Miracle, the comedown had been brutal. Felt mentally and physically annihilated. Took days to feel right again. He'd almost snorted more, *just a little,* to soften the landing, but then Samantha came over and he decided against it.

"Hey, Charlie!" Kenny stood before him, nodding and twirling his bat. His voice sounded hoarse, like he'd crossed a desert. "Can you bring some RC and tequila from the car, man?"

"*SNRKKT!*"

A snorting sound rose from the driveway.

"Sí!" said Charlie. *"Un momento!"*

Kenny coughed, then hocked a blood-loogie into the grass. He took off his aviators, wiped his eyes, slid'em back on—then nodded again, slower this time.

You're gettin' tired, ain't ya Kenny...

Bet your cowboy-boyfriends are, too...

He glanced at his cap, still floating on the blood-streaked surface of the kiddie pool.

Mikey...

What would you do?

In a situation this fucked up?

The pain-numbing haze of the Purple had begun to fade, but his thoughts sharpened. He reconsidered his situation.

Even *if* him and his Boys got free, they were too beat up and exhausted to take on Bill and Graham-fuckin'-Riley. Only Wiley still had fight left, and judging by the silence in the house, David, Jack, Mouse and Grant had probably fallen on their last legs, too.

Or…

…maybe they're hidin'?

Preparin' an ambush…

Napoleon-style, on Bill and Graham.

If they took out Bill and *especially* Graham, Kenny and Young wouldn't stand a chance. Kenny might have a *little* fight left, but he looked wrecked. Young didn't look nearly as bad, but he hobbled and winced a lot. *He was hurtin', too.*

They'd be a piece of cake compared to *Graham-fuckin'-Riley.*

At any rate, if they got out of these fuckin' ropes, they'd all need to snort a shit-ton of Miracle—fast.

Charlie returned, handing Kenny a can of RC. *"Bebe esta, amigo.* I done put the tequila in the can for ya."

"Danke…" Kenny took a long sip.

Charlie sniffed and rubbed cocaine off his mustache. He turned to Tommy.

"Cómo estás, Glick?"

Slowly, he dragged his cold metal bat across Tommy's face.

*"Cómo…*fuckin'*…estás…"*

He pressed the bat against Tommy's mouth, prying his lip upward. Rust and dirt seeped in. Metal scraped his teeth, sent a jolt through his jaw.

"No está bien, huh?"

Charlie grinned, eyes twinkling.

*"No-está-*fuckin'*-bien…"*

He and Kenny laughed and laughed like it was the funniest thing ever. Despite the knife-like pains across Tommy's torso, a surge of rage, *empowering rage,* coursed through him.

We're gonna show you no*-fuckin'*-bien, *Young…*

Once we get free of these ropes…

With his right middle finger, he loosened one of the rope-knots.

We'll tie you and your cowboys bitches up…

Snort a fuck-ton of Miracle and torture y'all for days...
Beat the livin' fuck out of y'all like piñatas.

He loosened another knot.

Young didn't tie'em near as good as Bill did.

BILL

The weedboy's screams had turned into cries for mercy once Graham teetered on the edge of crushin' his skull like a watermelon. Bill tied him up real easy after that.

"If you'd been skinnier," said Bill, tending to Graham's belly-gash, "he probably would've spilled your guts out..." He poured the bottle of hydrogen peroxide they'd found in the bathroom over the wound. White foam hissed as it hit raw flesh, running pink to the floor. Graham winced.

"Thank God you're a big ol' boy..." said Bill. "Who knows how to eat his momma's cookin'..."

He expected Graham's trademark chuckle, but instead, the big guy stared into space.

Ol' boy's probably gettin' tired...

Gotta get some food in him...

And some more cocaine, too.

Bill found gauze in the bathroom and wrapped it real tight around Graham's belly, somewhat staunching the blood. The cut wasn't that deep, but he'd likely need stitches later. Would have to make up a story about roughhousin' or horseplayin' later at the hospital. *"Boys'll be boys."* That kinda shit.

"Alright, Graham-cracker..." said Bill. "...there ya go..."

Bill patted Graham's belly for good luck. It echoed like a drum. He liked that sound.

"Thanks, Bill..." said Graham.

"Don't mention it, big guy..."

While Graham finished his purple Kool-Aid, Bill took the knife to the kitchen and rinsed the blood off, then tossed it in a random drawer filled with utensils.

What kinda lunatic tries to slice a guy's stomach open?

He shook his head.

That's what crystal meth does to ya...

I'll never mess with that *shit.*

BILL

The weedboy that had almost killed Graham squirmed as they carried him across the living room. Blood dripped from his ears, but other than that, he seemed alright.

Bill glanced at Mouse and the Asian boy on the floor.

Best tie them up next...

Just in case.

MOUSE

"They're gone now..." whispered Mouse. *"...they're in the front yard..."*

He could speak again.

Could barely move, but he could fucking speak again.

David lifted his head.

Blood streamed from his eyes, nose and mouth.

TOMMY

Three.

Three of my Boys left now.

After tossing a tied-up Grant beside Wiley, Bill and his bitch-ass cowboys slapped each other high-fives. Like they'd won a fuckin' ball game.

No.

No.

We *will win this.*

Not y'all fuckers.

We can still—

fucking—

win this.

Bill and his crew huddled out of earshot, probably discussing their next move, like they'd already won. A massive tear ran across Graham's shirt revealing blood-soaked gauze wrapped around his belly. Charlie seemed to ask what had happened, and although Tommy couldn't hear the reply, Graham's chubby finger pointin' at Grant told him enough.

Grant had hurt him.

Good Guy Grant had fuckin' *hurt* Graham-fuckin'-Riley.

He could be hurt.

***

Bill, Young and Graham headed back inside the Smokehouse while a shirtless Kenny sipped RC and tequila, grinning and nodding to some bizarre rhythm. Ugly bruises dotted the wannabe-cowboy's hands, arms and chest. Dried blood decorated his face like warpaint.

Tommy tilted his head back, absorbing the vastness of the almost infinite blue sky. He hadn't prayed in a long time—not since Mikey had died. He never stopped believing in God, but after he'd discovered his brother's brains splattered across the wall, he didn't feel like praying anymore, either.

Today, he would pray, though.

Pray with all his might.

Please, God...

Let us win this.

I know I haven't prayed to you in a long time...

But please...

Let us win *this.*

Suzie chanted under her breath, only a handful of words reaching Tommy's ears:

"...Mikey..."

"...make it better..."

"...we'll help you find it..."

"...the Temple..."

DAVID

David could barely see through the blood.

Everything *hurt.*

Every muscle, every bone, every fiber of his being hurt and felt weak, like a battered puppet with loose strings.

"...David..." whispered Mouse. *"...snort it..."*

Amidst a red haze, a small pile of white powder, tinged with blood and adorned with glass fragments, sharpened into focus.

"...snort it all, David..."

BILL

Bill entered the Smokehouse with Graham and Charlie at his side.

"Alright, y'all," said Bill. "Graham, you go find Jack over in that hallway and bring him here so we can tie his ass up. Might be hidin' in one of them rooms or somethin'. *Be careful.* Me and Charlie'll tie up Mickey Mouse and the Asian boy."

"Can I eat pizza first?" asked Graham. "I'm hungry..."

Graham picked up a mushroom pizza slice off the floor, cramming the whole thing into his mouth.

"Mmm..." he rested his hands on his gauze-wrapped belly. *"...so good..."*

Bill's stomach rumbled.

Pizza sounds pretty good right about now...

"...maybe more..." said Graham, chewing. "...in the fridge..."

"Alright," said Bill. "We'll go check if there's more pizza, you go fetch Jack."

The big ol' boy's been through a lot today...

He deserves some pizza...

As Bill and Charlie headed toward the kitchen, Charlie bragged about how he'd single-handedly taken out not only Wiley, but Glick and Longface, too. But Bill focused on the two weedboys lying absolutely still in the living room.

Had the Asian boy moved?

GRAHAM

Graham pulled down his pants and sat on the toilet. The seat creaked under his weight.

He stared at the closet before him.

Probably should've checked inside there before poopin'.

He released a stream of warm piss onto the inner side of the toilet.

Mmm...

Felt good.

Nothin' wrong with sittin' down to pee.

Not when you were poopin'.

It's *okay* when you're poopin'.

Errreeeeeeeeek...

The closet.

Did something just *creak* inside that closet?

Was that Jack guy...

...*hidin'* in there?

(jack)

(jack in the box)

Was that Jack guy gonna...

...*surprise* him?

("aaaaaaaaaaaaaaah!")

("ahahahahaha!")

He didn't like *surprises...*

("you don't like your new present, son?")

("ahahahahaha!")

Even though he could've squeezed out a few more, he wiped and pulled his jeans up.

Wasn't gonna be surprised while poopin'.

That would *traumatize* him from poopin' for the rest of his life.

He knew that.

And poopin' stood as one of his greatest joys in life.

SCHWRRRSSSH!

As the toilet flushed, Graham gripped the closet doorknob. For the first time in a long while, he felt *afraid.*

"Weedboy," said Graham, "if you're in this closet, you *better not* surprise me..."

He waited for a reply.

Nothing.

Flinging the door open, he steadied himself for a screaming, raving Jack to pop out like that awful, *awful* toy.

("you don't like your new present, son?")

("ahahahahaha!")

Instead, he discovered only toilet paper, cleaning supplies, and off in the back, vials of white powder tinged with a touch of blue.

Probably that crystal meth stuff they been snortin'...

He released a sigh.

Guess that Jack guy was in a bedroom, then.

"Huh huh huh..."

While washing his hands, he couldn't help but chuckle. After all these years, still scarin' himself over some stupid toy that—

"*Snrrk!*"

A sound.

From behind the shower curtain.

A *snorting so—*

CRRNKLE!

Darkness.

He gasped.

Darkness all around as light bulb fragments crashed to the floor.

Breathing, heavy and raspy—from behind the shower curtain.

(jack)

(jack in the box)

No...

He *hated* the dark.

("momma, can i sleep with my night-light on?")

("now graham-cracker, big boys don't do that...")

He *hated* the dark and he *hated* surprises—especially in the dark.

("graham, you're in high school now!")

("you're a big boy!")

("big boys aren't afraid of the dark!")

He whirled around and felt through the darkness for the shower curtain with his left while his right tightened into a fist, ready to *smash* anything that popped out.

("i'm not afraid of the dark, momma!")

("i just like sleepin' with my night-light on!")

("that's all!")

He ripped the shower curtain back.

The crowbar struck his mouth with such fury he didn't even feel it.

DAVID

Inch by agonizing inch, David pulled himself toward the blood-stained pile of Miracle.

"...so then I said, *'rally this, motherfucker!'*" said Charlie from the kitchen. "And I fuckin' wolloped that weedboy straight up the head, man! Now, I know I should've probably said that shit in Spanish..."

...close...

Blood wept from David's eyes, tickling his cheeks.

...so...close...

...just...gotta...

...snort it...

The crimson haze thickened before him. Each movement brought a fresh wave of torment.

"...you can do it, David..." whispered Mouse.

"...'cause that would've been a hell of a lot cooler," said Charlie, "but to be honest with ya, I don't even know how to say '*rally this*' in *español,* man. I mean, who actually says that shit? Other than weedboys, I mean."

...almost...there...

His body burned like fire.

"...snort it, David..." whispered Mouse. *"...I believe in you..."*

Charlie continued. "It's not like a word that comes up in daily fuckin' conversation, ya know what I'm sa—"

"The Asian boy!"

"Don't let him snort that shit!"

BILL

"...'cause that would've been a hell of a lot cooler," said Charlie, "but to be honest with ya man, I don't even know *how* to say *'rally this'* in *español,* man. I mean, who actually says that shit? Other than weedboys, I mean."

Bill nodded while pulling pizza boxes from the fridge. Charlie had a point—would've been a hell of a lot cooler if he'd said that shit in Spanish, but he couldn't be expected to know every single phrase in *español.*

Charlie continued. "It's not like a word that comes up in daily fuckin' conversation, ya know what I'm sa—"

Bill froze.

The Asian boy.

He had *fuckin' moved!*

While we were outside!

He whirled around, balancing five pizza boxes. Over in the living room, the Asian boy crawled toward something—

—a small pile of that crystal meth bullshit.

"The Asian boy!"

"Don't let him snort that shit!"

DAVID

"No drugs for you, motherfucker!"

"No está bien!"

Charlie's voice rang out as his boots *clomp-clomped* toward the living room.

"Snort it, David!" said Mouse. *"Snort it all!"*

David scooped the blood-soaked, glass-filled Miracle off the floor and crammed it into his face, inhaling as much as he could.

("GA-YA DWAE-YO!")

His eyes rolled back,

("JI-GEUM!")

and his mind turned inward,

("JI-GEUM!")
("JI-GEUM!")
("JI-GEUM!")

to ancestral memory.

1970s

CHAPTER VI

ANCESTRAL MEMORY

The Imjin War began in 1592 when Japan invaded Korea; a seven-year campaign of fire, steel, and slaughter.

SEONG

Fire.
Fire and waves of heat.
Burning, searing, roaring.
("ga-ya dwae-yo!")
("ji-geum!")
Through the flames—
her voice.
("ga-ya dwae-yo!")
("ji-geum!")
"You have to go!"
"Now!"
And then—
his son's.
("appa!")
"Daddy!"
From outside.
("appa!")
("appa!")
"Daddy!"
"Daddy!"
Hands.
Arms.
Pulling him away.
Away *from her.*
("ani!")
("ani!")
"No!"
"No!"
Smoke.
Sound.
Light.
"We have to leave!"
Voices.
Pulling him further.

"They've taken the village!"
"We're retreating!"
("ani!")
("ani!")
"No!"
"No!"
Gunshots.
Swords clashing.
Explosions.
Screaming, screaming, screaming—
—from inside his house.
Screams from Sun.
("nae anae!")
"My wife!"
His voice—
("nae anae!")
—no longer his.
He didn't *feel* himself talk.
("nae anae!")
("nae anae!")
"My wife!"
"My wife!"
"My wi—"
The earth shook.
A cannonball.
Dust.
Smoke.
Couldn't see.
Couldn't breathe.
Sun.
No longer screaming.
("ani!")
"No!"
"Sun!"
More voices.
Arms.
Grabbing, pulling, yanking.

"They have guns!"
"We have to retreat!"
"They're coming!"
Dogs.
Japanese dogs.
Clad in their dog-armor.
Emerging from the smoke.
("jug-il geoeyo!")
"I'll kill you!"
A sword.
On the ground.

("jug-il geoeyo!")

"I'll kill you!"

DAVID

(KILL KILL KILL)
(MURDER MURDER MURDER)
David no longer felt.

(GA-YA DWAE-YO!)
"You have to go!"
He didn't *feel* himself grab the crowbar.

(JI-GEUM!)
"Now!"
He only *moved.*

(JI-GEUM!)
"Now!"
He moved like liquid, sculpting the air with violence.

(JUG-IL GEOEYO!)
"I'll kill you!"
(JUG-IL GEOEYO!)
"I'll kill you!"
(JUG-IL GEOEYO!)
"I'LL KILL YOU!"

("nae anae!")
("my wife!")

The Japanese dogs would pay for killing Sun.

1970s

CHAPTER VII

CHAOS

"NAE-ANAE!"

(my wife)

"NAE-ANAE!"

(MY WIFE)

BILL

The Asian boy moved with surreal speed, swinging his crowbar at Charlie like a fucking cyclone.

"JI-GEUM!"

"JI-GEUM!"

"JUG-IL GEOEYO!"

That voice—metallic and wired now,

"*GA-YA DWAE-YO!"*

"*GA-YA DWAE-YOOOO!"*

no longer human.

"Fuck!" said Bill.

"Graham!"

"Get in here!"

Bill dropped the pizza boxes, grabbed his bat, and surged forward.

Mouse rose from the floor.

"Kill'em, David!"

"Fucking kill'em all!"

TOMMY

As Kenny sipped his tequila RC, nodding and smiling behind his fucking sunglasses, Tommy loosened another knot behind his back. He didn't dare check if Larry and the rest had progressed with their knots—not while Kenny watched him.

Grant and Wiley's mouths still moved all weird, a side-effect of the Miracle he'd almost forgotten. Wiley kept chantin' shit about *"grape-grape-jelly"* while Grant repeated *"Can't miss, won't miss, never miss again..."* Blood trickled from Grant's ears, slow and shiny. They'd both calmed somewhat after Kenny socked'em with his baseball bat.

And then there was Kevin.

Poor, poor Kevin.

Already had his eyes shut.

Already checked out.

Larry tilted from side-to-side, about to pass out like Kevin.

Or...

Is he fakin' it?

As he loosens his knots, too?

Kenny pointed his bat at Wiley. "Why'd he keep sayin' *'grape-grape-jelly'*?"

"...hell if I know, man..." Tommy loosened another knot. "...maybe he's hungry..."

Kenny snorted and spat a blood-loogie, landing just shy of Tommy. He tipped his cowboy hat and smiled as if he knew a secret.

"You know," he said, "you really shouldn't've thrown that chicken strip at Bill. Back at Dairy Queen. That was probably like, the worst mistake of your life."

"Charlie!"

"Don't let him snort that shit!"

Bill—Bill's voice.

Tommy's heart pounded as Young's rang out, too:

"No drugs for you, motherfucker!"

"No está bien!"

Kenny turned toward the Smokehouse as Bill yelled again.

"Fuck!"

"Graham!"

"Get in here!"

A cacophony of clanging and screaming in an Asian-sounding language filled the air.

"GA-YA DWAE-YO!"

"JI-GEUM!"

"JUG-IL GEOEYO!"

David!

He's still fightin'!

Didn't know he could speak Chinese and shit...

Tommy considered prodding Kenny to go help his little cowboy bitches, but no—*reverse psychology* would be the better play.

"I wouldn't go in there if I were you..." said Tommy. "...best stay out here, where it's safe...my boy Asian David knows *karate* and shit...he'll break all your goddamn bones..."

Kenny glanced back at Tommy, flashing a delirious, unhinged smile, like a carnival clown gone mad.

"We'll see about that!"

GRAHAM

Jack lay sprawled in the bathtub like a puppet with its strings cut. Graham had stomped him, good and hard. Froth coated the weedboy's mouth while his lips twitched like an insect's legs, post-squash.

Graham wiped blood from his mouth.

Weedboy had *surprised* him.

Just like that awful, awful toy.

Surprised him *in the dark.*

And knocked a tooth out, too.

He coughed, ejecting a crimson spray onto the shower curtain.

Fuck this shit.

Didn't even know where his tooth went—

Fuck this shit.

—but it was *gone.*

Fuck this shit.

Had to pay him back.

Make it even.

A tooth for a tooth.

He squeezed his hand into a fist, drew it back and aimed straight for Jack's—

"Charlie!"

"Don't let him snort that shit!"

Uh-oh.

"No drugs for you, motherfucker!"

"No está bien!"

More bullshit.

"Fuck!"

"Graham!"

"Get in here!"

More,

"Kill'em, David!"

endless

"Fucking kill'em all!"

bullshit.

He dragged Jack by his hair into the hallway, spraying blood onto the walls and carpet as he spat.

If you cause any more trouble, weedboy...

I'll rip all *your teeth out...*

One-by-one.

He spat blood onto Jack's face, wincing at the pain in his belly-gash.

BILL

Bill barely deflected the onslaught of strikes from the Asian boy, the weedboy's crowbar a black blur.

"GA-YA DWAE-YO!"

"JI-GEUM!"

"JUG-IL GEOEYO!"

"NAE ANAE!"

"Graham!"

"Fuckin' somebody!"

"NAE ANAE!"

"NAE ANAE!"

"NAE ANAE!"

"Fuck!"

GRAHAM

Dragging Jack behind him, Graham returned to the living room to find Charlie sprawled on the floor, clutching his chest. Beside Charlie, that Asian David kid screamed shit in Chinese as he swung the crowbar in a rapid blur.

"Motherfucker!"

The voice came from Mouse, wobbling as he struggled to stand.

"Motherfuckerrrrrrr!"

Mouse lunged toward Graham, hurling a clumsy swing.

"Huh huh huh..." Could've dodged that blindfolded.

Graham slammed his fist into Mouse's stomach, the impact immediate and satisfying.

"UUUNNNF!"

He shoved a keeled-over Mouse to the floor.

You are weak.

I am strong.

Next.

Wiping blood from his mouth, he stomped forward, but an abrupt *yank* pulled his left leg out from under him.

"Wha?"

He careened face-first to the floor, the entire house quaking upon impact.

BOOM!

Mouse reached for the baseball bat beside him.

KENNY

A shirtless Kenny stormed into the living room, cowboy hat low, sunglasses on. He gripped his baseball bat and tequila RC, nodding like he heard a chorus drop.

Damn...

Shit got wild again...

Mouse clung to Graham's leg and yanked him down—*BOOM!* The whole house quaked. The Asian kid screamed shit in Chinese as he assaulted the fuck outta Bill, his crowbar a black blur, voice metallic and electric, as if charged with guitar distortion.

"JUG-IL GEOEYO!"

"NAE ANAE!"

"ANI!"

"ANI!"

"ANI!"

Kenny gulped down the rest of his tequila RC, then tossed the can aside.

Time to fuck shit up.

He bolted forward, bat raised high.

"EIN SCHWEISSLAND!"

TOMMY

As Tommy freed the last knot binding his hands, a wall of screams roared from the Smokehouse:

"EIN SCHWEISSLAND!"

"NAE ANAE!"

"ANI!"

"ÁNDALE, MOTHERFUCKER!"

"FUCKIN' ÁNDALE!"

"EIN FLAMMENWAFFEN!"

"THE ASIAN BOY!"

"GRAB THE ASIAN BOY!"

His heart hammered.

Wiley.

First, untie Wiley.

Wiley rocked back and forth. *"Grape-grape-JELLY!"*

"That's right, Wiley..." Tommy loosened the knots. "You're gonna fuck'em up like grape jam and jelly and shit..."

Didn't know what the fuck that meant, but whatever. Dude still rolled on Miracle, could still fuck shit up.

"Go!" Tommy freed the last knot. "Go fuck'em up! *Like grape jelly!"*

Wiley tore toward the house, spit flying.

"Grape—grape—JELLLLYYYYY!"

Pain lanced Tommy's chest.

God...

He squeezed his eyes shut.

My Boys...

They need me...

We can win *this...*

He scooted across the lawn to Grant, the grass still wet with morning dew. Best to free the Miracle-fueled Possibles first.

Grant rocked in place, eyes wild, blood leaking from his ears. *"Can't miss, won't miss, never miss again..."*

"That's right, buddy..." said Tommy. "...you can't miss..."

Didn't know wh—wait, maybe *Grant* had missed with the water gun? Even though *Jack* was supposed to shoot?

Oh well.

Didn't matter now.

"You won't miss again, bro..." Tommy yanked the last knot loose. *"Go! And don't fuckin' miss this time!"*

Grant raced toward the Smokehouse.

"Can't miss! Won't miss! Never miss agaaaaaaaaain!"

Lightning ripped through Tommy's chest.

God...

He groaned, shoved it down.

The water gun—where would it be?

If we blasted that in Graham's eyes...

They still had a chance.

Especially with the water gun.

They could still *win* this.

"Shit!"

"More weedboys!"

Bill—Bill's voice.

Sounded panicked.

Good.

Kevin fell face-first into the grass.

Fuck!

Larry didn't look too good, either—and hadn't been untying his ropes like Tommy hoped.

"Larry," said Tommy, deciding to free his own legs first. "You good, bro?"

"I don't..." Larry's voice sounded thin. "...I don't feel good...Tommy..."

Blood dripped from Larry's nose. Drool clung to his lip. Looked like he might die, or at least pass out any second now.

Poor guy...

Gettin' thrown through a fuckin' window'll do that.

"I'll bring you Miracle, bro!" Tommy yanked at the last knot. "I'll bring a *shit-ton* of Miracle! And we can snort it together!"

A *boom* rocked the house.

"GA-YA DWAE-YOOOOOOOOOO!"

Tommy tried to stand.

"Ohhhh, fuuuuck..."

Everything spun.

The ground blurred, smeared into green streaks.

Holy shit...

Hard to even stand...

Agony, raw and soaring, lit up his torso; every bat strike screamed now, loud and clear.

Miracle...

Just gotta just make it...

To the Miracle...

The ground tilted beneath him.

He took a step—

—then stumbled.

Fuck.

Could barely walk.

He lurched toward the kiddie pool. Suzie didn't move—just stayed curled into a ball. Wincing, he fished his cap from the blood-streaked water and stared at the lone crow stiched on the front.

Help me, Mikey...

Help me win this...

The uproar from the Smokehouse exploded: howls, slams, unhinged battle cries over crowbars clanging into bats. Boots pounded floorboards. Glass shattered. Something heavy toppled, followed by a scream that cut off too fast. Shouts in Spanish *("ÁNDALE!")*, German *("EIN WANZERFAUST!")*, and what sounded like Chinese *("NAE ANAE, NAE ANAE!")*. Voices wild, cracking, barely human—and over it all, a deep, ragged roar, like an animal gone mad.

Tommy took a deep breath.

Chaos...

It's not a fight anymore...

It's chaos.

He put his cap back on,

and stumbled toward the chaos.

LESLIE

Leslie lay across on her beanbag, neither comfortable nor uncomfortable.

Just numb.

Numb.

Numb.

Numb.

The Purple shit.

Must've fucked her up bad.

Bad?

Fucked her up *good,* hadn't it?

Real good.

That's how she wanted to feel.

Numb.

But this—this felt *beyond* numb.

Detached.

Lifeless.

Inert.

Like a rock drifting through the void of space.

A void...

The Void.

This place is called The Void.

Within the perfect stillness of The Void, she turned her mind inward to *glimpse* things—fragments of people and places both familiar and unfamiliar:

A man.

A *faceless* man—his face a swirling distortion, surrounded by lush mountains, speaking with Tommy. A beam of light shined in the distance. That light—was it a good place? Or a bad—

An office—a really *nice* office, the kind you saw on TV. Jack, gazing out a window. Holding a magazine. He spun around, looked surprised. Not to see her, but to see—

A dumpster—the *Cracker Barrel* dumpster. The one she'd fucked Larry at. Felt *gross a*fter that. Cried after that. Then she kinda missed it. Like, *really* missed it. Then she cried more. *Because she fucking missed it.* A scent—*of* *what?*—a candle. One of them wood wick ones. *Mmm. Vanilla bean.* Dumpster hadn't smelled like that. If it had, she might've f—

A road—a *purple* road, the color of Kool-Aid, pushing through a pink-hued sky as if fueled by magic. Mouse and Lacey, arguing. The sky darkened. Lightning flashed. Cold rain on her face. Metal blaring—*heavy* fucking metal—the roar of distorted guitars ripping through the air, vibrating in her ribs, rattling her teeth—

"CROSS-ATTAAAAAAAAAAACK!"

The sky reverted to pink.

The metal lowered to a hum.

But something felt *wrong*, so fucking—

"My eyes!"

"The glass is in my eyes!"

That voice.

David.

The Asian boy.

Always thought he was cute.

But why was he scream—

"*—ALLY-UUUUUUUUUUUUUUP!*"

A *rally-up*.

The Boys were in trouble.

With who?

The heavy metal returned, pounding.

"ARRAAAAAAAAAAUUUUGH!"

Screaming.

Jack's screams.

Rising above the unrelenting metal.

"Huh huh huh..."

"No drugs for you..."

Graham.

Graham-fuckin'-Riley.

"CROSS-ATTAAAAAAAAAAACK!"

David.

Kevin.

A weird, manic energy behind their voices, like—

"EIN SCHMETTERLIIIIIIINNNNNNNG!"

German?

Someone yellin' in Ger—
BOOM!
Everything shook.
Violence.
She sensed it.
Blood.
She smelled it.
The heavy metal surged.
"...fuuuuuuuck..."
The word slipped her lips,
like a grain of sand,
shifting with the breeze.
"...fuuuuuuuck..."
She tried to speak again.
To say anything,
but *"fuck."*
"f..."
Couldn't.
Couldn't move.
Couldn't see.
Her eyelids, like concrete.
Her body, like stone.
Awareness.
Fucking *aware* now.
Aware of the *chaos* around her.
Clang-clanging.
Screaming.
Screaming in different languages.
Multilingual chaos—
—made symphony.
"EIN SCHWEISSLAND!"
"Nae anae!"
"Ani!"
"Ándale, motherfucker!"
"Fuckin' ándale!"
"The Asian boy!"
"Grab the Asian boy!"

"I got him!"
"Grab his legs!"
"Ani!"
"Ani!"
"Grab his fuckin' legs, Charlie!"
"Cálmate, motherfucker, fuckin' cál— "
"ARAAAAAAAAH!"
"He's bitin' me!"
"He's fuckin' bitin' me!"
"Grape-grape-jelly! Grape-grape— "
"EIN SCHMETTERLING!"
Blood.
Blood on her face,
blood in her mouth.
Tasted like metal,
like copper.
BOOM!
The earth shook again.
A guitar solo soared through the air.
"Can't miss, won't miss, never miss ag—aaaagh!"
"Another weedboy!"
"From the fuckin' yard!"
"A dónde vas, motherfuckers!"
"He's got the water gun!
"The water gun!"
"Go for his eyes!
"His fucking eyes!"
"EIN SCHNELL, EIN KRIIIIIIIIIEG!"
The chaos intensified,
"ÁNDALE!"
"ÁNDALE!"
descending into a whirlwind,
"JUG-IL GEOEYO!"
of desperation
"JUG-IL GEOEYO!"
and fury.
"NAE ANAE!"

"GLICK!"
"HE'S HEADIN' TOWARD THE HALLWAY!"
"HOLD DOWN THE ASIAN BOY!"
"HOLD HIM DOWN!"
"NAE ANAE!"
"NAE ANAE!"
"THAT OTHER WEEDBOY!"
"GET HIM OFF GRAHAM!"
"GET THE WEEDBOY OFF GRAHAM!"
"NEVER MISS AGAAAAIN!"
"STOP GLICK!"
"DON'T LET HIM SNORT THAT SHIT!"
"DON'T LET HIM SN—"
"MOTHERFUCKEEEER!"
"GRAHAM!"
"FORGET MOUSE!"
"STOP GLICK!"
"GET HIM!"
"EIN VOLKSTRAGGEN!"
"EIN VERACHTUNG!"
"EIN LIEBERSTRAGGEN!"
"EIN ZEIT—UGGH!"
"KENNY!"
"KENNY!"
"TE JODO, MOTHERFUCKERS!"
"TOMA ESTO!"
"GRAPE-GRAPE-JELL—*AAGH!"*
"THERE'S YOUR FUCKIN' GRAPE JELLY, MOTHERFUCKER!"
"EAT THAT SHIT UP!"
"HOW'S THAT TAS—*AOOF!"*
"CHARLIE!"
"CHARLIE!"
BOOM!
BOOM!
BOOM!
"STOP—"

“THIS—”
“FUCKIN’—”

“BULLSHIT!”

PART VII

BREAKING NEWS

1990s

CHAPTER I

BDK

Good ol' Sammy the bartender...

He'll fix me up good...

ROCK MUSIC BLARED and customers chattered as Sammy swept the floors of his bar, *Ol' Sammy's,* with more urgency than usual.

"When you gonna play it?" asked Tammy-Lynn, the buck-toothed, big-boobed waitress he'd hired last month. She smacked on gum while cleaning tables, occasionally blowing pink bubbles.

"I'll play it later," he said.

Tammy-Lynn held out a stick of cotton candy-flavored Bubble Yum. "Want some?"

"No thanks." Shit's bad for your teeth. Besides, he preferred the blue raspberry flavor. Or purple. Purple was good, too.

Tammy-Lynn blew a pink bubble that hung for a moment, suspended, before bursting.

"Why don't we play it now?" she asked.

"I wanna clean up first."

"Well, I'm poppin' popcorn before we watch it," she said. "Don't lemme forget."

"You actually brought popcorn?"

"Yeah, why not? It's a big deal."

Sammy gazed at the TV above the bar, feeling butterflies in his stomach. She was right—it *was* a big deal.

Might even be the talk of the town.

Sammy swept around the jukebox and yanked the plug. *"Killing in the Name"* died mid-chorus, the machine powering down like a spaceship dropping out of warp. He loved that sound. Reminded him of *Star Trek.*

Then came the next sound he loved: the moans and groans of customers not wanting to leave yet.

"Sorry guys!" he said. "Gotta close up!"

Most everyone shifted in their seats, but only a quarter got up to leave. Always a step-by-step process. *Like herdin' lethargic sheep.* He swept near Tammy-Lynn while she wiped her tables and whispered, "I don't wanna play it 'til everybody's gone..."

She blew a big bubble, smiled and turned to the remaining stragglers.

"C'mon, now!" she said. "Sammy's makin' everybody leave! Even me!"

"We're almost finished!" said Seth, playing a guy at pool. Seth was one of the regulars. He kicked ass at pool.

Slowly, the customers shifted in their seats and rose, moseying toward the exit while finishing stories and trading anecdotes about the usual bullshit.

"C'mon, now!" said Sammy.

A regular sauntered past him. "Gotta get home to your wife and kids, Sammy?"

Sammy emptied the dustpan into the garbage bin. "Yeah, they're waitin' for me..."

"Shiiiit," said another regular. "He ain't got no wife or kids..."

"He will one day!" said Tammy-Lynn. "He's just waitin' for the right girl to come along!"

Sammy smiled. "Oh, I might already have a kid or two." He winked. "Just don't know about'em yet."

Everyone laughed.

That was always a good one.

"Pray that you don't!" said an older guy. Everybody laughed again as they headed into the parking lot.

"Hey," said Sammy, "that Bobby guy is pukin' in the parkin' lot. Can you take a bucket and go cle—"

"Nope," Tammy-Lynn shook her head. "I ain't doin' that. You don't pay me enough."

"Well, all you gotta do is take a bucket and—"

"Nope!" She blew another bubble. "I already played nurse to him today and patched his ass up. I ain't playin' 'parkin' lot janitor' on top of that. That puke-shit's gross."

Sammy shook his head. All she had to do was throw of bucket of water or two on it, dilute the stink. But whatever. Keepin' good waitresses these days was tough, especially with them fancy-ass places like Applebees and TGIF and all that bullshit poppin' up around town. Lucky to even hire her.

"Fine," he said. "I'll do it, then..."

Just gotta be careful not to forget. If he did, all that puke would cook under the sun and smell like sour shit the next day.

He swept near Seth and the long-haired guy he'd been playing pool against.

"C'mon, guys!" said Sammy. "Finish it up!"

"Shit, Sammy," said Seth. "Why you makin' us leave so early tonight?"

"Y'all got money on the game?" asked Sammy.

"Yeah."

"How much?"

"Twenty."

"Whoooo."

Sammy's eyes widened.

That's why Seth sounded pissy.

"Alright, fine," said Sammy. "You got five more mi—"

The sharp crack of a cue ball striking its target cut through the bar.

"Fuck!" said the long-haired guy.

A sly grin crept across Seth's face. "That eight-ball's a bitch, ain't it?"

The long-haired guy put on his cap and thrust a crumpled twenty into Seth's hand, muttering *"Good game, asshole"* while storming out the door.

Seth leaned back against the pool table and chugged the rest of his beer, watching the guy drive off.

"D'you kick his ass?" asked Tammy-Lynn.

"Yep," said Seth.

Sammy snatched Seth's beer mug. "He's gone now. You don't gotta worry about him stabbin' you in the parkin' lot or nothin.'"

"Can never be too careful..." Seth sauntered to the door. "Y'all have a good night, now."

"You too, hun," said Tammy-Lynn. She watched Seth leave, then turned to Sammy.

"Can we watch it now?"

***

Sammy hit rewind on the VCR.

"Why didn't you just watch it when it was on?" asked Tammy-Lynn. She sat at the bar and reached across the counter to pour herself a tequila shot.

Sammy clenched his jaw.

Didn't like her doin' that.

But whatever.

"Nah," said Sammy.

Lots of reasons not to watch it earlier:

One—it would distract him from his job.

Two—wasn't sure if it was good. (And if it wasn't good, that would be *fucking horrifying.*)

Three—he wanted to watch it without any distractions, like in a movie theater.

Tammy-Lynn tossed back her tequila shot with an *"Ahh,"* then blew a massive pink bubble that burst on her face, the sticky mess clinging to her nose and mouth.

"Fuck!" She wiped bubblegum off her face. "Hurry up and play it, Sammy!"

The rewinding clicked to a stop. Part of Sammy yearned to watch it by himself, but Tammy-Lynn was an employee there, too. *Part of the team.* Her feedback might be valuable.

Besides, she was *in* it, too.

Only for like three seconds.

But she was in it.

"Alright." He took a deep breath, pressed play, and stepped back.

"Wait!" Tammy-Lynn bolted up. "The popcorn! I forgot the popcorn!"

Sammy sighed. "You ain't even popped it yet?"

"It's in the microwave! Don't play it yet!"

"Alright..." He pressed pause.

Tammy-Lynn dashed to the kitchen and returned with a full bag of popcorn. Smelled tangy, with hints of herbs and spices.

Mmm...

Might be that new flavored shit...

Tammy-Lynn spat her gum into a napkin then shot it like a basketball into the trashcan behind the bar.

"Alright." She crammed a handful of buttery popcorn into her mouth. "I'm ready. Play it."

Sammy pressed play.

A commercial for Crash Comics played first, followed by another for Mike Smith's Toyota.

"When's it gonna get to you?" she asked.

"It will..." Sammy's heart fluttered. An awful mix of both wanting and dreading to see himself on TV swelled within.

Did I even make the right call?

To spend all that money on a—

"It's you! It's on!" said Tammy-Lynn.

"Hi, my name's Sammy..."

Sammy stood in the empty parking lot with his bar, Ol' Sammy's, *behind him.*

"...and have you ever wanted a bar..."

The camera zoomed in on Sammy's face.

"...where everybody knows your name?"

Sammy stood behind the bar counter, his voice now narrating the action onscreen.

"Have you ever wanted a bar..."

He poured a whiskey shot, spilling a little over the rim.

"That has good drinks..."

He stared blankly at the camera, then crouched behind the bar and rose holding a plate of nachos.

"...and good food?"

The camera zoomed in and out on the nachos.

"...and pool?"

Sammy leaned against the pool table inside his empty bar, holding a cue stick while nodding and smiling.

"...and darts?"

The lights on an electronic darts machine flickered while he pointed at a dart stuck in the bullseye, nodding and smiling at the camera like Christmas had come early.

"...and how about..."

The camera cut to Tammy-Lynn, leaning against the jukebox. After several seconds of looking confused, she pushed her chest out and said, "...and good music, too!"

Tammy-Lynn clapped. "Haha! I'm famous now!"

"Then come on down to Ol' Sammy's!" Sammy strode across his bar's empty parking lot as a Dairy Queen takeout bag floated behind him. "We'll treat you right and we'll treat you good, so you can have a dang good ol' ti—"

"BREAKING NEWS" appeared in large, bold letters on the screen as an urgent news jingle played.

"What the fuck!" said Sammy. "They cut off my commercial!"

"Shh!" said Tammy-Lynn. "It was pretty much over anyway."

"But I paid for the whole damn time slot!"

"Shh!"

"WASD—your source for news in Western Alabama."

A stern-faced news anchor appeared on-screen.

"Good evening. I'm Todd Beaton and we're coming to you a little early this evening to deliver some breaking news. We're going to check in with Amy Watts, our correspondent who was on location earlier today when the Mapleville Chief of Police held a special press conference sharing a shocking update regarding the tragic death of Police Officer James McReynolds. Amy?"

Amy Watts stood in a pink pantsuit beneath a somber gray sky. Police tape cordoned off the small parking lot behind her and the woods beyond. Despite her blonde hair swirling in the wind, her face remained solemn and serious.

"Thanks, Todd," said Amy. "I'm standing here in a small parking lot right beside US Highway 71, where the mutilated body of Officer McReynolds was discovered last..."

"They're talkin' about that dead cop!" said Tammy-Lynn.

"Shh!" said Sammy.

"...with his throat ripped out. Just hours ago, Police Chief McDoogle of the MPD held a special press conference regarding the ongoing investigation."

Chief McDoogle appeared, an elderly man in a police uniform looking well beyond retirement age. Amidst a barrage of camera flashes he shuffled toward a podium, shadowed by an imposing deputy donning aviator sunglasses. The Chief tilted his head and leaned into the microphone, squinting with each camera flash.

"Thank y'all for comin'..." He spoke Southern and slow, his words like ancient molasses flowing from a jar. "We would like to share an update..."

His hand trembled as he pulled notecards from his shirt pocket, fumbling through them.

"...regarding the ongoing investigation into the brutal murder of Officer McReynolds, who was found..."

"See, they *are* callin' it a murder now!" said Tammy-Lynn. "At first they said it was a wild animal! Or bullshit like that!"

"Yep..." said Sammy.

"...we have uncovered a piece of evidence which we believe key to the investigation, and also important to the safety of the citizens of Mapleville."

Amy's voice narrated, "It was then that the Chief made a shocking announcement..."

"As mentioned in our initial report," said Chief McDoogle, "in a small

wooded area near the parkin' lot where the body of Officer McReynold's was found, we had uncovered a..."

Chief McDoogle paused, fumbling with his notecards.

"...we had uncovered...a..."

He cleared his throat.

"...a semen...crusted Barbie doll..."

A roar erupted from the journalists.

The barrage of camera flashes intensified.

"...hangin'...in the branches...of a nearby tree..."

Sammy shook his head. "That is so fucked up..."

"I know..." said Tammy. "I had a bad dream about it after I saw it in the paper..."

The deputy pressed in beside the chief, his hand settling on the grip of his holstered gun.

"Quiet!" he said. "Y'all be f-beep!-ckin' quiet now! Chief McDoogle is tryin' to speak!"

Camera flashes reflected off his sunglasses.

"Y'all shut the f-beep!-k up now!"

He kept one hand on his gun and held out the other, palm open as if to stop a surging crowd.

"Y'all show some f-beep!-ckin' respect! Respect to Chief McDoogle!"

"Let him fuckin' speak!" Tammy-Lynn stuffed popcorn into her mouth.

The journalists' roar lowered to a murmur.

"Thank you, Deputy Duke." Chief McDoogle cleared his throat again and looked at his notecards.

"As we reported earlier, we did not have any evidence that the Barbie itself was connected to the murder of Officer McReynolds, and in fact..." He switched to a new notecard. "...we had initially considered the possibility that it may have been a wild animal attack, due to the nature of the wounds on his throat."

"Bullll-shiiit," said Sammy. "Everybody knew it wasn't no wild-fuckin'-animal. Ain't no animal in the world would do that to a man's throat, but leave the rest of him untouched."

"Mmm-hmm," said Tammy-Lynn. "Would definitely eat his organs and guts and shit."

"...but after interviewin' numerous eyewitnesses," said the Chief, "and

conductin' a thorough investigation of the crime scene, we have discovered evidence of..."

He paused.

"...semen...on the gravel of the parkin' lot..."

He looked up from his notecards.

"Semen from a...a..."

He coughed.

"...human bein'."

The camera flashes intensified.

"Well, what'd they think?" said Sammy. "That a coyote was fuckin', beatin' off and jizzin' everywhere after it—"

"Shh!" said Tammy-Lynn.

"We do now believe that Officer Reynolds was murdered," said the Chief, "and that the semen-crusted Barbie, initially theorized to be unconnected, is possibly linked to his murder."

He looked up from his notecards.

"*In some...kind of way..."*

"No shit, Sherlock!" said Sammy. "What'd you think? That a *semen-covered Barbie doll* found at the crime-scene was a fuckin' coincidence?"

Tammy shook her head, munching on more popcorn.

"...and we would like to ask the public to remain vigilant, and to report any sightin's of any man carryin', or playin' with, or perhaps even..."

He glanced down at his notecards.

"...masturbatin'..."

The camera zoomed on his face.

"...on a...Barbie doll..."

He licked his lips and glanced up at the camera.

Amy's voice narrated, "Chief McDoogle then opened the press conference up to questions, revealing even more *intrigue..."*

"Chief McDoogle," said a journalist. "Do you believe the Barbie Doll Killer is only targeting police officers? Or is he also after the general public?"

"And will BDK strike again?" asked another journalist.

"First off..." The Chief held up a shaky finger. "...we do not refer to him as the Barbie Doll Killer, nor as BDK, as some of y'all in the media have begun callin' him..."He paused, as if he'd forgotten his train of thought. "... and we would like to ask the media, and the general public, to refrain from sensationalizin'...this heinous act of—"

"But will he kill again, Chief McDoogle?" asked the journalist. "And should the citizens of Mapleville be afraid?"

"We have no evidence of any kind of pattern yet," said the Chief, "and we'd like to ask the media to refrain from sensationalizin'..."

"Of course he's gonna kill again," said Sammy. "Guys like that don't stop." He glanced at Tammy-Lynn noshing on popcorn and snatched a handful, too.

Mmm...

This shit was good.

"Chief McDoogle! Chief McDoogle!"

"Yes, the woman in the blue dress," said the Chief. "With the cute little ribbon in her hair."

"Thank you, Chief McDoogle. Can you describe what outfit the Barbie doll was wearing?"

"The fuck does that matter?" said Sam.

"I wanna know..." said Tammy-Lynn.

The Chief paused.

"...she was naked."

He leaned into the microphone.

"...buck naked."

The journalists' chatter surged to a roar. Flashes burst in every direction. The Chief shielded his eyes.

Deputy Duke stepped up beside the Chief and placed his hand on his gun.

"Now what the f-beep!-ck did I just say! Y'all shut the f-beep!-ck up now and let Chief McDoogle speak!"

"That Deputy don't play," said Tammy-Lynn.

"He's probably mad that his buddy got killed," said Sammy. "Can't blame him. I'd be pissed, too..."

"Chief McDoogle! Chief McDoogle!"

"Yes, the woman in the Hawaiian t-shirt. Wearin' them cute lil' purple shorts."

"Thank you, Chief McDoogle. Could you tell us about the murder weapon? Have you determined what BDK used to kill the officer?"

"Due to the nature of the injuries sustained to the Officer's throat," said the Chief, "our forensics team has determined that a bladed weapon was used, perhaps even..."

He shuffled his notecards, then looked at the camera.

"...a pair of scissors."

Uneasy chatter rose from the journalists in waves.

"A scissor-wieldin' maniac," said Tammy-Lynn, "jerkin' off on a Barbie and rippin' people's throats out..." She shook her head. "What is the world comin' too..."

"Goin' to hell in a handbasket." Sammy grabbed another handful of popcorn. "I'll tell ya that right-the-fuck-now..."

"Chief McDoogle! Chief McDoogle!"

"Yes, gentleman with the pink shirt," said the Chief. "And the polka-dot-tie."

"Did the Barbie Doll Killer masturbate on the barbie before, *or* after *he killed the Officer?"*

"Well..." The Chief stroked his chin. "...we suspect before. But we're considerin' all angles at the moment."

"Doesn't that change everything?" asked the journalist.

"Excuse me?" asked the Chief.

"Doesn't the timing *of BDK's masturbation change everything?"*

The Chief looked perturbed. His tone sharpened. "Now, why would you say that?"

Deputy Duke brought his hand to his gun.

"If he masturbated on it after *the murder," said the journalist, "then he was possibly rewarding himself. For killing the officer. But if he masturbated* beforehand, *he...he might've just been angry..."*

"Angry, why?" asked the Chief.

"That, that—"

"Now you listen here," said the Chief, "if you think you're so smart, with your fancy a-beep!-ss college degree, and you wanna play detective, then go the f-beep!-k ahead!"

"Chief McDoogle!" said the journalist. "I wasn't trying to be rude, I just—"

The Chief scowled. "No, no! You go ahead and f-beep!-kin' tell me why!"

Deputy Duke nodded, slowly unfastening his gun holster.

"Now, Mr. Smartypants," said the Chief, "why would BDK have been angry? Huh?"

"Because..." said the journalist. "Because he was interrupted."

"What?" asked the Chief.

"Interrupted," said the journalist. "Angry that his masturbation was

interrupted. Or embarrassed, maybe. Because he got caught, and questioned about it. And maybe that's why he kil—"

"Well," said the Chief. "That's an interestin' little theory you got there, Mr. Smartypants. Maybe you should go write a f-beep!-in' book about it! Next question."

"Who does that journalist think he is?" asked Tammy-Lynn. "Needs to keep his mouth shut about his little theories..."

"That's a know-it-all-journalist for ya," said Sammy. "Like to act like they're fuckin', criminal psychologists or somethin'."

"Needs to stick to his day job," said Tammy-Lynn.

Sammy nodded. "It's obvious a serial killer wouldn't masturbate *before* he killed somebody. It *had* to have been after."

"Mmm-hmm," said Tammy-Lynn. "It *had* to have been after. Just common sense."

"Probably got excited by all the blood and stuff," said Sammy. "So he just, ya know, had to beat off. To release the pressure."

"And then jizz all over the place," said Tammy-Lynn. "Especially on the Barbie doll."

"Yep." Sammy nodded. "Especially on that."

"Chief McDoogle! Chief! McDoogle!"

"Yes, the man in the back," said the Chief. "With the Where's Waldo-lookin' shirt. And the tie with large pineapples on it."

"What if—"

"Now," said the Chief, "you ain't gonna be a Mr. f-beep!-in' Smartypants, too, is ya?"

"No, Chief McDoogle, I'm not, I—"

"Good. Now ask your question, son."

"Yes, sir. What if someone sees a man at a toy store purchasing a Barbie doll? Should they be alarmed? And should they call 9-1-1?"

"Uhh..." The Chief looked surprised. "Well, if a father is buyin' a Barbie for...legitimate purposes, for example...for his little daughter or somethin', then..."

"Nope," said Sammy. "Even if you *do* got a little daughter, if buy her a Barbie now, you'll probably get arrested or fuckin' shot, right then and there."

Tammy-Lynn narrowed her eyes. "Ain't a good time for dads to be buyin' their daughters that kinda shit..."

"Uh-huh..." said Sammy. "I wouldn't wanna be caught dead with *any* fuckin' Barbie dolls, I'll tell ya that right now." He grabbed another handful of popcorn. "This is pretty good. It's like, flavored and shit, right?

"Yeah, it's the new ranch flavor."

"Mmm..." He made a mental note to buy some later on. Shit was good.

"Chief McDoogle," asked a journalist, "can you share the description of BDK? Of the Barbie Doll Killer?"

"We have conflictin' reports of the man's appearance," said the Chief. "As we shared previously, Officer McReynolds was investigatin' reports made by people drivin' by a wooded area, claimin' they saw a man at night with his pants down, grippin' an object real tight-like *in his hand."*

"How'd they know he was grippin' it *real tight-like*?" asked Tammy-Lynn.

"How else you grip somethin'?" asked Sammy.

"...some say he was real big, some say real small," said Chief McDoogle. "This leads us to conclude he's about medium-sized. And regardin' his race, some claimed he was Black, but others claimed he was white, or possibly even Hispanic..."

"About medium-sized, and either Black, white, or even Hispanic," said Sammy. "That fuckin' narrows it down."

"At least we know he ain't Asian," said Tammy-Lynn.

Deputy Duke leaned in front of the Chief, speaking to the mic.

"I just got somethin' to say to you, BDK, because I know you're f-beep!-ckin' watchin' this."

"Oh shit..." said Tammy-Lynn.

"We're gonna find you, and we're bringin' justice with us," said Deputy Duke. "J-U-S-T-I—"

"Now, Deputy Duke—" said the Chief.

"And there ain't nowhere you can f-beep!-'in hide! McReynolds was one of us!"

Deputy Duke drew his gun and pointed it upward. The journalists erupted. Camera flashes surged.

"Sweet, sweet justice is comin' for ya, BDK!" he said. "And we don't care if you're Black, white or even Hispanic—"

Chief McDoogle snatched the mic back with a trembling hand.

"Thank you, Deputy Duke, for that little extra warnin'," said the Chief. "This press conference is over now. No more questions, please."

"Chief McDoogle! Chief McDoogle!"

The camera flashes returned.

"One more question! One more question!"

The Chief turned back to the microphone.

"Y'all have a good day, now."

The camera cut to Amy, striding across the parking lot with the woods in the background.

"I actually had a chance to speak with some of those key eye-witnesses myself," she said, "and here's what they had to say..."

The camera cut to a shirtless, mullet-haired, bearded white man. He wore a camo cap and stood by a pickup truck.

Amy's voice narrated, "We spoke with Darryl Holland, who often drove by the murder-site on his way from work..."

"And I called the po-lice, three or four f-beep!-in' times," said Darryl, "lettin'em know there was a guy in the woods. With his pants down. Grippin' somethin' real tight-like..."

The camera cut to an elderly black woman, rocking chair in a chair on her porch.

"And Esther Parker," said Amy, "a local African-American woman who's been a resident of the area near the grisly murder site for decades..."

"I tell ya," said Esther. "I been livin' here 'bout sixty, sixty-five years now. And I ain't never seen nothin' like it."

Amy's voice narrated, "Esther was the first to call the police when she noticed something strange..."

"I called the cops," said Esther. "Multiple times. They didn't believe me." She shook her head. "They didn't give no f-beep!-ks."

Amy continued. "Police received reports of a man with his pants down, standing in a wooded area beside US Highway 71..."

"Sir." Amy held a microphone to Darryl's face. "You're claiming that you saw BDK, is this correct?"

"Yep," said Darryl. "I mean, I dunno if he was no, f-beep!-in' BDK or nothin'. But yeah, I seen a guy."

"Where did you see him, sir?"

"Right there in them woods." Darryl pointed towards the trees behind him. "I'd be drivin' in my truck, on my way home, and more than a couple of times I f-beep!-in' seen him."

"Could you describe him for us?"

"I mean, he was just a guy with his pants pulled down...don't know how else to describe him..."

He paused, his mouth hanging open while he stared into space.

"...usually wearin' tighty-whities..."

"And Mrs. Parker," said Amy to Esther, "when did you see BDK?"

"Well, whenever I drove home or down to the grocery store, I'd see him at night." Esther rocked in her chair. "The lights from the cars drivin' by made his tighty-whities as bright as the moon..."

"And what was he doing, sir?" Amy asked Darryl. "With his pants pulled down? In his underwear?"

Darryl spat. "Couldn't tell. But he was always holdin' somethin' real tight-like *in his left hand..."*

"He was beatin' off on a muthaf-beep!-in' Barbie doll!" said Esther. She rocked faster in her chair. "I seen his a-beep!-ss! I seen his lil' pervert a-beep!-ss multiple times! Always had his big butt facin' the highway! With his lil' p-beep!-nis pulled through the pee-hole of his tighty-whities!"

"Was he holding a Barbie doll, sir?" Amy asked Darryl.

"...I mean...I don't know what he was holdin'..." said Darryl. "But yeah, it might've been."

"Do you think he was masturbating on it?" asked Amy. "On the Barbie doll?"

"What?"

"Masturbating," said Amy. "Was BDK masturbating on the Barbie doll?"

"I...uhh..." Darryl's eyes widened. "...ya know, I ain't no expert on masturbation'or nothin', so I can't say...I was drivin' real fast..." He shrugged. "...I mean, he could've been doin' anything."

Amy's tone sharpened. "Could he have been masturbating *on it, sir?"*

"...I mean...yeah, I guess...he could've been masturbatin' on it or somethin'...a little...I dunno..."

"He was jerkin' off on a muthaf-beep!-ckin' Barbie doll!" said Esther. "A hundred f-beep!-ckin' percent! And now he done killed an officer of the law! The people that's supposed to be protectin' us! And he's on the f-beep!-ckin' loose!"

"See?" said Sammy. "That Black lady knows whats up."

"Black people just tell it straight," said Tammy-Lynn. "They call it like they see it."

"I mean," said Sammy, "this white dude, he couldn't even put his shirt on for the interview? And we're supposed to trust him?"

"It has been real hot out lately, though," said Tammy-Lynn.

Sammy nodded. "Yeah, it has..."

Amy thrust the microphone in Darryl's face. He pulled back, squinting at the camera.

"And what did the Barbie Doll Killer look like?" asked Amy.

"Uhh...ya know, I mainly just saw his underwear," said Darryl. "It was real white. And real big."

"So he was a big man?" asked Amy. "Larger than normal?"

"Yeah, he might've been pretty big. But not real *big. Ya know, 'bout medium-sized, I guess."*

"Was he white?" she asked. "Or Black? Or possibly even Hispanic?"

"I mean, uhh..." said Darryl. "He might've been Black."

"So he was Black?"

"Yep, a big Black dude." He shrugged. "Maybe."

"Could he have even been Hispanic?"

"Yep, yep." Darryl nodded. "Definitely could've been Hispanic, too. Mixed race or somethin'. Definitely."

"He was white!" said Esther. "He wasn't no f-beep!-ckin' Black dude! Black people don't do weird sh-beep!-t like that! That's f'-beep!-cked up white people sh-beep!-t! That's some Silence of the Lambs *sh-beep!-t right there!"*

"And how do you feel, sir," Amy asked Darryl, "knowing that you're one of the few people to actually see *the Barbie Doll Killer, before he became famous?"*

"I mean, uhh..." said Darryl. "...pretty good, I guess..."

"And why is that?" asked Amy.

"What?"

"Why do you feel good about that, sir?"

"Well, everybody's talkin' to me about it now. Some guy's writin' a book about it. Wants to pay me good for an interview."

"Do you feel as safe as you used to?" asked Amy.

"What?"

"Now that you're a key witness in the Barbie Doll Killer investigation," asked Amy. "Do you still feel safe?"

"I mean, yeah. I guess."

"You're not afraid that BDK will choose you *as his next target?"*

Darryl's mouth dropped.

"You're not afraid*?" Amy shoved the microphone in Darryl's face. He*

recoiled. "You're not afraid," she asked, "that he'll do to you, what he did to Officer McReynolds? With a pair of scissors?"

"Well, I mean," said Darryl, "I got my double-barrel twelve-gauge, so I ain't afraid of no Edward f-beep!-in' Scissorhands, if that's what ya mean..."

Tammy-Lynn clapped and nodded. "Hah-hah! That's fuckin' right!"

Sammy shook his head. "But that dude's a *key* eyewitness. I don't care if he's got a twelve-gauge, he's stupid goin' on TV runnin' his mouth like that. If I was BDK, he'd be the *first* motherfucker I'd take out."

Tammy-Lynn shrugged. "Yeah, I guess so..."

"I bet BDK's watchin' this shit right now," said Sammy. "Playing with his Barbie doll, twirlin' his scissors, ready to take'em both out."

"Could be," said Tammy-Lynn. "You got a point. He's probably thinkin', *'Thanks WASD, "for tellin' me who I gotta* kill *next."*"

They both grabbed handfuls of popcorn.

"...but I guess I will tell my daughters." said Darryl. "Not to play with no dude, or talk to no dude, that's holdin' no f-beep!-in' Barbie doll. Especially if he's, ya know..."

He spat.

"...masturbatin' on it or somethin'..."

"Are you afraid?" *asked Amy to Esther.* "Afraid *for the lives of your children and grandchildren? And for yourself?"*

"Oh, I ain't worried about myself," said Esther. "I keep a Colt .45 under my pillow. Every night."

"But what about your—"

"If Edward f-beep!-ckin' Scissorhands wants to visit me, I'm f-beep!-ckin' ready!" She leaned back and cackled.

Sammy and Tammy-Lynn both cackled, too.

"But what about your children?" asked Amy. "And your grandchildren?"

Esther's laugh faded.

"Well, I don't let my grandkids play with no Barbie dolls no more..." She narrowed her eyes. "...I'll tell ya that right now."

"There you have it," said Amy, back in the parking lot. "Two innocent citizens of Mapleville, living afraid..."

Ominous music played.

The camera zoomed on Amy's face.

"Afraid for their lives, and for the lives of their children and grandchildren..."

A pixelated split-screen image of Darryl and Esther appeared.

"Afraid they'll become the next targets..."

Gradually, a naked Barbie materialized in the center.

"...of the Barbie Doll Killer."

Beneath the Barbie doll, the letters "BDK" *oozed into view, thick red blood dripping from them.*

The camera cut back to anchorman Todd Beaton.

"Wow." He shook his head. "Chilling. Now, police have released a sketch of the Barbie Doll Killer that they'd like shown to the public, which we'll show onscreen."

A sketch appeared of a pudgy, balding man gripping a naked Barbie doll. His race remained unclear; he could have been Black, white, or even Hispanic.

"That could be any guy in the state of Alabama!" said Tammy-Lynn.

"Yep," said Sammy. "I see fifty motherfuckers like that a week."

"For now," said Todd, "the police are recommending citizens of Mapleville and neighboring areas to avoid all wooded areas, and keep an eye out for any medium-sized man carrying a Barbie doll, especially *if he's masturbating on it. If you do see such an individual, they advise that you stay calm, avoid approaching him and immediately call 9-1-1. Remember that he is considered armed and dangerous, and could be Black, white, or possibly even...Hispanic."*

Todd's grave expression switched to a warm and sunny smile.

"Next up is Cal, with the weather," said Todd. "Cal, how are we lookin' next week?"

"Well, next week's looking hot and sunny, Todd, with a chance of rain on..."

"I'm headin' out." Tammy-Lynn tossed the popcorn bag into the trashcan. "Your commercial looked *real* good, Sammy."

She winked at him.

"Especially that hot girl you got starrin' in it."

"I'm glad you liked it," said Sammy. "Oh, and watch out for BDK!"

Tammy laughed, heading out the door. *"I will..."*

Sammy hit rewind. The tape whirred as the screen flickered past distorted frames until the police sketch jolted back into view. He pressed pause. Faint lines crawled down the suspect's face.

Somethin' about that sketch...

It did resemble lots of guys he saw all the time, for sure, but it also looked *just like* someone he—

"Hey, Sam?" Tammy-Lynn poked her head through the front door. "That Bobby guy's still in the parking lot. He's lookin' kinda weird."

"More than usual?"

"Yeah."

"Alright, I'll check on him."

She said bye again, closing the door. Sammy stared at the police sketch a bit longer, lost in thought. After a few moments, he shook his head, then headed outside.

"Hey Bobby," he called across the parking lot. "You alright, man?"

Bobby stood behind his car, frozen, like he forgot where he was. Vomit and drool dangled from his chin.

"Hey!" said Sammy. "You alright, man?"

Bobby didn't answer.

Didn't even blink.

"Hey, brother?" Sammy took a step forward. "You good to drive?"

Bobby shuddered, then sucked up his dangling drool-vomit with a loud *slurping* sound. He turned to Sammy and smiled, chin glistening in the moonlight.

"Y-yep, yep..." he said. "...I'm al—riiiiiight, *brotherrr...*"

"Okay!" Sammy nodded. "Well, see ya next time, man!"

He waited for Bobby to get in his car, but Bobby just stood there.

Not moving.

Not blinking.

Just smiling.

A glob of vomit slid off his chin, splattering on the gravel.

"...o-kayyy..." said Sammy.

He went back inside and locked the door, watching Bobby stand in the parking lot, still *smiling.*

"Man, am I gonna have to call that motherfucker a cab or somethin'..."

The police sketch remained paused on his TV, casting an eerie glow across the bar.

Something about that sketch...

He stared at the sketch a moment more, then turned his gaze back to the parking lot. Bobby had finally driven off.

"Wait a minute..."

Balding.
Pudgy.
Belly stickin' out.
Round face and weirdo-lookin'.
Kinda like—
Nah...
He switched the TV off.
Bobby was a weirdo, alright.

But he wouldn't hurt a fly.

PART VIII

FORTUNA BRUTALIS

"Even the Romans knew how to act like Blackbeard, ese! They didn't play around!"

Blackbeard: The Man Who Scourged the Seas
By: Roberta Stevenson
CHAPTER 14
Across Eras: Examples of Blackbeard-style Brutality Throughout History

(pg. 128) Not only Blackbeard, but various nations and leaders throughout history have understood that brutality not only *saves* lives, but can truly *finish* a conflict, as well.

Japan: The Empire that Started It

On December 07th, 1941, Japan launched a surprise attack on the US Naval Base at Pearl Harbor, killing more than 3000 Americans. *They didn't even declare war before attacking.* But this proved a strategic blunder, as their surprise attack enraged a nation which knew how to wield *brutality* to end a conflict.

America: The Nation that Finished It

What was America's response?

They retaliated in full force, defeating Japan in numerous epic battles across land and sea, pushing the Japanese Empire back all the way to their home islands.

But when asked for an unconditional surrender, Japan promised to fight on: every man, woman, and child stood ready to die defending their nation, fighting hand-to-hand, house-to-house if need be!

→ ***Did You Know?*** *The Japanese government handed out pamphlets urging families to prepare for an American invasion. Civilians were taught to fight to the death with makeshift weapons. Even children were trained to use their small size as an advantage: grab something sharp, aim for the legs!*

At this point in history, America faced three epic choices:

1) Make peace with Japan, but agree to some of their terms.

Instead of demanding unconditional surrender, the U.S. could have relented, allowing Japan to keep parts of its empire. The war would have ended sooner, but it may have laid the groundwork for future vengeance; a never-ending cycle of conflict and retaliation waiting to ignite.

2) Invade Japan and fight every last Japanese citizen in brutal house-to-house combat.

With overwhelming military superiority, the U.S. would have likely prevailed, eliminating the threat of future retaliation. But the cost would be staggering: estimates projected up to 1,000,000 American soldiers and nearly 20 million Japanese dead, making it the bloodiest invasion in human history.

3) Do something unspeakably brutal, saving lives on both sides.

We'll never know if President Harry S. Truman was a fan of Blackbeard or not, but his decision would have made the legendary pirate proud. Truman ordered an *atomic bomb* to be dropped on the Japanese city of Hiroshima, obliterating it from existence.

→ ***Did You Know?*** *An atomic bomb is like a normal bomb, but way more powerful. Just one can destroy an entire city, wiping it off the face of the map!*

After Hiroshima, America demanded Japan accept an unconditional surrender, *but Japan still said no!* Even after such awful destruction on a scale never before seen in the theater of war, they still refused. Maybe they thought America only had *one* atomic bomb, or maybe they were simply *so hardcore they didn't care.* (We'll never know.) But America didn't give up, either: they dropped *another* atomic bomb on the Japanese city of Nagasaki, obliterating in a sea of fire just like Hiroshima.

"Next time, it's Tokyo," said America, threatening Japan's very capital with annihilation.

After losing two entire cities to the most destructive weapon in world history, Japan *finally* relented, agreeing to an unconditional surrender.

→ ***Did You Know?*** *America actually bluffed when they threatened Tokyo. That was their last atomic bomb! Good thing Japan fell for it, or one of your grandpas might have died in the invasion, and you wouldn't be born.*

Although a staggering 110,000 Japanese citizens died due to the atomic bombings, *millions* would have perished in a land invasion. By committing two of the most brutal acts in the history of warfare, America actually *saved* millions of lives.

America may not have started it, but they sure did finish it!

Rome and Carthage: War Over Centuries

Even civilizations long before the era of Blackbeard understood that brutality saved lives and prevented further conflict. Let's travel back in time, to the days of the Roman Republic and the Carthage Empire!

Carthage: The Empire that Started It

You may have learned about the Romans in school, but did you learn about Carthage? The Carthaginian Empire spanned northern Africa and southern Europe, rivaling the Roman Republic for dominance across the Mediterranean.

Over the course of an entire century, Carthage and Rome fought three separate wars called "The Punic Wars." The First Punic War began when Carthage, nervous of Rome's growing power and expansion, declared war on Rome and launched an attack on Sicily. At the time, the Romans barely even had a navy, but despite the odds, they somehow secured victory.

After losing the First Punic War, Carthage thirsted for revenge and nearly destroyed Rome in The Second Punic War when their top general, Hannibal, invaded Italy.

→ ***Did You Know?*** *During the Battle of Cannae, Hannibal orchestrated one of the most devastating defeats ever inflicted upon a military force in history, slaughtering nearly 80,000 Roman soldiers in a single day. It wasn't until the Battle of the Somme, more than two thousand years later in World War I, that more soldiers died in a single day.*

Even after such a history-making defeat, Rome refused to discuss *any* terms of peace. After seventeen years of endless warfare, Rome finally defeated Hannibal at the Battle of Zama, ending the Second Punic War.

Rome: The Republic that Finished It

In the aftermath of the Second Punic War, Rome decided *enough was enough.* Instead of waiting for Carthage to attack them, *they* attacked Carthage, beginning the Third Punic War. After a string of hard-fought victories, Roman forces finally surrounded the capital city of Carthage, demanding their unconditional surrender.

Just like Japan in World War II, however, Carthage refused.

So what could Rome do?

As we did with America, let's review Rome's choices at the time:

1) Make peace with Carthage, agreeing to some of their terms.

Rome could have relented, agreeing to some of Carthage's terms and allowing them to retain portions of their Empire. This would have ended the war and greatly weakened Carthage, but over time, they would have recovered—just as they had after the First and Second Punic Wars.

And—*just as they had before*—Carthage would have thirsted for vengeance, leading to countless more Punic Wars.

2) Lay siege to the city of Carthage, starving them into submission.

Rome actually attempted this, laying siege to Carthage for three whole years. Keeping their own massive army fed and supplied for so long posed a massive challenge, though, placing a significant strain on their own resources. Roman soldiers likely got bored and homesick, too!

3) Inflict unspeakable brutality on Carthage, saving lives on both sides.

Although we'll never know how Blackbeard felt about The Punic Wars, we can assume he approved of Rome's ultimate decision to *inflict brutality* on the Carthaginians, ending their conflict forever.

But what *brutality* could Rome have wrought upon Carthage?

After all, atomic bombs didn't exist back then—they didn't even have airplanes!

In an act of brutality unrivaled in nearly all of history, Rome invaded the city of Carthage, taking *no prisoners.* This means they fought house-by-house, street-by-street, killing every single Carthaginian they came across: every man, woman, and child. They even killed the babies!

But they didn't stop there!

After committing genocide, Rome systematically razed the entire city to the ground, demolishing every last building and statue. They even set the rubble on fire!

And did they stop there?

Nope!

Rome sought to erase the very *memory* of Carthage from history, destroying all Carthaginian literature, art, and historical records. They even struck the name "Carthage" from their maps.

Wow!

Carthage simply ceased to exist after The Third Punic war. It's estimated that nearly 750,000 Carthaginians died in the slaughter, far more than even in the atomic bombings of Japan!

Rome didn't play around, did they?

But after fighting Carthage for more than a century, we can understand why Rome took such drastic measures. If they had simply given Carthage a slap on the wrist and taken territory and gold as tribute, the conflicts would have never ended! *They might even be fighting to this very day.* It took an act of Blackbeard-style inhumane brutality to truly end things.

Rome may not have started it, but they sure did finish it!

→ ***Vocabulary Question:*** *Do you know what "inhumane" means? "Inhumane" describes actions or behaviors exhibiting extreme cruelty and a lack of compassion towards others, disregarding their well-being, dignity, or fundamental rights as human beings. To act inhumane toward someone is usually a bad thing, except when it's not.*

Brutality: Saving Lives Across History

These two historical examples, both modern and ancient, showcase just how many lives Blackbeard-style brutality can *save* when applied effectively and decisively. Blackbeard may not have lived during the times of Ancient Rome or World War II, but his strategy of inflicting *true brutality* can be discovered throughout the rich pages of history.

Now let's return to the present and learn how you can be awesome and legendary, just like Blackbeard!

Turn the page to become brutal!

Discussion Exercises—Talk With Your Friends!

1. Japan went from being America's worst enemy to one of its strongest allies and economic partners, and is now one of the most peaceful countries in the world. Why do you think Japan changed so much?

2. Some people feel that Rome and Carthage were destined to be enemies, that America and Japan were destined to go to war. Do you feel that some people are destined to be your friends, or your enemies? Why or why not?

3. Have you ever had an enemy who later became your friend?

4. What about the opposite: a friend who became an enemy?

1970s

CHAPTER I

THE OATH

"A man is only as good as his word."

LA HACIENDA

Charlie held the Blackbeard book high as he stood on the living room table with his shoes off.

"This book has got all y'all need to know! About life, and how to fuckin' live it!"

Bill, Graham and Kenny sat before him, like a congregation.

"Do y'all wanna live like a fuckin' *Posse?"* asked Charlie. "Or like a bunch of bitches?"

"Like a fuckin' Posse!"

Charlie shot his finger at the stain on the carpet.

"That, right there! What the fuck is that?"

"Disrespect!"

"That's disrespect, Charlie!"

"We don't tolerate that!"

"That, right there, is fuckin' disrespect," said Charlie. "And *hellll no* we don't tolerate none of that!"

"Hellll no!"

"We don't tolerate none *of that!"*

"You tolerate disrespect," said Charlie, "even once, then it invites *more* disrespect!"

"I ain't about that shit!"

"Me neither!"

"Let's fuck shit up!"

Charlie bent over and locked eyes with each of them, holding their gaze.

"Y'all know what we gotta do..."

BILL

Bill stared at his reflection in Charlie's car window. Dark circles ringed his bloodshot eyes. Somehow, *by the grace of God*, his sunglasses and cowboy hat remained intact.

The rest of him, not so much.

All his fingers had been fuckin' *smashed* and just about every other body part had gotten fuckin' *thwacked* by the crowbar of a crystal meth-pumped weedboy more times than he could count.

He pulled up his sleeve. A ring of human teeth marks encircled a bruised-black core. Blood and yellowish-clear liquid seeped from the bite.

Need some hydrogen peroxide on that shit...

"I can't..." Charlie winced as he reached for the bag of cocaine on the floorboard. "...I can't even bend down, man..."

'Cause your ribs are probably fractured, Charlie...

And it's gonna hurt worse as the day goes on.

They all needed to visit the hospital after this—and tell'em they did a whole lotta roughhousin'.

"Fuck it..." said Charlie.

Charlie gave up and dropped to his knees, cussing in Spanish and English ("motherfuckin' *puta madre!")* before he finally grabbed the cocaine.

"You okay for this last part?" asked Bill. "You sure you still wanna do *everything?"*

Surely, Charlie wouldn't need to do *everything* now.

Not after today.

Charlie tilted his head back, as if searching the sky for an answer. After a moment of silence, he tossed his broken sunglasses into the car, then locked eyes with Bill.

"I sure fuckin' do."

LESLIE

Leslie could finally move.

Barely.

It took a shit-ton of effort, but she could *move.*

"...fuuuuuck..."

Her eyelids clung together as if sealed with cement. Through sheer force of will, she pushed them open.

Light.

Light spilled through shattered windows.

People.

People groanin'. Stirrin'. Wakin' up.

Lacey...

Lacey lay on the floor, mouth agape and drooling, still asleep, stoned as fuck.

The Boys...

That chaotic nightmare shit she'd heard earlier—

—was that *real?*

("charlie!")

("don't let him snort that shit!")

Shards of glass mixed with blood-caked powder lay on the floor. Flecks of red dotted the carpet, walls and sofas.

Fuuuuuuck...

Maybe that shit *had* been real.

Even her purple bracelet had dried, crusty blood on it. *Gross.*

Clomp-clomp!

Heavy boots behind her.

She turned toward the front door.

That Kenny guy, Skinny Kenny or whatever, stood there shirtless in a cowboy hat and aviator sunglasses, wearing a lopsided grin. He had that off-kilter look—skin tanned and cheekbones sharp, like an outlaw Comanche from a Western, but wavy brown hair brushed his shoulders, too smooth for the rest of him. Dried blood streaked his face like warpaint and his lower lip had swollen to the size of a roll of nickels. Ugly bruises mottled his arms and torso, blotched like camouflage.

Holy fuuuuck...

That shit was *fuckin' real...*

"Sup, Leslie..." His voice sounded cracked and hoarse. He scanned the living room, then hit rewind on the boombox by the door.

"...whaaarrt..." she said. "...whaaarrt harrppened..."

Fuck.

Could barely talk.

Could barely move her fucking tongue.

"Thur....Borrys..."

The Boys.

Had they gotten their asses whooped?

Then why were Bill and his guys *still* here?

A single fly buzzed by her face, slow, lazy, and loud. It circled once. She flinched and batted it away.

The tape clicked. Kenny heaved the boombox on his shoulder and pressed play.

The speakers hissed. A soft pop.

Then—*metal.*

Heavy fuckin' metal, the kind she'd heard in her dreams, ripped through the house.

Kenny flashed a demented smile.

"We got a show for y'all today."

BILL

As various dudes and chicks groggily pulled themselves up to the windows of the Smokehouse, Bill couldn't help but feel recharged.

An audience.

Destiny had granted'em an *audience* for this.

Just like his dreams had shown him.

Despite his pain, his pace quickened as he and Charlie strode up the hill toward Kenny, Graham, and the tied-up weedboys. Something about an audience, it *gave him* something, a kind of energy he needed now.

Just enough to finish the job.

***

Bill nodded to the heavy metal jamming from Charlie's boombox. For the fourth time since they'd tied their asses up, he re-counted the weedboys—this time in *español,* to keep his Spanish sharp:

Uno—Glick.

Dos—Longface.

Tres—Mickey Mouse.

Cuatro—The Jack dude.

Cinco—Asian boy.

And...

He furrowed his eyebrows.

Couldn't remember Spanish numbers after that.

Fuck it.

Six—Grape-grape-jelly dude.

Seven and Eight—Two other "Possibles." Forgot their names.

Eight.

Eight fuckin' weedboys.

Not a single one missin'.

Most of the Possible boys couldn't even sit up, instead just lay face-planted in the grass, frothin' at the mouth like rabid animals and shit. They'd thought the Jack guy had died at first, but later realized his pulse just beat *real* fuckin' faint. Apparently spasmed a ton after he knocked Graham's tooth out. Guess that crystal meth shit didn't sit well with him.

Kneelin' and tied up, Glick, Longface, and Mickey Mouse looked like them German kid-soldiers he'd seen in his history books, dragged from the sewers in the Battle of Berlin. Bewildered, but defeated, with a thousand-yard stare in their eyes. Maybe finally graspin' just how defeated they really were.

He coughed.

His ribs burned like fire.

Y'all fought hard...

He spat, locking eyes with Glick.

But in the end...

Y'all fuckin' lost.

Glick glared right back, seething with hatred.

"How's your arm?" asked Kenny. His voice sounded hoarse and raspy, like he'd crossed a desert.

"Fuckin' hurts," said Bill. "Remind me to never fight an Asian boy fucked up on drugs again..."

Blood wept from the Asian kid's eyes, nose, and mouth. Little dude knew how to fuckin' *bite.* Still mumblin' in Chinese under his breath, *"nae anae, nae anae"* or shit like that.

"I *knew* that boy spoke somethin' Asian," said Charlie. "I mean, he is fuckin' Asian, after all."

He handed Kenny a tequila RC and Graham a baggie of coke. "Here's y'all some refreshments."

Like Bill, Kenny had somehow managed to preserve his sunglasses, but the fucking Possibles had made it a *priority* to get rid of Graham's. One of'em—the grape-grape-jelly dude—stomped'em on the floor before takin' a potshot with the water gun.

The water gun.

What was *that* bullshit about?

"Now wait a minute," said Bill. "Who's got that water gun they kept tryin' to shoot?"

"SNRRK!"

Graham snorted coke off the back of his hand with a crumpled dollar bill. Bloody drool swayed from his mouth. He'd thrown his sunglasses back on, not givin' a damn they only had one lens. Looked kinda ridiculous. But whatever.

"I think *you* got it, Bill." Kenny gulped his tequila RC, his rhythmic nod returning.

"Oh."

Bill patted his jeans.

Shit had gotten so crazy he'd forgotten.

"...the hell's in this thing?" He examined the water gun from all sides, like it had a secret switch. A thick red liquid flowed from one end to the other like magma.

"Kentucky Blood sauce," said Graham.

"BRAAAAP!"

He belched.

"They were tryin' to shoot my eyes," said Graham. "I think..."

"Kentucky Blood sauce?" asked Bill.

"*SNRRK!*"

Graham snorted another line, then narrowed his eyes at the weedboys while wiping blood from his mouth.

"Yeah," said Graham. "The *extra-hot* kind..."

"Es delicioso, amigo," said Charlie. "You ain't tried it before?"

Bill shook his head, gazing at the water gun.

So that's *what the water gun shit was about...*

If they'd actually shot Graham in his eyes...

He shuddered, imagining how things might've gone in a very different, terrible direction for him and his Posse.

Could've been trouble.

Real fuckin' trouble.

His dreams hadn't shown him anything about a water gun, and if they hadn't shown him *everything*—if they'd missed important fuckin' details like the water gun and that crystal meth bullshit—what *else* had he missed?

What else would he miss—

—in the future?

He tilted his head to the sky.

We barely won this...

Why didn't I see everything?

He lowered his head back down, meeting Glick's hate-filled stare.

And what am I gonna miss next?

"Whose idea was this?" asked Bill. "Huh?"

Bill strode to the front of the weedboys, raising the water gun in the air.

"Whose idea was it," asked Bill, "to fuckin' squirt Graham in the eyes with this shit?"

"...mine..." said Mouse. "...it was mine..."

He coughed blood.

"...gay-ass cowboy motherf—"

In one liquid motion, Bill lowered the water gun and flicked his wrist.

A sharp stream hit Mouse square in the eyes.

BILL

At first, Mouse only blinked.

Then, after a few seconds, he let out a deep, guttural scream.

"AAAAAAAAAAAAAAAAAAAAAAARRRRRRRRAAAAAAAAGH!"

"How's that feel, motherfucker?" asked Bill.

"AAAAAAARRRRRRRRRRRRRRRRRRAAAAAAAAAAAAAA AGH!"

"Ándale!" said Charlie. "That's for tryin' to bust Graham-cracker's kneecap!"

"Huh huh huh..." chuckled Graham.

"OHHHHHH GODDDDDDDDDDDDDD!"

"That's right, motherfucker!" said Kenny.

"IT BURRRRRRRRRRRRRNS!"

A crooked grin crept across Kenny's face. He brought his tequila RC to his lips and snickered. Longface and Glick started yellin' some bullshit, but who gave a fuck.

"God, shut their asses up," said Bill. "Charlie, you still got them bandanas?"

"I sure fuckin' do, Bill." Charlie pulled out three Kentucky state flag bandanas from his backpack and tied'em around the weedboys' mouths, muffling Mouse's screams and the whinin' from Longface and Glick.

"Alright, boys," said Bill. "Let's get that Colombia marchin' powder in us, then do what we gotta do."

More people ambled to the shattered windows and front porch. Bill stood a little straighter, jaw tight.

Time to finish the fuckin' job.

He nodded and tipped his cowboy hat at the onlookers on the porch.

They nodded back, looking confused.

ZANE

"Zeke..." said Zane.

Zane gave Zeke a shove.

Nothin'.

Still dead to the world.

"Buncha crazy shit went down. Wake up."

He shoved him again, harder this time.

Fuck.

Fuckin' lightweight when it came to drinkin' and drugs and shit. Wild like a bobcat, but a lightweight. Would leave him be, then.

Zane ripped off that stupid purple bracelet the birdboys made him wear *(gay as fuck...)* then patted his head.

Bandana still on.

Rebel flag, still facin' straight.

Good.

He scanned the room. Dudes and chicks sprawled out everywhere. Some wakin' up, some not. Mainly Crows. A few he knew.

Oh.

A Zion bitch.

In the corner, passed out on a beanbag.

An idea slithered in; a good one.

Still high and groggy as fuck, Zane stumbled over to the Zion bitch and unzipped his fly.

"Here's your breakfast drank..."

A hot stream splashed the Zion bitch's cheek: sharp-smellin', dark yellow. Perfect.

"...uhhhrrmmf..."

Barely twitched.

Just moaned like a zombie while gettin' pissed on.

Look at you!

Moanin' like the little Zion bitch you is!

Zane snickered, aimed lower, right at that dumbass Polo logo.

Who wears Ralph-fuckin'-Lauren to a house party?

Zion bitches.

That's who.

Who best keep to themselves in Zion.

He shook out the last drops, spat on the bitch's face for good measure, then zipped up, nice and slow.

Good way to start the mornin'.

TOMMY

Tommy bit down on the Kentucky state flag bandana stuffed in his mouth, cotton soaked with spit, tasting like old denim. Mouse screamed and writhed beside him. Graham, apparently unsatisfied with the back of his hand, tried snorting coke off the stairway banister—

"SNRRK!"

— with a crumpled dollar bill. Between snorts, he spat blood, grinning through the gap where a front tooth used to be.

Good.

We knocked one of your front teeth clean out...

And sliced your belly open, too, you fat fuck...

We fuckin' hurt *you.*

Him and his Boys may have lost—

"AAAAAAAHHHHRRRRRRRMMMM!" screamed Mouse through the bandana.

—but they put up a hell of a fight.

"...nae anae...nae anae..."

Especially David.

Fuckin' went *wild* on'em, then bit the shit out of Bill's arm.

Would make him an honorary Smoketown Boy, ASAP.

Would make *all* the Possibles full-fledged Smoketown Boys, but especially David.

"...nae anae..."

After they'd bought him a new pair of glasses.

"...nae anae..."

And gotten his eyes checked by a doctor and shit.

"BRAAAAP!"

Graham belched after a swig of Kenny's tequila RC, then sat down and pulled up his jeans to reveal red shin guards—hard plastic ones, the kind catchers used in baseball.

Tommy's jaw dropped.

Fucking *shin guards?*

How *the fuck* did they know?

Did one of his Boys let it slip?

Their *cross-attack* strategy?

That would've fucking worked?
No. Not one of his Boys.
They would never...
Maybe Leslie?
Or Lacey?
He glanced at Larry, wearing the same look of disbelief.
"Mmfh d'y'all kn'w?" asked Tommy through the bandana.

"Mmfh d'y'all *fuckin'* kn'w?"

LESLIE

"Lacey..."

Leslie shook Lacey's arm.

"Lacey, wake up..."

Dried flecks of blood crusted Lacey's cheeks. Leslie touched her own, discovering the same. Crumbly. Dry. *Gross.*

"Lacey..."

Fuck it.

Lacey was out cold. Figured, since she'd smoked more Purple than anyone else. Straight up hogged that shit.

Leslie forced herself up, knees wobbly, head swimming. Small crowds gathered near the shattered windows and porch, everyone half-dazed, murmuring and gawking at something outside.

"Holy shit..."

"What're they doin'..."

"Should we call the cops?"

No, *don't* call the fuckin' cops. With all the drugs and underage drinking, everybody would go to jail and get in a *shit-ton* of trouble with their parents. Bill and his little Posse might be fine; his dad's the fucking sheriff. But Tommy and the Boys would be truly fucked.

She wobbled through the crowd, glass crunching underfoot.

Can barely walk...

After making it to the window, she leaned on the shattered pane to look outside—

—then gasped.

"Holy fuuuuuck..."

So that's *why y'all wanted to call the cops...*

Tommy, Mouse, and Larry were on their knees, hands and legs bound with rope. Beside them, Jack, Wiley, Kevin, and Grant lay faceplanted in the grass, while David hunched over, rocking back and forth while he mumbled in Chinese or something.

"...nae anae...nae anae...."

They looked like they'd been in a car wreck, or maybe tortured and shit: busted lips and eyebrows, bloodied foreheads and ears. Unsightly blue, black and green bruises marred their arms and hands. David was the worst, though. Blood wept from his eyes—

("my eyes!")

("the glass is in my eyes!")

—nose, and mouth.

His skin looked drained, a ghostly pale.

"Who's the little girl?"

"Think it's Tommy's little sister or somethin'..."

That was Suzie, right? Had only met her twice. Now she was curled in a ball in a fucking Barbie-themed kiddie pool.

"Who's the big guy?"

"That's Graham-fuckin'-Riley! You don't know him?"

"Damn, he's huge!"

"That's the biggest boy I ever seen!"

"Who's the other guy? With his shirt off?"

"Isn't that Kenny? Skinny Kenny or whatever?"

"Why're they all wearin' cowboy hats?"

Graham turned his gaze to the window; Leslie almost looked away. His sunglasses had lost a lens, giving him a half-crazy, half-stupid look. He grinned. One of his front teeth was missing. A thick strand of bloody drool dangled from his chin.

"What the hell happened this mornin'..."

"Dude, I fuckin' heard it while I was sleepin'..."

"I heard it, too!"

"It was like the most, epic fuckin' fight ever..."

"Dude, I saw it..."

"You fuckin' saw *it?"*

"Dude, I saw it all..."

"What happened?"

"Shh! Be quiet!"

"More shit's about to go down!"

Bill Cunningham and Young Charlie hobbled up the hill. Also looked tired and beat-up as fuck, but tryin' not to show it. Young handed Kenny an RC and Graham a baggie of what looked like cocaine.

"Who's the other dudes in the cowboy hats?"

"It's Bill, Bill Cunningham..."

"And that Young Charlie dude..."

"Man, I heard about these guys, they call themselves the 'Posse' or somethin'..."

"Oh yeah, don't they sell coke?"

"SNRRK!"

Graham used a crumpled dollar bill to snort coke off the back of his hand.

"Hey y'all, what the fuck's goin' on?"

The voice—a thick, snot-filled drawl—came from Zane, that Hazard Maf guy who'd touched her arm last night, leering in a way that gave her goosebumps. Reeked of chewing tobacco and truck exhaust, not to mention looked dumb as fuck in that Confederate flag bandana. But that's Hazard people for ya.

"Dude, look at that Asian kid..."

"He's bleedin' from his eyes and shit..."

"These cowboy dudes really fucked shit up..."

"SNRRK!"

Graham switched to snorting coke off the stairwell banister. Sounded like a pig. He grinned as a thick, syrupy strand of bloody drool swayed to his jeans, then clung to it, like slime. A ragged tear in his shirt revealed blood-soaked gauze wrapped tight around his belly.

"We gotta call the cops!" said some underclassmen chick. "Somethin' bad's gonna happen! I can *feel* it!"

Bill and his Posse looked like they were talking about that water gun Jack had brought to Cracker Barrel. The one filled with Kentucky Blood sauce—the *extra hot* kind.

"Why's he got a water gun?"

"Looks like there's red shit inside it..."

"Why would they put red shit insi—holy fuck!"

Bill's hand snapped down in a blur. A blast of red sauce hit Mouse square in the eyes.

"AAAAAAAAAAAAAAAAAAAAAAARRRRRRRRRAAAAAAAAGH!"

Leslie and the others gasped.

"AAAAAAARRRRRRRRRRRRRRRRRRRRAAAAAAAAAAAAAA AGH!"

Graham chuckled while Bill yelled shit about the Boy's plan to shatter Graham's kneecap.

"OHHHHHH GODDDDDDDDDDDDDD! IT BURRRRRRRRRRRRRNS!"

Murmurs grew around Leslie, swelling to a clamor.

"Holy fuck..."

"What's in the water gun?"

"I dunno, maybe fuckin', hot sauce *or somethin'?"*

"That's gotta fuckin' burn, *dude..."*

"These cowboy dudes are crazy..."

Bill glanced at the onlookers on the porch, then tipped his hat at them.

ZANE

The weedboy's house looked like a warzone. Blood on the walls, glass in the carpet, furniture busted to shit. Nearly every window shattered. Cowboy dudes knew how to fuck shit up, it seemed.

He'd recognized one of 'em: Graham-fuckin'-Riley, the boy with the body of a bank safe. Biggest motherfucker in the whole of Tri. Didn't know the other guy, the dude who'd said earlier, *"We're just lookin' for a weedboy,"* but he'd heard the ruckus, unsure if it was real, or a weed-dream. It had all sounded too fuckin' *epic* to be real, though. People screamin' shit in a bunch of languages amidst all that *clang-clangin'* while the whole house shook with loud-ass *booms.*

His feet crunched over broken glass as he crossed the kitchen. Still hard to walk. Felt like his legs weren't his. Purple Dream shit had fucked him up good. *Real good.* That shit would *sell.* More than worth comin' out to birdboy territory to buy a bunch. Would flip that shit back in Hazard real easy.

He peered over an overturned kitchen table. A jet-black crowbar lay on the floor, slick with blood.

Damn.

Shit got wild...

Groups gathered at the shattered front windows as metal—*heavy* fuckin' metal—blared from the front of the house.

"Who's the other dudes? In the cowboy hats?"

"It's Bill, Bill Cunningham..."

"And that Young Charlie dude..."

"Man, I heard about these guys, they call themselves the 'Posse' or somethin'..."

"Oh yeah, don't they sell coke?"

He shoved past people until he could see.

"Hey y'all," he said. "The fuck's goin' on?"

Ho-ly shiiiit...

On the front lawn, a cowboy hat-wearin' Graham-fuckin'-Riley snorted coke off the stairwell banister while another cowboy dude gave a speech, wavin' a...*water gun* in the air?

Zane narrowed his eyes.

One of the dudes kept nodding—not to the metal blasting from the boombox, but to some internal rhythm. *Kenny. Kenny Moser.* Used to go to North Hazard Middle with him. Nodded his head like a psycho back then, too.

Before the dress-up cowboys knelt *all* the weedboys, tied up and lookin' beat up as fuck. Half of 'em couldn't even sit up—just lay face-down on the grass.

"...nae anae...nae anae..."

Chink boy was bleedin' from his eyes and shit.

"We should call the cops!" said some stupid bitch. "Somethin' bad's gonna happen! I can *feel* it!"

Zane shook his head.

Ain't nobody callin' no fuckin' cops, you dumb fuckin' sl—

"AAAAAAAAAAAAAAAAAAAAAARRRRRRRRAAAAAAAAGH!"

Zane's jaw dropped.

These cowboys didn't play around.

BILL

"Mmfh d'y'all kn'w?" asked Tommy through the Kentucky state flag bandana. "Mmfh d'y'all *fuckin'* kn'w?"

"*SNRRK!*"

Bill followed Graham's lead and snorted a line off the stairwell banister, then wiped his mustache and stared at Glick through his sunglasses.

The *arrogance* of these weedboys.

Damn glad they beat their asses today.

Fuckin' deserved it.

He glanced at Charlie, noddin' and smilin', probably thinkin' the same thing.

"Weedboys thought they was fuckin' smart," said Bill, "with that *cross-attack* bullshit, huh?"

"They sure fuckin' did, Bill," said Charlie.

"Well, guess what, Glick?" asked Bill. "*We* can think like Napoleon, too..."

"*SNRRK!*"

He snorted another line.

"And we straight up *out-Napoleon'ed* y'all."

Wiping his nose, he blinked against the burn behind his eyes.

"Didn't we, Charlie?"

"We sure fuckin' did, Bill," said Charlie.

Bill glanced at the water gun, then at Mouse screamin' and cryin' about his eyes.

That could've been Graham-cracker...

"Daaaamn," said Kenny. "They cracked the shin guard..."

Graham unfastened the cracked shin guard, revealing a blackened and bruised, but unbroken, kneecap.

Glick and Longface stared at the shinguard in disbelief, still lookin' dumb as hell. Still not *gettin' it.*

Bill sipped from Kenny's tequila RC, letting the carbonated sweetness and the tang of cheap tequila sit in his mouth before swallowing. *Hit the spot. Would help numb the pain, too.*

"Y'all ain't half as smart as y'all think y'all is," said Bill. "Saw that *cross-attack* bullshit comin' a mile away..."

And thank God I did...

Bill's dreams had shown him the crowbars, but nothin' about the *cross-attack* strategy itself, which was fine—that was plain common sense. Once he saw the crowbars, he knew it'd be good to equip everybody with shin guards, shit like that. That's what crowbars were good for: *bustin' kneecaps.* And that they'd try to focus on takin' out Graham-cracker first was a no-brainer, and *of course* they'd try to use their advantage in numbers and fuckin' pincer attack or *cross-attack* him and shit. If he was Glick, he'd train the little Possibles to do the same damn thing. 'Bout the only way you could take out a boy as big as Graham-fuckin'-Riley—had to go for his knees.

"Guess wearin' the shin guards *was* a good idea," said Bill. "Huh, Graham-cracker?"

Graham rubbed his knee. "Yeah, yeah..."

Bill smiled. Graham had bitched about the shin guards, callin'em *"pussy guards"* or somethin'. But good thing he fuckin' wore'em.

"How's your *pussitis,* Graham?" asked Kenny.

"Wha?" asked Graham.

"Your *pussitis."* Kenny grinned. "In your knee."

Graham stared at Kenny, then kinda smiled. Still looked ridiculous with a missing tooth and only one lens in his shades. A bloody strand of spit dangled from his chin like it didn't know where to go.

"Yeah." Graham spat blood. "And pussitis in my *mouf,* too..."

"Atentos, y'all." Charlie nodded toward a shattered window. "It's Gina. And that Sarah chick. Those Hazard chicks we hung with at Dairy Queen."

Bill stood a little straighter.

Oh, shit...

Gina with the nice tits...

And Sarah and Tracey, too...

Hot, stuck up as hell, but hot, *Tracey.*

Kenny waved. "Hey Gina! Hey Sarah!"

"Hey Tracey!" said Bill.

"Hey..." said Gina, looking confused. Sarah and Tracey peered from behind her, cautiously raising their hands in greeting.

"Uh..." said Gina. "...what'd y'all squirt in his eyes?"

Mouse's muffled screams had died down, now just moans of anguish, like his damn momma had died or somethin'.

"Oh, him?" Bill tapped his bat on Mouse's shoulder. "Just some Kentucky Blood sauce."

"The extra hot kind!" said Kenny.

"...oh..." said Gina.

A cool morning breeze swept across the lawn.

Birds flew by.

"Es delicioso!" said Charlie. "That means, 'it's *real* fuckin' good!' In Spanish!"

All three girls kinda nodded.

A moment of silence passed.

"Have y'all tried that?" asked Charlie.

"Tried what?" asked Gina.

Charlie laughed. "The Kentucky Blood sauce! The fuck you think I'm talkin' about?"

"The extra hot kind!" said Kenny.

"Uhh..." said Gina.

"I have!" Sarah poked her head from behind Gina.

"I just..." said Gina. "...don't really like spicy stuff..."

"Oh..." said Charlie. "Well, they got other flavors and shit, too..."

Bill cleared his throat. "Yeah, anyway, we'll call y'all later to hang out! Gotta take care of business today!"

He nodded and ran his fingers across the brim of his hat.

Fuck.

Had to act extra cool now that *they* were watchin'.

ZANE

"We should call the cops!" said the stupid slut. *"Those cowboy dudes are crazy!"*

She wandered like a drunken zombie to the kitchen phone and picked it up.

"That's Bill Cunningham!"

"His dad's the Sheriff!"

"What?"

"His dad's the fuckin' Sheriff?"

"Don't fuckin' matter!"

"Call the police!"

Zane yanked the phone cord from the wall.

"You ain't callin' no cops, bitch."

He ripped the phone from her hands.

"We gonna see how this plays out..."

BILL

Suzie was still in the pool. That part of his dreams had held true.

Thank God.

Hopefully the rest would, too.

Please, God...

Let the rest of this shit go easier than it has been...

Little Suzie wasn't screamin', though; not like at first, like in his dreams. She had been chantin' some bullshit about *a temple* like a lunatic, but then she fell catatonic again, withdrawin' into herself like a turtle.

Oh well.

Still in the pool.

That's the most important part.

Maybe she'll scream again soon enough...

"Alright boys," said Bill. "We got our audience startin' to form. Huddle up."

Time to get this show on the road.

Bill's Posse hobbled and limped over to him at varying speeds, trying to look cool now that they had an audience, but clearly exhausted and in pain.

Bill leaned on his bat like a crutch. "Now, I know what y'all are thinkin'...this mornin' has been a lil' bit more *wild,* a lil' bit more fuckin' *epic* than we all fuckin' imagined..."

He expected a smart-ass reply or two, like *"No shit, Sherlock"* or *"Why didn't your dreams tell us half the shit that happened today?"* but his Posse only nodded wearily.

"So let's just get this over with," said Bill. "I'll pull Glick aside and talk to him where nobody can hear, 'cause I know that fucker's pride's so goddamn high he still ain't gonna agree to swear to shit. At least, not at first."

Kenny spat and nodded, not to the heavy metal but just nodded. "And what if he *still* won't swear to nothin'?"

Bill squeezed his baseball bat the way he squeezed his guns at home. His hands, swollen and bruised and fucked up as they were, still ached with a kind of *lust* to hurt someone, despite all the shit that'd already happened today. He didn't like to hurt people, but his hands did.

Slowly, he turned his gaze to Glick.

"He will. He fuckin' will."

He brushed cocaine from his beard and turned to the new onlookers near the shattered window, making sure to tip his hat.

And if he won't...

I'll introduce him to Wild Bill.

LESLIE

Leslie stood with a group near the remnants of a shattered window, watching Bill grab Tommy by the back of his neck and drag him across the yard, halting at the forest's edge. He spat, then removed his cowboy hat and ran his fingers through his long hair.

"Why'd he take Tommy away from the rest?"

"I think he's tryin' to talk to him..."

"Or he's about to fuck him up some more..."

As he spoke, Bill pointed at the Smokehouse, then at Tommy, and turned his hands palm-up, as if to say, *"That's the situation, deal with it."*

Tommy shook his head and looked off into the forest.

Bill took off his sunglasses and rubbed his temples.

"He's tryin' to convince Tommy of somethin'..."

"Of what? They already beat their asses, what more could they want?"

"I bet he wants their drugs and shit..."

"He wants the Purple! I bet they're here to steal the Purple!"

"Then why don't they?"

"Probably don't know where it is..."

Leslie bit her lip. Bill and his cowboys weren't here to steal drugs. At least, that wasn't their main reason.

They came for *revenge.*

Revenge for what the Boys had done to Young Charlie's house.

But this...this was *overkill,* wasn't it?

Maybe there'd been other stuff, other shit that'd gone down she didn't know about...but what else could Bill possibly want? After all this?

"Dude, I bet this has somethin' to do with Prom..."

"Prom?"

"Yeah, that Bill dude took Tommy's girl to Prom. As friends and shit."

"Ohhh..."

"That Samantha Henson chick? Why didn't she go with Tommy?"

"'Cause they broke up or somethin'. 'Cause she wouldn't fuck him."

"Wouldn't give him no blowjobs, neither?"

"Dunno. Guess not."

Bill flailed his hands, yelling something she couldn't make out. But he seemed more frustrated than angry, and seemed to...*plead* with Tommy.

"I bet he's tellin' Tommy that Samantha is his *girl now..."*

"Yeah, just makin' him fuckin' accept it and shit..."

"Nahhh, there has to be more than that. It was fuckin' epic shit *today. No way they'd all get in a fight* that fuckin' epic *over some girl..."*

"I dunno, man...girls make dudes do crazy shit..."

Leslie shook her head. There was *no way* this was about that stuck-up bitch Samantha. Had to step in and correct this shit.

"It ain't over Samantha," she said. "They fucked up Young's house. Real bad. 'Cause Young and them talked shit in the Dairy Queen parkin' lot. And there might be other shit goin' on, too. But it's probably 'cause they fucked up Young's house."

"What'd they do to his house?"

"They—"

Holy shit.

She almost didn't believe her eyes.

Tommy Glick was *crying.*

Shaking his head and fucking *crying.*

She'd never seen Tommy or one of the Boys *cry* before.

"Holy shit, is Tommy cryin'?"

"What the fuck?"

Bill lay his hand on Tommy's shoulder, seeming to console him.

"Dude!"

"What'd that Bill dude say to make him fuckin' cry?"

Bill removed the bandana from Tommy's mouth, patting him on the shoulder.

"Maybe it's about that Saman—"

"ARRRAGH!"

Bill's scream echoed across the yard.

"Holy fuck!"

"Holy fuck!"

"Tommy bit his hand!"

"He bit his fuckin' hand!"

"Dude, he was like, fake-*cryin'!"*

Leslie's heart swelled with pride.

That's my Tommy...

Fightin' 'til the end.

Bill slammed his boot into Tommy's gut. A wet grunt burst from

Tommy as he doubled over *("ugh!")*. Gasps rippled through the crowd around Leslie.

"Oh, daaaaamn!"

"He's wearin' cowboy boots, too..."

"That's gotta hurt..."

Bill shook his head in disgust. His voice roared across the lawn, sounding much older now:

"Alright, weedboy!"

"You wanna play that way?"

"Huh?"

"I gave ya a chance!"

He grabbed Tommy by his throat and dragged him across the yard—

—toward the kiddie pool.

LA HACIENDA

Kenny twirled his bat while sipping his tequila RC.

"Guys, this is the most crazy fuckin' thing I ever imagined doin'. But if this fuckin' works—"

"It will." Bill paced around the room, nodding to the heavy metal from Charlie's boombox.

"It sure fuckin' will," said Charlie. *"Seguro que sí,* y'all. *Seguro que-*fuckin'-*sí...*"

"SNRRK!"

He snorted a line of coke.

"If it fuckin' works," said Kenny, "if Bill's dreams are actually, fuckin', *prophetic,* then Bill, Bill-fuckin'-Cunningham is our *prophet,* man! The prophet of our fuckin' Posse!"

"Huh huh huh..." chuckled Graham. "Prophet Posse."

Charlie and Kenny's eyes widened.

"Eso es brillante, Graham-cracker!" said Charlie. "That's fuckin' genius, man!"

"Huh huh huh..." chuckled Graham. "I just thought it. Then I said it."

"Prophet Posse!" said Kenny. "That's what we'll start goin' by! The Prophet Posse!"

"Prophet Posse!"

"Prophet Posse!"

Bill picked up a baseball bat and squeezed the handle.

"Prophet-fuckin'-Posse!"

"Prophet-fuckin'-Posse!"

A chill ran through him.

("we follow your dreams, man...")
("just tell us what to do.")

His blood felt like ice.

TOMMY

"STAAAAHP!"

Suzie had started screaming again.

Bill dragged Tommy by his throat to the kiddie pool while Suzie screamed and screamed and screamed.

Tommy gagged, his windpipe crushed by Bill's grip. He tried to look at Suzie.

It's gonna be okay...

Don't cry...

Behind Suzie, fucking Young Charlie smoked a cigarette while he grinned and grinned and fucking grinned.

("I like the way your sister cries, Glick...")

Tommy gasped for air.

I'll kill you for this, Young...

I'll kill every last one of ya...

But you first.

At the edge of the kiddie pool, Bill slammed Tommy's face into the water, then yanked back.

"Yulgfff..."

Tommy gasped for air, then gurgled and coughed blood into the pool. He glared at Charlie.

"Glick," said Bill. "Don't ya look at Charlie, now. Look at me. *Look at me, now.* I'm the one talkin' to ya."

"When Bill talks to ya," said Charlie, "you fuckin' look at him!" He drew his bat back.

"Charlie!" Bill held out his hand.

Tommy turned his glare to Bill. Sharp stabbing pains ignited across his torso as he coughed and sputtered up water and blood. The numbing effects of the Purple had all but vanished, and his entire ribcage now screamed with pain.

"...ne...ver...swear...that..." he said.

"Okay, Glick, have it your way." Bill twisted Tommy's head to face his sister.

"Look at her," said Bill. *"Look at her."*

"Why d—"

Tommy's head plunged beneath the water's surface.

("live through it, tommy...")

("live through it...")

Water flooded his nose and throat and lungs and he couldn't breathe he couldn't breathe he couldn't breathe *he couldn't fucking breathe* and then light again. Light. And Suzie. Screaming.

"Swear it!" said Bill. *"Fucking swear it!"*

Tommy coughed up water and blood.

"...ne-ver...swear...it..."

"Goddamnit, Tommy!" said Bill. "I will fucking *drown you* in front of your little sister!"

"BUBBAAAAAAAAAAAA!"

Bill slammed Tommy's head past the blood-streaked surface to the bottom of the kiddie pool and held it there, grinding his cheek against the slick plastic. Suzie's screams, warped by the water, sounded almost otherworldly—

"BU-BAAAAAAAAAAAAAA!"

—as if from a different dimension.

You'll have to kill me, motherfucker...

I'll never *swear to that shit...*

Never.

This time, he managed to hold his breath before Bill slammed his head underwater—but his lungs rattled, and it took everything he had not to cough or suck in water.

Bill yanked his head back up.

He gasped for air, coughing and choking.

"Damnit, Glick!" said Bill. "I will fucking *drown* you! I am *not* fucking playing!"

("tommy...")

Mikey.

Mikey's voice again.

"Do you fucking *understand* me?"

("live through it, tommy...")

"I will *drown* you in front of her!"

("live through it...")

"It will *traumatize* her, Glick!"

("find it...")

"She will need *therapy* the rest of her fucking life!"

("find the temple...")

Bill slammed Tommy's head into the water again and held it there, pressing his face against the bottom of the kiddie pool.

("find it...")

("the temple...")

Suzie's distorted screams faded.

Only Mikey's voice remained.

("temple above all...")

Bill pulled Tommy's head back up and yelled some more.

Suzie screamed and screamed and screamed.

Larry yelled, too, but Tommy barely heard him.

He only heard *his* voice—

("temple...")

("find the...temple...")

—the voice of his dead brother.

Why are you sayin' that, Mikey?

How am I supposed to find a fucking Tem—

(FIND IT)

For one stunning second—

(FIND THE TEMPLE)

—Tommy understood.

(TEMPLE ABOVE ALL)

Only for a *second.*

(TEMPLE)

(ABOVE)

(ALL)

But that was enough.

"...and we will bury your body," said Bill, "in front of your sister, so she'll fuckin'—"

"...ok-ay..."

"What?" asked Bill. "What'd you say?"

"...I'll..."

Tommy coughed, spraying the pool's surface with blood.

"...I'll...swear it..."

"What?" asked Bill. "I can't fuckin' hear you, Glick!"

"...I'll fuckin'..."

He coughed again, barely able to breathe.

"...swear it..."

"In front of *everyone?"* asked Bill. "You'll fuckin' swear it in front of *everyone*?"

"...y-ess..."

"Good boy, Glick..." Charlie crushed his cigarette beneath his cowboy boot.

"...bam, bam, bamba..."

LA HACIENDA

"Charlie," said Bill. "I understand you're pissed, man. I am, too. So, later on, *after* we rob Stevie Baker, we'll fuck up their Smokehouse *real* fuckin' bad, *twice* as bad as what they did here, and we'll—"

"Nope." Charlie took a drag of his cigarette. "Ain't enough."

"And," said Bill, "*of course,* we're gonna beat their asses, too. Real good, and *real hard,* in front of everyone. Ambush'em somewhere, straight-up Napoleon-style, *with* the fuckin' baseball bats, because I don't care anymore about—"

"Nope, nope..." Charlie shook his head. "Ain't *enough...*"

He looked Bill straight in his eyes.

"We gotta go Blackbeard on'em."

Bill stared at Charlie for a moment. "What does that even *mean,* man? Huh?" He paced the room. "*How* are we gonna go Blackbeard on'em? Like, tie'em up and *flay* their asses? Rip off their fuckin' skin? Like Blackbeard did?"

"Nah..." said Charlie. "...that'd be messy..."

"Then what do ya mean, *amigo*?" asked Bill. "I mean, if we fuck up their Smokehouse and beat their asses real bad—"

"Don't fuckin' play with me, Bill," said Charlie. "You *know* that shit ain't enough."

Bill flinched.

Charlie had never spoken to him like that before.

"Okay, okay..." said Bill. "What do ya wanna actually *do,* then? I mean, you wanna take your dad's gun and go *shoot'em* or somethin'? Is that what ya fuckin' want?"

Charlie stayed silent, blowing smoke from the corner of his mouth.

"Here, I'll fuckin' get it." Bill went inside and came back with Charlie's dad's revolver, yanked from between the couch cushions.

"You wanna take this and fuckin' *shoot* all of'em?" asked Bill. "Huh?"

Charlie shifted his gaze from Bill to the revolver, silent, contemplative. Then he turned back to the moon and took a long drag from his cigarette.

"So, we do nothin', for now," said Bill. "And focus on robbin' Stevie Baker *first.* Snatch his coke and sell it to help pay for your windows and shit.

And *I'll* pay for all your windows, man, with my cut from the coke profits. And the money I'm gonna make from doin' chores for old people, and—"

"You ain't even dreamt it yet," said Charlie.

"What?" asked Bill.

"You ain't even dreamt *how* we're gonna rob Stevie Baker yet," said Charlie. "Or even *when.*"

"I'm sure I will, soon," said Bill. "So we wait. Until my dreams tell us to. And once we take care of that, we fuckin' *attend* to Glick and his weedboys. Their guard'll be down by then, so it'll be better. Won't be expectin' shit."

Charlie shook his head. "Nope. That's fuckin' *ni hablar* with me, *ese...*" His hand trembled as he brought the cigarette to his lips. "...straight up *ni*-fuckin'-*hablar...*"

"Why *ni hablar,* Charlie?" Bill didn't know what *ni hablar* actually meant, but it sounded negative. "Tell me why it's fuckin', *ni hablar...*"

"It's *ni*-fuckin'-*hablar, ese,* 'cause we can't just fuckin' roll up and beat their asses for this shit..." said Charlie. "We can't just, fuckin', egg their house and poop all over it and shit. *That ain't enough, Bill.*"

"Why not?" asked Bill. "We'll fuck up their Smokehouse *twice* as bad, and it'll be—"

"'Cause that'll just invite *more* shit!" said Charlie. "*More* fuckin' retaliation, and then *we* gotta retaliate again, and then it's fuckin' retaliation after retaliation, and it'll never fuckin' end and it'll destroy our entire summer. Our entire fuckin' summer'll just degenerate into a never-endin' cycle of that bullshit!"

He spat, then returned his gaze to the full moon.

"We gotta do somethin' *big,*" said Charlie. His voice shook now. "Somethin' so big, so epic, so fuckin' *legendario* that they'll never forget it. Send a message so loud, and so fuckin' clear, that it'll spread all across Crow, and maybe even across the Tri..."

He turned to Bill, meeting his eyes head-on.

"We gotta go *Blackbeard* on'em."

His words hung in the air.

"You said that before," said Bill, "but what do you *mean* by that, exactly? We shoot'em? We kill'em? Like Blackbeard killed people?"

He gave Charlie a hard, no-bullshit stare. Maybe reverse psychology would calm his ass down.

"I mean," said Bill, "you wanna commit *murder,* Charlie? Here's the gun if ya do." He handed the cold, heavy revolver to Charlie. "You really wanna commit *murder?"*

Charlie tilted the revolver, staring at it.

"Nah..." said Charlie. "...probably go to jail if we did that..."

"Yep," said Bill. "We most assuredly fuckin' would."

Charlie's gaze lingered on the revolver, as if hypnotized.

"...you sure your dad, ya know..." he said. "...couldn't get us out of it somehow?"

"Out of goin' to jail?" asked Bill. *"For fuckin' murder?"*

Charlie nodded.

"No, he couldn't fucking do that, Charlie," said Bill. "Nor *would* he, even if he fuckin' *could!"*

Charlie shrugged, still gazing at the revolver.

"So," said Bill, "what else can we do? We just gotta get'em back, man. The way they got us, but with a real nice ass whoopin' on top."

Charlie narrowed his eyes and shook his head, like he'd tasted something bitter.

"What else *can* we do then, Charlie?" asked Bill. "Huh?"

As Charlie tilted the revolver, moonlight caught the metal chamber, flickering shadows across his face.

"...I'll tell ya what we can do..."

TOMMY

Tommy coughed and coughed, unable to expel all the water from his lungs as Bill dragged him by the neck across the yard toward the tree line. Charlie still stood beside the kiddie pool,

("good boy, glick...")

lighting a cigarette with that shit-eating grin of his.

Young...

You'll pay for this...

I swear to God you will...

Upon reaching the tree line, Bill grabbed Tommy's face, forcing him to meet his gaze.

"Glick..." said Bill. "...don't want no bullshit, now. You fuckin' with me? Or you serious?"

Tommy glimpsed his reflection in Bill's sunglasses. For a moment, he saw *her* face—

("i love you, tomm—")

("you're the on—")

—but averted his gaze, looking out into the woods.

Did you really fuck her, Bill?

Did you really rub your bloody dick across her f—

"Damnit, Glick!" Bill forced Tommy's face back toward him. "I don't got all day, now!"

Tommy squeezed his eyes shut.

Mikey's voice rang loud and clear:

("live through this, tommy...")

("all for the temple...")

"...I'm...se-rious..." said Tommy, coughing.

He'd only understood Mikey for one second, *one brilliant, stunning second,* but that was enough.

Bill studied his face with skepticism. "Alright...I'm gonna say *exactly* what I want ya to swear to in front of everybody. And then you're gonna repeat it back to me, just to make sure that we're on the same fuckin' page. And you sure as fuck better remember it all."

Bill forced Tommy's gaze upward, where his own pitiful reflection stared back, warped in the lenses of Bill's sunglasses.

"And I swear to God, Glick," said Bill, "if you try some bullshit, if you try to fuckin' *bite* me again, or if you even fuckin' *say* some bullshit, I will squirt you, Longface, and every single weedboy in y'all's goddamn eyes with that Kentucky Blood shit."

He grabbed a fistful of hair just beneath Tommy's cap.

"*I will bring pain and chaos into your world,*" said Bill. *"Do you understand me?"*

Tommy glanced over at Mouse, still moaning in agony.

"...I understand..." he said.

"...but I want one thing from you, too."

TOMMY

Tommy stared at the grass.

He stared at the grass because whenever he flicked his eyes up, even for a fucking second, the slack jawed faces of all the spectators reminded him of just how far and fast he'd fallen.

Only twelve hours earlier, him and his Boys had been the *Kings of the Tri-County.* Holding the biggest house party anyone had ever seen, smoking the most legit weed anyone had ever smoked, and receiving *tribute* from both the Hazard Mafia and the Zion soccer team.

Now, before all those people who'd previously respected the shit out of him, *he kneeled.* Him and his Boys fucking *kneeled* to these gayass cowboy-wannabe motherfuckers who'd just *barely* fuckin' won, he fucking *kneeled* in front of everyone watchin' like spectators in a goddamn colosseum.

Might as well hold a Roman triumph...

Parade us through the streets...

He stole a glance at the gawking faces, then dropped his gaze to the grass, slick with blood and spit.

("live through this, tommy...")

("find the temple...")

The *only* reason he fucking agreed to this bullshit was because of Mikey. *Mikey's voice.* And that Temple shit. Didn't know if it was real or not—probably not—but for one second he *understood* something, something grand and awesome and beautiful, and that understanding changed him.

That, and he had a plan.

A plan for his Boys to come back from this.

They would.

They would come back from this.

It'd be tough, but they still had the entire summer to plan shit out. Still had plenty of Monkey and Purple and even Mira—

Hot breath blew into Tommy's ear.

"You ready, Glick?" asked Bill.

Tommy sighed.

Fuck.

He nodded.

A red ant crawled up a blood-streaked blade of grass and perched, wiggling its antennae.

Bill lowered his voice to a whisper.

"Don't want no bullshit, now..."

Tommy grit his teeth.

He nodded.

BILL

"For those of y'all who don't know me...." Bill gestured to his audience. "I'm Wild Bill. And this here's my fuckin' Posse."

Heavy metal blared from Charlie's boombox as Bill's Posse hooted and hollered. Kenny jumped in place, screaming the loudest.

Bill raised a hand to calm his Posse. "Now, I know some of y'all might be wonderin' what the fuck is goin' on today..." He straightened his posture and began to pace. "...so lemme break it down for ya."

The voices of his Posse rang out in support:

"Break it fuckin' down, Bill!"

"Break it down for 'em, now!"

"Not too long ago," said Bill, "me and my Posse, we was just mindin' our own business, out over in Dairy Queen parkin' lot..."

"Just mindin' our fuckin' business!"

"Wasn't startin' shit with no one!"

"I was eatin' a banana split!"

"And little *Tommy Glick the Prick* over here..." A smile escaped Bill's lips. He'd come up with that just now, but it was good. Could've said Glick the Dick, but no. *Prick hit better.*

"...came over and started talkin' shit."

"Glick the Prick!"

"Fuckin' talked shit to us!"

"When we was just mindin' our business!"

"And he threw a chicken strip!"

"I ate it!"

"Now, me and my Posse," said Bill, "we don't start shit..."

He shook his head, allowing for a dramatic pause.

"...but just 'cause we don't *start* shit," said Bill, "don't mean we won't fuckin' *end* it!"

"That's goddamn right, Bill!"

"We don't start shit!"

"But we sure do know how to fuckin' end *it!"*

"Ain't no cowards in this motherfucker!"

"So we challenged these 'lil dipshits," said Bill, "to a fuckin' fight! Over on the baseball field!"

He pointed his bat at the weedboys.

"And their pussy-asses didn't even show up!"

"Didn't even show up!"

"Bitch-ass pussies!"

"Fuckin' bitchass pussies is what they is!"

"And they had *eight* fuckin' guys!" said Bill. "And we only had *four!"*

"Twice our fuckin' numbers!"

"And still didn't show!"

"If you's a weedboy, then you's a bitch!"

"And instead..." Bill shook his head in a slow, sorrowful way, then sighed as loudly as he could. "...they fuckin' *trashed* Young Charlie's house..."

"They trashed our Hacienda!"

"Our La Hacienda, *man!"*

"Too afraid to fight, so they fucked with our shit!"

"And I mean fuckin' trashed it..." said Bill. "...did *thousands* of dollars worth of damage..."

The crowd stirred—gasps, low whistles, cries of *"holy shit..."* and *"thousands of dollars?"*

Tommy scrunched his face.

Bill paused. Maybe not *thousands* of dollars, but whatever.

"And I don't know 'bout y'all..." Bill pointed his bat at the audience, sweeping it left to right, making sure everyone felt the weight of his gaze.

"...but my momma didn't raise no bitch."

"Hellll no!"

"Momma didn't raise no bitch!"

"Hell-to-the-goddamn-no!"

"And when people fuck with me," said Bill, "and especially, when they fuck with *my Posse..."*

"Prophet Posse!"

"Prophet Posse!"

"Ain't nobody fuck with the Prophet Posse!"

"Then I fuck'em right back!" said Bill. "Ten times what they did to us!"

"Ten fuckin' times, Bill!"

"A thousand times that shit!"

"Mil veces-*fuckin'*-eso!"

"That means a thousand times!"

"In Spanish!"

"And me and my Posse," said Bill, "we fuckin' *ended* shit today!"
"We ended that bullshit!"
"We don't start shit, but we fuckin' end it!"
"Fuck with us, see what happens!"
"Lo terminamos, *y'all!"*
Bill pressed the cold metal bat against Glick's cheek.
"You tell your boys!" he said.
"All your little weedboys!"
"And everybody here!"
"What you fuckin' agreed to!"

"Swear it!"

TOMMY

"Swear it!" said Billy Badass, givin' a speech all dramatic-like, like he was actually someone important. A guitar solo whined from Charlie's boombox, too loud and annoying as fuck.

Tommy squeezed his eyes shut.

This is the biggest bullshit in the history of bullshit...

"...I swear—"

The voices of Bill's Posse rang around him.

"Can't hear you, Glick!"

"Can't fuckin' hear ya!"

"Talk loud like a fuckin' man, Glick!"

"Glick the Prick!"

"Glick the Prick!"

Tommy cleared his throat and raised his voice.

"I swear," said Tommy, "that—

"Swear to God, Glick!" said Bill.

"I swear to God," said Tommy, "that neither me, nor my Boys, will ever fuck with Bill and his Posse—

"in any—" said Bill.

"in any way," said Tommy, "shape, or form, ever again."

"That's fuckin' right!"

"This is what happens!"

"This is what happens when y'all fuck with us! "

"Don't ever fuck with us!"

"Don't ever fuck with the Prophet Posse!"

"Prophet-fuckin'-Posse!"

"Prophet-fuckin'-Posse!"

"And what else?" asked Bill.

"I swear—"

"—to God!" said Bill.

"I swear to God," said Tommy, "that neither me, nor my Boys, will ever..." He clenched his jaw.

"Say it!" said Bill.

"...will ever..."

He swallowed.

This is the biggest bullshit ever...

The biggest bullshit in the history of fucking bullsh—

"Fucking say it!" said Bill.

"...will ever..."

Tommy bit his lip.

It bled.

"Goddamnit, Glick!"

Bill reared his bat back and aimed the water gun at Tommy's eyes.

"I told ya I didn't want no bullshit, now! *Fucking say it!"*

Tommy took a deep breath, then forced himself to fucking *say it.*

"...will ever hang out..."

"Where?" asked Bill. *"Where won't y'all hang out?"*

The sharp taste of blood hit Tommy's tongue. Metallic. Warm. He swallowed. It slid down his throat, slow and bitter.

"...in the Walmart parkin' lot again..."

Gasps and murmurs erupted from all the fucking spectators. Bill's cowboy bitches pranced around, yellin' like goddamn monkeys. Beside him, Larry, still barely conscious, managed to widen his eyes in shock.

"That's goddamn right!"

"I got so goddamn tired of seein' y'all everytime I went to Walmart!"

"No more of that shit!"

"None of that bullshit, now! No fuckin' more!"

"And where *else?"* asked Bill. "Where *else* won't y'all fuckin' hang out?"

"Nor..." said Tommy. "...will we hang out in, or nearby, the Crow County Dairy Queen parkin' lot, either..."

"Ever again!" said Bill.

"Ever again," said Tommy.

"That's goddamn right!"

"That's our territory!"

"Prophet Posse territory!"

"Y'all want some Dairy Queen y'all go through the goddamn drive-through! Y'all don't even eat inside!"

The murmur of the spectators swelled to a clamor.

Tommy lowered his head and tried to focus on The Tem—

"Not in any *Crow County parkin' lot!"*

"Make him swear to that, Bill!"

"Yeah!"

"No more parkin' lots, period!"

"Y'all keep to y'alls goddamn selves!"

Tommy grimaced. "That wasn't *part of the deal,* Cunningham. The deal was that—"

"Just fuckin' swear it," said Bill.

"Y'all can still hang out in Zion!"

"*Or Hazard!"*

"Just keep out of Crow County parkin' lots!"

Tommy again swallowed the blood trickling from his lip, searching for his brother's voice.

("live through this, tommy...")

("the temple...")

("temple above all...")

"And," said Tommy, "I swear to God, that neither me, nor my Boys, will ever hang out in any Crow County parkin' lot, ever again."

"You're goddamn right ya won't!"

"Don't even wanna see y'all's asses no more!"

"No más, *motherfucker! No fuckin'* más!"

"Go hang in Zion! With Zion bitches!"

"Hazard rednecks'll give ya a real good fuckin' welcome!"

"*...and?"* asked Bill, the satisfaction in his voice so fuckin' apparent. "What about y'all's bullshit music?"

Tommy inhaled, then exhaled. The ropes binding his arms creaked with pressure.

"And," he said, "I swear to God..."

He swallowed.

"...that we will keep our hippy music to ourselves, and won't play it loud from our cars and trucks no more."

"That's goddamn right!"

"Fuck your hippy bullshit!"

"We don't wanna listen to that shit!"

"Keep y'alls pussy-ass-music to y'all's pussy-ass-selves!"

"And," said Bill, "one last thing, weedboy!"

"And..." Tommy sighed. "I swear to God, that neither me, nor my Boys, won't ever sell any drugs, other than weed."

"Damn straight!"

"Weed bitches only sell weed!"

"Leave the cocaine and the real *fuckin' drugs to us, you little bitch!"*

Bill turned to the onlookers. *"We* are the providers! Y'all want some *real* drugs, like fuckin' cocaine, y'all come to us!"

"And *only* us!" said Charlie. *"Solo nosotros!"*

"And Glick *swears to God* on all this shit!" said Bill. "Don't ya, Glick?"

Tommy spat on the lawn, avoiding the gaze of the onlookers.

"...I swear to God..."

"Good!" Bill turned back to the audience. "This shit ends today! *That's* why we did all this today! Not to *start* shit, but to fuckin' *end* it! 'Cause we don't want no more bulls—"

"Swear on your brother's grave, Glick," said Charlie.

BILL

"What?" asked Tommy.

Bill's Posse fell silent.

Confused murmurs rose from the audience.

"You heard me," said Charlie. "Swear on Mikey's grave."

A chill ran up Bill's spine.

Didn't know Glick used to have a brother...

The heavy metal tape jammin' from Charlie's jukebox switched to a slower, mournful song. Bill tried noddin' to it, like he didn't give a fuck, but he wasn't sure if—

"Fine," said Glick. "I swear on my brother's grave."

"Say his name," said Charlie.

Glick shook his head, and for a second—*a split second*—something flashed in his eyes.

"I swear on the grave of my brother, Michael Glick."

"And on your sister's life, too," said Bill.

What?

What the fuck?

Did I just say that?

Even Charlie, Kenny and Graham looked surprised.

Why the fuck did I just say that?

Maybe it was the cocaine,

(you know why you said it...)

or a speck of darkness, waiting,

(this makes it real...)

for moments like this.

Longface started yellin' some bullshit from behind his bandana.

"Longface." Charlie pointed his bat at Larry's long face. "Best shut the fuck up, now. *Cállate.*"

Bill glanced at Suzie, who'd returned to her semi-fuckin'-catatonic state, and then at Glick, who seemed to be weighing the situation.

"I swear on the life of my sister," said Tommy, staring straight at Suzie. "Susanne Glick."

Bill nodded, feeling like he'd *almost* pressed things too far, but still tryin' to act cool about it, like he didn't give a fuck. He ran his fingers across the brim of his cowboy hat and checked the audience: slackjawed, watchin' everything play out like it was goddamn Shakespeare.

Gotta end the show on a high note...

"Now, all y'all heard it!" Bill turned toward the audience. "All y'all *witnessed* this shit!"

He pointed his bat at Glick and his weedboys.

"*They* started it!" said Bill.

He pounded his chest with his fist.

"And *we* finished it!"

He turned back to the tied-up weedboys.

"No more bullshit from y'all!" he said. *"Ever!"*

Out of the corner of his eye, he glimpsed Gina, Sarah and Tracey. Seemed maybe impressed with him. *Good.*

"We finished this shit!" He swung his baseball bat through the air for dramatic effect. *"We fuckin' end—"*

"Nope," said Glick. "We ain't finished yet, Cunningham."

"What?" Bill whirled around, gripping his baseball bat. *"The fuck'd you just say to me, weedboy?"*

Glick lifted his gaze, his face now serene.

"You gotta swear, too, Billy boy..."

Bill froze, the bat heavy in his hands.

Shit.

Forgot about that.

TOMMY

"Huh?" asked Graham.

"The fuck?" asked Kenny.

Tommy spoke with a deadly calm. "If you *really* wanna stop the bullshit, then *you'll* swear, too, Cunningham. Not to fuck with us, either."

"Nope," said Kenny. "Bill don't gotta swear shit."

"Glick," said Charlie. "I think you fail to understand who's got the power, the fuckin' *leverage* here. I'm talkin' *ventaja, ese."*

Tommy tuned out the cowboy bitches, the gawkers and the bullshit heavy metal blaring from the boombox, focusing only on Bill.

You told me, Cunningham...

You told me right over there, beside those woods...

That you'd swear, too.

"If you're *serious* about endin' shit," said Tommy, "then you'll swear, too. Swear to God."

Charlie raised his baseball bat. "Now, you listen *here,* motherf—"

"Fine." Bill looked away from Tommy and spoke quickly: "I swear to God that neither me, nor my Posse will ever start shit with y'all, nor ever do bad shit to y'all, after today."

He turned back to Tommy.

"Happy?"

"Swear on your brother's life," said Tommy.

The heavy metal tape clicked to a stop.

Bill and his Posse's eyes widened.

An eerie silence fell across the lawn.

Despite the agonizing pain in his chest, Tommy smiled.

Didn't think I knew about him...

...did ya, motherfucker?

BILL

"Swear on Wayne's life, Bill," said Tommy. *"Swear on the life of Wayne Cunningham."*

Charlie shook his head. "You don't gotta swear on shit, Bill. That's some bullsh—"

"Fine," said Bill. "I swear on my brother's life."

"Say his fucking name!" said Tommy.

Bill sighed and looked out into the forest.

"I swear on my brother, Wayne Cunningham's life—"

For a split second, Bill *felt* something—like an anvil heavy and hard and *wrong* sink inside him—but he pushed it away.

"—that we won't ever start shit with y'all, nor do nothin' bad to y'all after today."

He looked at Glick.

"There. Ya happy?"

He turned back to the audience.

"This shit ends today!"

"Forever!"

BILL

Bill paused to let the weight of everything sink in, surveying the weedboys and the spectators watching from the house and porch.

Hazard Maf guys.

Zion soccer team dudes.

And a shit-ton of Crows.

They all saw what happened today.

They all *witnessed* it.

Even *better* than what his dreams had shown him.

"Huh huh huh..." chuckled Graham. "We should take their drugs, too."

"Fuck yeah!" said Kenny. "We can sell their shit for a ton of money!"

Bill paused. Stealin' the weedboys' drugs wasn't part of the plan, and he didn't wanna *push* things, but Kenny had already laid his bat on top of Glick's head.

"Where's y'all's drugs?" As Kenny raised the bat high, something flashed in his eyes, something fucked up and not right, someth—

"Locked in a closet," said Glick. "In the spare bedroom on the right side of the house..."

Graham stomped up the porch stairs into the house.

Glick glared at Bill.

"But this wasn't part of our deal, Cunningham..."

Kenny's face lit up with a delirious grin, bat held in triumph as the sun rose behind him.

"We done changed the deal, weedboy..."

TOMMY

As Graham stomped into the house, Tommy gazed upon his Boys in various states of misery. Mouse still moaned like a wounded animal, even during the fucking oath. Larry looked like he might pass out at any moment. Probably had a concussion. The rest lay face-down in the grass.

Good.

Glad they didn't have to see that bullshit.

Today was the worst fucking day in the history of the Smoketown Boys.

("find it...")

But he'd heard Mikey's voice.

("find the temple...")

And for a second, just a *second—*

("temple above all...")

He'd *understood.*

("temple above all, tommy...")

If he could *talk* to Mikey again, if he could—

"You said it was locked." Kenny still held the bat high. "Where's the keys, weedboy?"

Tommy fought to keep his poker face. He just wanted the day to be fucking over, but these wannabe cowboys weren't getting *their fucking drugs* on top of everything.

No fucking way.

"It's locked with four deadbolts," said Tommy. "But I don't got my key on me, and I dunno if the rest of my Boys have—"

BOOM!

A crash erupted from inside.

Kenny's grin widened. He snickered like a demented clown.

"Guess we don't need y'all's keys no more..."

The crowd on the porch parted for Graham as he returned carrying two huge bags of Purple Dream.

"This wasn't part of the deal, Cunningham," said Tommy. "I've sworn to *every-fuckin'-thing* you—"

"Shut the fuck up!" Kenny sprayed Tommy's face with spit and blood.

His eyes gleamed with something wild and unhinged. For some reason, he began nodding.

Graham dropped the bags to the ground. "There's more weed in there. And that crystal meth stuff in the bathroom, too. We can—"

"No," said Young.

Kenny looked at Young like he'd just spit in their food. "No, what?"

"He didn't fuck with our drugs." Young turned his gaze to Suzie. "So we don't fuck with his. I wanna keep this *justificado.*"

Tommy breathed a sigh of relief.

Thank God.

The *one* silver lining to the worst fucking day ever.

Horse People would fucking kill him if he didn't deliver on that shit.

He looked upon Jack laying face-down on the lawn, mouth surrounded with froth, twitching intermittently.

Thanks for helpin' me make the right call back then, Jack...

About not stealin' their drugs and shit...

You were right.

You were right about every-fuckin'-thing from the very-fuckin'-beginning.

Graham bitched some, but shut his trap once Bill backed Young. Kenny looked like his fucking mom had deprived him of a bedtime story, but finally lowered his bat, the *maniac-flash* in his eyes fading. Still kept nodding, though.

"Alright," said Bill. "Let's go, boys. I'm fuckin' tired."

He headed towards the driveway.

"Nope, nope," said Young.

"Una cosa mas."

BILL

"Alright," said Bill. "Let's go, boys. I'm fuckin' tired."

He glanced at Kenny and Graham's exhausted faces, hoping they just wanted to go home, too.

They'd done enough today.

More than enough.

He strode toward the driveway and tried to look as cool as possible despite feelin' like an old man wracked with battle wounds. Just wanted to eat, take a hot shower, then go the fuck to sleep. Maybe go to the hospital first, get shit checked out. Could pick some Dairy Queen up on the way. Chicken strip basket sure would hit the sp—

"Nope, nope," said Charlie. "*Una cosa más.*"

Bill halted.

Charlie...

This should be enough, now.

Today should've been more than enough.

He narrowed his eyes behind his sunglasses.

"...you *still* wanna do that?"

A terrible smile crept over Charlie's face.

"I sure fuckin' do."

1970s

CHAPTER II

FORTUNA BRUTALIS

"Y'all know what we gotta do..."

"You can call yourself Wild Bill, but you best live your life like Blackbeard, ese..."

Blackbeard: The Man Who Scourged the Seas
By: Roberta Stevenson
CHAPTER 15
You Can Be Like Blackbeard!

(pg. 138) By now, you're probably thinking, *"How can I become someone famous and legendary, like Blackbeard?"* or maybe, *"How can I be somebody that no one messes with, just like no one messed with Blackbeard?"*

Although you may not be able to become as famous and legendary across the world as Blackbeard, you can increase your reputation amongst your local community, even without becoming a pirate!

Be Like Blackbeard! Eight Easy Steps

Just follow these eight easy steps, and you and your friends can be the Blackbeards of your hometown!

Step 1) Give yourself and your friends a nickname.

If Blackbeard had called himself Francois L'Ollonais, he wouldn't have been as famous, and no one would have cared about him. Come up with short and memorable nicknames for yourself and your group of friends, so people can remember you easily!

Step 2) Develop your own unique style.

If you dress like everyone else, then people will see you like everyone else. Try to come up with a *style* that you and your friends can adopt. Unique clothes, hairstyles, and even tattoos can set you apart from the crowd!

Step 3) Make yourselves known.

Blackbeard didn't keep it a secret that he captured ships; in fact, he did his best to ensure that all of his exploits gained recognition far and wide. Your nicknames and style, no matter how cool, won't matter if nobody knows about you! Here's some easy things you can do to become well-known in your community:

Be loud: Cruise around town with your buddies and play your music loud to draw attention. If you don't have your driver's license yet, strap your boombox to your back and play it while riding your bike!

Be Seen: Hang out at places where you'll be seen by lots of people, like parking lots, shopping malls and roller-skating rinks. No one will know who you are if you just sit at home like a couch potato!

Be Social: Throw parties and get-togethers—everyone loves a party! By hosting them, you'll increase your branding and recognition amongst your local community.

Be Cool: Once you're old enough, you can even start hanging out at bars! Bars are often the best places to see and be seen, helping you develop a reputation and expand your social network.

→ ***Did You Know?*** *Blackbeard loved to take his crew for wild times on shore, igniting excitement wherever they went. When you hang with your friends in public places, make sure to keep the energy level high, so people notice!*

Step 4) Do something epic.

Did you know that in 1718, Blackbeard and his pirates once blockaded the entire port of Charleston, South Carolina for *a whole week?*

Can you imagine that?

Not the Spanish Armada nor the French Navy, but *pirates* blockading the port of one of the most important British colonies of the New World.

"I will bring you chaos," wrote Blackbeard to the Governor of Charleston. *"I will bring pain and chaos into your world, such that you have never seen..."*

Wow!

Blackbeard didn't play around, did he?

Even decades after sailing from Charleston, Blackbeard's name stayed on the lips of everyone—people just couldn't stop talking about him! To this day, his daring blockade is hailed as the *most epic event in pirate history,* helping make his legend larger than life.

So try to be like Blackbeard and do things no one has ever done before: *epic, unforgettable, next-level* things which boggle the mind!

And when you do, don't forget *Step 3,* and make sure that whatever awesome thing you've done is *well-known* throughout your community.

You've got to be the talk of the town!

Step 5) Never hurt people without a good reason.

Blackbeard never hurt anyone who complied with his demands. If word gets around that you and your friends like to hurt people who never harmed or disrespected you, you'll develop a bad reputation. Pretty soon people may even turn against you. *Nobody likes a bully!* That's why it's important to *never* hurt people unless you have a good reason. What are some good reasons? Here's some examples:

- If someone harms or threatens you or your friends or family.
- If someone damages or steals your property.
- If someone says mean or hurtful things about you or to you.
- If you really need someone to do something, but they won't do it.

Step 6) Never tolerate disrespect.

Disrespect, when tolerated, only invites more disrespect. Blackbeard understood this, and so should you. Show the world that you have *zero tolerance* for disrespect!

Step 7) Don't start conflicts—only finish them.

Unless you have a *good reason* to hurt someone (see Step 5), don't go around starting conflicts with people. That could ruin your reputation! Show respect to everyone around you, even your rivals and enemies. This way, if conflict *does* arise, it won't be your fault, and you can apply Blackbeard-style brutality free of guilt, able to rest at night with a clear conscience.

Step 8) Exercise Brutality! Always finish conflicts in the style of Blackbeard.

When someone steps on your toes, cut off their head. Any disrespect, any slight, *must* be paid back in multiples.

It may sound harsh, but that was how the world worked during the times of Ancient Rome, and how it still works today.

Ask yourself, if someone wronged you, what choices would you have?

You could do nothing, or you could do *something.*

And if you do *something,* you *have* to make it count. You must do something so horrible, so *uncompromisingly brutal* that the person who wronged you would never even *consider* wronging you again. Remember what America did to Japan, or what Rome did to Carthage?

Japan started it, but America *finished* it.

Carthage started it, but Rome *finished* it.

Both nations *went Blackbeard* on their enemies. They understood that brutality both saves lives and prevents future conflicts, and by now, hopefully you do, too.

Never be afraid to exercise brutality—always *go Blackbeard* upon those who've wronged you!

Exercising Brutality: Use the Power of Your Imagination!

"But what can I do to exercise brutality?" you might be wondering. *"I wanna go Blackbeard on my enemies, but I don't know what to do!"*

After all, you probably don't have an atomic bomb, an army, or even a pirate ship! But that's okay—you have something *far greater* than all of those things:

The power of your imagination.

With the power of your imagination, you can do anything!

Discussion Exercises—Talk With Your Friends!

1. Why is it important to avoid starting conflict?

2. If conflict is forced upon you, why is it important to be the one to *finish* it?

3. What is the best way to *finish* a conflict, and truly end it, to avoid a cycle of retaliation?

4. Have you ever *"gone Blackbeard"* on someone? Has someone ever *"gone Blackbeard"* on you? How did it feel?

5. *Open your history book!* Try to find times in history where the victor failed to *"go Blackbeard"* on their enemy, causing more trouble for them later on. What should they have done differently?

ABOUT THE AUTHOR

Dr. Roberta Stevenson is a former social studies teacher and current educational author with a passion for bold, uncompromising stories from history. Born in 1941 in Southern Virginia, she holds a PhD in Historical Education from the University of Kentucky and spent years in the classroom before turning her focus to writing full-time.

Her books, often controversial, challenge young readers to examine leadership, fear, and moral responsibility through the lens of real-world conflict. *Blackbeard: The Man Who Scourged the Seas* is her fifth book and the first in her "Command and Consequence" series, which explores how acts of controlled force can prevent larger spirals of violence.

She lives in Murray, Kentucky, with her husband Arthur and their aging collie, Jasper. When she's not writing or researching, she enjoys fencing, collecting maritime antiques, and making lesson plans for teachers seeking to teach history "without watering it down."

LA HACIENDA

"...and so that's why Blackbeard is one of the most badass motherfuckers who ever lived."

Charlie stood before a sitting Graham and Kenny. "But there's a lot more shit to it than that, I can't explain *everything* that's in the fuckin' book. So once Bill's finished with it, I'll let y'all borrow it so y'all can read it, too."

Graham shrugged. "I'm okay with just the explanation."

Kenny raised his hand.

"Kenny," said Charlie.

"So, what you're sayin'," said Kenny, "is that you want us to get revenge on the weedboys, in the style of Blackbeard?"

"I sure fuckin' am," said Charlie.

"And get revenge on'em *so bad,*" said Graham, nodding like he maybe understood, "that they don't even, ya know, ***think*** about gettin' back at us?"

"Eso es correcto, Graham-cracker," said Charlie. "I'm glad you was fuckin' listenin'."

"So, what're we gonna do?" asked Kenny. "Like, cut off their heads, and stick'em on the bow of a ship or somethin'? Like Blackbeard would?"

"Maybe on a boat," said Graham, nodding. "Out on Lake Gilead..."

"No, no..." said Charlie. "...we ain't go no ships for that, nor any fuckin' boats..."

"Then you're sayin'," said Kenny, "we just, ya know, like...*kill'em all?* Like how Blackbeard killed people."

"Straight-up kill'em all," said Graham, nodding.

"No, no..." said Charlie. "...I ain't sayin' we gotta *kill* them weedboys... we'll go to jail if we do that..."

Graham raised his hand.

"Graham," said Charlie.

"Couldn't Bill's dad, ya know," said Graham, "keep us from goin' to jail and stuff, since he's the—"

"No," said Bill, *"he fuckin' couldn't!"*

"I already asked that, actually," said Charlie. "It's a good question, though, Graham-cra—"

"Well, y'all stop fuckin' askin' it!" said Bill.

The room fell silent.

After a few moments, Kenny spoke.

"So, what do you want us to actually *do*? If we ain't gonna, like, ya know, *kill* them weedboys, I don't understand how we can actually *'go Blackbeard'* on'em and shit."

Charlie shifted his gaze to the brown spot on the carpet. Something cold and terrifying crossed his face.

"Alright, *amigos,*" he said. "I'm only gonna explain this one fuckin' time. So y'all listen real closely, and don't interrupt me until I'm finished."

Charlie fell silent, flicking his eyes between Kenny and Graham, studying them. He then explained, in great detail, the awful thing he planned to do.

Neither Kenny nor Graham said a word.

Bill stood behind them, leaning against the wall, staring at the brown spot on the carpet. He took off his cowboy hat and ran his fingers through his long hair, secretly hoping they'd refuse to go along—that Kenny would try to *reason* with him, to talk him out of it and even Graham would say, *"That's too much, Charlie-boy. That's too fucked up."*

"...and then we leave," said Charlie. "Any questions?"

Silence.

A cardinal landed on a nearby windowsill, tilting its head at Bill before pecking at the glass.

"What do y'all think of that?" Bill stared at the cardinal. "Of what Charlie wants to do?"

He turned toward his Posse.

Please say y'all are against that shit...

Please.

Slowly, Kenny and Graham turned to face Bill.

Their grins told him his answer.

BILL

A cold knot tightened in Bill's stomach. He approached Charlie and lowered his voice so the audience couldn't hear.

"You still wanna do that?" he asked.

"Sí," whispered Charlie.

"Dude..." Bill glanced around him. "Graham's bleedin' bad from his belly...and weedboys probably need to take that Asian boy to the eye doctor, ya know, for his eyes and sh—"

"Justo lo que..." said Charlie.

He laid a hand on Bill's shoulder.

"Justo lo que..."

"...recetó..."

"...el médico."

TOMMY

"Una cosa más."

The fuck did that mean?

Una...sounded like *uno.* That meant "*one,*" but didn't understand the rest, the fuckin' *"cosa más"* or whatever. Cunningham asked Young if he was *"sure"* about something and then they had a little pow-wow, whisperin' and shit so he couldn't hear.

He glared at Young and spit on the grass.

What more...

What more could you fucking want after all this?

Young and Cunningham walked back to their car while Kenny and Graham stared at Tommy, grinning like they knew a secret.

Somethin' about those grins...

An ant crawled across Tommy's face, tickling his cheek.

He shook it off.

Something about those grins bothered Tommy.

TOMMY

Cunningham and Young returned carrying a blue-and-white cooler, the kind used to keep beer cold. Kenny and Graham snickered like fucking children as they placed it in front of Tommy.

"Cunningham..." The pain in Tommy's torso sharpened by the second. "The fuck is this? We're *done* here, right? I swore to *everything* you asked!"

Bill stared out into the woods.

Tommy cast a worried glance at his two remaining still-conscious Boys. Mouse lay face-planted on the grass, his screams of anguish now occasional moans. Larry, his mouth still bound by a Kentucky state flag bandana, gazed wide-eyed at the cooler.

Charlie flung off his backpack and pulled out two pairs of pink dishwashing gloves.

LESLIE

"What's the cooler for?"

"Maybe it's got beer in it?"

"Nah, there's somethin' other than beer in that..."

Leslie's throat tightened.

She swallowed.

Bill and his crew should have left by now. They got everything they wanted and more—even Tommy swearin' that him and the Boys wouldn't hang out in the Walmart parking lot *ever again,* nor in *any* fuckin' parking lot in all of Crow.

Some *true* bullshit, if there ever was any.

She turned to see Lacey still gonked out on the living room floor, mouth agape and drooling. Lots of shit to catch her up on once she finally woke up. Shit she wouldn't believe.

"Pink dishwashin' gloves? What the fuck?"

"I told ya there ain't no beer in that fuckin' cooler..."

"What could it be, then? Snakes?"

"Dude! I hate snakes!"

Leslie's eyes widened.

She hated snakes, too.

But something told her it wasn't snakes in that cooler.

("something bad is gonna happen!")

("i can feel it!")

TOMMY

Young Charlie donned the pink dishwashing gloves and stared at his hands, as if seeing them for the first time.

The fuck?

Dishwashing gloves?

"Cunningham..." said Tommy. "Now, you're a man of honor, ain't ya? You just now *swore* y'all wouldn't do nothin'..."

He tried to steady his voice.

Something wasn't right.

"Here." Charlie tossed Bill the other pair. "You're gonna need'em, too."

Bill sighed and slipped them on.

Tommy narrowed his eyes.

Why?

What the fuck is going on?

"I'll help, Charlie!" said Kenny. "And I'll—"

"Nope. *No bueno,*" said Charlie. "It's gotta be Bill."

Bill stared off into the fucking woods, refusing to even look at Tommy.

Look at me, you dickless wannabe cowboy...

We just swore an oath...

You fucking look *at me.*

"You fuckin' *swore,* Cunningham...." said Glick. "Everybody here saw ya, now! You fuckin' *swore* in front of *fucking everybody* that shit was over!"

Charlie crouched and knocked twice on the cooler.

"He swore *after today,* motherfucker."

BILL

Bill slipped on the dishwashing gloves. Kinda weird that they were pink, but whatever. That's all Walmart had left.

"He swore *after today,* motherfucker," said Charlie. "And last time I checked, Glick..."

He smiled and winked.

"...it's still fuckin' today."

Bill sighed.

Charlie...

We ain't Blackbeard.

We don't gotta do this.

Glick flicked his eyes between Charlie and Bill, his face a mix of confusion and fear.

Charlie gripped the cooler. He didn't blink.

Something twisted tight in Bill's gut. Felt like they were on the edge of somethin', an *atrocity,* somethin' they couldn't undo and would carry for the rest of their—

Without opening the cooler, Charlie rummaged through his backpack. He tossed Bill a cassette tape.

"Switch the tape," he said.

"Fuckin' *vamos."*

TOMMY

Why do they need to switch the fucking tape?

Bill's eyes widened. "You wanna do *that part,* too?"

What "part?"

What the fuck is going on?

"Sí," said Young. *"Como hablamos."*

"Charlie," said Bill, "after everything we—"

"I been fuckin' practicin'!"

Bill sighed, looking old and weary now. Not the self-righteous, dramatic speech-giver he was earlier.

Tommy winced as pain bolted through his ribs like lightning.

He didn't know *what the fuck* was in that cooler or why Young wanted to change the fucking tape, but a sense of dread overwhelmed him, and within that dread rose a single command:

Run.

BILL

Bill turned to address the audience. "Alright, y'all. We're 'bout finished here today. But, before we leave, Young Charlie's got, uhh..."

He glanced at Charlie, facing away from the audience with his eyes closed, murmuring in Spanish.

"Something else he wants to, *uhh...*" said Bill. "...ya know, fuckin' do..."

Charlie raised his finger and pointed at the boombox.

Bill pressed play.

♪ *Para bailar La Bamba...* ♪

LESLIE

♪ *Para bailar La Bamba…* ♪

Bill hit play, and Charlie whipped around—

♪ *Para bailar La Bamba…* ♪

—singin' to fuckin' *La Bamba.*

"Holy shit!"

"He's singin' La Bamba!"

Leslie's mouth fell open.

What the actual fuck?

♪ *Se necesito una poca de gracia…* ♪

Amidst his Spanish serenade—

♪ *…una poca de gracia…* ♪

—he pointed a pink dishwashing-gloved finger at everyone in the house. Squeals erupted from the girls. One of them clutched Leslie's arm, nails digging in like she couldn't believe what she saw.

"This is insane!"

Leslie shook the bitch's arm off as Charlie limped across the lawn, every step looking like it hurt, but he wore that grin anyway—like he'd rehearsed the whole damn thing.

♪ *Pa' mi, pa' ti, arriba, y arriba…* ♪

The beat caught hold of everyone.

Even the girls started nodding along.

♪ *Y arriba, y arriba…* ♪

Charlie gestured toward the three Hazard whores (the ones who sucked dick on the side of the house) and winked at'em.

He fucking *winked* at'em.

♪ *Por ti seré, por ti seré, por ti seré…* ♪

Leslie's stomach turned. All three whores giggled like they'd just been winked at by Elvis himself.

"Daaaamn, he sings that Spanish shit so fuckin' good!"

"Is he part Mexican or somethin'?"

One of the sluts even waved.

♪ *Yo no soy marinero…* ♪

With his melody in full swing,

♪ *Yo no soy marinero, soy capitán…* ♪

Charlie moseyed over to the stairs,

♪ *Soy capitán, soy capitán…* ♪

whipped out a cocaine baggie,

♪ *Ba-ba-bamba…* ♪

and poured some on the banister.

♪ *Ba-ba-bamba…* ♪

People sang along,

"*SNRRK!*"

while Charlie snorted fucking coke.

♪ *Ba-ba-bamba…* ♪

Still grinning like a little shit, he wiped his mustache, nodding and singing without missin' a beat.

♪ *Para bailar La Bamba…* ♪

♪ *Para bailar La Bamba…* ♪

Graham chuckled and clapped, bloody drool dangling from his mouth.

♪ *Se necesito una poca de gracia…* ♪

Kenny started clapping, too. *"Come on, y'all!"*

♪ *Una poca de gracia…* ♪

One by one, *everyone fucking joined in the clapping.*

♪ *Pa' mi, pa' ti, arriba, y arriba…* ♪

Bill stared into the woods, half-heartedly bringing his hands together. Charlie limped over to Mouse, still face-planted on the grass, and yanked his head up by the hair.

♪ *Y arriba, y arriba…* ♪

He placed the cocaine baggie under Mouse's nose, turned to the audience and mouthed, *"Want some?"*

♪ *Por ti seré, por ti seré, por ti seré…* ♪

Mouse half-nodded, eyes crusted shut, tears still streamin' down his face.

♪ *Ba-ba-bamba…* ♪

Charlie mouthed "*No,*" then let Mouse's face plop back to the ground.

♪ *Ba-ba-bamba…* ♪

The house erupted in laughter.

"That Young Charlie guy's somethin' else!"

"Dude, he's fuckin' hilarious!"

Charlie stuffed the baggie in his pocket and shot everyone a playful wink.

♪ *Ba-ba-bamba...* ♪

While singing and nodding, he gravitated toward the cooler.

"He's gonna open the cooler!"

Leslie stepped back from the window, heart pounding in her ears. She felt light, floaty, like she might pass out.

"He's gonna open it!"

"He's gonna open it!"

♪ *Ba-ba-bamba...* ♪

TOMMY

Unreality washed over Tommy.

♪ *Ba-ba-bamba...* ♪

Clad in pink dishwashing gloves, Charlie sang to fucking *La Bamba* as he moseyed over to the cooler, rapped his knuckles on top *("knock-knock!")* and smiled.

Tommy's mouth hung open.

This...

This isn't real...

Charlie *acted* like he'd open the cooler, but then mouthed *"Wait!"* and rummaged through his backpack. He pulled out a Ziploc bag with a piece of paper inside.

♪ *Ba-ba-bamba...* ♪

The paper bore a scrawled message on one side. Flecks of brown dotted the back.

♪ *Ba-ba-bamba...* ♪

Tommy furrowed his eyebrows.

The fuck is that?

A note?

Did he write a fucking note?

♪ *Ba-ba-bamba...* ♪

Charlie held the note out to the spectators.

His smile faded.

LESLIE

Almost everyone except Leslie fucking clapped and sang to *fucking La Bamba.*

♪ *Ba-ba-bamba...* ♪

Charlie dug through his backpack and pulled out a Ziploc bag with a folded piece of paper inside.

"The fuck is that?"

"Looks like a...piece of paper..."

"Is there somethin' written on it?"

"It's a note!"

"Why's it in a Ziploc bag?"

He pulled the note from the bag and held it toward the house.

♪ *Ba-ba-bamba...* ♪

Leslie squinted, trying to read it.

"Dude, what's it say?"

"I can't make it out!"

Leslie raised an eyebrow. What *the fuck* was Young doin', holdin' out some kinda *note* like that? Was this a fuckin' joke?

"Why's he just...just holdin' it out like that?"

"Maybe he's gonna do a magic trick!"

"I love magic tricks!"

Charlie's smile faded.

"I don't think he's gonna do a magic trick..."

TOMMY

♪ *Ba-ba-bamba...* ♪

Charlie held the note out toward the spectators, no longer singing, no longer smiling.

♪ *Ba-ba-bamba...* ♪

He wore the face of a sad clown about to pull off one last, cruel trick.

"Young," said Tommy. "What *the fuck* are you—"

Charlie whirled around and jammed the note in Tommy's face. The paper crinkled against his nose. His stomach dropped.

In Tommy's own handwriting, it said:

"BILL AND CHARLIE'S FAGGOT ASS POSSE SUCKS BIG DICK"

LESLIE

Young Charlie gazed down at Tommy, holding the note inches from his face.

"What's on the note?"

"I couldn't read it!"

Leslie bit her lip.

("somethin' bad is gonna happen!")

("i can feel it!")

Maybe that chick had been right.

Maybe they *should* have called the fuckin' cops.

"Why'd he show us the note when we can't fuckin' read it?"

"Fuck if I know, man...dude is on a different level..."

"What's he doin' now?"

Young stared at Tommy for a while—*just fucking stared*—then said something in Spanish.

"Dude, look how intense-like he's starin' at Tommy..."

"Man, I just wanna know what's on the fuckin' note..."

Young turned to his Posse. "We best put on our clothespins now."

Kenny cackled. "Almost forgot about those!"

"What'd he say? 'Clothespins?'"

"Why would they need clothespins?"

"I don't think he said 'clothespins,' dude..."

"Dude! He said fuckin' 'clothespins!'"

"Nah, I think he said somethin' else, man..."

Young, Bill, Graham, and Kenny each produced wooden clothespins from their pockets.

Goosebumps prickled Leslie's arms.

He said fuckin' *"clothespins."*

TOMMY

Charlie spoke in a voice Tommy didn't recognize anymore.

"Glick," said Charlie.

His mouth twitched, just for a second.

"Desayunaste?"

Tommy squinted.

Desayunaste...

He'd heard that before.

In his fucking mind.

In his *dreams.*

But what did it mean? What did it fucking m—

"Best put on the clothespins, now," said Charlie.

Kenny cackled. "Almost forgot about those!"

Tommy stared, dumbfounded, as the wannabe cowboys pinched their noses shut with clothespins. *La Bamba* continued to play. Most people in the house still fucking nodded to it.

"Ya desayunaste, Glick?" Charlie nodded to the rhythm.

Tommy cycled through what little Spanish he remembered, but to no avail.

"My *español* is rusty, Young..." said Tommy. "...you'll have to ask me in *inglés...*"

"Ba-ba-bamba..." sang Young. "Bill, help me hold his mouth open."

Tommy's eyes widened.

What?

My mouth *open?*

Bill looked hesitant.

"If Bill don't wanna do it," said Kenny, "I'll help ya, Charlie, I'll fuckin'—"

"No," said Young. "I done told ya, it *has* to be Bill."

Why the fuck they need to hold my—

Bill seized Tommy's face from behind, gloved fingers digging into his cheeks.

"Open your mouth, Glick."

Young locked eyes with Tommy.

"*Ya desayunaste*?"

He opened the cooler.

BILL

"Ya desayunaste, Glick?"

Bill clamped the wooden clothespin onto his nose. Forgot he even had that. Didn't think they'd actually need'em—not after everything that happened today.

"Ba-ba-bamba..." sang Charlie. "Bill, help me hold his mouth open."

Bill hesitated. That *feeling* gripped him again—of moving in slow-motion toward the brink of something they couldn't undo.

"If Bill don't wanna do it," said Kenny, "I'll help ya, Charlie, I'll fuckin'—"

"No," said Charlie. "I done told ya, it *has* to be Bill."

(do it, bill...)

Feeling the weight of Charlie's gaze, Bill forced himself to move behind Glick.

(it's about sending a message...)

With hands clad in pink dishwashing gloves, he seized Tommy's face, digging his fingers into Tommy's cheeks.

"Open your mouth, Glick," he said.

(a message no one forgets...)

Charlie locked eyes with Glick—

"*Ya desayunaste*?"

—and slowly opened the cooler.

Oh, God...

Bill could barely even fucking *look at it.*

But he did.

He looked at it.

And he noticed the maggots first.

BILL

Bill had never seen maggots before, not really, probably because he'd never stared at roadkill for more than a few seconds. They crawled real slow, them maggots, likely eatin' while they moved.

The ants drew his attention next: tiny red ones that crawled faster than the maggots, but occasionally stopped to wiggle their antennae. Seemed to co-exist just fine with the maggots, even though he assumed they competed for food.

"Desayunaste, Glick?"

Both the ants and the maggots explored every inch of the huge pile of shit they'd discovered on Charlie's living room carpet. Layered on top lay the remains of the eggs the weedboys had thrown at Charlie's house.

"Ya desayunaste, Glick?"

The eggs now resembled something from outer space, the yolk an otherworldly, puke-green color, the egg white a bluish slime, carpeted in fur-like mold.

*"Desa-*fuckin'*-yunaste, Glick?"*

Broken glass from Charlie's windows glittered on top, scattered like sprinkles; a last-minute ingredient thrown in for good measure. *"To give it a little crunch,"* Charlie had said.

Glick trembled. Bill dug his fingers into Glick's jaw, then looked past Kenny and Graham's leering grins toward the woods.

Don't struggle, Glick...

Just let it happen.

"Like I told ya at Walmart, Glick..." said Charlie. "...it took me a loooong time to clean up them eggs..."

Charlie inserted his pink-gloved hand into the pile of shit.

"...so..."

A swarm of baby flies emerged, disturbed by the sudden movement.

"...damn..."

Charlie lifted his hand and cupped it, making sure he had a good, generous amount.

"...long."

He turned toward the audience, gesturing at them with his handful.

Kenny's squeal rang across the lawn. *"That's the shit Glick took on Charlie's carpet!"*

Some of the audience gasped, some laughed, some murmured variations of *"Oh my God..."*

Charlie's expression stayed the same: cold, unforgiving. A man who no longer gave a fuck.

"*Gaack!*"

"*Gaaaack!*"

Glick started gagging.

Bill pressed his fingers deeper into Glick's cheeks.

"And when I had all them eggs cleaned up," said Charlie, "I thought to myself, *'Now, that's a shame to throw these away...'*"

Longface started gagging, too. Saliva dangled from his bandana-bound mouth.

"*Gaack!*"

"*Gaaaack!*"

Charlie shoved his maggot-infested, shit-filled hand toward Glick's face. A chunk of corn, bright and yellow, jutted from the top.

"And I thought to myself," said Charlie, "*'ya know, I bet Tommy Glick would like to have these eggs back...'*"

Glick squirmed and squirmed and yelled some bullshit but Bill squeezed his face good and hard, ready to pry his fuckin' mouth all the way open.

"'And,'" said Charlie,

"'I bet he'd like to have his shit back, too...'"

TOMMY

Tommy's insides churned.

"Gaack!"

"Gaaaack!"

The stench—God, *the stench*—was so fucking bad that—

"*Bluuagh!*"

Beside him, Larry retched and puked—

"*Bluuaaaagh!*"

—the bandana around his mouth breaking the vomit's flow.

"...en—*gaack!*—enough......" said Tommy.

A cold, dead smile spread across Charlie's face.

"What's that, Glick?"

"...you've...d-done enough..."

"Sorry, *ese!*" said Charlie. "Can't heeeear yaaa!"

"...s-stop..." said Tommy.

Bile crept up the back of his tongue, bitter and burning, like battery acid.

"...p-lease..."

Charlie turned to the spectators, grinning.

"D'yall hear that? He said *'please,'* now!"

The spectators laughed.

Kenny slapped his knee. *"Motherfuckin' Tommy Glick said 'please!'"*

"Y-Young..." said Tommy.

Charlie said, "Sounds like he's *beggin'* us, Bill!"

The spectators hooted and hollered.

"....w-we...we used to..."

Charlie spun around.

"Used to *what?*"

He shoved his shit-filled hand close to Tommy's face. Sour, meaty. Unbearable.

"*We used to fucking what, Glick?*"

"...we, we used to..."

Tommy gurgled.

Vomit slicked the back of his throat.

"...s-smoke together..."

Charlie froze.

His grin vanished.

For a moment, mercy flickered in his eyes.

Maybe he remembered when they'd smoked weed and chilled and talked about life together. When Tommy had taught him to blow smoke rings, and he tried to teach Tommy *español.*

Maybe he remembered when they used to be—

friends.

Amigos.

("you can come to my place anytime...")

Mejores amigos.

("we'll fuckin' chill and smoke, like mejores amigos, *man...")*

But only for a moment.

Like a cloud passing over a last ray of sunlight, the mercy vanished, leaving only cold hatred, a message conveyed by his eyes:

You fucked with us.

"Do it, Charlie!"

And you fucked with my carpet, Glick.

"Make him eat his breakfast!"

And now, you pay.

You fucking pay.

Kenny bounced up and down, chanting. *"Break-fast! Break-fast!"*

The spectators joined in.

"Break-fast!"

"Break-fast!"

"Break-fast!"

The whites of Charlie's eyes flashed; his teeth showed beneath his mustache. He placed Tommy's note atop the pile of shit in his hand.

"Glick," he said.

"Ya desayunaste?"

LESLIE

"Open your mouth, Glick!" said Bill. *"Open your fuckin' mouth!"*

No...

Leslie couldn't believe her eyes.

This...

This ain't real...

Charlie's screams pierced the air.

"Ya desayunaste?"

*"Ya desa-*fuckin'*-yunaste, Glick!"*

Everyone chanted.

They fucking *chanted.*

"Break-fast!"

"Break-fast!"

"Break-fast!"

"No!" she said. "We gotta stop this!"

Everything around Leslie melted; the house, the people, and every-fucking-thing melted into a blur, *a swirling blur.*

This is insane...

This isn't real...

How could they chant that?

"Stop sayin' that!" she said. *"We gotta stop this!"*

She ran toward the front door, but someone grabbed her from behind and squeezed her arms.

"Ain't nobody stoppin' nothin', weedslut..."

Zane.

The Hazard Maf guy.

Leslie struggled to break free.

"Let go of me!"

Zane snickered and squeezed her tighter.

"We gon' watch us a show, now..."

He licked her face.

TOMMY

"Break-fast!"

"Break-fast!"

"Break-fast!"

Tommy stared into Young Charlie's eyes.

"Desayunaste?"

Amidst his panic, *his utter physical revulsion,* something dawned upon him:

"Ya desayunaste, Glick?"

This wasn't the same Young Charlie he used to smoke with.

*"Ya desa-*fuckin'*-yunaste,* Glick?"

This was someone else.

"Open your mouth, Glick!" said Bill.

Or maybe,

"Open your fuckin' mouth, now!"

he never really knew *the real* Young Charlie.

"Just let it happen, Glick!"

"Just let it fucking happen!"

Tommy lifted his gaze to the unforgiving sky.

God...

Mikey...

Help me....

Suzie screamed.

Where are you?

"Open his mouth, Bill," said Charlie.

Why can't I hear your voice anymore, Mikey?

"BUBBAAAAAAAAAAAAA!"

Suzie splashed across the pool towards him.

I'll find The Temple...

I'll find it, Mikey...

"DON'T HURT MY BUBBAAAAAAAAAAAA!"

I'll find the fucking Temple!

"Keep that bitch away!"

Please God,

help m—

"Open his fucking mouth!"

BILL

Suzie screamed and splashed across the pool while Glick squirmed and squirmed.

"Open his fucking mouth, Bill!" said Charlie.

"I can't!" said Bill.

He squeezed Glick's jaw and pried at his teeth, but the fucker's mouth stayed clamped shut.

"Break-fast!"

"Break-fast!"

"Break-fast!"

"I can't get his fuckin' mouth open!" said Bill.

"Huh huh huh..." chuckled Graham. "Poke his eyes."

"What?" asked Bill.

"Poke him in his eyes!" said Kenny. "That'll make him open his—"

"AAAAAAGH!"

Glick screamed as Bill pressed his eyeballs into their sockets.

"Therrrrre ya go!" said Charlie.

TOMMY

"Break-fast!"

"Break-fast!"

"Break-fast!"

Tommy saw himself reflected in Bill's sunglasses, bloodied and pitiful, on his knees and no longer a leader, no longer the leader of anything,

"Open his fucking mouth, Bill!"

about to be force-fed *human shit* in front of a chanting audience,

"I can't!"

then *her* face appeared, Samantha's face, smeared with cum and blood,

"I can't get his fuckin' mouth open!"

smiling and telling Bill the same thing she told him *("only you...")*,

"Huh huh huh..."

"Poke his eyes."

then the *stench* of rotten eggs mixed with human feces and the bacterial overgrowth on top,

"What?"

tinged with the metallic taste of his own blood,

"Poke him in his eyes!"

overwhelmed his fucking senses and,

"That'll make him open his—"

"AAAAAAAAAAGH!"

"Therrrrre ya go!"

as the first bitter drop of egg slime and maggots and shit chunks and glass shards fell upon his tongue and the vomit surged up his throat, everything spun and swirled and a voice emerged—

"Break-fast!"

not Mikey's,

"Say 'Aaah!'"

not God's,

"*Desayunaste,* Glick!"

but *hers.*

("i love you, tommy...")

("you're the only one I'll let do this.")

BILL

"Break-fast!"

"Break-fast!"

"Break-fast!"

"BUBBBBBAAAAAAAAAAAAAAAAAAAAA!"

Just as Suzie reached the kiddie pool's edge, Charlie shifted to Glick's side—

"AAAAAAAAAAAAAHHHHHHHHHHHHHHH!"

—barely dodging the projectile vomit that nailed her right in the face.

"AAAAAAAAAAAAAAAAAAAAAHHHHHHHHHHHHHHH!"

She screamed and screamed and screamed, drenched in her brother's hot yellow puke.

The scent of Domino's pizza wafted through the air.

BILL

"Break-fast!"

"Break-fast!"

"Break-fast!"

"Alright, now..." Bill watched Tommy vomit into the kiddie pool while Suzie screamed and screamed and fucking screamed, drenched in her brother's hot pizza-puke.

"Let's go, Charlie..."

Something twisted inside Bill.

His right hand trembled.

"We've done enough, now..."

He squeezed his right hand with his left.

A vomit-covered screaming Suzie stepped out of the pool, but Glick puked again—right onto her bare feet.

"BUBBBBAAAAAAAAAAAA!"

The audience's laughter swelled to a roar.

Something flashed in Charlie's eyes. He turned toward the seven other weedboys.

Bill's right hand trembled harder.

Charlie...

No...

"Charlie..." said Bill. "We've done enough, now..."

Kenny hopped up and down, squealing.

Graham wiped blood and slobber from his mouth, belly heaving.

"Nope..." Charlie scooped another fistful of shit. "Still got seven more weedboy mouths to feed..."

"Break-fast!"

"Break-fast!"

"Break-fast!"

"Charlie..." said Bill. "You don't really wanna do that...to *all* them weedboys, do ya?"

Charlie smiled and winked.

"I sure fuckin' do."

THE STORY CONTINUES IN BOOK III: IT'S ALWAYS SUNNY IN KENTUCKY

ABOUT THE AUTHOR

Ashley is the award-winning author of the Kentucky Blood series, a gritty, uncompromising Southern Gothic saga that explores complex characters and raw emotion. Raised in the rural enclaves of western Kentucky, he survived for 11 years in Tokyo's cutthroat corporate world and now splits his time between countries. He often roots for the bad guys in stories and hopes his books inspire you to do the same.

You can connect with Ashley on his official Facebook / IG accounts, as well as on his website, ashley-thomas-sheikh.com.

www.ingramcontent.com/pod-product-compliance
Lightning Source LLC
Chambersburg PA
CBHW031026030726
47497CB00004B/1018

* 9 7 9 8 9 9 0 7 0 3 7 4 2 *